tuesday's child

Forthcoming Sequel

Tuesday's Child II: Redemption

After serving time in jail and testifying at Jenna's criminal hearing, Lane is now expected to master the complexities of her newly identified family life.

Can her real father's love and her uncle's continued support get her through this time of transition? Will the identification of all the players in her life help her sort out years of secrecy, confusion and abuse?

Continue to follow Lane's arduous journey as she desires to withdraw, hide in the forest and perhaps identify her own self-worth.

But, as her father warned, "Things were far from over." Financial power and revenge drive her mother to relentlessly target anyone and everyone associated with the Keates family.

Lane survived before. Will continued survival lead to further pain or much-needed redemption?

tuesday's child

CAROLYN GIBBS

Legwork Team Publishing
New York

Legwork Team Publishing
80 Davids Drive, Suite One
Hauppauge, NY 11788
www.legworkteam.com
Phone: 631-944-6511

Testimonials

"The flashbacks are handled like a seasoned pro, and they help set the stage for a sympathetic character. The author has done a nice job defining the character and the drama/trauma that was introduced into her life. Another thing that I find interesting is that this is a YA novel, but it has a decidedly mature tone. I am sure that teenage readers will appreciate a novel that speaks to them as adults and not mindless readers."

—Amazon Breakthrough Novel Award,
Expert Review

"Tuesday's Child is an engaging portrayal of human nature in which the characters exhibit a range of motivations and behaviors that hit home. In a world that seems to be trying to mimic fiction, it is a pleasure to read a book so dedicated to the concepts of individual perseverance and realistic emotion."

—Davin R., IT Consultant

"I'm impressed that this first-time novelist was able to build her characters, plot, and suspense with such success! Usually I find one of them lacking. I would highly recommend this novel not just to YAs, but to readers who enjoy suspense!"

—Diane, Very Satisfied Reader

Testimonials

"This is one for my high school students. Easy reading, identifiable characters, interesting plot. The story really draws us into their lives."
—Benjamin Dancer
Author, *Fidelity*
(http://www.BenjaminDancer.com)

"This book was very well-written. I enjoyed the author's writing style. She made me hate certain characters and love others. The author also does a good job of throwing in a twist or two along the way, leading to a satisfying and slightly unexpected ending. I would definitely recommend this book to those who like a character-driven story."
—www.FlamingNet.com Reviewer,
Reviewer Age: 16

"Well done, Carolyn Gibbs. Tuesday's Child *is full of sorrow, heartbreak, domestic abuse and violence. What clinched it for me, though, was that despite all of the hardship, there was always a bit of hope mixed in as well as some very uplifting figures, which was where Gibbs really excels as a writer. The main character, Lane, is extremely likable. She's very independent, strong, and defiant when she needs to be, yet you can also see the vulnerable, afraid, weak girl she is. She makes for an excellent protagonist, and I just cheered her on the entire way.*

Then, I thought the end of this book was perfect for the kind of story it was. Gibbs filled all of my needs as a reader. I shut the book not only with a sense of closure, but also with satisfaction and even a good feeling. Tuesday's Child *is a very moving story for someone looking for something a little bit more emotional and edgy."*
—A. Kelly
(http://www.GoodReads.com) Reader

Testimonials

"Wow! A great read from a promising up-and-coming new author. The book captivates you right from the start. Never does it disappoint. There is always hope in the darkness of life. Once you start through the journey of this story, you will never want to put it down."

—Deb A

"It is so refreshing to come across a novel in the Young Adult genre that doesn't rely on vampires or dragons to move the plot ... the market is saturated with those. This is about real situations and people, which is so much more tragic. This is a real gem of a find. It is the sort of book a young adult would rip through in one night! It has down-to-earth characterizations, dialogue and talented writing."

—Liz Hoban
Author, *The Cheech Room, A Fine Pickle*
(http://www.lizhoban.com)

"I just finished reading Tuesday's Child, *and I am floored. The attention to detail is wonderful. The storyline and characters are just so engaging; it was hard to put the book down."*

—J. Ackerman, Satisfied Reader

*"*Tuesday's Child *reveals some of the many secrets our young people face even today, secrets that are shared only with a trusted peer. Carolyn has gotten into the minds of these young people.* Tuesday's Child *is a must read if only to realize that things are not always what they appear to be. You must meet Lane. Parents, this is a book you should also read, maybe even before your teenager."*

—Mary Brodeur
Director of Religious Education,
St. Thomas Church

Testimonials

"Congratulations on the book; what an accomplishment! It was packed full of action, drama, and great characters. What an incredible achievement to write a book as good as this.

—Patty, Steve, and the Kids

"I just finished reading Tuesday's Child. *I enjoyed it immensely. Carolyn is a gifted storyteller. The imagery was amazing. I felt like I was watching Lane's life from the sidelines and felt all of her emotions. I admired Lane's strength and perseverance to survive at all costs.*

—Patty, Satisfied Reader

"Hooray for new author Carolyn Gibbs. Her storytelling style kept me reading on into the wee hours of the morn. This teenage girl is so mistreated that my mind couldn't conceive of such extreme parental abuse, yet the author made it perfectly believable. The scenic descriptions of the Washington forests are vivid and awe-inspiring, including the bone-chilling cold of winter with which Lane Harris must contend.

This is a story where you root for the heroine, no matter her survival techniques. You hate the villains and are mystified by the parts the other characters play in Lane Harris's life. An excellent read for all who like storytelling at its best."

—Betty Nearing
Contributing author to the *Patchwork Path* anthology series
Wedding Bouquet, Christmas Stocking, and *Treasure Box*

"Dear Carolyn, I have just finished reading your novel, Tuesday's Child, *and I must tell you how much I enjoyed it. It is a captivating delight filled with surprises. I plan to read it again!"*

—M. Minns, Avid Reader

Testimonials

"Gibbs hit the ball out of the park on her very first novel—a gripping story about a teenage girl, Lane Harris, who is abandoned by her family, shunned by her peers, and fighting for life one day at a time. Gibbs' descriptions of Lane's socialite home, the streets of Seattle, and the raw wilderness of Washington State will transport you to an alternate reality. The story runs the gamut of emotions; from pity and despair to rage and ultimately hope. The in-depth and shocking detail of what could happen will leave you hanging on the edge of your seat, not wanting the story to end but praying for Lane's salvation. This story, though geared for young adults, should not be missed by adults, especially those with teenage girls."

—Lori Young, Writer

"I purchased Tuesday's Child *as a Kindle for my PC. Reading anything from a computer screen for any period of time is not very pleasant, so it says a lot about this book that I read it in two sittings. The second sitting was a marathon session. I couldn't put the book down; I really wanted to find out how the story ended. I quickly cared about the main character; I appreciated Lane's strengths and worried about her vulnerabilities. The plot's momentum grew as the story unfolded. It drew me in and kept me engaged. The writing was crisp and concise. I enjoyed the story, and I look forward to reading more from this author."*

—Penny, Writer and Satisfied Fan

To Mom: My glue. My sword. My shield.

Tuesday's Child is full of grace.

—Nursery Rhyme, Author Unknown

(First recorded in A. E. Bray's *Traditions of Devonshire,* 1838)

Acknowledgments

I acknowledge the dedicated efforts of Yvonne Kamerling and Janet Yudewitz of *Legwork Team Publishing*. I extend my gratitude to them and their team of design, editorial and technical professionals for transforming my story into the book you hold in your hands.

Introduction

We live in a disposable civilization. If a better model is released, upgrade. If it breaks, get a new one. If we don't want it, throw it away.

Parents abandoning their children is far more common than we'd like to admit. This story is not an attempt to explain that tragedy, though in the course of the telling, the excuse for this particular situation will be revealed. The reason isn't important to me—the children are.

When we hear about an abandoned child, we think of teenaged mothers who are ill-prepared for their responsibilities; we think of toddlers left by neglectful guardians who are too concerned with their own needs to worry about someone else's, or six-year-olds roaming malls alone. But when we discuss runaways, we think they've put themselves in harm's way because they didn't want to do their chores or follow their parents' rules. They didn't want to be home by midnight or they didn't want to go to school. We fail to realize that teenagers can also be victims of abuse and neglect. They can be tossed aside by parents who are seeking the fulfillment of their own desires, and we assume that a teenager is mature and experienced enough to handle being emotionally abandoned.

Introduction

With apologies to cross-country runners who will no doubt pick up on a little poetic license, this exploration is a fictitious account of one teenager who is tossed aside to fend for herself; she is about to find out the price she's willing to pay to survive. Is she mature? Sure. Experienced? Some. Ready for life on her own? That remains to be seen. During her trials and tribulations, she'll find the will to survive and the grace to remain human.

chapter one

The gunshot echoed through the Olympic foothills. With that, teenage runners haloed in their own breath bolted from the line and quickly sorted themselves out into groups, clustered together by team. Stronger teams competed with each other, blocking, jockeying, fighting for dominance of the trail. Weaker teams hovered at the rear, hoping for nothing but to finish. Mills Valley High raced in dead last.

Lane Harris found herself shut out, breathing the dirt kicked up by other runners and deflecting the branches they swept aside and released. It wouldn't matter, not in the long run. Time and terrain favored her. And preparation as well. The forest held footprints as evidence of her daily visits, during which she pounded the trails, memorized the ins and outs, and befriended the treacherous tracts and easy go-aheads. At just seventeen, nothing remained to this trail that she didn't know—intimately.

For now, the best strategy relied on staying back, keeping pace, and conserving energy for the long run ahead. She dipped into the past, fueling her desire to win with the pain of her childhood memories. Her thoughts drifted.

chapter two

The wrought-iron security gate peeled open, its low hum barely audible inside the late model Volvo as it drove through. The mansion, a three-story white structure with pillars, blotted out much of the mountain range behind it. The rain stopped earlier that day, and the peaks not blocked from view stood shrouded under a heavy mist.

The Volvo puttered up the drive and stopped in front of the main entrance, and six-year-old Lane hopped out and skipped through puddles, leaving her school bag, sweater, and beauty accessories for their housekeeper Camilla to carry, along with all the groceries.

Her first kindergarten masterpiece fluttered in the breeze she created as she rushed into the house, leaving the ornate front door open behind her, just one more task relegated to the staff. Camilla would close it—*if she ever catches up*, Lane thought. The youngster did not worry about the tiny, wet footprints following her as her patent leather shoes clacked along the hardwood floors.

The teacher's instructions had been specific: put the pictures up on the refrigerator for Mommy and Daddy to see. But the master and mistress of this house never went into the kitchen; Morgan and Jenna Harris spent their time in the study, the den, the parlor, occasionally the billiards room, the library, or even the great room, but never the kitchen. That is, unless someone got yelled at or fired. *That sometimes happens in the kitchen.*

It was a Thursday. Mother spent the day in Olympia, returning home late in the afternoon after hours of primping and pampering. Father also worked in Olympia as the Vice President of a local bank. When he arrived home, he unwound with a drink or two—or more—with his wife, monopolizing her time completely. They'd play billiards, snuggle while reading the daily newspaper, or stroll the grounds arm in arm.

Interaction with their daughter happened at dinner. Father sat at the head of the eight-person table, Mother at the foot, and Lane at the chair to Mother's left. She and Mother chatted about their respective days; Father kept silent, finished his dinner, and left quickly. Usually. Sometimes he just glared at Lane, his eyes burning holes in her skin.

But today, Lane had a mission that couldn't wait for dinner. *This is important*, she thought, searching the house for them. She peeked into the assorted rooms as she skipped by, her dress billowing and her footfalls muffling as she passed into carpeted areas.

Jenna lay draped across Morgan's lap, and they cuddled on a velvet settee in the corner of the bar. Rich mahogany paneling adorned the walls; four table sets, two additional settees, and several window benches provided seating. The room could host an entire gentlemen's club or provide a hideaway for a quiet rendezvous.

Even while reclining, Morgan was a giant. He towered over most adults, making Lane feel even smaller. Well into his fifties, white had already obscured most of his natural hair color, and his dark eyes resembled holes the size of dimes.

Jenna stood a foot shorter than Morgan and, at nearly twenty years his junior, retained her natural brown hair. In quiet moments, Lane liked to run her hands around Mother's face, tracing the elegant and delicate bone structure, and staring into her amber-colored eyes.

Right now Lane had other plans, and she rushed over with her artwork; Mother displayed mild interest, Father not so much. His face got all pinched up and his eyes narrowed as Mother faked pleasure and lavished praise on the youngster.

Lane didn't care that it was bogus; she just liked to hear it, liked to be the center of attention. But something snapped in Father, and the anger he usually saved for the hired help lashed out at her.

The openhanded and swift slap jerked the child's head around, spinning her sideways. Instinctively, her hand sprang up and cupped the stinging skin, but not until after a scream pierced the quiet ambiance. And Father liked that even less; he dismissed Mother from his lap.

The windows behind him framed his body as he rose. The signs were all there; the smoldering eyes, the clenched jaw, and balled-up fists. But even at six years of age, Lane knew better than to run.

Her father latched onto her arm and hauled her away, the brightly colored drawing fluttering behind her.

Sometimes her feet touched the ground, sometimes not; it didn't matter to Morgan if he dragged her all the way. His long stride covered the distance to the front door in seconds, and they climbed the grand staircase with its half-circle base sweeping upward to the second floor. Lane struggled to stay ahead of him; as long as she did, she spent more time on her feet than on her knees.

They ignored the second floor and continued to the third floor, which held the family quarters. The master suite took half the floor for itself, extending from the outer left wall to the grand staircase. The rest of the rear wall hosted an open-faced library, which sat opposite the staircase and took most of the remaining floor space. The little area on the wall opposing the staircase held a bathroom and access to the attic. Morgan veered into the hallway on the right and marched past the two bedrooms reserved for any additional children Morgan and Jenna might conceive. The final room, Lane's bedroom, stood at the very end of the hallway, abutting the servants' staircase.

Lane assumed that he would lock her in her bedroom; he did that occasionally, though she never understood why. It had actually been happening more often in the month since Gamma and Pop-Pop died, and Lane headed for her door.

But Morgan didn't stop; he tugged her across the hall to the attic, straining her shoulder and eliciting a yip from the youngster. With a quick turn of the knob, the button lock popped; he ripped the door open and threw Lane inside, slamming and locking it behind her.

The stairwell lacked natural lighting, and the darkness enveloped the six-year-old swiftly, blinding her before she even turned back to the door. Pounding and kicking it didn't produce the freedom she expected. But the door did swing back open. Lane took a step away, and spasms of fear shook the artwork from her hand.

Morgan loomed in the doorframe, using his size and words to terrify her. "I know you're not running from me."

Jenna moved into the doorway. "For God's sake, Morgan, she's just a child."

Morgan whirled on Jenna, one hand rising but stopping short of striking. "You are my wife, Jenna, first and foremost. She"—Morgan's finger jabbed down at Lane—"does not come between us. Ever."

Jenna cooed, trying to smooth his ruffled feathers, but the door slammed shut.

Lane huddled before it. She sucked up her runny nose and listened to her parents fight in the hallway. She heard a rousing slap catch Jenna's face, followed by the sound of Mother's quiet sobbing. Something slammed against the door, and the vibration rippled through the wood and into the child's flesh. Lane backed away, tripped up the stairs in the darkness, and lay still. Shadows played along the floor, moving slowly left and right, forward and backward, revealing the characters even if the action remained hidden.

The fight escalated. The sound of tearing cloth seeped into the attic stairwell, followed by a mild slap; *Oh, Momma, you shouldn't hit Daddy.*

The next strike, even more harsh than the one that rocked Lane in the bar, brought louder sobs from Mother. Another bang sounded on the door, higher, closer to the top, and Morgan yelled, his words unmistakably meant for the child. "I don't want to hear another sound out of you. You understand me?"

Shuffling, stumbling, the muffled rubbing of skin against floor. Father dragged Mother down the hallway, and with the distant slam of the master suite door, silence returned to the dark attic staircase.

Light slivered under the door, and Lane eased her way toward it one baby step at a time until her hand bumped wood. Tiny whimpers escaped her as she twisted the knob, but it refused to turn. And then she heard something. Soft footsteps. Creeping closer.

She snapped around but saw nothing; she worked harder at the door, pushing and leaning against it as if desire alone would free her. The footsteps neared.

Lane cocked her head, listened. She dropped to her knees and peeked under the door. *Someone's coming.*

The door popped open, and Camilla stepped in holding a small bag. Lane pushed her aside, but Camilla held her steady.

"I will have you fired," Lane said, casually assuming Father's air of authority.

The delicate French accent gave Camilla's voice a fluid melody. "Better count your friends where you can, Little Miss. You are no a princess. No anymore. This will get you through tonight." She held the bag up. "I will come back tomorrow with more, unless they let you out. I no think they let you out tonight."

Camilla reached past the child and flicked on the light switch. "There is another light at the top. Turn this one off so Mr. Morgan no sees it. There is also a door. Close it behind you, or the environmental sensors will tell Mr. Morgan that the temperature has changed, and then he will come up, and you will be sorry again."

She held the bag of food out to Lane, but the youngster refused to take it. "Carry it upstairs." Lane folded her arms across her tiny body and stepped aside, thoroughly expecting the maid to take the order.

Camilla smiled and set the bag down on the second stair. "When you are hungry, you will learn to carry it yourself. Just no let Mr. Morgan find it. Inside the door, you will find light switches. Turn them on so you can see. There is furniture and a bathroom. You will be comfortable at least." Camilla turned to leave.

Lane bolted to the door, but Camilla held her at bay and slipped out. "If you pound on this door, Mr. Morgan will come back. I no think you will like it." The lock clicked behind her.

Lane stared at the knob for a few minutes, then at the door at the top of the staircase for another few. She took a tentative step up, the wood creaking beneath her. The bag remained on the stairs, silent, crumpled, looking more like an offering to the homeless than a meal for the heir of the Harris family fortune. *Carry it myself. Really?*

But what will Father do if he finds it, she wondered. She pinched the folded-over top edge of the bag between two fingers as if it were the diseased body of a dead mouse, holding it away from her body as she climbed up to the attic.

The door at the top of the stairs squeaked open into a black abyss. Trembling fingers eased along the wall, finding the light panel. An overhead light came on when she snapped the first switch. Once able to see her surroundings, she shut off the stairwell light.

Next to the row of light switches, another panel displayed the temperature and humidity. A solitary green light started to blink, then abruptly changed to red, flashing out in panic mode. The panic transferred to the child, and she quickly closed the door; with the environment sealed, the light popped back to green.

Beyond the little bubble of light, the attic loomed dark. *And scary.* The switches snapped on one by one as tiny fingers urged them up. In response, a row of lights came to life, glowing softly at first, then brighter as the fluorescent bulbs warmed up. With the flick of the last switch, the light spread to the left, completely illuminating the attic.

A bathroom of sorts sat directly across from the entry. It contained no counter, a tiny over-the-sink cabinet, no door. *Who could use such a terrible little bathroom?* Lane's face scrunched up, as if someone had just suggested live toads had become the new caviar.

A small window graced the wall next to her; peering out, she looked down on the driveway and the servants' quarters three flights below. She made a half turn and found a matching window on the far wall. *It must look over the meadow and the mountains*, she thought.

The rest of the attic was little more than a warehouse. The first section held eight rows of metal storage shelving, spaced four feet apart with a larger walkway down the center. Cardboard boxes, all neatly arranged and labeled, covered most of the available space.

Lane tiptoed along the wooden boards, tiny steps designed to reduce noise, but it didn't work. Her shoes hadn't been made for stealth mode; she slid them off and left them behind.

The clatter of pots and pans startled her, and she jumped,

crushing the paper bag against her body like a shield. The rattling came from a vent pipe that hugged the wall near the stairs. The pipe continued out of the house through the roof but transported sounds as well as steam, smoke, and cooking odors through the attic. *I wonder if anybody knows.*

Lane continued down the center aisle, gawking at the eight-foot-tall army of steel and wondering what might be in the boxes, but knowing better than to touch Father's things.

No walls marked room divisions here. The shelving simply ended, and in the approximate center of the attic lay an assortment of furniture. Some she recognized from Gamma and Pop-Pop's house, antiques that needed a new home after they died.

More shelving lined the furthest end of the attic, mimicking the first section. Subdued noises came from these shelving units, not sharp and crisp like the sounds traveling along the kitchen pipe.

The buzz grew louder as she drew closer. Her parents' voices drifted into the recesses. They varied, sometimes soft, sometimes yelling. She followed the cadence to the far wall but didn't see any pipes; rather the sounds bled into the attic from a series of fixtures installed in the attic floor.

Searing white light bulbs blocked most of her vision, but she could catch glimpses down into the master suite by leaning left and right. Her parents lay on the bed. Mother cried out a couple times; Father held her down. *Maybe they're wrestling, but why is Momma crying?*

Bits of the conversation filtered up into the attic. Mostly, Father yelled while Mother protested and cried. Morgan said something about "humping everything in the state to get ahead," and Lane wondered what that meant.

Then something about Jake Olsen, whom Mother had referred

to as a dumb ox when they encountered him at his brother Vic's gas station. She said he swept the floors at Vic's sometimes to make extra money because he wasn't smart enough to get a real job.

His son, Jason, attended school with Lane. *But he's mean*, she thought. *A bully.* Then she heard something about the Keates brothers. *Yes! Momma should call Sheriff Keates if Daddy's hurting her.*

Lane twirled and scanned the room, but she had no idea where to find the phone up here. By the time she knelt back down, Mother lay alone on the bed, all wrapped up in the sheets, crying. No matter how Lane twisted or turned, she couldn't see Father, and powerless to change anything, she wandered away.

Pop-Pop's gun cabinet stood along the wall, smothered in bubble wrap so thick that she couldn't see inside—couldn't tell if Pop-Pop's beloved guns were there or not, even if she pressed her face against it.

Further along, Gamma Jo's old easy chair sat discarded against the front wall. Lane hugged it, wishing Gamma and Pop-Pop hadn't left her. She climbed up into the chair, plopping down and arranging her dress in an appropriately ladylike fashion.

The paper bag unfurled in her hands, presenting her with limited choices for the night's meal: a package of Pop-Tarts, raisins, an apple, and two juice boxes. It was no contest: the Pop-Tarts fell victim, followed by the grape juice. The fruit found a new home on the floor, and the tired youngster snuggled into the chair, lulled to sleep by whiffs of Gamma and chocolate chip cookies.

In the morning, Lane ran down the stairs, gathered up her forgotten artwork, and found the door unlocked. She scurried down the hallway as Mother came out of the master suite.

"Momma!" The masterpiece led the charge, offered up for review by arms open wide for a hug.

She hadn't expected Mother to slap her, hadn't expected those delicate eyes to fill with such rage. And hate.

For the life of her, Lane couldn't figure out what she'd done to deserve it. Her hand rose halfway to the stinging skin before her eyes locked on Mother's. And then those amber slits went empty, devoid of any emotion or concern.

Lane's hand fell to her side. A tear brimmed, slipped down her cheek, but she refused to cry. The slap didn't hurt nearly as much as the betrayal, the loss of the only person who even pretended to care about her.

Father slipped out of the master suite, snuggled up against Mother's neck, and smiled wickedly. Mother's face remained frozen.

chapter three

The gurgling waters of the river brought Lane out of her trance and created a breeze that cooled the surrounding air, dropping the temperature several degrees. The chill invigorated her, though most of the other runners barely noticed it as they rounded the bend and charged toward the last series of hills.

The first hill rose from level ground to a steep, sixty-degree incline that presented a grueling climb. At the top, it immediately dropped into a gully, followed by a lesser incline at just forty-five degrees. After that, the ground leveled out for several yards, then fell into the last gully before presenting the final sixty-degree climb. If the grades weren't difficult enough, the ravines trapped runners unfamiliar with the course.

The wind picked up, dancing along the branches of the trees. Trapped in the valley, it swirled against its captor mountains and raced back and forth across the trail, pushing against the runners as it swept past. It took some measure of joy when the scrawny mortals stumbled and knocked each other off stride while it pranced off to find another playmate.

Lane welcomed it. With the wind knocking the competition around, she'd get even further ahead once she made her break.

Her teammates, nominally smarter than the visitors, gathered around her, anticipating her moves. They closed up ranks and shadowed her like a pack of wolves chasing down a lamb.

Lane smiled; they hated her, but they also knew she'd win this race. *Yahoos.*

Their sole commitment to this meet culminated in a slow walk-through so the coach could point out the pitfalls. They hadn't even run the course this year, relying instead on their coach's instructions: "Watch Harris."

But that casual forest stroll occurred two weeks ago. Since then, spring rains had swollen the rivers and streams, soaked the ground, and left gigantic mud marshes throughout the forest. The hills retained so much moisture that climbing up them bordered on pointless. And the wind rose up suddenly these days, lashing out and tossing debris along the paths.

The opposition hadn't bothered to scope the trail at all. They came to Mills Valley, nestled in the foothills of the Olympic Mountains, knowing that the local team hadn't placed in thirty-plus years.

And no one outside the town expected them to do so now— mostly because no one outside the town knew about Lane, or that she had joined the team ...or that she was their most promising runner since the Keates brothers those thirty-plus years ago.

The runners neared the first rise, where the trail split into three tracks. Most runners took the shorter main route. A few took the second path, believing it would give them the ability to pass. Just as steep as the main trail, it provided no real advantage except lack of bodies.

No one took the last fork; longer than the other two trails, it zigged fifteen yards into the forest, then zagged another eighteen yards back to the main trail. But the incline rose more gradually; a runner expelled less energy on the longest of the three trails.

Lane broke ranks; her teammates followed. She tracked easily along the outer path as her competition dug in and pummeled their way up the main hill, spewing dirt into each other's faces.

In the middle of the second leg, she picked up speed and vaulted a six-foot muck hole she'd discovered days earlier. Behind her, a runner fell. The catching of breath, the thump, the plop—Lane didn't look.

Whoever had fallen hadn't reacted quickly enough, or hadn't believed it necessary. The mud grabbed her, sucked at her and planted her face down before spraying brown goo on the rest of the team.

The fallen runner yelled at her teammates to keep going, and they did, leaving her struggling to pull herself free. No one worried about her; volunteers manned stations along the trail to aid runners in distress. They came in handy for the occasional sprain or broken bone—or bear.

Her competitors clawed the dirt near the halfway mark of the first ascent. Lane rejoined the main trail at the top of the hill; running at near full speed, she sailed into the air and jumped the twelve-foot ravine. She landed a few feet from the top of the opposing hill and quickly scurried over.

The rest of the Mills Valley High team followed, throwing themselves over the chasm, thumping into the ground, grunting and groaning as they grappled their way up the second rise.

Lane noted the sounds, determining the order in which her teammates landed, but she didn't wait for them. The twenty-yard stretch to the next gully fell away quickly, and she leapt into the air one last time, solidly planting herself just inches from the top of the last hill.

The intensity of the noise behind her grew, signaling that the out-of-towners had finally crested the first rise. Without any speed built up, they had no choice but to drop into the ravine and then tackle the second hill from the bottom up.

Focused on the win, Lane scrambled easily over the top of the final rise and tore up the remaining course. She ventured a quick peek over her shoulder; mist swirled up on the mountainside. *No time to lose,* she thought.

The wind swept down at them. Out here in the open, it held the power to strip seconds off a runner's overall time, or slap minutes on. Branches whipped to fury urged the wind forward; it stampeded the meadow, mowing blades of grass flat. Nothing on the plain challenged it. It raced among the runners, pressing against their backs, fluttering through their clothes and hair. One girl stumbled into another; both went down in a tangle of arms and legs.

In its zeal, the wind raced ahead of them, and unable to slow itself to toy with them any more, it began chasing their leader. Still several dozen yards behind her, its tendrils shot forth, tousled her short hair, and tugged at the back of her shirt. It surged forward, steamrolling closer, ready to devour her.

A split second before its power unleashed, the leader merged into the tree line, seeking asylum from nature's force among the trunks of Douglas fir and Western hemlock.

Disappointed, the wind threw a few halfhearted shots in among the trees. It continued on its path, racing toward the mountains where it would have one final chance to swirl back and wreak havoc on any unfortunates still on the field.

Happy with her lead and the protection the forest afforded her from the wind, Lane funneled back into her thoughts, storing up anger from the past and energy for the rest of the run.

chapter four

On that morning so many years ago, Father slipped out of the master suite, snuggled up against Mother's neck, and smiled wickedly down at Lane. He kissed the back of his wife's neck, eased her aside, and turned on Lane, snatching her masterpiece and crumpling it in his hand. "Come with me."

The muffled sounds of retreating footsteps weren't enough to break Lane's focus. She hesitated, staring at Jenna, waiting for some show of affection, understanding, sympathy perhaps. Something. None came.

The emotion fell from Lane's face, and she stared at her mother with cold, dead eyes. Morgan and Jenna had been good teachers, and as it turned out, the look wasn't that hard to imitate.

Morgan bellowed. "Now!"

The pivot flipped her hair around behind her, producing an air of disdain that dismissed Jenna's presence altogether. Lane followed Morgan down the hall to her bedroom.

White lace curtains, fine mahogany furnishings, and delicately flowered pink wallpaper beckoned her in, welcoming her home. She stomped past Morgan, her back facing him as he spoke. "The attic is your room now. Take all your crap out of here. Use the furniture that's up there. And use the servants' entrance and stairwell from now on." Morgan grabbed her by the shoulder and spun her around. "Do you understand?"

Cold, dead eyes stared back at him with not an emotion to be found—not even a hint that the red handprint brightening the side of her face caused any pain at all. She nodded at him, and he chucked her wadded up art onto her bed before walking out.

"You've got until the end of the day." He stopped suddenly and whirled back around. "And just one more thing. Anything that happens in this house stays in this house." A menacing finger jutted in her direction. "You breathe a word to anyone and you'll regret it. And so will they. Trust me."

Work began immediately. Several trips later, she'd made no real headway, what with carrying just a few things at a time. But unaccustomed to manual labor, it wasn't long before she was hot, tired, sweaty, and very cranky.

Camilla met her in the stairwell midmorning, smuggled her some breakfast, giving her some advice and a box full of shopping bags for carrying clothes and such. Lane didn't want to take advice from the maid; she still wanted to be the princess of the house. *But who would know better about these things than the maid?*

After that, anything small enough to fit in a bag was allotted to one—clothing, toys, books. Filled bags ended up on the floor in the vestibule while larger items lined the stairs. All the transplants would get carried up to the attic after the bedroom had been cleaned out.

Camilla met her again at lunchtime, bringing her a cold bologna sandwich and a glass of milk. Lane sat on the stairs beside the maid, a boo-boo face marring her normally pleasant-when-not-smug features.

"You no have time to pity yourself. Eat, and get back to work."

Lane practiced her newly acquired dead stare on the maid, but it only made Camilla laugh.

"I will no be back today. If you need something, you come down to the kitchen before five this evening. You understand?" She paused, but Lane remained silent.

"Well before Mr. Morgan gets home. Otherwise, you no come down until after nine. After they have eaten and retired. You no want him to see you. You understand? *Oui*?"

Lane nodded.

"You take this stairwell. You make sure that door is closed." Camilla pointed toward the master suite. "You stop at the second floor, and you make sure no one is around. Then you go to the kitchen." Camilla patted the girl's leg. "I will leave a plate for you in the refrigerator. Hurry, now. Get this done before Mr. Morgan gets home from work." She took the plate from Lane and headed back down to the kitchen.

When Morgan arrived home at six p.m., he immediately went to Lane's former bedroom, inspected it, and found the drawers and closet empty. All her knickknacks and toys were gone. Even the pillows and linens had been removed. Only the crumpled drawing remained, sitting stoically in the center of the bed.

Halfway up the stairs, Lane jumped a little, but she refused to look back when the attic door opened behind her. She dragged a bag of books, pausing at every step to rest the heavy cargo before hauling it up to the next stair.

Sweaty and disheveled, she brushed her tangled hair out of her face and hoisted the bag up. She envisioned Morgan's wicked smile, his lips curling back to expose his pearly white wolf fangs. The door closed with a dull thud.

Moonlight poked through one attic window long before she'd carted all of her possessions from the bottom of the stairs to the top. Worn out by a hard day of manual labor, she snuggled up with her pillow and blanket in Gamma Jo's chair. Sleep came quickly, preceded by the fleeting concern of what she'd tell the other children at school if they asked why she'd been absent on Friday.

The cackle of a bird outside the window woke her at six a.m. A weary hand scrubbed across her eyes, and she stumbled down the attic stairs and let herself out. She'd forgotten all the rules regarding the master suite door and the second-floor landing; she continued down the stairwell oblivious to the possible dangers.

The kitchen sparkled. It spanned an area large enough so that several cooks could handle food preparation during a major soirée, yet the design enabled one staff person to handle normal mealtimes without racing from one end of the room to the other.

Camilla stood at the stove, preparing the family's regular Saturday morning feast. Bright-eyed eggs stared out of a shiny aluminum pan, bacon bubbled in its own grease, potatoes fried in oil, and Lane's eyes grew wide with anticipation.

Camilla spied the girl and pulled a plate from the fridge, its foil wrapper emblazoned with an 'L' in permanent marker, and she stuffed the cold plate into the youngster's hands.

Eager to quiet the growling of her stomach, Lane ripped it open, uncovering a turkey sandwich and a garden salad.

Camilla's face held no emotion at all. "You need to learn no to waste food. Now take it upstairs before Mr. Morgan catches you here."

Lane's angry scream ripped through the kitchen, echoed around the room, and bounced off the appliances.

The plate sailed through the air, and as it lost momentum, it shattered against the floor.

Camilla carried on as if nothing extraordinary had occurred; she retrieved a broom, and as Lane continued screaming for a real breakfast, she swept up the food and glass.

The belligerent six-year-old's foot stomped the floor. *Why does she keep moving away? Why isn't she listening to me?*

Rough hands grabbed Lane, yanked her off the floor, and tucked her under a powerful arm. Morgan threw open the kitchen drawers, one then another. Not immediately gratified by the object of his search, he whirled on Camilla, thrust his hand out, and growled at her. "Spoon!"

Camilla had warned the girl, and she wasn't about to throw away the job she and her husband had left France for. She obediently retrieved a wooden spoon from a drawer several feet away from Morgan, and slapped it against his palm like a nurse assisting a surgeon. She returned to her cooking without a sound, her eyes fixed on the eggs.

Morgan perched on a nearby stool and drew one leg up to brace himself and to create a shelf. He draped Lane over the leg and paddled her bottom soundly with the spoon, leaving little oval welts on her backside and legs.

Her yelping and wailing did nothing to assuage his anger, and when he was done, he threw the spoon across the room and dragged her back to the servants' stairwell.

Lane struggled and pulled against Morgan's hold. He smiled a broad grin full of white teeth and released her suddenly, letting her fall backward onto her already bruised backside. She yipped, rubbing her butt as she rose slowly to her feet.

She spent the rest of the day locked in the attic. With nothing else to do, she amused herself by getting even with Morgan, a deliberate but pointless act of defiance.

Father's things had always been off-limits; look, but never touch. Now, the satisfaction outweighed the risk; she opened all his storage boxes, peering inside at the treasures he'd hidden there.

Many of the boxes held nothing but paperwork. *Boring.* But some of the boxes held items that required a closer look. Paintings, vases, African masks, coins encased in plastic. Even an occasional gold brick. It would be worth the spanking just to see the look on Morgan's face when he found her greasy little kid-prints all over them. Better still—when he figured out it wasn't an accident.

A rack against the rear wall held empty boxes waiting to become homes to future treasures. In the meantime, they'd make a perfectly good wall, and Lane spent a few minutes stacking four of them inside the bathroom entrance.

When completed, the cardboard privacy curtain blocked casual sight, but Lane viewed it from assorted angles to make sure that no one would be able to see her when she was in the shower. *Or on the potty.*

Stupid little bathroom. Stupid little shower stall. Can't even take a bath. She supposed when they let her out of the attic, she'd be able to use the *real* bathroom, but in the meantime, the toilet flushed, and the sink worked, so that was really all that mattered. *For now.*

The furniture provided an additional albeit small distraction before she turned her attention to the light fixtures. She spied through all of them, learning what rooms lay below. By the time she finished, she had scoured and categorized every square inch of the attic, and the sun had set. Her stomach protested its mistreatment, growling repeatedly for her attention since her last meal had been a cold bologna sandwich yesterday at lunch. The raisins and apple from Thursday night didn't help at all. And no one had come to let her out or bring her additional provisions. There had to be a way out, a way to open the door—a way to provide for herself.

Possessions heaped into piles on the floor as Lane upended bag after bag, pushing through the contents until she found her jewelry box. Inside, she fingered her way among necklaces, bracelets, and rings—none of them real gems. But her eyebrows danced high on her forehead as her eyes landed on the key to the box. She grabbed it, hurried down the stairs, and found that it fit into the lock on the lower door. It wiggled freely and snagged against something inside the knob. Lane nearly shrieked when she heard the button pop open, but her throat clamped down on the tiny screech and prevented it from alerting anyone to her escape.

She gently pushed the door open; being more diligent this time, she snapped off the light, peered down the hallway, then snuck down the servants' staircase.

The kitchen sat empty. All the cooking and cleaning for the day had long since been done, and the staff and owners had all retired to their respective quarters for the night.

The fridge door resisted the youngster's attempts to open it. Tiny fingers pried into the rubber seal and pulled; the fridge popped open and bathed both kitchen and child in a wedge of light.

The racks held the Sunday roast, a quart of milk, vegetables, several jars of delicacies, artichoke hearts marinating in a bowl of oil. And a chunk of Brie. The pantry yielded some crackers; *together, they'll make a delightful snack.*

Unable to reach the counters, Lane sat down on the floor, pried free an oval-shaped wheat crisp, and stuffed it in her mouth while she struggled to remove the Saran Wrap from the cheese.

"Lane!" Morgan's voice bellowed through the house. "When I find you, you won't be able to sit for a week!"

The crackers skittered across the floor, kicked out of the way as Lane panicked and ran for the kitchen door.

A harsh red light shone from the alarm panel. Her hands flailed in desperation. She didn't know the code and had only three options: take the beating, hide, or set off the alarm. The deadbolt twisted easily; the alarm beeped its displeasure when the door opened.

The twelve-foot-high security walls blocked the property on three sides and partially along the front of the house. The driveway held the only possibility of escape, ending at the wrought-iron bars of the main gate.

The rear lights blinked on, illuminating the entire backyard. A whimper of fear rose in Lane's throat. She slipped a leg between two of the bars and squished herself through—scraping her legs, belly, and ears—and watched for Morgan.

But the rear lights went out. No engines revved. No garage doors opened. No one followed. Intent on escaping, Lane hurried away, her focus alternating between the mansion and the two other homes on the street that bore Father's name.

The house nearest the mansion belonged to the Olsens. An eerie bluish light flickered in the living room. Hopefully, the TV claimed their attention and they wouldn't look out the window.

No light at all poked out of the other house, and its "For Sale" sign jutted prominently out of the front yard. It had been for sale as long as Lane could remember.

The cross slates of the street sign that sat on the corner of the lot identified Harris Lane and Mill Road. She'd driven with Camilla enough to know that left on Mill went to the highway and ultimately Hoodsport or Shelton, while right led to Mills Valley Township. With a final glance over her shoulder, she headed into Mills Valley.

The countryside caught slivers of moonlight, but darkness shrouded the edges of the road and the forest beyond, hiding potential dangers, hiding wild animals. The security walls at the mansion kept bears and coyotes out, but it hadn't been designed to restrict mountain lions. Periodically, Camilla's husband Anton called the Department of Fish and Wildlife to extract cougars that had scaled the walls and made themselves at home in the backyard.

Now Lane walked openly on the dark road, nothing more than a tasty morsel for whatever sharp-toothed creature might be around. Her march down Mill Road at eight p.m. suddenly trumped all as the worst decision of the day, more so than throwing a hissy fit over cold leftovers. *But really*, she thought, *who eats leftovers?*

She dwelt on the possibility of attack, her head and eyes jerking back and forth, her body jumping at every sound, convincing herself that at any minute some creature would streak out of the night and eat her face off. Too busy worrying about them to focus on the ground, she tripped over a branch on the black highway, stumbled sideways, and fell into the dirt at the side of the road.

The insolence. *Stupid branch.* She climbed up, dusted off her dress, and winced as her palms stung where she'd scraped them against the tar.

The whine of a car engine echoed through the forest. *Morgan.* He'd find her out here on the road. Her hands flailed. *Hide. Hide.*

But there was no time. The vehicle sped into view, rounding the bend out of Mills Valley.

It can't be Father. And since it couldn't be Morgan, she continued her journey. Headlights fell on her, blinding her, forcing her to shield her eyes with her hand.

The car drove a little farther and made a big U-turn in the street.

Older than any vehicle she had ever seen, the black car pulled up close to her. The man inside turned on the interior light, and Lane recognized him from town.

Camilla's job entailed cooking, cleaning, and babysitting, so it wasn't uncommon for Lane to accompany her on whatever errands she had to run. In fact, it was far more common than Lane liked, and so she made a science out of ignoring the people in the stores, the laundromat, and at the gas station. Pretty much everywhere and everyone. If they made the mistake of addressing her directly, she would look at them briefly and with a flip of her hair, dismiss them into the realm of unimportance. They were simply not her concern.

But this man was also one of Pop-Pop's friends, and Pop-Pop had taken her to this man's house specifically to meet him. She frowned, suddenly missing Pop-Pop and Gamma very much, wondering why they had never come back.

The man leaned across the car, fought with something, and very slowly the window rolled down. *Must be broken*, she thought.

"You're quite a ways from home." He had a pleasant and friendly voice, but Lane decided to keep moving toward town.

The car followed her, and the man called to her again. "I'm Father Ray. Ray Keates. I see you in the grocery store sometimes, with Camilla."

I know that. She graced him with a glance. "You're Pop-Pop's friend."

Ray smiled. "That's right. I wasn't sure you'd remember. You running away? I can give you a lift. As far as town anyway."

Lane stopped and turned toward the car. Her lips pursed, and she glared at him. "You'll take me back," she said.

"No, no I won't. Not unless you want me to."

"I don't." Long hair flew out behind her as she pivoted on her heel and resumed her trek.

Ray eased off the brake, and the car drifted up to her again. "No worries then. I'll just take you to town." He popped open the passenger side door.

Lane considered the offer. Camilla always enjoyed talking to this man, his clothes all black save for the white square at his neck. And Pop-Pop made him the guardian of something or other, although she'd been too busy throwing rocks in the lake to pay any attention. Plus there was the matter of mountain lions waiting to eat her face off. She climbed into the front seat and winced a little as she sat.

Ray's eyebrows rose just a little. "Got yourself a spanking?"

She didn't answer, but she did wonder why he drove with the inside light on and why he looked at her so much—at her dress, her hair, her dirty hands and knees, and her eyes.

He pulled the car up in front of Marigold's Diner and shifted the gears into park. His body twisted sideways and leaned against the door, one arm draped casually along the back of the seat. "You hungry?" Lane's eyes grew wide, and her head bobbed up and down. "Let's go."

Ray swung his door open and stepped out. His left hand perched on the door while his right hand extended into the car to help her. She slid over, grabbed his hand, and swooshed out of the car in a flurry of hair and billowy dress, becoming a princess once again.

Marigold's Diner stayed open until midnight, and several patrons sat around chatting and eating. Lane had never been in the diner and thought that it looked rather dim and dirty. "Where do we sit?" she asked.

"I've got a favorite spot back in the corner, if nobody's there." He ushered her toward the last booth at the back of the restaurant and scooted in with his back to the door. Lane hopped in on the other side.

"Why do you like it back here?"

"I'm usually alone, so I come back here, and I talk to God while I wait for Marigold to fix my dinner."

"Who's God?"

Ray chuckled. "I'd love to introduce the two of you. I think you might like him."

"Why would I like him?" Lane's shoulders shrugged up, and her palms rose elbow-high toward the ceiling. "I don't know him."

"I think you'd like him *after* you got to know him. He's kind, and he takes care of us, and he loves you very much."

Lane's face screwed up and her nose wrinkled. Ray smiled. "You'll just have to trust me on it. But you'd have to stick around awhile. Can't do God justice over burgers and fries."

Marigold showed up promptly with menus, and Lane remembered her from the grocery store, too. The long hours of cooking, cleaning, and waiting tables made the waitress look much older than her forty-some odd years.

She compensated for her exaggerated age with vibrantly dyed hair, and tonight jet black tresses bordered her bloodless face. Grayish roots peered out from the hairline; no doubt she'd dye them again soon.

"Got a new friend, Father?" Marigold remembered Lane and her flippant attitude, the way she flicked around and ignored their first introduction.

"Hitchhiker. A hungry one, I think. I'll have my usual. And a cup of ice. How about you, little lady?"

Lane couldn't read the captions, nor did she recognize any of the pictures. "What is this stuff?"

Marigold scoffed. "Come on, those pictures aren't that bad. That's a hot dog."

"A hot *dog*?"

"Yeah, you never had hot dogs? Frankfurts? Tube steak?" When Lane shook her head, Marigold shrugged and pointed to another picture. "Not surprising. Them's chicken nuggets, comes with fries. This one"—her finger shifted to another picture—"is macaroni and cheese. Very popular with clientele like you."

Marigold blushed ever so slightly; she meant it to sound impressive rather than the snobbish way it came out. "I sell more mac and cheese to the four- to twelve-year-old crowd than any other single menu item. Make vats of the stuff," she said, quickly correcting herself.

Her clientele liked it. "I'll try it. And a glass of ice water, please."

Marigold almost laughed. "Cheese tubes and tap on ice for the young aristocrat," she said as she scribbled on her pad.

In the bright lights of the diner, Lane could see Ray better, especially his gorgeous eyes—light blue, almost gray—and sandy brown hair that was thinning at the top. He'd twisted sideways and leaned against the wall, resting an elbow on the table and cupping his chin in his hand.

Lane copied the pose, but her arms were too short to accomplish the task. He smiled at her antics, and his attention made him all the more appealing.

"So, what'd you do to get yourself a spanking?"

Lane frowned, pushing her lips out. "Not supposed to say."

"Ah. Can you say if you deserved it?"

She sucked her lips in, thought about the dinner plate sailing through the air, and Camilla stepping out of the way. "I threw a plate at the maid."

"Camilla? How did she take that?"

"I don't know. She's the maid."

A subtle change washed over Ray's face, but it vanished quickly. "She has feelings too, you know."

Lane shrugged, dismissing the notion that servants were as important as her.

"It was Camilla who called me. Told me you'd run away."

Lane looked up at him, eyelashes fluttering. "Camilla?"

"She was worried that you'd get hurt. You should trust her."

Marigold returned with their drinks, the ice, and a booster seat, which she simply slid onto Lane's side of the booth without a word. The youngster quickly figured it out, climbed into it, and found she could reach the table better. She took a big sip of water, slurping loudly when the straw pulled free of the glass.

"My fath—," Lane stopped mid-word. "Their bosses don't treat them very well."

Ray nodded his agreement. "I know. All the more reason for the rest of us to treat them better. Make up for it. Might be a good reason to stick around, unless you're dead set on heading out on your own. Learn a little about God, and maybe help Anton and Camilla in the process."

Ray let it sink in, pulling an ice cube from the cup. "Let me see your hands." His wiggling fingers urged her to agree. He circled her wrists and turned her hands over.

The ice cube melted across her right palm, initially sending pain impulses through the nerves and to her brain. Lane winced and tried to withdraw her hand, but Ray refused to let her go. He held her tight, sliding the ice cube around. A moment later, her struggling ceased.

"Better?" he asked. She considered it and nodded. "You try."

Lane helped herself to a fresh ice cube and slowly applied it to the damaged skin as Ray had done, sliding it over the irritation until the pain lessened. She studied his features, his broad smile and kind eyes. "What does 'died' mean?"

Ray's mouth fell open, forming a small *o*. "What?"

"Gamma and Pop-Pop 'died.' What's that mean?"

Ray folded his hands on the tabletop. "No one explained that to you?"

Lane shook her head and continued stroking the ice cube around her raw palms.

Ray took a deep breath, letting it out very slowly. "I can help you with that, but it's gonna require us to talk about God first. The two kinda go hand-in-hand, at least for me. And for your Gamma and Pop-Pop, too. You willing to stick around a while?"

Lane considered it briefly, but the food arrived, sparing her from having to agree to anything too quickly.

Marigold set several items down on the table; before Lane sat a bowl of golden ooze, wiggly pale tubes covered with gobs of yellow cheese. The spoon slid in easily, but Lane didn't quite trust that her clientele would even look at this gooey mess, let alone eat it.

But when it hit her tongue, her eyes opened wide, and a smile creased her face. She ate it all, right down to the last bit of goo stuck to the spoon. "How long do you think it would take to learn about God. And 'died'?"

Ray looked surprised that she'd brought the subject back up, but he shrugged and finished his last bite of burger. "Long as you want." He pulled a business card from his wallet, pushed it across the table to her.

"Fry?" He slid his plate into the center of the table while stuffing his mouth.

Lane examined them and noted the grease glistening in the light. Her chin dipped down to her chest, and she declined with an earnest shake of her head.

Ray nudged the business card closer to her. "Call me, or e-mail me, or come visit me any time you want. Put that in your pocket so you don't lose it." He waited while she tucked the card in the pocket of her dress. "So, you think we're friends now?"

She grew pensive, her head tipping toward her shoulder. Then she nodded. "Do you think you might run away again?" Ray asked.

Lane shrugged, and Ray queried further. "Can you promise me just one thing? If you ever decide to run away again, can you let me know first?"

"So you can talk me out of it?" Her face wrinkled up in an I-know-what-you're-up-to fashion.

"Not really. Just so I know. I have lots of friends. I can probably help with almost any problem you have. Deal?"

Lane liked this man. She liked the way his eyes twinkled, the way he held her hand and smiled, and the way his eyes absorbed every little thing she did. She liked that he cared about her even though he had no reason to. After a moment, she nodded, losing herself in his blue-gray eyes again. Maybe he could replace Morgan. "Can you be my new father?"

Ray just smiled. "I sort of am. I'm your godfather."

"What's that?"

"I'm the guy your parents asked to teach you about God. They just haven't allowed me get started on that yet."

"Really?" Lane felt a twinge of excitement and anticipation at the thought of spending more time with this man.

"Absolutely."

"*Absolument*," she said, mimicking words she'd heard Camilla and Anton use. She would keep her new friend, though she wouldn't tell Morgan or Jenna about him. She worried that it might earn her another spanking. *I guess I could hang around for a little while. And if it still doesn't work out, I can always run away again.*

Lane fell asleep in the car while Ray drove her home. The wrought-iron gate swung open as the car approached; Ray had called Camilla to let her know they were on the way, and he could see her in the front window waiting for them. *Just as well not to encounter any other Harrises tonight*, he thought.

Concern tormented him. She'd objectified Morgan and Jenna, referring to them as employers and deliberately not calling them her parents. At so young an age, that kind of distance didn't bode well for a normal relationship with them, and probably not with anyone else either.

The sleeping child nuzzled into Ray's chest as he carried her into the house, his arms firmly wrapped around her tiny body. *"Merci,* Father Ray, *Merci."* Camilla took the groggy child from the priest and stood her up on the floor. "Quickly, quickly. Up to your room."

She kept her voice low, but it didn't matter. Heels on the hardwood floor alerted everyone to Jenna's approach.

Eyes sweeping Ray from toes to crown, Jenna made no attempt to hide her disdain. "I suppose I should be thankful you and not some pervert found her." She whirled on Lane. "Go to your room. We'll deal with this in the morning."

Lane headed for the kitchen but eyed the cascading grand staircase. She shot a glance over her shoulder and snuck a wave to Ray. The corner of his mouth twisted into a smirk, and his eyes twinkled again. She delayed for another second, basking in Ray's attention, until Jenna turned around and gave her a cold stare.

Lips all scrunched up, Lane planted a deliberate foot on the grand staircase. She stopped, daring her mother to say or do anything with the priest in the house. She took another step, then another, and for a few minutes at least, she was the princess again, bouncing up the stairs with her long hair whipping to and fro.

She rounded the baluster, triumphant, but the victory proved short-lived; Morgan leaned against the wall at the top of the next flight of stairs, his arms folded across his chest and his lips curled back to reveal his teeth. *Wolf fangs.*

Lane counted on Father Ray's presence to keep Morgan from spanking her again, but when the front door closed downstairs, she ran for the servants' staircase.

chapter five

*L*ane always thought that first sprint through the house fore-shadowed her current love of running. That might have been the last time she ran from Morgan, but running gave her a feel of freedom and peace that she couldn't get any other way. It gave her a way to channel the pain and forget her past, if only for a little while. And by the time she turned seventeen, she'd grown really, really good at it. All of it.

Lane sprinted from the forest and ran easily toward the finish line. Now fifty yards ahead of her teammates and seventy yards ahead of any of the other competitors, no one could challenge her.

The wind bore down on her, chasing her across the field, bobbing and darting like a dog with a toy. It pressed against her as she dug a wider churn with her arms to keep her balance and pace.

The crowd remained quiet; the entire town hated her because of Morgan, and none of them would give her any credit for this achievement. *Well, there is one*, she reminded herself. An earsplitting whoop broke the morbid silence, and Lane smiled. In response, she pulled another burst from her gut and charged home, racing as hard and eager as if she'd just left the starting line.

Ray continued to cheer, his voice getting coarse and his cheers turning to screams. Lane pointed at him as she threw herself through the tape, then jogged to a stop and sank to her knees to thank God.

The crowd finally erupted with their own screams. No doubt her teammates had finally come into view, straggling out of the forest in dribs and drabs, winded and struggling. *And beaten*, Lane thought. *Wicked beaten.*

The team coach stared down the field with one of many individual trophies clutched in her hands, waiting for someone else, anyone else, to finish. It didn't matter. Ray crushed Lane with a fierce bear hug and whisked her away toward the parked cars, deliberately taking the long route past the trophy table. Ray strode past the coach, an arm still draped around Lane's shoulders, and snatched the trophy from the coach's hands in Lane's honor.

chapter six

*V*oices, laughter, and the clattering of dishes echoed through Marigold's Diner. Lane drifted back to the present, letting go of the shadows of humiliation she'd endured after her runaway attempt; they hacked off her hair, replaced all her delicate clothes with jeans and shirts, and gave her chores to do like the hired help. It wasn't the worst thing they had done to her; the haircut, the jeans, and the tee shirts proved practical considering her lot in life. On top of that, the chopped hair and unstylish wardrobe constantly reminded Morgan and Jenna of their sins, and Lane rather liked that idea. She smiled, shook it off, tuned her attention to the present.

Mills Valley hosted several year-round restaurants, but Marigold's stood out as the local favorite. It often filled to capacity, but seldom had it hosted a party that streamed out to the street and wrapped around the building. And never had it drawn the attention of the local sheriff's office to monitor traffic, drunkenness, and disorderly conduct. No one who frequented Marigold's cared about the old furniture or the heavy smell of grease in the air, which had long ago stained the wallpaper and curtains a yellowish brown. And no one cared about the calories, the trans fat, or the cholesterol-laden dishes guaranteed to cause a coronary. Marigold's held the distinction of being comfy; everyone just liked the place and its familiar sights, sounds and smells.

Usual celebrations included weddings, graduations or birthday parties, even homecomings for soldiers; tonight, the diner hosted the local high school's girls' cross-country team, fresh off the town's first win in decades. Throngs of family, friends, and other proud citizens streamed in slowly, their bodies keeping the door open. The line snaked around tables and gradually made its way toward the counter and the object of everyone's attention: the team trophy.

Ringed by a rotation of mustard and ketchup bottles, the trophy sat atop the counter in the place of honor, which was usually reserved for the pie case. Every well-wisher entering to congratulate the team stopped by the counter first, just to pat the trophy's head.

The double-columned statue stood nearly two feet tall and touted a runner on top, a winged angel below. Each girl on the team had a miniature version, single columned sans the angel, topping out at just ten inches high.

Father Ray beamed like the proud dad of a newborn. He unbuttoned the top of his shirt and slid a finger under his Roman collar to loosen it. Sitting opposite Lane in their favored corner booth, he tried, but failed, to wipe the "Cheshire cat" grin from his face.

He hadn't aged poorly in his fifty years, but neither could he deny that he'd earned those years with his graying hair and the deep-enough-to-grow-corn wrinkles that troughed his forehead. His blue-gray eyes had lost their youthful vibrancy, but not their crystal clear focus.

To Lane, he always resembled a pixie, and she mumbled at him as she stuffed the last bite of burger into her mouth.

"Stop." She wiped away the grease trailing down her chin.

"Can't help it."

"Try eating."

Ray laughed, pinched a few fries between his fingers, and stuffed them in. He munched on them for a few seconds, the grin disappearing briefly.

"See? Already you don't look so dorky. See any scouts?"

The smile returned, ear to ear, wide and toothy. Teepees made from sugar packets circled Lane's individual trophy, one side white, one side pink Sweet'N Low. Ray tossed a glance at the team trophy, checked the placement of his last teepee, and happily rubbed the statue's head.

Lane scruffed a hand through her short, jagged brown hair, slouched down, and kicked her feet onto the booth next to Ray.

She'd just turned seventeen back in December, joining the team this year only because of Ray's encouragement, but she now ranked as the town's best runner, pushing out the high school records of both Ray and his brother Richard for the top honor. Ray eyed her feet. "Need more room?"

Whooping from the front of the diner drew Lane's gaze, but Ray ignored it. "Saw two scouts in the crowd today." He glanced across the table, at the sadness in her hazel eyes, her desire to belong. Just another friend or two and she'd be like other kids, but all she had was him.

And his friendship had been the only thing keeping her from delving headfirst into an abyss of self-pity and depression. With his eyes shooting briefly to the ceiling, he apologized silently for not granting any recognition to God for his part, and he reminded himself that Lane teetered on the edge of that abyss regularly. He followed her gaze and found her teammates back-slapping and guffawing over their win—a win they owed entirely to Lane.

"They took Dorey to task on your time. Said she padded seven seconds on. They were hopping mad—threw their credentials at her and everything." He trailed off, waited.

Lane heard everything; the only issue to resolve was whether or not she'd acknowledge what she heard.

"They called her an ugly, old goat," he added.

Lane's focus came back to Ray, slowly. First just her eyes shifted, locking on his with the dead stare that she only used when somebody had gotten her dander up, or when she couldn't believe what she'd heard. Then her head followed, snapping sharply to face him. "She *is* an ugly old goat."

He shrugged. "Uh, yeah. Anyway, they made her fix it." He leaned across the table and folded her small hands in his. "I am so proud of you."

"For kicking the crap out of your record?"

"Never any doubt of that. No, for kicking the crap out of Richard's record." From his pocket he withdrew a metal strip engraved with the meet, the date, and Lane's name. The wax backing peeled off easily, and he pressed the metal strip onto her trophy.

A smile broke Lane's face. "You didn't?"

"Course I did. Went down to Olympia. Got it myself. Not like those jokers are going to make it a point to get it for you. And"—he pulled a small, wrapped box out of his suit jacket—"I got you this."

Her smile challenged Ray's for the most teeth displayed. She slid her finger under the scotch tape and slowly unwrapped the present. A tiny silver cross stared out at her, and she carefully slipped it over her head. "It's beautiful. Thanks. And for dinner, too. This was really great."

"Not done yet." He pulled the menu from its holder, slapped it on the table, and planted his finger on the diner's signature dessert, *Mountain of Mud.* His eyebrows danced up and down on his face,

39

daring Lane to accept the invitation.

"Sometimes you are such a dork."

On cue, Marigold arrived at the table, her freshly dyed hair cutting a bright red swath against the drab wallpaper. She set down a deep bowl holding twelve scoops of ice cream, six toppings and whipped cream.

"I'm gonna be so sick."

"Good thing you ain't racing tomorrow," Ray laughed, shoveling a big scoop of Rocky Road into his mouth.

chapter seven

*T*he black Falcon idled by the side of the road with only its parking lights on. A pull-off attested to its routine visits; the car's tires ground away the vegetation over the years and left nothing behind but worn tracks. Moisture condensed on the inside of the windows, fogging them up a little and forcing Ray to flip on the defroster every now and then.

Beside the car stood a narrow grove of woods, one hundred feet across at its widest point. The white lights of the Harris Mansion's exterior lighting system blazed out over the security wall, shooting fingers of light amongst the trees. Ray twisted and draped one arm over the back of the seat and the other along the door. "Musta been a helluva party. Hope you cleaned the pool."

Lane nodded. "Before the meet this morning."

His fingers toyed along the steering wheel, and he studied Lane as she rambled on about her classes, the additional work for the Early College Program, and her worries and hopes about leaving Mills Valley. The odd shadows cast by the dashboard light couldn't hide the emotions playing on her face. His watch chimed the hour, and he absently glanced at it: two a.m. "I'm only a phone call away."

"And a ferry ride and a long-ass car drive."

Ray chuckled. "I think you string profanity together just to see my reaction."

"You know what I mean. We aren't gonna be able to just *visit*."

"Yeah, uh, phone call?"

"Not the same." She leaned against the door. "You're, like, my father. Well, better than my father." Lane tossed him a haphazard glance and pinched her eyes into a tight squint in response to his silly grin. "You *know* what I mean."

"We discussed all this. Why the cold feet? I'll wire you the money so you can come home for Christmas. Besides, for all you know, you're gonna meet some boy and forget all about me. You'll end up spending every spare minute with him." Ray glanced out the window, blinking quickly to overcome the sadness stinging his eyes.

Lane sighed. "Yeah, you're probably right. All these years with no friends at all, I'll probably grab hold of the first boy I see, and hell, just never come up for air."

Ray's head jerked back to Lane, his finger pointing at her sternly. "No sex."

Lane laughed nervously. "So *this* is what it's like to talk sex with your father," and she buried her face in her hands.

"I'm serious. On second thought, I'll just drive out and get you myself."

"Relax, will ya? You'll be the first one I tell if I'm thinking about it, OK?"

"OK, OK. I can live with that. Wait. *Live with* may be the wrong choice of words. Coming over after Mass tomorrow, uh, today?"

"*Absolument.*"

"Bring your license. I'll let you drive after dinner. You need to keep your skills up."

"Cool. It's great the way your mom trusts you with the car."

Ray lunged across the Falcon and swatted her playfully. "You get the hell outta my car!"

"Whose car?"

"Out!" He swatted her again, then pulled her close, planted a kiss on top of her head. "You know you're the daughter I can't have, right?"

Lane nodded. "I'm sorry."

Ray cocked his head to the side. "For being the daughter I can't have?"

"For ruining your whole life."

Ray dismissed the allegation. "My congregation may be a tad smaller than it was, but I didn't lose the sheep that needed me most."

Lane hugged him fiercely and whispered, "I wish you were my real dad."

"I love you," he said.

"Love you more."

Ray countered, as he always did in their playful style. "Doubt it, but I loved you first."

Lane smiled. "Can't argue with that."

A car rounded the bend behind them, its headlights stabbing through the darkness. Ray glanced in the rearview, concerned only that the oncoming vehicle could see the parked car and avoid it.

The car veered right, pulled to the side of the road, and approached slowly. Ray slid his arm off Lane and reached for the on-the-column shift of the car's Ford-O-Matic Transmission.

Lane sensed his increasing nervousness and slid back to the passenger side so that Ray would have room to maneuver if he had to put the car in drive. Seconds later, the darkness yielded to the flashing blue lights of the newcomer.

The private moment was destroyed; Lane scrunched down in the passenger seat, hiding in the little space available.

Ray glanced out his window at the sheriff's dark sedan, which inched forward and pulled up alongside them. "Unbelievable." Ray cranked down the manual window and waited.

A moment later, the cruiser's power window slid down and the interior light clicked on.

Ray kept his voice upbeat and friendly. "Hiya, Richard. What's up?"

Sheriff Richard Keates, Ray's younger brother, leaned forward to see around Ray. "Having car trouble?"

"No."

"Kind of late to be out here, what? Parking?"

Lane muttered under her breath. "Jerk."

Ray reached over, patted her knee. "Just relax." Turning back to Richard, he smiled pleasantly. "Thank you for checking, Sheriff. Good night."

Richard smiled back. "Move along."

"Oh for God's sake, Richard. What do you do? Follow me around town?"

Lane returned Ray's pat on the knee. "Just relax." She threw open her door, jumped out. She leaned across the top of the Falcon and stared at Richard, not that she could see him very well. "What's the problem, Dick?"

The sheriff's face twisted with his displeasure and he didn't like her attitude at all. "I could just arrest you."

"For what? Standing on my own property, minding my own business? Run with that one."

Ray leaned across the seat, shushed at her. "Don't make it any worse."

"How can it be worse?" She ducked into the car. "Can I leave my pack with you until tomorrow?"

Ray nodded. "I'll wait 'til you're over the wall."

With a parting wave, she headed into the woods, much to Richard's chagrin.

"I'm not done with you."

Lane whirled, flipped him off. "So shoot me." She headed further into the woods and stopped abruptly. She spun back around, flipped him off again in stereo. Both hands high and deliberate. Ray's chuckle drifted to her on the night air but faded quickly once she entered the trees.

The path wound through the strip of forest, meandering around trees and rock outcroppings on its way to the security wall. Years of use, starting very shortly after her first meal with Ray, kept the ground packed hard and the weeds at bay.

She'd quickly grown independent, far faster than other children her age. While their mothers or fathers waited with them at the bus stops, Lane marched there on her own, having regressed from chauffeur-driven luxury to public transportation. The days ended much the same, Lane tramping down Harris Lane alone while moms in other neighborhoods collected their chicks and ushered them home. That is unless Lane missed the bus; if Ray was around, he'd give her a lift, otherwise she hiked all the way from town. The natural progression grew exponentially: sneaking out of the house to visit the priest, climbing trees and scaling the security wall, and hiding out in the pantry to discover the code to the alarm.

Those skills precipitated visits to the priest without Morgan's or Jenna's knowledge. Back in those days, Ray didn't approve of her behavior, and that required another skill—blackmail—she threatened to simply run away. He got over his uneasiness. And she developed muscles most little girls didn't use.

The tree had been chosen years ago because it filled all the requirements for climbing: a low initial branch with an easily accessible first joint, close placement of secondary branches spiraling around a stout trunk, and proximity to the security wall.

Lane caught the lowest limb and hauled herself up into the tree, climbed the twelve feet, and peered over the wall near the servants' quarters to see if any dangers lurked in the backyard.

With no one in sight, she eased out toward the wall, and with her hands upon the cold, smooth stone, she shifted her weight onto her arms and pulled herself onto the wall.

She turned back to the street, upset that she'd left her best friend in the lurch again. Ray waved; Richard stood by Ray's window with his arms folded across his chest.

Getting down from the wall no longer included fear as it had when she was younger. The length of her arms added to her overall height leaving just over four feet between her and the ground, which just happened to be the height of the cordwood stacked neatly between the servants' quarters and the wall. And since the cordwood lay covered by bins that Anton had built to hide the wood and protect it from the weather, the drop was easy and stable. Crouched low, she double-checked for guests, then crept to the corner of the servants' quarters. The gentle puttering of the Falcon and the roar of the sheriff's V-8 faded into the distance.

The servants' quarters, a small bungalow decorated to complement the main building, housed only Anton and Camilla, even though Morgan designed it to hold more servants if the need ever arose. To that end, it boasted three bedrooms, three baths, and a common living/kitchen area. All of its windows were dark.

From the corner of the building, Lane peered out over the extensive and well-manicured property. Hedged walkways meandered about the grounds, and guests as well as owners often indulged in pleasant evening strolls. The hedges periodically scooped out into the lawn and provided alcoves with benches and private seating among picturesque gardens.

With her back to the wall, Lane ducked around the corner in a tight ball, sliding in behind a row of shrubs. She leaned forward into the greenery, pressing her face into the newly trimmed boughs and breathing the sweet aroma. *Funny that they didn't smell this good when I trimmed them.*

The side and rear of the main house sprawled out before her. Three porticos announced the grander entrances to the rear of the house while a simple door near the servants' quarters allowed Anton and Camilla access to the kitchen.

Parties had been a mainstay as long as Lane could remember— though she'd never actually been allowed to attend any of them— and tonight's was no different than any other. They were mostly held on Saturday evenings, allowing guests and hosts alike a chance to recover before going back to work.

Lane learned many things from earlier parties, most notably not to attempt to sneak into the house until all the guests had departed. Failing to heed Morgan's warning was the quickest way to earn a whack in the head. But she also learned to absorb and process the clues that the yard and house provided.

At that moment, the mess in the backyard told a story of wanton disregard for the house staff and the property of the homeowner. Plates with discarded remnants, half-empty glasses, and napkins scattered about told Lane that the guests couldn't even bother picking up after themselves.

It also revealed that Camilla and Anton had gone to bed; not having cleaned the premises immediately after the party meant that the master of the house had retired and didn't want to hear them scurrying about.

From her hiding place, Lane searched each floor, window and door, and studied the patterns of light and dark, scanning for movement in the shadows and along the curtains. Sporadic lights dotted the first and second floors, but the master suite windows glowed with slivers of white at the edges of the curtains. *Not that uncommon*, she thought; Morgan and Jenna often stayed up after a party, recalling events and comparing notes, and planning how best to utilize the information to their advantage.

With each dark window and still curtain, Lane's confidence grew that she would safely reach her bedroom. She crawled out of the shrubs and headed swiftly toward the servants' door.

Camilla always locked and armed the door when she retired for the evening, and the alarm began its chirping as soon as Lane entered. She quickly punched in the disable code to silence it, then just as quickly reset it. And she flicked off the exterior lights, not wanting to hear a lecture about wasted electricity in the morning.

A foil-covered plate sat on the counter nearest the door, an *L* blazoned across the top in black marker. Lane scooped it up as she crept across the kitchen, rounded the prep table, and headed down the servants' passage toward the great room.

The passage—a hallway that provided a buffer between the kitchen and Morgan's office—kept the chaos of the kitchen hidden and provided a secret entrance and exit for the house staff. Recessed lights in the ceiling provided illumination during busy times, but at night, button lights near the floor showed the way, reminding Lane of a movie theater.

She reached the end of the hall and peered out. The dim light in the great room assured her that no guests remained.

Running two-thirds the length of the house, the great room—

normally the picture of high society style—had been laid to waste. The partygoers had left swill, plates and glasses all over the room. Water rings marred the wood surfaces, plates balanced precariously on the backs of sofas, and appetizers and wine stained the rug.

Lane prayed that Camilla and Anton would have time to clean the mess before Morgan got up; God knew the hell he'd put everyone through if he saw his precious house this way.

The track meet and celebrating with Ray had left her physically drained; she desperately wanted to sleep, but she put off her own needs and decided to give Camilla a hand.

The bar held an assortment of serving trays as well as trash bags, and Lane toured the great room, cleaning up the litter. Half an hour and several trips to the kitchen later, the visible swill had been cleaned up, but Camilla would still have to tend to the stained furniture and carpeting.

She slid the last tray load of dishes onto the kitchen counter along with other findings: a purse, a pair of eyeglasses, and a single, lonely earring. She gathered up the foil-covered plate and headed up the servants' staircase.

Wine footprints and a solitary piece of cake marked the path taken by a guest; why they'd been in the servants' staircase was anyone's guess, but the tracks continued all the way to the second floor.

They ended at a guestroom. Lane rolled her eyes, muttered under her breath. "Harris Hotel. Plan all your affairs with us." One more thing Camilla would have to clean up.

She continued up to the third floor. *No turning back,* she thought as she peered down the hallway to the master suite. Lights still showed under the door, but no shadows revealed any movement inside.

The attic door beckoned from across the hall. The button lock wasn't engaged, nor did any obvious booby traps scream "Danger! Danger!" No bells, no additional locks, no issues to be considered before running headlong through. Nothing to slow her down or let Morgan catch her.

She darted across the hall and ducked into the stairwell. The dim light from the hallway illuminated the entry space just enough to see that no one lay in ambush, and she eased the door into the frame without making any sound at all.

The light remained off; she knew the way. *Three steps forward, slide the foot 'til it bumps wood, then grab the rails.* Not that she needed the handrails; they just provided a way to lift her weight off the stairs and kept the wood from creaking as she tiptoed up.

At the top, she pushed open the final door and snapped on two lights, one at each end of the attic. She peered in. The coast remained clear; no one lurked in here either, and she breathed a sigh of relief as she padded quietly down the center aisle.

Over the years, the room had multiple looks, eventually resulting in an approximation of what Lane thought an apartment would look like. Excess furniture jammed along the walls and into corners created a border effect, a corral of sorts. The simple arrangement of furniture yielded a bedroom area on the front wall of the house, though she hadn't been strong enough to manhandle the mattress onto the frame until she was twelve. A TV tray near the bed pretended to be a night stand.

A couch served double duty as the footboard for the bed and as divider between the bedroom and living room. A coffee table sat beyond the couch, complete with neatly stacked magazines, a doily, and two small trophies. Gamma Jo's easy chair kept a watchful eye on Pop-Pop's old box TV, opposing it from across the coffee table. Lane set it up that way because it reminded her of the one time she'd heard Gamma and Pop-Pop fight, something about Lane's future. They'd argued for a few minutes, then their mouths clamped tight. They just stared at each other wide-eyed from opposite sides of their kitchen table, and they kept it up until their granddaughter's giggling broke the standoff.

On the other side of the center aisle, the dining area snuggled up against the rear wall of the house. An oak-colored hutch hugged the wall with a minifridge on the floor next to it. It claimed no expensive china; instead, it hosted paper- and plasticware, a teapot, a hot plate, and an assortment of nonperishable and easily prepared food items.

An oblong table with six matching chairs completed the dining room. Lessons for the Early College Program sat in three piles: waiting to be turned in, waiting for grades to come back, and being ignored in favor of just about anything else.

The bathroom had been updated as well. Several milk crates stacked against the wall between the toilet and sink held her towels, toilet paper, and toiletries. The closet-sized room still lacked a door, but a spring-loaded curtain rod and an old blanket gave it the illusion of privacy.

Lane set the plate on the table, peeled the foil off, and revealed a cupcake—chocolate with vanilla frosting. Little sprinkles covered the top, and gel icing scrawled "Congratulations" across the top edge of the plate. Both Anton and Camilla had signed their names across the bottom edge, Anton in blue icing, Camilla in red.

Lane smiled, glad that she, Camilla, and Anton had become friends, even though they had to keep it hidden from Morgan. She wolfed down the tiny cake in three massive bites and licked the remnants of frosting from her fingers.

She moved to the end of the table, leaned her hip against it, one foot under, one foot stretched behind her, and applied steady pressure. The table moved.

In the attic, which ran the entire length of the house, any noise generated would be heard on the third floor. If that wasn't bad enough, any noise made near the pipes or ducts ran the risk of being heard in all the bathrooms on the first and second floors and in the kitchen.

With steady pressure, the table shifted—millimeters, fractions of fractions of an inch—without any noise at all. Its leg moved past a spot only Lane could identify. She kneeled on the floor, slid her fingers under the lip of the hutch, and pulled her pocketknife from its hiding place.

Two sections of floorboards had to be removed to reveal the hiding place of her most precious possessions. The laptop PC she had bought for school nestled inside the hole along with an assortment of items that needed protection from Morgan and Jenna.

Over the course of the day, her pocket amassed a wad of crap: her trifolded paystub, a deposit slip, and the bank envelope holding her leftover cash. She pulled the mass out and sorted through it.

Lane's job hours had changed some as she grew older and now required her to put in a minimum of twenty-five hours per week, more if she wanted or needed to. She seldom wanted to and only occasionally needed to, but it provided a dependable way to earn ten dollars per hour.

She'd worked since the day they hacked off her hair, but when she turned fourteen Morgan put her on his employee rolls and took taxes and social security out of the check. And he demanded the same exacting standards of her as he did from any of his employees. Worse ways to make a living existed, but better ones did, too. The kids at school all talked about minimum wage, and why anyone on earth would expect them to do all that manual labor for just seven sixty-five per hour. Paint jockey at the hardware store or waiting tables at Marigold's certainly sounded more desirable than yard worker and custodian. But she did have them beat by two-plus bucks per hour. And she didn't have to chew up her paycheck buying gas to get to work, be that in Mills Valley, or Shelton, or Hoodsport.

On top of that, her job entailed mostly outdoor work. Three seasons of gorgeous or tolerable weather gave her outstanding views of the Olympics and the forests. She enjoyed the feel of the wind caressing her face and the smile of the sun as it toasted her skin to a golden hue; most of the time, there was nothing not to like about it.

Those three good seasons provided Anton with yard help, and he had shown Lane how to manicure the shrubbery, create topiaries, how to mulch, fertilize, and provide general care for the gardens. He also showed her how to clean and shock the pool, monitor the chemistry of the water, and open and close it depending on the season. She became the "pool girl."

Once she had completed any necessary lawn or pool maintenance, she focused on the equipment, buildings, and fences. Something always needed tending, whether it was washing equipment, painting walls, tuning engines, fixing light fixtures, replacing plumbing, or patching mortar.

When the more brutal days of winter struck, equipment and building maintenance continued, but the work focused on the interior areas of the buildings. Camilla welcomed the help but usually gave Lane tasks designed to keep her out of Morgan's sight, like cleaning the basement or the pantry.

But the hardest winter job remained shoveling, and ten dollars per hour didn't adequately compensate for the backbreaking, viciously cold task of clearing snow off the massive driveway, walkways, and multiple patios. Even with Anton fighting alongside her to get it done, it took hours, and they were both numb from the cold by the time they finished.

Lane consoled herself with the paycheck, much of which remained in the bank for future college expenses. But she usually kept some on hand for her own personal needs. Morgan and Jenna supplied her food, though Lane often wondered if they knew it; it was possible that Camilla still snuck nourishment to her after all these years. Everything else she had to buy for herself—clothes, school supplies, and anything else she wanted or needed. She almost bought a new mattress, but Ray convinced her that she didn't need it; she'd be going off to college, and her new school would provide the bed.

She carefully dropped coins into a recycled pickle jar, and split the currency bills into two piles. Twenty went back into her pocket in case she needed it during the week, and the other thirty went into an envelope. She added the "deposit" to the tally written on the outside of the envelope and added up the new total, pleased that her stash of "mad money" had grown to nearly four hundred dollars.

She yawned and stretched widely, ready for a good night's sleep. She filed away the paystub and deposit slip in their designated folders, dropped her wallet in with her treasures, then grabbed the floorboards and fit the first one back in its spot.

The second board lay across her lap, bottom side up, and she admired the etchings she'd carved with her knife. Her name was there, along with Ray's, Gamma's and Pop-Pop's. She ran her fingers along their names, wished them goodnight, then set the board back in place.

From the opposite side of the table, she slowly and carefully pushed the table back to its original spot, covering the loose floorboards and keeping them secure from the casual prying of her landlords.

She tiptoed across the floor, nudged off her shoes, and crawled into bed with both her clothes and the lights still on.

chapter eight

*T*he overhead light mixed with the diffuse natural sunshine to create a murky visibility in the attic, like a bar during the day before the lights go on. The environmental system hummed softly as it cycled off and on. Lane slept face-down on the bed, breathing slowly, dreaming of Disneyland.

The crowd pressed in on her, separating then fifteen-year-old Lane from Ray as they disembarked the Canal Boats. She pursued him, twisting around the masses determined to keep her from him, and he waved at her from the entrance to Sleeping Beauty's Castle. The gate swung closed as she reached it. Just barely squeaking through as it clanged shut, she ran for the classroom, taking a seat at the rear of the auditorium as Ray lectured the students on helping those less fortunate. The floorboards creaked as he paced before the chalkboard. Odd that the plush carpeting didn't prevent the noise.

Lane's eyes snapped open.

Thick fingers wrapped around the back of her neck before she had time to react. Morgan yanked her out of her bed in a single motion, and shock immediately replaced her grogginess. Lane tensed as the offending hand dragged her backward.

Morgan suddenly released her; momentum carried her into the center aisle. Lane stumbled backwards and landed on her butt. Her eyes fixed on his legs as she rose slowly.

His arms folded across his chest, but they didn't hide any of his two hundred fifty pound, six-and-a-half-foot body. His hair had all gone white in the last ten years, but his age hadn't yet softened his demeanor. His coal-black eyes burned into her, and Lane prepared for his worst.

But his voice remained calm and soft, betraying no hint of his smoldering anger. "I asked you to do one simple thing."

"I cleaned the pool." Lane's shoulders shrugged up, her hands turning palm forward.

Morgan pierced her with a glance; her hands immediately dropped back to her sides, and she fell silent. "Any idea how embarrassed Jenna was? How embarrassed I was?"

Lane opened her mouth to speak, but Morgan cut her off. "Did I ask you for an explanation? It's always about you. No matter what I give you, no matter what I do for you, how well I treat you. All I ask is that you clean the pool. If you were an employee, you'd be fired by now." He stepped forward; she took a nervous step away.

"I know you're not running from me."

Run, run, run! Her brain screamed, but the next few moments would only be worse if she listened. Footsteps echoed, and Morgan's body grew larger with each stride closer to her. And then his hand rose.

The slap rocked her face to the side, and she sagged to her knees. Instinctively, one hand rose to protect her while the other reached for the floor.

The defense failed, and the backhand hammered the other side of her face; Morgan's square, black onyx ring caught the corner of her eye. The blow knocked her off balance, toppling her. Morgan dragged her up, wrapped his hand around the back of her neck, and forced her across the attic.

The next few minutes blurred by. Impacting the door at the bottom of the stairs. A friction burn across her elbow when he dragged her to the servant's stairwell. Terror choking the air out of her lungs by the time they hit the first floor.

His fingers never wavered as they dug into the sides of her neck and controlled her every move like a puppeteer with his favorite puppet, and he dragged her across the room and out the kitchen door.

She had one chance; she let her body sag to the ground. The dead weight on the end of his arm slowed him, but it didn't stop him. Morgan swapped his grip on her neck for a handful of her shirt and continued dragging her to the pool.

Lane lived in this house her whole life and tended to the pool for years, but she'd never been in it, forbidden even to sit on the edge to cool off on hot summer days. Swimming was a skill she never acquired. Panic welled inside her, and she pounded on his arms and hands.

Morgan didn't notice. He dragged her to the edge of the pool. And he threw her in.

Slapping around in twelve feet of water didn't bring Lane any closer to the edge. A small frog swam past her, determined to escape the commotion she created.

"There he is. Did you miss him, or did you think he wouldn't return?" Morgan's lips peeled back, pearly whites flashing out in a rabid smile.

With her arms thrashing wildly, a single thought popped into Lane's mind as she sank below the water: *Only Ray will miss me.*

Instead of her life, Ray flashed before her eyes: his voice, his smile, the laughter in his eyes, the touch of his hand. His attempts to teach her to swim at the lake.

Every instinct in her body demanded that she fight, but Ray's voice thundered in her head. *Relax! Find the bottom!*

She focused on the memory, his features distorting as she drifted below the murky surface of the lake. A rope draped down off the dock and tethered her waist to his hand, just in case.

Her thrashing arms slowed and hung in the water. Morgan's shifting image danced above as she slowly sank to the pool floor. Outstretched toes touched the bottom; her heart leapt, but she resisted her first impulse. She needed more leverage, and so she waited, letting the soles of her feet find the smooth surface. Then her heels touched down. She bent her knees, sinking even lower, and prepared to spring.

Well out into the middle of the pool, Lane gathered what little strength she had left and pushed off the bottom. She prayed the angle would carry her close to the pool's edge, but as she broke the surface, she remained too far out. She windmilled, arms slapping desperately, spraying water in all directions; Morgan took a step away and frowned at the solitary drop that spattered his pant leg. But the windmilling did the trick, moving her the few inches necessary so that her outstretched fingertips found purchase. She pulled herself in, hung over the edge, and gasped for air, too tired to even attempt climbing out.

"Moron." Morgan stared down at her.

Her lungs ached as they refilled over and over, compensating for the lost breaths. But when Morgan took a step in her direction, she found enough air to ease away and head for the stairs.

Morgan followed, taking a step every time she pulled herself closer to the exit. "So you *are* running from me."

Lane spit pool water from her mouth and sputtered at him. "No, I'm just getting out."

He continued to shadow her. When she reached the stairs, she climbed up just two and waited.

He pointed to a spot on the concrete in front of him, like ordering a dog to sit or stay. Lane took a tentative step in his direction, then another, but not fast enough for Morgan's liking.

Despite his size, Morgan was surprisingly fast, and a single step put him within arm's length of her. His hand wrapped around her windpipe, and he dragged her away.

Hungry lungs sent panic racing back to the brain. She yanked on his forearm but couldn't dislodge the hand cutting off her air. She moved on to more direct measures.

Punches and slaps bounced off his arms, but her limbs were too short to reach the intended target—his face. Unfazed by her futile attempts, he ushered her down the driveway, out the gate, and into the street, where he simply released her.

Lane gasped for air. Over Morgan's shoulder, she spied an emotionless Jenna in the window of the second-floor landing.

With one final act of defiance, Lane lunged at Morgan. He countered, and the backhand toppled her to the ground.

Clouds floated peacefully by, a gentle wind tousled tree limbs. Birds chirped. The neighbor kids across the street laughed merrily. A hornet buzzed about her face, and for some strange reason, she didn't care. The wrought-iron gate clanged shut.

Several moments later, the euphoria wore off and realization set in. Her head throbbed where it touched the ground. She struggled to rise, rolling onto her hands and knees, then sat back on her heels.

Her face stung where Morgan's giant hands had slapped her, but her eye hurt, and her touch caused a wince as she gently probed it. Blood dripped onto her jeans from her split lip. She didn't feel any broken bones or other serious damage, and she pulled her shirt up to wipe away the tears and blood.

Wobbly from the ordeal, she balanced on one hand as she rose to her feet. The laughter grew louder, and three of her schoolmates rode toward her on their bikes.

They steered circles around her, laughing and mocking her, taking pictures with their camera phones. The largest of them, quarterback Jason Olsen, drove in close and bumped her with his bike as he threw a towel over her head.

"Looking better already."

On any other day, a day when her blood wasn't busy staining the street, she would have considered clotheslining him as he rode past. He wouldn't see it coming; one quick jolt to the neck would knock him clean off that pretty green ten-speed.

But today, she couldn't outrun him. He'd beat the crap out of her for sure. *Another day, Jason.*

Jake, Jason's father, called the boys back and their laughter faded. Lane pulled the towel down to her shoulders and pressed it against her lip. A bright red splotch spread across the terry cloth. With her bike tucked safely away from Morgan in Ray's garage, walking the four miles to Ray's house became Lane's only option: the lack of shoes and the pain throbbing in her head precluded running.

She began her trek.

Mill Road provided the easier route, but Jason and his buddies would have free access to her. Without a doubt, they'd dog her all the way to town, and there was no end to the damage Jason could inflict when his father let him off the leash.

The forest, even with its wild animals, was likely the safer route. Posted as private property, she wouldn't have to worry about Jason, his friends, or any of the town's other citizens.

Lane cast a last glance toward the house. Jenna still stood guard in the window. Her arms dropped to her side, and with exaggerated flourish, she twirled from the window and vanished from view.

The wind danced along in the treetops as Lane headed into the forest, daring her to run with it. She eyed the tousled leaves but ignored the invitation.

The pain in her head eased a bit after the first mile, but she still needed time to pull herself together before she arrived at Ray's. She thought about swinging down to the Keates' homestead to get cleaned up, but the sheriff usually drove over to the cabin on Sundays, either before or after his weekly visit to his mother's house. Sometimes he fished; most times he toured the property, checking for damage and vandalism. He seldom stayed long, but if Lane took the detour down to the lake and found him there, not only would she be unable to get cleaned up, she'd have killed the time for no reason.

Her slow journey gave her time to consider her life, or lack of it. Morgan and Jenna hated her, the town sheriff spent every waking minute punishing her for Morgan's sins, and her schoolmates tormented her. Her teammates tolerated her, though. Sometimes. But

Lane was sure it was only because she won meets.

The Early College Program that Ray had helped her enter would enable her to skip her senior year of high school altogether, but her only way out of Mills Valley depended on a scholarship that she wasn't sure she wanted.

If she continued to run well and win her meets, college scouts would camp out, preferably on Ray's doorstep, to induce her to attend their schools. But that meant leaving Ray, the only person on the planet she could talk to about anything. He assured her over and over that she'd meet kids at school, kids who didn't know anything about Morgan, kids who wouldn't punish her for being his daughter.

The plan meant finishing the last two months of her junior year and enduring two months of summer. Ray had already called in favors and gotten her a conditional acceptance to his Alma Mater, the University of Washington. The only kink in the plan was the funds to pay for college and Lane's ability to endure the isolation, loneliness, and emotional abuse of her current situation. "And the occasional well-placed slap," she exclaimed to herself. Lane blotted an arm against her eyes, soaking up the tears. But the more she thought about it, the more her eyes welled up. With each tear that escaped down her face, her nose congested even more, and no amount of sniffing freed it up.

A small stream blocked the trail, its width dotted with stones. Normally she would just cross to the other side, but today she stopped halfway, dipped Jason's towel in the cool water, and mopped up her face as best she could.

The wind continued to dance in the treetops, challenging her, calling her, wooing her back to play even as she crested the final rise. Mills Valley Township sprawled below.

Mill Road coursed west from Highway 101, halfway between Shelton and Hoodsport. Ten miles in, it swung north, transected Mills

Valley Township, and ended in the national forest just two miles past the downtown area. Main Street intersected Mill Road, and the spot proudly boasted the town's one and only traffic light.

The narrow band of land on the south side of town abutted the foothills and road embankments. Unsuited to residential outcroppings, the narrow band held several businesses, the post office, and the sheriff's office.

The north side of Main sprawled out with about half the businesses in town on or very near Main Street.

Pearce's Grocery was visible from here. It was the oldest building in town, and people still preferred it to the Harris Grocery Outlet, even though Morgan's store had the only pharmacy in town.

Crisscrossed streets jutted back from Main and into residential neighborhoods, and the sprawl expanded east, west, and north toward the national park. The west side also held the town's elementary and high schools, while the east side, nearest her, held the church.

But this area held fewer than 200 homes. Another 400 houses, cabins, and trailers stood apart from the confines of downtown, preferring more rustic and secluded locations.

Little pockets of humanity dotted the landscape, some in single home settings, others in clustered cul-de-sacs of three to five homes. Native Mills Valleyans always said that one could tell the hardiness of the soul by the number of houses in the cluster.

The outlying areas closer to the national park boasted several more businesses. Restaurants, stores, a campground/trailer park, even a second gas station had been built to serve both locals and the steady stream of tourists.

Lane picked her way down the slope, heading straight for the church and the rectory where Ray lived. The fading sound of the wind rattled the leaves.

It normally wouldn't have taken as long as it did to get to Ray's. It could have been embarrassment, the pain in her head, or the way she watched the trail to protect her feet from rocks and branches that slowed her down.

Half an hour later, she pulled herself up the rear porch stairs. The windows of the rectory were all open, letting cool air in and cooking aromas out. Unable to smell them, she wondered what delicacy Ray had cooked for dinner.

She closed her mouth and tried to draw a sucking breath through the congestion but failed. She gave up, wiped her face with the towel, and tried to make herself presentable.

Ray called to her from inside the house. "There you are. I missed you at Mass. I shouldn't have kept you out so late." The door peeled back as she reached the threshold; Ray's mouth dropped open.

The two-seat table stood by the window just inside the door, and it held a wash basin of blood-tinged water, which attested to Ray's ministering. Every time he tried to wipe more blood from her lip, she pulled away.

"I think maybe you cut it on your teeth. Could probably use a couple stitches."

Lane took a deep breath and choked back a sob. "I can't do this anymore."

Ray pulled a chair over and sat near her, his hands on her knees. His eyes exhibited compassion, understanding, and what she believed was the sort of love a father should have for a child. He waited.

"He threw me in the pool again."

Ray gathered her into his arms, hugged her tightly, and

whispered to her. "Let me call Richard." Lane shook her head, pulled away, and settled back into her chair. "He won't help, Ray."

"Put to the test, he'll do his job without prejudice."

"No, he won't."

Frustrated, he didn't know what else to do but try to convince her. He placed a hand behind her neck to pull her closer, but she cringed and stiffened.

The cloth splashed into the basin, spilling water onto the table. Ray moved Lane's shirt collar out of the way so he could see her neck. Matching bruises striped both sides.

"How bad is this?"

Lane shook her head.

Ray inspected her neck, front, back, and sides. He grabbed the handset off the wall phone by the kitchen door. "That's it. That bastard's going to jail."

"Ray."

But he didn't hear her; he was too busy banging on the keypad. Lane's hand rubbed across her eyes and massaged her brow. "Don't call your brother."

He jabbed in the final numbers. Lane twisted around in her chair, lightly touched his elbow. "Please."

Ray glanced down, absently slid the receiver around until it found the cradle, and hung up. "It'll only make it worse," she said with fresh tears threatening her eyes.

Ray moved back to the table and rubbed his hands across his scruffy face. "Is doing nothing making it any better?"

Lane lost her battle, broke down, and wept openly.

Again, Ray wrapped her into a hug. "Richard isn't the monster you think he is. I told you about him and Morgan." Lane cried into his chest, but he could feel her nodding. "Morgan stole Jenna from Richard, and Richard thinks he's getting back at Morgan by tormenting you. If he knew about Morgan, I think you'd see a different side of Richard."

Lane clung tightly to the priest. "Morgan knows hundreds of people. He's got friends in important places. Brags about bribing people. I hear him sometimes. He'll crush you. Both of you if he has to."

"I don't care if he comes after me."

"But I do. He'll destroy you, and that'll destroy me. And then he wins."

Ray blinked back disbelief. "So we just let him hold us for ransom?"

"What can you say? What can you say that won't get you in trouble? You have to let this go."

He crushed her into his chest. *Nothing. There's nothing I can say.* Richard would freak; he had been dropping callous hints for years. The church hadn't reacted well the last time there'd been a hint of impropriety mentioned in the same sentence with his name. This would be the end of his ministry for sure. And the townsfolk already cast him odd sidelong glances amid hushed whispers. *No, there's nothing I can say without getting into trouble. And lots of it.*

He always had a backup plan, but he had always hoped he wouldn't have to use it. "If I find you a place to stay, do you think you could hang on 'til summer break?"

Lane gasped as she tried to speak. "Who's gonna take me in? Morgan closed the town's freakin' mill."

"OK, here's the deal. My Mom will take you in."

Lane scoffed. "That should sit really well with your brother."

"Listen to me, will you? She'll take you in. Richard only visits her on Sundays, so we'll just make sure you're here when he's there. He'll never even know. School's out in two months, then I take you away from all this. We'll go find an apartment near the school."

"And your job?"

"I've got a buddy who can get me a position in his firm, and another who thinks he might be able to get me a teaching position at the university."

Lane started to protest.

"It'll only be 'til you're all set. I'll take a sabbatical, sort of. And when I know you're safe, I can always come back here. Or, maybe not. Maybe I'll get myself transferred to a church closer to you."

"I'm seventeen, Ray. They'll just come get me."

"Then we'll file a petition for emancipation."

Lane shook her head. "He knows too many people. Judges even. It'll never happen. And they'll put you in jail."

"I used to be a lawyer, remember? I know people, too. Judges even. And I've got pictures of you all beat to hell. And I think my judges are gonna kick his judges' asses."

Lane snorted, choked, laughed, and cried all at the same time. She pushed away from him. "He'll still destroy you, even if he doesn't win. I can't let you give up your life for me."

"I haven't given up anything. I've made a conscious choice to help you. But I would gladly give up my life for you." He smoothed the hair from her face and used his thumb to dry her tears.

"Go on upstairs and take a nice hot shower. Get cleaned up. We can eat when you're feeling up to it."

Lane nodded and headed down the tiny hallway to the stairs.

"Oh!" He called to her, poking his head through the kitchen door and craning to see her halfway up the stairs.

"Moved your room. Got sick of my neighbors calling Richard and telling them I had women in the house. Well, not that you're not *women*."

Lane smiled, then winced as it pulled on her split lip.

He mimicked her behavior when her words didn't come out quite right. "You *know* what I mean. I put you in Monsignor's old room."

He ducked back into the kitchen. Pots and pans rattled and cupboards opened and shut as he packed up dinner and stored it away in the fridge.

Lane felt badly for ruining the meal he had worked so hard to prepare, worse for causing him this trouble. And she still didn't even know what he'd cooked. At the top of the stairs, she turned left and headed down to the end of the hallway.

All the upstairs doors, except for Ray's bedroom, were kept shut and locked to prevent casual spying by rectory guests. That made it easier for him to avoid answering questions.

Lane pulled the carpet runner back, slid out the key, and let herself into her new room. She'd only been in the room once some eleven years ago on her first tour of the rectory.

This had been Monsignor Dunlevy's sanctuary; he died before Lane had ever been born. She wondered periodically why Ray hadn't moved his possessions into this larger room, but Ray always said he didn't need the bigger room because he had nothing to fill it with. Now Lane's stuff adorned the room: her furniture, her books, her trophies.

The statuettes decorating the room presented an odd mix of sizes, colors, styles, and sports, and they stood in two straight lines along the top of the dresser. Ray always found new things for her to try, and had gotten her hooked on track, cross-country, and competitive shooting, with an occasional foray into basketball, karate, archery, and soccer.

In her previous guestroom, he had periodically rearranged the trophies, sometimes by color, sometimes by sport, sometimes by date.

She expected he'd continue his game in her new room as she found the trophies lined up by size.

The dresser, a twenty-dollar salvage, held her clothes. She remembered the weekends spent helping him sand and paint it, and how little help she'd been when they moved it upstairs to her room.

She opened the drawers; all of her clothing was placed exactly where she expected, and she withdrew clean jeans and shirt. She popped open the matching cabinet, pulled out a large bath towel, and dropped everything at the foot of the bed.

Ray was more than just her best friend. He had been there for her all these years, helping her, coaching her, taking an active part in her life. And he was in her daydreams, packing up her possessions and carting her off to college, walking her down the aisle and giving her hand to the groom, standing by her side through thick and thin. She'd name her firstborn child after him, be it a boy or a girl.

For all her intents and purposes, Ray *was* her father, and she treated him that way. And he treated her as a beloved daughter, the way good fathers treated their children.

Weariness pressed against her eyelids, and she stripped off her filthy socks and crawled up the side of the bed. She didn't want to soil the sheets, but the pillow didn't stand a chance. She wrangled it away from the bedspread and crushed it against her face and chest.

The absence of running water piqued Ray's curiosity, or perhaps his concern, and drew him upstairs to check on his young ward. He found her curled up at the edge of the king size bed, her eyes still moist from crying.

Tears brimmed his eyes and flowed freely down his face. He

moved her clothes and towel to the top of the dresser, then unfolded the extra spread that lay across the footboard and pulled it over her. He didn't care how dirty she was. *That's what the washing machine is for.*

He kneed his way across the mattress, the dents jostling Lane as he moved, and he settled down next to her but atop the blanket. He wrapped one arm around her—protecting her, comforting her—and wiped his own tears away with the other.

She let go of her grip on the pillow, rolled over to face him, and snuggled in closer, her arm sliding across his rib cage. Her body shuddered against him as she inhaled deeply against the fading grief.

Ray thanked God for being in the position to help her, but couldn't fight down the uneasiness his secret brought to him and to those around him. And he was glad that he'd moved Lane's room away from the prying eyes of his neighbors.

chapter nine

Monday morning brought back the hardships of reality. Lane tugged her jacket close around her to ward off the coolness of the spring mountain air as she hurried along the sidewalk, scanning the area, the students, the stairs, and the campus. She noted the locations of the most hostile students, mentally plotted her path to the school, and without pause, headed off toward the building.

Some students went inside, but some packed up into groups, mingling with their friends. Lane sidestepped her way through them, intent on attracting as little attention as possible and on reaching the relative safety of the school halls.

Her high school life thus far had been a living hell; teachers and students alike made it their personal responsibility to remind her every minute of every day that Morgan was a heartless, self-centered bastard. Her sophomore year had brought an increase in the harassment after he'd bought and closed the last remaining mill, rendering hundreds unemployed. It escalated further in her junior year. Unemployed mill workers couldn't pay their mortgages. A holding company in Olympia swooped in, offering poor deals to those not yet in foreclosure and snatching up every property that had been foreclosed, all for a mere fraction of their true value. Then they bought the mill land from Morgan for three times what he'd paid for it and announced plans to hire a consulting firm to develop the region's newest resort property.

Fortunately, junior year would be the last year she had to endure. With Father Ray's help, she had enrolled in the Early College Program at the end of her sophomore year. Since that time, she funneled every spare minute into the program, and she earned enough credits to skip her last year of high school altogether ...provided Morgan didn't prevent it out of spite.

The best part was that, except for Father Ray, no one else knew: not the teachers, not the students, not even Morgan and Jenna. The townsfolk would all be raving about deforestation as the new resort went up, Morgan and Jenna wouldn't even miss her, and Lane would be long gone. Ray had promised to end her nightmare when school ended for the summer. For now, she would endure.

The distant roar of construction machines signaled that work on the preconstruction access road had begun. The rumble of trees hitting the ground reached her partly as sound and partly as vibration. The smell of diesel fuel drifted on the wind. The distractions helped her ignore the taunts, shoves, curses, and the occasional wad of spit.

The remnants of a coffee smashed at Lane's feet and sprayed up onto her black jeans. Students in the immediate area laughed, but she quickly calculated a new route toward the building. More students picked up the harassment, ringed her, and blocked her escape.

"Think you can get my old man a job?" Jason, cocky as ever, pushed his way through the crowd and gave her a shove as she passed, knocking her off balance.

Lane stumbled into a few students, who eagerly pushed her back toward Jason.

"Least you could do. Maybe he can scrub your toilets."

"Take it up with Morgan." Lane stepped out, but Jason blocked her, matching every step she took.

"Taking it up with you." He shoved her back and advanced on her. At a good foot taller than Lane, he glared down on her, his hostility clear. "Unless I get a scholarship, I can kiss college goodbye."

"Makes two of us."

"Really? Your daddy's got all the money in Mills Valley. Like you need a scholarship." He stepped closer, using his size to intimidate her.

"Beating the shit outta me won't bring back the mills."

A small hole opened behind Jason as students moved around, vying for position and a good view. Jason turned his back on her for a brief second, addressing his friends. "Yeah, but it'll sure make me feel better. Besides, if your old man can do it, why can't I?" His friends laughed.

Lane bolted. The first stride put her next to Jason, who turned back to her just as she drove her leading shoulder into him. Her second stride swept her past him as he stumbled into his friends. The third stride came high on her toes, and she charged headlong for the hole that had opened up behind Jason. The spectators reacted too late. One managed to grab ahold of her jacket but couldn't hang on. No one bothered to chase. Instead they threw more coffee cups, stones, and a couple of books. The coffee cups fell harmlessly behind her, too light for the journey. The books, not designed for air travel, splayed open and dropped to the ground. A couple of stones succeeded in finding her, but they bounced off her back without doing any damage.

Jason's face flushed with anger and embarrassment, and he grabbed a water bottle from a nearby student and twisted it into his hand like a football. He judged the distance and her speed and chucked it at her like a quarterback to his wide receiver.

A cheer rose from the crowd behind Lane as she raced toward the front door of the school. Students nearby stared into the sky while racing out of the way. Their heads tilted up then slowly came back to a level bearing.

Lane planted her right foot solidly and pushed away, veering left. She vaulted up three stairs, stopped, and turned. The water bottle slammed into the stairs and spewed water in all directions. Lane glanced back at her tormentors as she casually climbed the last few steps.

"Bitch!" Jason screamed from across campus. "I'll fix your ass. You just wait."

Lane turned toward the door, flipping him off with both arms high over her head as she entered the school.

chapter ten

*C*alculus could be exciting. Just not at Mills Valley High. The teacher droned on, her monotone voice making the subject matter more boring than it needed to be.

Lane sat in the back corner and waited for lunch, killing the time by staring out the window at the mountains where the wind played along treetops.

A soft knock interrupted the lesson. The door squeaked open, and the principal stepped in, flanked by Sheriff Richard Keates.

Heat rose up Lane's neck and surfaced on her face, flushing her skin a bright red. She turned away, abnormally interested in her textbook. Peripheral vision tracked her nemesis, but her head remained down as Richard scanned the students trying to find her.

The principal apologized for the disruption. "Lane Harris, please."

The instructor put down her chalk and sauntered in Lane's direction. "We knew it was just a matter of time. Don't just sit there, you little delinquent. Your fan club is here."

Students guffawed. Jason slapped the desktop and jabbed a "gotcha" finger in Lane's direction as she gathered her possessions and slowly trudged down the aisle and out of the room.

The sleek lines of Richard's crisp, tailored shirt disappeared beneath his bulky utility belt. His hands perched on his hips, but he didn't move out of the way, forcing her to squeeze past him. He pointed her to a spot on the floor.

She bristled. Morgan did that. *Thinks he has a right to do that. Nobody else gets away with it. Nobody.*

She moved to a different spot, one she chose, and she crossed her arms over her chest, glaring at the sheriff defiantly as the principal shut the classroom door.

Though he was a year younger than Ray, Richard Keates stood a good six inches taller than his brother. His square, clean-shaven jaw tucked in toward his chest as he stared down at her with pale blue eyes that pierced into her and forced her to turn away.

Richard loomed over her and studied the bruises on her face. "Where are you staying?"

Lane feigned ignorance and threw sarcasm and caution into the wind with an arrogant flick of her hand. "Uh, the mansion on the hill?"

Richard drew himself up straight and tall, adopting his most intimidating stare. "I have it on good authority that's not the case."

Lane shrugged. "Don't know who could have told you that."

"Jason Olsen."

"Yeah." Lane's eyebrows rose high on her forehead, and her eyeballs rolled around in their sockets. "There's a reliable source."

"He says your father beat you up and threw you out."

Lane shifted and stared off down the hallway. "That's a bit of an exaggeration."

"Really? Hmm." Richard reached into his shirt pocket and pulled out a stack of time stamped pictures. He shuffled through them, withdrew one of Lane's bloody lip and bruised eye, and flashed it in Lane's face. "Nothing like a camera phone."

Lane's defiance grew. "I'm going home tonight, just like every night."

"Not last night." Richard rifled through the stack and produced a picture of her entering the church rectory, Father Ray in the background.

"I went over for dinner."

"And never left," Richard said.

"You don't know that."

"Think I do." Another photo. Lane stepping out the rectory door. Time stamped at seven-fifteen a.m. Twenty minutes before school started.

Lane swallowed and fell silent. Richard reached out and grasped her by the arm, but she pulled away.

"Don't fight with me, little girl. I can assure you, you won't like the results."

"You don't know shit."

Suddenly stirred to life, the principal jumped in. "Watch your language." Balding, thin, and just inches taller than Lane, he lacked any real power to intimidate.

"Or what? You'll give me detention? Just when the hell you think I'm gonna serve it, Einstein? Huh? Maybe I can serve it while I'm in juvie."

Richard interjected himself, amused. "Juvie? You're not going to juvie. Not unless you've committed some crimes I should know about." He waited for a moment, but Lane remained quiet.

"No, this is a simple case of child abuse. I do know that your father's going to be seriously annoyed when he finds out I turned you over to the state. That will certainly ruin his picture-perfect business image."

Lane snorted. "Screw you, Dick."

A smug twist pulled at Richard's lips, and delight crept across his face. The principal, flustered by the outburst, grabbed her by the arm. "That's it."

She yanked herself free. "In fact," Lane pointed her finger in the sheriff's face, "screw you and Morgan." Lane's entire body tensed.

The rippling of muscles didn't elude Richard. "Don't even consider it."

And in a split second, Lane flew into motion, streaking down the hallway. Richard pursued. Pounding footsteps echoed in the hallway as Lane spun around the corner and headed for the stairs. She slammed through the door and jumped down several stairs at a time, hitting the landing with a loud bang.

Richard slid through the doors behind her before they had a chance to close and followed her leap for leap down the stairs.

She glanced up, shaken by his proximity. No one ever got or stayed that close. The fear etched on her face spurred Richard forward.

Her only chance was to get out of the building and hit open, uninterrupted terrain, where she could turn on her speed. She raced for the door, but his longer stride brought him closer with every step.

Lane slammed against the front door and launched herself off the stairs. Dirt spewed as her feet dug into the ground, and she pumped her arms as if the air had gone solid and she could pull herself through it.

Richard landed seconds behind her. He reached for her and missed, and then she pulled away. He pursued for another few seconds, but the open terrain gave her the advantage, and he knew it.

chapter eleven

The sun refused to yield the sky, but the moon didn't care. Already ascending into the heavens, the crescent sliver ignored the sun's futile attempt to hold dominion and knew that time alone would force the hot orb to loosen its grip on the horizon.

The battle lasted another fifteen minutes; ever humble, the moon declined to gloat as darkness spread slowly across the sky.

The tree line by the side of the road provided ample cover as Lane waited for the final shreds of light to fade. Any cars traveling on Mill Road now would have their headlights on, and she'd see them miles before they saw her.

Tree frogs and crickets trilled in the darkness. A pair of owls gossiped across the highway, but there were no signs of humanity. Lane hitched her hand through the carry loop of her backpack, eased out of the forest, and jogged across the highway while moonlight reflected off the tiny particles of mica and quartz in the tar.

The pull-off scooped into the woods, and Lane ducked out of sight, taking cover behind the low scrub. She waited a few moments before picking her way along the rocks and pathway.

The security lights remained dim. The mansion seldom hosted a party on a Monday, but a dark compound during the week meant the master and lady of the house weren't sitting on a patio or strolling the grounds. She reached up to grab her climbing tree. *WHACK!*

The blow to the back of her head sent her careening into the stone wall. A pair of gloved hands grabbed her and threw her backward to the ground. A black-clad body fell atop her, pressing her into the dirt and leaf litter.

Lane fought to open her eyes so that she could see her attacker, but her head roared like a freight train running full bore. All she could manage was a squint.

Her attacker loomed close to her, his face completely covered by a knit cap. He pressed even closer, holding her down with his body while he cuffed her hands around a small tree.

He leaned close to her ear, his mask brushing her skin. He traced a finger along her face, grabbed her by the jaw, and turned her face to meet his. "I've been waiting a long time for this." He unzipped her jeans.

Lane focused on the man, but his whisper was bland and unrecognizable. She had no idea who he was. She struggled against him weakly, trying to rise, but his body was too heavy, and her hands wouldn't move. "No."

A hand clamped over her mouth. "Oh, yes, little girl. Just relax. I'll take good care of you." With his free hand, he pulled her shiny gold trophy from her backpack. "I bet you're mighty proud of this, huh?" He laid the trophy across her throat and pressed, cutting off her air and her ability to protest.

Fighting the lack of oxygen, Lane pushed against her attacker and the trophy. As her mind clouded, her body relaxed. Darkness claimed her, momentarily ending her struggles.

The pressure eased off the trophy, and as air found its way back in, she came to a dim consciousness. Tousled around by the removal of her clothing, she shivered in the cold night air, goose pimples welling up on her flesh.

The man toyed with the chain around her neck, straightened it out, and brought the tiny silver crucifix back to the center. He smoothed it against her body, his hands lingering where they didn't belong.

The trophy lay against her throat again, and the attacker pushed it down hard against her windpipe, silencing her scream just before the sudden and searing pain in her loins.

Pebbles bit into Lane's backside with each thrust of his hips, and the handcuffs cut deep into her wrists. The pressure against her neck made it difficult to breathe and swallow, and the salty taste of blood flooded her tongue and pooled at the back of her throat.

Time faded. The ordeal could have lasted five minutes or an hour, but as suddenly as it began, the torment ended. The man removed the handcuffs, wrapped her up in a blanket, and threw her over his shoulder like a side of beef.

Lane's head bounced off his back, rousing her a little more. The security wall receded from view as the man carried her to a car waiting near the highway. She caught a glimpse of dark metal but couldn't identify the vehicle.

Her assailant dumped her onto the floor in the back of the car, stuffed her feet in behind her, and slammed the door shut. Seconds later he climbed in the front. Dirt and pebbles spun out from under the wheels as the car sped off, and Lane pondered what she had done so wrong that this would be her last night on earth.

Consciousness faded in and out. Her breathing grew more and

more strained. A new pain surfaced, this one in her throat. A sucking like air through a straw accompanied every breath, and a fleeting thought whispered that she wouldn't wake up again if she fell asleep.

The squishiness of blood oozed everywhere, matting her hair to her skull, down her face, and between her legs.

The blood pool at the back of her throat sprayed loose as she choked on it. Droplets of airborne blood filtered back down like the early morning mist in the forest.

The forest. Trees stretching to touch the face of God. Slivers of sunlight flickering in the canopy. Jays dogging hawks to protect their young. Bambi frolicking near his mother. The wind rustling the mountain meadows. Her mind knew death was reaching up for her at the same time Heaven was reaching down.

The roar of a commuter train snatched her from Heaven's door. Lane's eyes popped back open as the vibrations rippled through the car. *Seattle?* Seattle had good hospitals. *But why do this to me and then take me to the hospital?*

Buildings flashed past in the rear window, transitioned from tall and new, to short, old, and rundown. Well-lit areas gave way to lesser-lit areas. Lane's eyes grew heavy, found the projector screen under her eyelids, and watched the wind drift along the wildflower meadow, high up in the Olympics, calling to her, wooing her back, telling her to give up her struggles and come play.

The car pulled to the curb and jacked the brakes, slapping Lane against the base of the front seats. The door opened, and a strange tapping noise, dull and distant, drilled into Lane's head. She wrapped her mind around the sound, focused on it, and dragged herself toward consciousness on its threads.

Her attacker grabbed her feet and hauled her out of the car, banging her chin on the ground as he dumped her near the curb. The strange tapping ended, and a shadow passed over her. Lane wanted to see him with the hope that she might identify him, but she couldn't raise her head and couldn't get a good look. The door shut and echoed, then silence followed.

The car retreated into the city, becoming smaller and smaller until it vanished from view. She lay on her side, and the blood continued to flow freely from her mouth.

The drag from the car had loosened the blanket, and she freed one hand and pressed it to her throat. She found the wound and figured out that if she covered the hole with her hand, she could breathe a little better.

Her eyes shifted from the street to the skyscrapers beyond. Drifting out again, she expected that death would shortly claim her. In one final act of defiance, she pushed a finger into the hole in her neck.

chapter twelve

*D*espite the efforts of the EMTs, blood streamed out of the puncture wound and down along the side of the neck collar.

They left her finger in place, knowing not to try to remove it. They'd packed gauze around it and strapped her arm to her body so she couldn't involuntarily pull her finger from her throat during a spasm or from a bump during the ambulance ride. Overhead lights whizzed by. A cacophony of voices bounced off the walls. Covered by a sheet stained with her blood, she lay quietly as the EMTs rushed her to an open trauma bay.

"Puncture wound to the larynx. Looks like the perp held her down with something so he could rape her. We're assuming she plugged the hole herself. Took a blow to the back of the head as well. Good size laceration. Pupils are equal and responsive, but passersby found her unconscious." Lane's eyes tracked the sound, locking onto a hefty EMT as he continued talking about her. "Guessing her at sixteen to nineteen years old. No ID."

The gowned figures all spoke at the same time, grabbing equipment and needles, tubes and kits. They moved quickly, efficiently. Except for the hefty EMT standing next to her, she had difficulty tracking their voices to their bodies; all of the chatter mixed together.

"Get me a stat cross-type, and put the blood bank on standby. Start the rape kit, Dr. Michael." The voice of an older, confident male barked orders nearby.

"Detective Glenn's here," came a young female's voice, farther away from the male.

"Blood pressure is eighty over sixty, Dr. Edwards," said a second male near Lane's arm.

The trauma team loosened the straps holding Lane and moved her onto the exam table. The police detective walked in, flipping the curtain aside with a wave of his arm. "Gonna need pictures, Doc."

Lane's eyes flitted around the room and saw the shiny gold badge. The detective's face blurred, fading in and out, morphing into Sheriff Richard Keates.

Lane couldn't mistake the piercing eyes, the sweep of dark hair across his forehead, the perpetually clean-shaven, square jaw. Panic and adrenaline flooded her body. She flailed against the trauma team. Hands tightened on her, pinching into her flesh.

"Restrain her. Quickly, people. Before she rips her finger out of her throat."

Straps cinched down, squeezed her into the table. Lane quieted, her head falling back to the table. The detective's face shifted again, grew older, tired, and haggard. He wasn't Sheriff Keates at all; his hair was much too light, and his elongated chin was fuzzy, spotted with day-old stubble.

Lane drifted, the incident shrouded in a dull fog. *What happened? How did I get here?* Her eyes lagged behind as doctors and nurses darted around, flashing in and out of her field of vision, popping in and drawing blood then popping out again. The action reminded her of Father Ray's collection of old, silent movies.

Ray. Saliva and blood gurgled in her throat as she tried to speak his name.

A doctor with the old, kind eyes eased closer to her, his voice thunderous but slow. "Don't try to talk."

She fought to bring clarity to his words, but all she saw was his eyes; his mask and gown covered the rest of his body. *Eyes like Ray's.*

"Do you understand? Don't try to talk just yet."

Suddenly the kind eyes vanished, and a more sinister expression emerged. His light blue medical cap and gown faded to black, and he pressed down upon her. His voice remained pleasant and reassuring, but the lights faded to black, and tree branches and stars fought with ceiling tiles for possession of the sky.

"Just relax. We're going to take good care of you."

The ceiling tiles won. The intensity of the room lights rose, and blinding white bulbs washed away the black-clad assailant and returned Dr. Old-Eyes to his place.

His head buzzed around her for a moment as he visually inspected the neck wound, careful not to touch it directly or apply any pressure near it.

Beyond him, a nurse moved other people out of her way. "Stirrups coming up." She slid a metal pole out of each side of the table, lifted it up, and locked it into position. Each post held a small plastic scoop into which the nurse placed Lane's heels.

The beefy EMT stepped back into her view. "We didn't try to get her finger out. Figure it's the only thing keeping her from bleeding to death."

Dr. Old-Eyes nodded, replaced the gauze. "Good call."

Dr. Michael conducted his rape exam, combing hair, inspecting the injuries. At his first light touch, Lane jumped.

"Bruising of the fourchette."

Lane lifted her head from the gurney and tried to find the owner of the voice, but Dr. Old-Eyes inserted himself into her line of vision, took her hand, and spoke softly and calmly.

"I'm Dr. Edwards. We have to examine you to see what kind of damage you've sustained. You should feel some light sensation right now, maybe some pressure as Dr. Michael obtains some swabs."

His explanation continued, but pain split up Lane's gut, starting at her genitals and stabbing upward. She winced, and a shriek disguised as the gurgling noises of a drowning girl startled the staff. She tried to pull her legs back to protect herself from the invasion, but nurses kept her feet planted in the stirrups.

"Try to relax. I know this is difficult for you. We need to gather as much evidence as possible if the police are going to catch and convict your attacker."

The meaningless words bounced off Lane, who struggled to free herself from the violation.

"Got 'em." The speculum withdrew, the pressure eased.

"There," Dr. Old-Eyes patted her hand. "Relax. All done."

The younger doctor stood up and handed the samples off to a nurse as he shot a quick glance at Lane. His mask covered most of his face, and his dark eyes were distant and empty.

The young doctor morphed—he put on a hundred pounds and grew a foot taller. His shoulders squared off, like a professional linebacker. He transformed into Morgan, then seconds later morphed back into himself. His attitude and voice remained detached. "Vaginal tearing. A lot of it. Second degree."

Dr. Old-Eyes glanced over at him. "Done?"

"Just need a head sample for comparison." He slid to the top of the gurney, and Lane got a better look at him as he separated a few strands of her hair for plucking.

"You've got about ten seconds." Dr. Old-Eyes pointed a finger at a nurse. "We're going to need a head CT."

He whirled on another attendant. "Pack the vagina. And get my cross-type."

The detective inserted himself into the melee as the trauma team packed Lane up for transport. "Hey, I need presurgery pictures!"

Dr. Old-Eyes swept past him. "Then you better come with us, because smart as she was to stick her finger in that hole, she's still bleeding to death."

chapter thirteen

*T*he cruiser parked underneath the budding branches of a bigleaf maple, its girth partially shielding the car from view of the rectory. Richard practiced the next few minutes in his head—what he'd say, what he'd do.

Danny, less than half Richard's age, stared at the house from the passenger seat. "Going 'round back?"

Just under six feet tall and skinny, his muscles hadn't yet grown to fill out his frame. He'd graduated from college and returned to Mills Valley less than a year ago to join the sheriff's department, but Richard knew that a lot of Danny's education came from observing his fellow officers. He spent a great deal of time guessing their moves and anticipating their needs.

Richard nodded thoughtfully and murmured his agreement.

"OK. I'll watch the front, case she makes a run for it."

The afternoon rain splattered against the windshield, the semisolid splotches reminding the world that winter hadn't yet given way for spring to claim the mountains.

Danny pulled two Stetsons from the dash clip and slapped one into Richard's hand as the sheriff popped open the car door and stepped out.

Richard surveyed the area as he slid the hat on, letting the Stetson funnel water away from his head. Without looking, he knew that Danny matched his movements on the opposite side of the car; he knew all too well why the other deputies referred to the youngest officer as "Junior." *Hell, half the town calls him that.*

Danny took his station on the front porch, and Richard slowly moved down the width of the house, peeking in windows as he went. The front room stood empty, but pots and pans rattled in the kitchen.

He rounded the rear corner of the house, giving it a fairly wide birth, and from the new vantage point he could see Ray's head bobbing around as he prepared dinner.

The stairs creaked with each step Richard took. The door swung open as he reached for the knob.

"Dinner's almost ready." Ray stopped dead in his tracks.

"Not who you expected?" Richard didn't wait to be invited in, brushing past Ray and into the old-fashioned but homey kitchen. "She here?"

Richard didn't miss the change in Ray's breathing as the priest inhaled deeply and exhaled slowly. As a law enforcement officer, Richard's training included recognizing the subtle signs of guilt—nervousness, flitting eyes, and stalling tactics. Obviously, Ray knew he'd been trapped, and even his voice betrayed him. "No."

"Having company for dinner?"

"You know I am, Richard." Ray sidestepped his brother and stirred a pan of sauce spouting tiny lava fountains on the stove.

"Who?"

Ray used the same spoon to stir the pasta, introducing pink swirls into the boiling foam. "I think you know that, too."

He laid the wooden spoon across the sauce pan and retrieved a loaf of bread, tucking it under his arm along with butter and

Parmesan cheese from the fridge, which he often said was older than him. He dropped the three ingredients on the table, arranging them near the heirloom oil lamp he'd confiscated from their mother's attic.

He snagged a stick match from the box he left on the window sill—he made sure it was always close at hand and easy to find but far enough from the lamp so that he didn't set the house on fire.

Sparks flew as the match slid against the striker, and sulfur permeated the air. Smokey tendrils drifted toward the ceiling, dissipating long before reaching their destination.

Ray lifted the chimney and set the match to the wick, which grabbed the flame easily. The lamp cast a warm, amber glow around the room.

Richard waited for Ray's hands to empty, then he grabbed two handfuls of his older brother's shirt, spun him around, and slammed him into the wall. Pictures shook, and loose panes of glass in the window rattled.

"Are you freaking stupid?" Richard's face loomed just inches from Ray's.

The two grappled for a moment, each fighting to get the upper hand. But Ray's days of physical conflict remained in the past. He spent his days caring for the spiritual needs of his tiny flock, and aside from jogging with Lane, he had little interest in exercise.

Richard, on the other hand, kept himself in peak physical condition by jogging, boxing, and lifting weights, and he quickly won the conflict, subduing Ray by pressing a forearm across his throat.

"Are you nuts?"

Ray protested. "She needs my help!"

"And that includes overnight stays?"

Ray sputtered, not quite willing to admit it. Richard pushed away from him, pulled out the pictures Jason had printed out, and threw them in Ray's face. He stalked to the other side of the kitchen.

Ray straightened his clothing and slowly gathered the pictures off the floor.

"She spent the night with you."

Ray balked. "She spent Sunday night *here*."

"You think a jury will see that distinction?"

Ray thumbed through the pictures, pulled one out, and flashed it at Richard. "Then you know Morgan's been slapping her around."

"That would explain why I tried to take her in."

"Her?" Ray's voice carried his confusion.

"She needs to be placed into state custody."

Ray shook to his core. "No. You can't. You have to help her."

"I would have, but she ran. Tell me where she is."

"Putting her into the system isn't going to help her, Richard."

"No? Well, that's what the state does with abused children. Tell me where she is."

"I don't know where she is."

"Would you tell me if you did?"

Ray thought for a moment, shrugged. "I dunno."

Richard nodded. "Great. Just great. Was she here last night?"

Ray inhaled deeply, buying time to think. "She came by for dinner. I dropped her off when I left for the city."

"So, you let a kid being abused by her father go back to her father's house. Why would you do that? Why wouldn't you call me?"

Again Richard watched as Ray hunted for a response. "Wait. A minute ago you were bitching because I didn't send her away, and now you're bitching because I let her go?"

Richard shot him a heart-stopping stare.

Ray's dander rose; he fought to keep it in check as a pink hue crawled across his skin. "He slaps her around sometimes, and he treats her like shit. And he's got really powerful friends with lots of money and lots of contacts. She's working on a plan, but she thought he'd know something was up if she didn't go home. She always goes home."

"This little plan include running away?"

"Wow. Make it a point to always think the best of her, OK? She's planning on going to college in the fall."

Richard absorbed the information and filed it away, another morsel of information stored for future use. "Mind if I take a look around?"

Ray's face froze, all the muscles pulling tight.

"Unless you've something, or someone, to hide."

Ray shook his head and wagged a finger in Richard's direction. "Don't even. I may be an ex-lawyer, but I'm not some seventeen-year-old you can intimidate with lines like that."

"You're gonna make me get a warrant, Counselor?"

Ray motioned him to the stairs. "Didn't say that. But don't, not for one minute, think that I've forgotten the law. Not any of them. You can look, if that means you'll leave when you're done."

Richard shrugged, followed him upstairs. "Deal. Let's start with your room."

Without a word, Ray ushered him down the corridor and swung the door open. Richard snooped around the cramped room, which was little more than a monk's cube. A chair sat near the window with a sweater over the arm and a book on the seat. The chair's position took full advantage of the natural light.

Little floor space remained for the plain double bed and the four-drawer dresser. Only one thing concerned Richard; a lone picture of Lane sat atop the dresser. Taken from across the table at Marigold's Diner, the sleepy-eyed teenager's head rested on her hand, her fingers entwined in jagged tufts of hair.

Richard turned slowly, his eyes shifting between the picture, the bed, and Ray. He didn't have to say what was on his mind; the flush to Ray's skin screamed volumes. Point made, he headed back into the hall. "Lane's room."

Ray hesitated.

"I'm not the stupid one, Ray. We both know this isn't the first time you've had overnight guests. Hell, all your neighbors know it."

Ray led Richard down the hall and unlocked the door for him.

Richard twirled around the room. "Wow. This is"—he paused for emphasis—"bigger." He strolled past the king-size bed, the student's desk, the cabinet, and the dresser topped with trophies. "You get her into all this stuff?"

He examined a shooting trophy, fingered the green belt neatly folded before a statuette executing a front kick, and tipped a golden runner back to get a better look at it. He continued through the room, not really expecting Ray to offer any comments that weren't required.

"Why's her bed so much bigger than yours?"

Ray sighed. "It was Monsignor Dunlevy's."

Richard nodded, remembering the old priest and his excessive girth. "Why didn't you take it?"

"Don't need it."

"You like sleeping on the same bed you've had since you were, what, fifteen?"

"I just don't need a bigger bed, Richard. I sleep in it. That's all. Why would I need a bigger bed?"

Richard strolled around the bed, his hands in his pockets. "If I sweep that bed, how many contributions will I find?"

Anger clawed its way up from Ray's stomach to his head, flushing his skin a deeper red along the way. It threatened to pop out from behind his eyeballs but settled for furrowing his brows and narrowing his pupils.

"Just doing my job, Ray." Richard headed back down the stairs.

"Oh, no you don't." Hot on his younger brother's heels, Ray grabbed him by the shoulder. "You're gonna wait right here until Lane gets back."

Richard shrugged loose. "I'd like to, but I don't think that's going to happen. She hasn't been seen by anybody but you since she ran from me yesterday morning."

Ray's mouth fell open, and his anger fell away. His heart froze in his chest, and his lungs clamped down against the cold rush of empty terror.

"What?"

Richard wormed his way through the house, opened the front door, and invited Danny in. "Far as I can tell, she ran from me yesterday morning and had dinner with you last night. That makes you the last person to see her." He turned to Danny. "Obviously, I can't be involved in this particular case right now, Dan."

Dan's eyebrows rose high on his face, and his eyes darted between the brothers as he placed a light grip on Ray's arm. "Charging him?"

Richard shook his head. "Nope. Just talking."

Ray pulled his arm away from Danny, causing Richard to turn and stare him down.

"What if she comes back? I should be here."

"You shouldn't resist, Ray. Go. Have a chat with Dan. I'll stick around here awhile. Maybe have some dinner since you went to all this trouble."

Danny ushered Ray out of the rectory amid Ray's protestations. "Turn the stove off."

Richard muttered under his breath. "Like I said, Ray, I'm not the stupid one here."

chapter fourteen

*L*ane spent three weeks in the hospital. Walking got easier as the vaginal tearing healed, and she had started speech therapy to relearn how to speak and swallow.

The therapists didn't worry about the odd noises she made when she spoke or the preponderance of *H* sounds that preceded or followed many words, which happened because she couldn't control the amount of air she expelled as she spoke. Lane likened it to a lisp, only not with the *S.* Words beginning with vowels or soft consonants often made her sound like she was trying to speak and sigh at the same time. Sometimes hard consonants at the beginning or end of words got dropped off completely. She controlled it better when whispering, but they insisted she actually speak. She hated the sounds she made.

They also placed her on semisolid foods—mashed vegetables, cream soups, applesauce, pureed meats, and the like. Baby food without the jar. But she failed to make any real progress in the few days she'd been eating. Even the semisolids got stuck in her throat, and she gagged and choked her way through every meal.

The nurses encouraged her to continue trying, and the doctor insisted she keep at it regardless of the unpleasantness of hacking up food all over herself and the bed.

The therapists worked with her daily, showing up at mealtime to coach her through sips of soup and slurps of Jell-O. They warned her to take small bites, "The kind of bites you wouldn't bother with if you could eat without thinking about it."

They insisted she chew until the food was absolutely pulverized, almost liquefied, even though it was the kind of food that didn't require much help to swallow.

In response, she showed them that she couldn't even swallow water properly; she sounded much like a drowning victim choking on the first gulp of water after the air gave out and the mouth gaped open. It wasn't uncommon for the therapist to leave the session with just a bit of Lane's attempts on his or her uniform.

But they returned faithfully, or at least the woman did. The male therapist reached for her throat one morning to show her which muscles to target. Thoroughly professional, he carried on as if nothing had happened, as if she hadn't recoiled in terror and jumped off the bed, pressing her back into the wall. He completed the demonstration using his own neck, but he never came back after that.

The hospital staff didn't know for sure if Lane had been unable or unwilling to shed light on her identity, so her official records referred to her as Jane Doe with traumatic amnesia. The nurses took turns calling her different things to see if it might jog her memory. Lane admitted that some of the trial names were better than her own; not every kid on earth got named after a street.

But even though her real name wasn't recorded anywhere, she worried that the attacker might find out that she was alive, and he might come after her again. That fear manifested itself in the form of nightmares. She doubted that anyone knew about them since her screams issued forth as nothing more than strangled whimpers in the sparsely staffed hours of the late night shift.

After three weeks in the hospital, the doctors deemed her healthy enough to relocate and discharged her into the care of social services, and she spent another three weeks under their protection.

Too old and too damaged to have been willingly accepted into a traditional family setting, she found herself a guest in a group home. They tried diligently to help her, spending hours each day in therapy and an assortment of counseling sessions designed to deal with crisis, rape, and anxiety. But Lane wasn't the only damaged soul in the facility. Other teenagers with their own assorted problems lived there, too. Each walked his or her own personal tightrope of reality, and overlaps were unavoidable.

There had only been one real incident, but that was all it took. A teenager copped a feel of Lane's butt as she came out of the girls' lavatory, triggering her first flashback. Terror gripped her as the ordeal replayed in vivid detail. She screamed as the black-clad man ripped her clothes off and forced himself upon her. She doubled over in the hallway, clutching herself, feeling the penetration, and reliving every moment, every sensation.

The flashback ended with a flash of light. She found herself staring at the floor, hands plastered to her groin, her lungs refusing to inflate.

Sound filtered into her brain. Chuckles. Whispers. Her eyes shifted up and scanned the faces of her fellow residents, who had gathered close, drawn by the screaming.

Lane could understand the whispers, the nervousness, even the pointing. But laughter? Snickers? Her stomach rolled at the thought, and she barfed, spraying liquefied food and bile all over the boy who'd provoked the flashback.

His face flushed scarlet as the others turned their laughter toward him. He surged toward them like a defiant grizzly defending his turf with his hands out wide to the sides, daring them.

The others just laughed all the harder. He whirled on Lane, his dark eyes burning with hatred and embarrassment. He strutted up to her with his arms still open wide, and Lane flung herself at him. She'd been in fights before, but not like this. She usually found herself embroiled in combat with some weak willed sissy girl who would pull her hair or scratch at her like a ferret in heat. Only God knew how long she'd last in a no-holds-barred throwdown against a boy.

Lane's first lunge reminded her of the forceful and perfect punches she'd thrown to acquire a green belt from her dojo. The strike hit the boy center chest, at the solar plexus.

He sagged to his knees as the blow knocked the breath clean out of him, but Lane wasn't content with dropping him. Rage and terror consumed her, and the mixture frightened everyone in the area, including her.

Her second punch caught him in the nose, and he toppled over, howling and spurting blood. Her third punch chased him to the floor, and she fell atop him, pummeling him with both fists.

By the time the security guards forced their way through the crowd, the young groper lay unconscious, but Lane hadn't stopped beating the crap out of him. The first guard grabbed her by the shirt, ripped her off the boy, and tossed her backward down the hall.

She scrambled quickly to her feet, ready to take on the newcomer, unconcerned in her frenzy that he stood a good foot-and-a-half taller than she and outweighed her by at least one hundred fifty pounds. It hardly mattered; the second guard caught her, tossed her against the nearest wall, and pressed his forearm across her throat.

Another bright flash of light, and the black-clad man pressed her trophy into her neck. Her body convulsed; she lost consciousness as a shrill voice screamed at the guard to "Watch her neck!"

Lane awoke strapped to the bed in the hospital; one of the security guards from the group home watched her from the door. Dr. Old-Eyes breezed in, professional but harried, and unfastened the restraints.

"You've strained that larynx. I expect it'll give you trouble for a few days." He shone a light in her eyes; she squinted.

"How much trouble are you having with flashbacks?"

Lane pressed her hand against her throat and felt for the tremor as she spoke, hoping she could regulate her speech as the therapist had shown her. It didn't work. "Just started."

The doctor didn't seem to notice. At least he didn't laugh at her. "And the nightmares and vomiting?"

"Couple weeks."

He wrote notes in her chart. "We'll start you on a mild antidepressant. It may take some time to get the dosage right. But it's more important that you take full advantage of your counseling. Those sessions can help you deal with your memories, but you have to let them."

A light spasm pulled against her lower abdomen. She resisted for a moment, then gave up and pressed her hand against it and massaged it.

"Pain?"

Lane nodded.

"Use your voice. How much?"

Lane struggled with the words. "Stabbing. Brief."

"Blood? Discharge? Any pain during urination?"

Lane shook her head and forced out a tiny "No."

"Probably nothing serious, but we should take a look while

you're here."

Lane swung her legs off the bed and rose, backing away like a trapped deer.

He didn't react. "I can have one of the women doctors do it, if you like. We had to repair a lot of damage. It could be that you've got some scar tissue building up, or maybe one of the sutures pulled the vaginal walls too tightly. Doesn't sound like an infection, but we should rule that out."

Lane shook her head.

"OK, but if it gets worse, spreads, or if you develop fever, chills, bleeding or discharge, come back so we can check it out."

The doctor dropped the chart back on the footboard of the bed. "And keep practicing with your voice. It won't get better unless you actually use it."

The doctor headed out, stopping long enough to tell the guard Lane would be free to go as soon as the discharge paperwork was done.

The guard nodded, thanked him, and took a few steps into the room. "Don't know how we're going to keep the two of you apart. Not like he won't be looking for some payback."

Three hours later, the guard escorted Lane out of the hospital. His confidence amused her; he barely kept a hand on her as he lightly steered her through the hallways and out the front door.

She considered bolting right there, but she couldn't be sure her abdomen would hold out and didn't know if the pain would pull her up short. If she split, it had to be a clean getaway, not a half-ass attempt where even this lumbering tree of a man could catch her.

Back at the group home, the guard deposited her in the director's office. As a no-nonsense kind of guy, Director Shephard rode a thin line between authoritarian and mentor. He had to help them, mold them, keep them out of trouble, and get them back out into society as responsible and productive adults.

He pointed her to one of two chairs sitting before his desk and scrutinized her as she decided to obey him or not.

Lane didn't like the scrutiny and most certainly didn't like him pointing her to sit. *Another one*, she thought. She bypassed the chair he suggested and sat quietly in the other.

When he finally did speak, his voice conveyed his authority, but he kept his words civil and professional. "What Simon did was inappropriate."

Lane felt a twinge of satisfaction, but she couldn't get over the feeling that the other shoe hadn't yet fallen.

"Beating the crap out of him was equally inappropriate."

Lane's mouth fell open, but he silenced her with a finger. "There are no excuses. I know he started it, I know you felt compelled to respond. I also know that once you got started, your memories took over."

She nodded, but he shook his head, waggled his finger, and dismissed her apparent agreement. "Just because I understand it, doesn't make it acceptable. Simon will be back later today, and I'm going to give him this same speech. Leave each other alone." His finger jutted in her direction for emphasis.

"I expect you both to let this situation lie. But if you can't, I'll quarantine the both of you. I'll lock you each in your rooms half the day so that you can't interact, and the first chance I get, one of you gets transferred out, probably you. Got it?"

Lane focused on the edge of his desk because it was easier

than looking at him, but he continued anyway. "To that end, he'll be going to sensitivity training while you go to anger management. And the hospital sent over a new script for you. Nurse Eugenia's at the pharmacy picking it up. From now on, somebody does something you don't like, you find a staff member. Understood?"

Lane nodded again just to make him happy, and when he dismissed her, she headed out to the common areas. The other kids eyed her and whispered about her as she passed by. A few sneered at her and called her dirty names. A few others gave her a silent deference, almost a respect for having stood up for herself. The rest just got out of crazy girl's way.

Weary from the ordeal, from the adrenaline fight, and from the vivid flashback, she longed for a nap, but she knew that would just bring the nightmares. She turned into the multi-use room and headed for the snack table.

An assortment of fruits, cookies, and granola bars lined the table, none of which she'd be able to eat easily. A hand stabbed out of the kitchen window and thrust a chocolate pudding cup at her. She mumbled her best imitation of *thank you* and took a juice bottle as well, then found an empty chair near a window.

People outside the group home swept past. A UPS man hustled up the front stairs of a building across the street. Two women laughed heartily, clutching multiple shopping bags in each hand. A double-decker tour bus drove by with the people on the upper deck snapping pictures as the tour guide pointed out the architecture of the area.

Lane licked dime-sized spots of pudding off her spoon, eating carefully and slowly to make sure the pudding actually made it down to her stomach instead of becoming decorations on the wall and floor.

Daydreams slipped into memories then flipped on themselves and turned back into daydreams. An hour later, the supper bell rang.

All the residents without special dietary needs ate first. After they were all seated and out of the way, the rest of the residents lined up: the diabetics, the anorexics, the obese, and the kid with the feeding tube.

And Lane. She waited her turn, took her plate of mush, then found a seat apart from everyone else. If her luck held out, no one would bother with her today, leaving her to play with her food without their comments.

She pushed the mush around with her fork and wondered why the kitchen staff had even bothered to separate the mashed peas from the mashed potatoes from the mashed cauliflower. Everything on the plate had the same consistency, even some beige goo that must have been turkey or chicken but resembled baby crap, whipped up smooth and lump-free to keep her from choking on it. Because of her inability to just eat and be done with it, it took a solid hour to clean the plate. Most of the other residents had long since finished and moved on to other things. Some played cards in the corner, some watched TV, a few even studied.

Lane carried her dishes to the basins, watched as they slipped below the surface of the soapy gray water, and wiped her fingers on her jeans.

A couple quick glances from assorted residents reminded her that she didn't belong to any of the groups mingling around the room. She headed to the second floor and then down the hall to the dorm room she shared with four other girls.

When she reached it, she pushed the door open and peered in. God smiled down at her. The room was empty. *A little solitude right now will do the body good.* She turned to close the door and found Simon standing in the threshold.

She immediately saw a flash of light, which was as blinding

as the flash of a camera, and Lane felt the pebbles biting into her backside. She heard her attacker grunting over her. Another flash, and Simon charged toward her.

Blackness. Then footsteps pounded up the stairs. Lane's vision cleared.

Simon lay on the floor, a gash on his forehead. Smears of Simon's blood stained Lane's hands as well as the shattered desk chair that she gripped. She quickly set the chair back down and rushed out of the room.

The guard who took her to the hospital grabbed her arm as she reached the landing in the middle of the staircase. "What was that?" he demanded.

Lane rubbed her hands together, eyeing the blood. In her crackly voice, she squeezed out a lie. "Chair broke. Cut my hand." She pointed down the stairs.

The guard nodded and let her go. "Yeah. Have Nurse Eugenia call me if you're going to need to go back to the hospital for stitches." He watched as she continued down to the first floor.

From the corner of her eye, she saw him step down a few stairs then hesitate. He turned and headed back up.

Panic threatened to turn her stomach inside out, and little voices in her head grew louder. *Run. Run. RUN.* She fought them down, cornering them and keeping them at bay long enough to reach the first floor.

No one down the hall seemed particularly interested in her, and the guard hadn't yet made it to the top of the stairs.

Lane bolted.

The first floor hallway led past the director's office, just ten feet from the front door. Seconds later, she raced into the heart of the city.

She didn't stick around to see if anyone noticed, nor did she care if the guard had found Simon, or if Simon was even alive. She had to get away, and she had to do it quickly. She'd hoped not to attract any attention because she still wasn't sure how much running she'd be able to do. The element of surprise gave her a head start, and the busy streets provided ample cover.

She didn't relax until she'd put several blocks between her and the group home. She walked quickly, taking occasional peeks over her shoulder and finding reasons to stop to see if anyone followed. A shoelace needed to be tied. A store window needed to be inspected. *So far so good,* she thought.

She leaned against a street sign, donned an air of nonchalance as she watched traffic, and considered her life options.

She couldn't go home to Mills Valley. *At least not yet.* She had no idea who'd attacked her; she could have ticked off suspects but knew it meant nothing. Anyone could have done it, and if she suddenly showed up in town, she'd just be putting herself in more jeopardy. She couldn't go back to the group home, either—not with Simon hell-bent for revenge. She had no money, nowhere to go, no way to feed herself or keep warm at night. Thankfully, June seldom brought snow to the lower elevations in Washington, but nights could still be downright cold. She needed clothes, shelter, and food in any order she could get them. And since she'd most likely have to steal them, she had better be sure she could run for her life.

Ray had taken her to Safeco Field once to see a Mariner's game, pointing out landmarks as they cruised along the highway. The freight yard, International Sector, and the industrial park stood to the west of the highway; the church he visited on Monday nights, its spires barely visible above a stand of woods, laid to the east.

He fed her hot dogs and pretzels; the phantom smell of spicy mustard rose up in her nostrils and set her mouth to salivating. They had a great time sitting nearly alone way up in the cheap seats. And it hadn't hurt that the Mariner's squeaked by the Red Sox. Ray would know what to do and how to end this nightmare, but every time she thought of him, or of going home, waves of nausea and anxiety rocked her. *No*, she thought. *It couldn't be Ray. It couldn't be.*

She held no illusions of mouthwatering franks and salty pretzels; finding Safeco would help her find the church, and that meant nothing more than a free meal from their soup kitchen.

She turned around and eyed a shopkeeper taking in his sidewalk rack for the night. She popped between the foot traffic and excused herself to him. "Safeco?"

He glanced up, pointed west, then swung an arc south. "Not the shortest route, but it's the simplest directions. Take Union to Fourth, then just follow it south. Can't miss it."

She nodded and whispered her short version of thank-you. "Q," she said.

"You're welcome."

Lane headed west. Three blocks later she found Fourth Avenue and turned south. She decided to try a test run and set off at an easy jog toward the ball field. A twinge stabbed into her abdomen, and she immediately stopped, pressing her hand against it and continuing on at a casual stroll. From the north, Qwest Field would rise into sight first, visible from quite a distance. Beyond that would be Safeco Field, and east of those two would be the junction of highways 90 and 5. Once she'd lined up on either stadium, she'd be all set.

Even jogging part of the way, she didn't find the church until very late that night. No people lingered on the street, and no lights shone from the houses. She couldn't even identify the rectory because the church sat smack-dab in the middle of a residential neighborhood. She hunted around for an open door on the church, but she found none, so she curled up in a side door alcove to wait.

Nightmares, noise, and the cold kept her awake half the night. Morning brought more noise and more cold air, but she hoped that if she could avoid confrontation, she might be able to at least avoid the flashbacks. Her stomach growled its displeasure, and cottonmouth halfway down her throat gagged her.

She drank from the church's exterior spigot, which only produced a trickle of rusty water when fully turned on. But beggars couldn't be choosers. Any thought about long-term side effects played second fiddle to the primary concern: drink or go thirsty.

The water only made her stomach growl louder. She carefully turned the spigot fully off before wandering off to survey the area. *I have to find something to eat*, she thought. *But I don't want to get too far from the church. Gotta find out about the soup kitchen.*

The sign in front of the church sported the Mass schedule, which was meaningless since Lane had no watch. But there'd be three services this morning, and if she was lucky, she'd get an angle on a free meal for today. If not so lucky, she'd at least know where to show up on Monday. She'd head back to the ball fields and the abundance of restaurants outside their walls. Perhaps she could wrangle her way into a hot dog.

She decided that by now, the police had been informed of her sudden departure from the group home. They'd be out looking for her along with anyone else they had BOLOS and warrants for. To make sure they didn't find her, she returned to the side door, coming back to the street only after the arrival of cars foretold an upcoming Mass.

A minivan pulled up; the young teens in the backseat threw the doors open despite the mother's attempts to rein them in before they ran headlong into Lane. The mother's eyes shouted her fear, and Lane took a step away. The father rushed around the car to protect his brood but recognized the teenager's plight instantly. "Are you OK?"

"Soup kitchen?" Lane strained to get the words out clearly.

"Monday nights, around back."

Lane nodded. "Q," she said and turned to leave.

"Hey, wait."

Lane slowed, glanced over her shoulder, but suspicion kept her from stopping.

He dug in his pocket, removed a five from a small fold of cash, and stretched his hand out to her.

She stopped, his fingers wiggling the bill in her direction. "Tide you over. Talk to Father Zavier when you get here tomorrow. He'll get you off the street."

Lane took the money, tears filling her eyes. She worked harder to get the words out right. "Thank you."

chapter fifteen

*M*onday afternoon, Lane stood in line at the soup kitchen with twenty-three cents left in her pocket. She queued up with others in assorted states of disrepair or disrepute. Some were homeless, some jobless, some schizophrenic. Most smelled and needed a change of clothes.

She didn't dwell on them for long; she had put herself in this situation when she fled the group home, an unfortunate but necessary choice. She couldn't help but wonder how long it would be until she looked and smelled like the rest of them. *Maybe I already do.*

Lane stepped forward, roused back to reality by the proximity of the priest's voice. She kept her head down, not really wanting to see the person doling out food to the unfortunates. She reached out and took the offered sandwich and bottle of water.

She focused on the priest's black shirtsleeve, which was rolled back a couple turns on rich brown skin. She nodded her thanks and mumbled her abbreviated gratitude, hoping her words would be understood.

A deep warm voice with a thick Spanish accent answered. "You're welcome, and God bless you."

She didn't want to look at him because she didn't want to make a connection with anyone, but his voice stirred her from the inside out with warmth, kindness, and genuine caring. She focused on the black shirt, ventured a peek, and found a young, handsome, black-haired priest staring back.

His features were rugged, his olive skin nearly flawless save for a tiny pockmark that blemished his right cheekbone. The sight of him ripped at her, and though she didn't know him, she couldn't help but transpose him into her own life.

Ray. She missed him with an intensity that sometimes seared deep into her heart. She stared at the young priest in front of her with his easy, unchallenging smile. His calmness reassured her. *No, it couldn't have been Ray. But if it couldn't have been Ray, why do I have to keep telling myself that?*

"How long have you been out here?"

Lane wasn't sure if he meant in line, on the street, or in the city. She shook her head, whispered "Not long."

"Do you have a place to stay?"

"Yes." She lied; the priest knew it.

"Rizal Park and the freight yard aren't safe at night. Watch yourself there. Soup kitchen is here on Mondays, at the Baptist Church on Wednesdays, and the Episcopal Church on Fridays." He pointed off to the north and west as he spoke.

Lane nodded and avoided his eyes.

He handed her a business card. "When you're ready, call me." The priest brought his hand up and traced the sign of the cross in the air in front of her.

She copied the cross on herself, met his eyes briefly before leaving, then sought out a secluded place to eat her meal.

chapter sixteen

*I*n the six weeks since Lane had vanished, Ray had been ostracized and vilified by everyone in town. There was no proof linking him to Lane's disappearance, but that didn't stop anyone from blaming him for it. Residents avoided him on the street and in stores, and all but five had stopped coming to Sunday Mass. He ran into Richard at their mother's house for Sunday dinner twice, but on both occasions, Richard had immediately departed.

Mom had told him not to be "silly," but Ray stopped visiting her on Sundays. Instead, he switched to midweek visits, Wednesdays being his first choice but switching to Thursdays if Mom was meeting her cronies for their monthly dinner/movie date in Shelton.

His bruised feelings almost accepted the idea that his mother needed extra company during the week anyway. *Now I know how Lane felt.*

But at the moment Ray sat quietly in the rectory as the vicar general expressed deep concerns about Ray's behavior. The vicar paced back and forth with his hands clasped behind his back and his arms pinching the sides of his suit jacket.

The vicar general's assistant and another young man, both priests, sat in the chairs across from Ray. Both presented a polished and proper image in their clerical blacks. The pale assistant focused his attention on the vicar while the olive-skinned priest studied Ray.

"You will have nothing further to do with this girl."The vicar came to an abrupt halt in front of Ray's chair. "Any of her belongings not currently in police custody will be turned over to them immediately." He pulled a picture of Lane from a coffee table and slapped it against Ray's shoulder.

Dutifully, Ray took the picture. He tried to interrupt; the vicar silenced him.

"Further, until this situation is resolved satisfactorily, you are relieved of your duties. You are to have no interactions with children that are not supervised. You are to conduct no church affairs." He strode toward the olive-skinned priest and waved a hand at him. "I believe you have worked the soup kitchen with Zavier?"

Ray nodded. He and Zavier Esperanza had spoken at length at the soup kitchen, exchanging stories of both a personal and a professional nature, sharing secrets.

Ray had limited his secrets to minor incidents, stealing the answers to the Latin test during his sophomore year of high school, taking his first drink of beer at sixteen, and sneaking into a movie theater in Seattle the night before he turned eighteen.

But Zavier had been more forthcoming with the escapades of his life, and Ray knew that the blemish on his cheek was a scar from an amorous encounter as a teenager in Spain.

He'd always liked Father Zavier, but he knew he'd have to work very hard not to blame him for what was happening. And the suitcase at Zavier's feet told Ray exactly where this meeting was going.

"Good. Zavier has been reassigned. He volunteered to help us through this. He will fulfill the needs of this parish as their temporary pastor, and you will provide him whatever assistance he requires."

Ray stood and forced himself into the conversation, struggling not to jump clean down the vicar's throat. "The girl needs help. If she comes back here, I am damn well going to help her."

The vicar's face turned scarlet from the tiny, white square at his neck all the way to his hairline. "You will call the police *if she shows up.* You will remove yourself from her presence *if she shows up.* You will have nothing to do with her except pray for her safe return. If you disobey this edict, you will be relocated, or worse, dismissed."

The vicar stormed out, his young assistant in tow. The front door slammed shut, followed by the dull thud of the car doors.

An engine fired up, but Ray didn't watch them drive off. His feet remained fixed on one point on the carpet, unable to move and unwilling to accept the vicar's decree. He raised the picture frame and stared down at the smiling face of the only person in the world who truly needed him.

"Ramón." The Spanish lilt in itself uttered the apology.

"Don't worry about it, Zavier. I know. But you might have to remind me occasionally to butt out."

Ray gathered up all the photos of Lane that he'd scattered around the room. Danny hadn't actually missed them; he had confiscated everything in sight. But these pictures had all been packed away, not coming out of their storage boxes until Ray couldn't stand the empty house anymore.

Lane's smiling face stared out at him. "I'll be damned if they take you away from me."

Zavier retrieved one from the top of the TV, eyed it, and brought it to Ray. "Is this her? I have seen this girl."

chapter seventeen

*F*ive and a half months of surviving alone in the city had transformed Lane into a scrawny, dirty street urchin willing to do almost anything for a meal. She'd made good use of the soup kitchens, but eating every other day during the week and skipping meals altogether on Saturday and Sunday hadn't worked out very well.

She'd eaten out of the garbage during her first weekend alone on the streets, climbing into a dumpster behind a store and consuming a loaf of moldy bread. After that, she graduated to low-level criminal activity, snatching food and beverages from street vendors and outdoor displays.

Then she learned to steal food from the hands of tourists and business people who milled around on the street. She merely jogged up, reached in, and took it, turning on the speed after her hand closed around the hot dog, grinder, soda, or whatever it was she wanted that someone else had.

Once she mastered that art and discovered that the easiest way to elude foot traffic in the city was among the moving vehicles in the street, she shifted easily to stealing money. First, she snatched greenbacks from the hands of people too dumb to put their change away before leaving stores. But opportunities like that didn't present themselves often, and she quickly moved on to snatching purses.

But purse snatching could be such a bother. The female victims invariably screamed, though most often failed to pursue their attacker themselves. Instead, their screams drew the attention of men, who were trained from birth to react in brave and heroic ways and thereby gave chase.

The bag itself was nothing more than dead weight. Once relieved of its wallet, Lane chucked it over her head, a move calculated to draw the pursuer's attention.

The pursuer usually slowed to recover the handbag, which gave Lane a few extra seconds to rifle the wallet and snatch the bills. Then it, too, soared airborne over her shoulder. After three such foot chases, she learned to lift purses only during heavy traffic hours, no matter how loud her stomach growled.

When easy money sources thinned out, she shoplifted food, careful never to hit the same place twice. When stealth failed, she just stole what she needed and ran. She'd even used the promise of sex as leverage, though she hadn't been forced into having it again. Today she shuffled along, eyed storefronts, and waited for an easy mark, ever vigilant for an opportunity.

An old man approached her, smelling of liquor and ogling her with his eyes. He walked all around her, taking an occasional puff off a cigarette. The salt-and-pepper of his buzz cut stuck out from the sides of his knit cap.

"Hundred bucks for the night."

Lane sized him up. He was only a few inches taller than her, and his clothes fit his slender frame well. She pegged his age around sixty, and with the smell of alcohol wafting around him, she decided she could roll him easily. It wouldn't be the first time she mugged someone after promising sex to them.

She already knew what he'd do if she failed to subdue him. She nodded, flicked her fingers out for the cash.

"What am I? Stupid? You get the cash when we're done."

Lane shrugged. She'd heard the answer before. She hoped one day to run into some dope who'd give her the money first; that way she wouldn't have to bash him over the head. Tourists, or hill boys maybe, coming into the big city for a wild night. Too bad they'd be looking for something in better condition to spend their money on, like a woman in tight, shiny clothes and high heels with big hair and lots of makeup.

She followed the old man down the street for several blocks before turning into a low-rent apartment building with a dingy entry and a dark stairwell. She followed him up the stairs. Six flights up, the old letch ushered her into a rundown, filthy studio. She jumped when he stripped off her outer coat. He didn't seem to notice, and he dropped it over the back of a chair, adding his outer gear to the pile.

She suffered his touch as he steered her toward the bed, wanting to recoil but barely resisting the impulse. He flipped on a photographer's lamp, turned on four cameras stationed around the room, then headed to the fridge and pulled out a beer.

With his eyes stripping her, he twisted the cap off and fondled the bottle suggestively before guzzling the contents in one long drink. He dropped the bottle into the sink, already overflowing with dirty dishes and empties.

Lane quickly realized she may have misjudged this mark. *I could have to go through with this.*

The fridge held little food but plenty of beer. He twisted the caps off two bottles and handed one to Lane. "Step back."

Lane obeyed.

"Again. Good." He took a swig off the new bottle. "Obviously, this is a business." He gestured to the cameras. "So first things first. In case the FBI shows up. Are you eighteen?"

Lane lied. "Yes." He didn't seem to know or care.

"Great. And as an actress, do you agree with what we're doing here?"

Lane nodded.

"You're not being forced to do this against your will?"

Lane shook her head.

"Great. Let's get started." He motioned her to the bed and put the beer down on the nightstand covered with sex toys and lotions. A pair of handcuffs sailed onto the bed, skittering across the satin spread.

Terror spread through Lane's body like a plague creeping across a continent. Her leg muscles refused to obey, and she inched forward, the rubber soles of her filthy sneakers dragging across the floor.

Moisture condensed on the cold beer bottle, causing it to slide down her palm. Instinct took over and clamped her fingers into a fist around the neck. A flash of blinding light preceded a vision of the black-clad man slapping the handcuffs onto her wrists. Her mind went blank, and her body took control. Her hands switched possession of the bottle; her right hand brought it up high above her head, then swiftly down.

The man cried out and cursed her, dazed but not subdued. The bottle rose up and crashed down on his head again, and a third time before he collapsed. Lane stood poised above him, ready to deliver another if need be.

He didn't move. The bottle slid from her grasp and crashed to the floor. It pitched over and spun away, rolling under the bed and spreading yellow fluid across the floor like cat pee.

Conscious thought returned. Lane stared down at him, her body trembling, not quite believing what she'd done. Again. She snatched the handcuffs from the bed and quickly cuffed the man's hands behind his back.

She swept the paraphernalia from the nightstand and pocketed the key to the cuffs, just to make sure the man didn't wake up and set himself loose before she got away.

His wallet bulged out of his back pocket. Lane ripped it free, relieved him of the promised hundred plus the remaining thirty-eight, then tossed the leather carcass with its assorted credit cards on the bed.

A little money went into each of her front pockets, but she tucked the twenties inside her shoe, five under the sole cushion, one on top. It would be easily visible if someone pulled off her shoes.

But money wasn't the only item of value here. Clothing. Food. Odds and ends. Searching yielded clean tee shirts, crisp white socks, an old Cable knit sweater, and a belt to cinch up her baggy pants.

An unconscious man didn't matter, and time in these circumstances was a precious commodity. Modesty hit the road. She ripped off her filthy, ragged shirt and slipped into two fresh tees. The excess material tucked in halfway down her legs and, with the pants strapped up and the Cable knit sweater pulled down; the new clothes trapped more body heat than the ones she'd worn into the apartment.

She shrugged into her coat and jammed two pairs of socks into the pockets for later. The old man's scarf stared at her from the kitchen chair; two twists around her neck and it completely hid the ugly scar that had, on multiple occasions, caused complete strangers to gasp out loud. She snagged his knit cap as well and pulled it down over her short, greasy hair.

That left the fridge. Mr. Wannabe Porn King didn't have much use for food, but half a grinder and a carton of lo mein graced the top shelf. They'd get her through the night, probably breakfast, too.

Her victim hadn't moved at all. Worry set in. Fear. They weren't usually out for very long. *Then again*, she thought, *I don't usually have to hit them three times.*

She performed a quick check; his pulse beat against her fingers, but a thin trickle of blood lined the side of his face.

She swung by the phone, dialed, and waited for the emergency operator to answer. She worked hard to issue intelligible sounds. "Help me."

The operator asked for her name and address, but Lane said nothing more. She set the receiver on the tabletop, leaving the connection open, then quickly left the apartment.

A drunk lay asleep across the hall. Two men openly dealt drugs at the top of the stairs. Their clients stood on the stairs, some shooting up, others waiting to purchase. Lane fixed her eyes on the floor as she sidestepped around the assorted obstacles.

Urgency rose in her like a scream, and she knew she had to get out of the building before the police arrived to answer the emergency call. She jumped down the stairs several at a time, pushed past a "john" soliciting a hooker in the lobby, and burst through the front door.

Outside proved no better than inside; she picked her way through a gathering of pushers, hookers, and pimps as well as their potential clients. Sirens in the distance caused her more concern than usual; these could be coming for her.

She flipped her collar up to block the cold November wind biting at her neck. It blew less playfully here; it didn't dance at all. The cold, harsh torrents rushed malevolently on those it found along its path.

Lane stuffed her hands in her pockets, hunched her shoulders up, and defied the wind. With her head down, she pushed away, fighting for every step.

chapter eighteen

The ax struck a piece of wood, cleanly splitting it, and the two halves toppled away. A car horn broke Richard's concentration.

Another family of seasonal campers waved at Richard from their station wagon, which they'd crammed full with boxes and bags of items they didn't want to leave behind. He stopped working long enough to be civil, waved goodbye, wished them a safe trip, and said he hoped to see them again in the spring. Not that he really cared if they came back. *Tourists. Weekend warriors.*

A determined swing embedded the ax in the chopping block and freed his hands to add the latest pile of choppings to the neat cords piled four feet high, four feet wide, and eight feet long. Six cords stood covered by green tarps with a seventh uncovered stack in progress.

He remained confident that the six cords would heat his trailer for the winter and that the seventh was precautionary only. He headed up to his deck for a short break.

Professionally carpentered, the deck snugged against the trailer with solid flooring to prevent ground drafts. It also boasted backplates, designed to block the large open spaces under the camper. Enclosed by a permanent, four-season room, it ranged the entire length of the camper, was twelve feet wide and hosted the wood-burning stove.

The trailer possessed two doors, one near the front end, the other near the back. The rear door opened into the bedroom and remained closed most of the time, but the front usually remained open, and along with all the windows on this side of the trailer, allowed the transfer of heat from the wood stove.

Richard spent the bulk of his time in the deck room. Comfortably appointed with his rocker, a small sofa, his TV, and indoor-outdoor carpeting, he could watch the goings-on around the campground and remain protected from the elements.

And near his rocker sat the minifridge whose top did double duty by holding whatever snack or beverage he wanted as well as all the accessories he needed for work: his cell phone, service revolver, badge, wallet, keys, and handcuffs.

The boot tray corralled debris set loose when Richard kicked off his shoes at the door, and he padded across the floor in his stocking feet and slid down into his rocker. Its fifteen years had transformed it from a mere chair to an intimate friend, conforming to his body and enticing him to stay a while. He obliged, pulled open the fridge, and snapped a beer from the plastic ring that bound it to its siblings. Air swooshed into the vacuum when he popped the top, and his taste buds sprang to life, eagerly awaiting the golden fluid.

His cell phone rang. His eyes shifted toward the sound, then back to the beer. The phone rang again, and he ignored it, indulging himself in a slow, relaxing draw from the ice-cold can. A third ring. Richard's lower lip wrapped up and smacked the foam from his upper.

The fourth ring earned a killing stare, but its persistence paid off. "Keates. Hey, Danny. So?" He liked Danny, liked his young and eager attitude, but sometimes the kid just didn't use the brain God gave him. "He's like anybody else. If he wants to break the law, he can sit in jail."

Richard pulled himself out of the rocker and padded into the main trailer, dropping his work gloves on the purple and mauve swirls of the sofa. With the phone tucked between his ear and shoulder, he swung open the freezer and pulled out a box of Hot Pockets.

"Nope. No. I'm working tonight. I'll see him then." He slid the meat-stuffed pastries out of their box, peeled off their cellophane wrappers, and dropped them on a plate. "Danny, I'll see him tonight. Bye." Richard flipped the phone closed without waiting for confirmation from Danny.

The Hot Pockets twirled around in the microwave as Richard sat down at the kitchen table. Weary of his brother's antics, he rested his chin in his hand and stared out the window.

Another seasonal camper drove by and slowed to look for him. Richard was glad that he didn't have to wave goodbye to yet another tourist who thought they were locals.

The microwave chimed, and he reached for its contents. He returned to the comfort of his rocker with his lunch in hand. Three bites in, the campground owner showed up with the honey wagon.

Wes, an affable mountain of a man, let himself in.

"Ready? Got three more tanks to dump before lunch."

"How do you do that?" Richard asked.

"What? Empty toilet tanks? You get used to it."

"No. Show up when I'm eating."

"Just part of the job." Wes took a seat on the sofa, eyed a picture on the coffee table, and tossed it into the trash.

"You know I hate it when you do that," Richard said.

"Yeah." Wes helped himself to a beer, kicked his legs out and propped them up on the table. "But you need to get over that."

Richard didn't bother to finish chewing before replying. "Nothing to get over."

"Really?"

Richard stuffed another bite into his mouth.

Wes knew Richard's tactics for ignoring topics and people. "Fine. But I don't believe you. We still on for the game?"

"Yep. You supply the beer, I supply the food."

"Good deal. Hear your brother's in jail."

"Good to know your scanner still works. What else you hear?"

"Heard he violated his restraining order." Wes tipped his beer can in Richard's direction.

"No big surprise that he's in jail then, is it?"

chapter nineteen

With the sun down, the temperature dropped another twenty degrees. Lane's teeth chattered while she waited on the theater stairs for the show to end; then a throng of the well-to-dos would rush forth into the night.

The sign around her neck asked only for spare change, but every now and again she got bills. She preferred them because transport was easier, but she'd take whatever she could get.

The doors burst open, and the first few patrons popped out. They laughed, talked, and decided where to eat dinner as they trooped down the stairs, completely oblivious to the beggar awaiting them. Then they spotted Lane.

The women shied clear of her, but one of the men stepped down to her and dropped a few coins in her cup before rejoining his group and heading off down the street. She mumbled her thanks.

A few more came out the doors, then a few more, and within moments, dozens of people streamed out into the darkness. Some of them wore casual clothes, others sported more elegant attire, and most of them simply stepped around her. A few didn't see her until it was too late, running headlong into a panhandler with her hand out. Most of them, too, just split apart like the Red Sea, going around her on either side.

Coins dropped and jingled in the cup. If the night proved generous, she'd eat for three, maybe four days, letting her save the money stashed in her shoe.

A middle-aged man in a fancy suit bumped into her and recoiled, wiping at the front of his jacket as if she'd soiled him with her touch. "Get a job, you loser." He shoved her back.

Rough hands grabbed Lane from behind and hauled her away toward the alley. Immediately, she crushed the cup shut and stuffed it into her pocket so she wouldn't lose any of the precious money.

In the flurry of hands and bodies, she caught just a glimpse of the security guard, but she recognized the chubby white rent-a-cop from prior encounters.

He threw her against the wall. "I told you not to come back here."

Her palms scraped against the brick as she sagged, but the guard drew her back up and leaned one arm against the back of her neck to keep her still while he retrieved his handcuffs.

A cold metal bracelet slapped against her wrist, circled it, and locked shut. It clicked repeatedly as it tightened down on her hand. Lane panicked; her body shuddered involuntarily. Goose pimples rose on her skin.

Then the arm wrenched up behind her back, and Lane braced herself against the wall, leaning her torso against it as the guard reached for her other hand.

Her leg rose; her foot shot back and slammed into the guard's knee. The bones shifted, and the crunch elicited groans from the few people within earshot. The guard buckled, his howl reverberating through his arm and into Lane's body.

Spurred on by the success, she drove her foot down along his shin and smashed her heel into the top of his foot. He pulled away to protect himself. Lane fled.

Most of the witnesses to the dislocation of the guard's knee moved out of the way, two made a halfhearted grab for her. One actually chased.

Her coat fluttered behind her as she jumped down the stairs, several steps at a time. People crammed the sidewalks, making them impassable; Lane stayed in the street, tracking the narrow channel between moving traffic and parked cars, but a hundred yards later, a stitch in her abdomen pulled her up short. Further back, the theater patron still chased, getting closer by the minute.

Unable to run any further for the pain in her belly, she swept the hat off her head and stuffed it into her coat pocket, leaving the cuffed hand in there as well.

A quick jump up the curb and onto the sidewalk put her among normal people, and she slowed down, shuffling in and around them. The simple trick confused the would-be hero; his head bobbed around as he tried to find her in the slower moving crowd.

Experience told her he'd give up quickly; heroes needed a target, an object, a perp to catch, and a victim to save. And now, there were no perps.

The hero jumped further out into the street, and took a few rambling steps. His hands went up in defeat, and he headed back to his friends.

Lane relaxed, and within a few moments the stitch eased. A group of tourists stopped in the middle of the sidewalk to gawk at the Space Needle; Lane snatched a cup of soda from one of them, jumped into the street, and jogged away.

chapter twenty

The exterior lights of the Harris Mansion blazed out into the night, illuminating the yard like a mall parking lot. There wasn't a dark corner or shadow to be found, and several guests strolled around the grounds and gardens, talking, laughing, taking a break from the elbow rubbing and political games going on inside. They'd stepped out discreetly for a breath of fresh air, but they stayed close to the propane heaters and brass firepots stationed around the property.

From the back of the mansion, the guests had free egress between the house and gardens via the twin sets of double sliding doors on either end of the house. Each of the twins opened onto a small patio, and elegant porticos provided protection from the elements.

In the middle of the house, opening from the great room, stood a double-wide, extra-tall set of sliders. Its portico matched the smaller versions in elegance, but on a much larger scale, and its patio held three dozen chairs arranged in little sociable groups, each sporting its own heater.

Inside the house, business associates and friends of both Morgan and Jenna talked and mingled, lording praise on their host and generally sucking up big-time. The serving staff resembled penguins in sleek, black pants with crisp white tuxedo shirts, and they coursed the room with trays, some with drinks and some with canapés. They stopped near the guests and offered their wares like street hawkers, only less obnoxious.

More guests arrived every few minutes, handing their outer garments off to dignified swarms of the "penguin workers." The penguins split the function; some dutifully whisked away all the furs and wools to the coatroom tucked underneath the grand staircase while the rest escorted the guests to the great room, presenting them into the party. Had the penguins announced each guest instead of just bowing them into the room, the gathering could have been mistaken for Cinderella's ball.

The great room contained a soft murmur of life and multiple conversations. Well-dressed men puffing expensive, host-provided cigars lounged in overstuffed chairs, discussing banking, politics, social, and international affairs. Some wives sat with them, impressing the other husbands with their intelligence or their business savvy. Those bored with the game mingled in women-only groups and had more genteel conversations, discussing their pet charities, or the latest styles, shoes, or handbags.

Other women, who were paid by the host to entertain and titillate, prowled the room in their seductive evening dresses, mingling, touching, brushing against the businessmen, focusing more on the unmarried but tempting the married as well, even sidling in among the band playing in the corner.

Morgan, wearing his most expensive Armani tux, strolled the room, wove among his wealthy guests, glad-handing and pumping them more for investments than for friendship. One hand stroked a cigar while the other caressed elbows, massaged shoulders, and slid up and down the backs of men and women alike.

A calming hush swirled through the room, and everyone turned toward the grand staircase. Morgan followed their gaze, his eyes locking on Jenna. Her brunette locks cascaded along her face, framing her classical Roman features and draping over her shoulders. Her black gown had been custom designed, not only to show off her incredible body, but to complement Morgan's tux as well. Jenna reigned as queen of this house, and she carried herself like royalty, smoothly gliding down the grand staircase, drawing all eyes to her. Like moths or minions, guests and servants alike became spellbound, mesmerized by her presence.

Morgan intercepted her at the bottom of the stairs, laced her arm around his, and squired her around the room—Arthur to her Guinevere.

Around the room, women whispered to their friends, and men appreciated her with their eyes. Jenna smiled sweetly, satisfied that she had everyone's attention.

"Having fun?"

Jenna nodded and batted her long lashes at him. "Mm hmmm."

"They'd all sleep with you in a heartbeat." Morgan confiscated two champagne glasses from a passing waiter and handed one to Jenna.

"Does it bother you that I haunt their dreams?"

He leaned in close and gave her a peck on the cheek. His hand pressed into the small of her back and drew her close to his body. "I rather like it."

He released her into a throng of rich investors and drifted away, deposited his unfinished champagne with another passing waiter, and headed to the bar for a real drink.

Hours later, Morgan watched from the master suite windows as the last of the catering vans departed. He pulled the knot loose and stripped the tie from his neck. "I got tired of answering questions about Lane."

Jenna emerged from the master bathroom, slipping into a silk, spaghetti-strapped nightgown. The diamond earrings that had graced her face all night dropped unceremoniously into their case.

She brushed by Morgan, touching him ever so lightly with her body as her hand traced along his arm and handed him the box. "I suppose they think they're being helpful. They don't know what it's like, having to answer the constant questions. It's like living in a shadow."

Morgan unbuttoned his shirt and added his diamond cufflinks to the case before stowing it in the wall safe. "Even if we want to go on, we can't. They keep throwing it back in our faces."

Jenna turned down the bed and took Morgan by the hand. "One of the ladies thought I was 'oh so strong' for being able to resume social events this soon."

Morgan chuckled and shook his head. "Brant wondered how we could even think of retiring to the islands once the resort is finished."

Jenna stopped dead in her tracks, her mouth falling open. Morgan wrapped his arms around her and pulled her close. "It's all right. I told him we still hoped for the best, but we have to face the possibility that she may never come back. We still have lives to live."

"That sounds so cold." She tried to push away, but Morgan refused to release her.

"Is any of it a lie?"

Jenna pushed again.

Morgan let her go. "We do hope for the best, right? But she may never come back. Right? We've been through all this. They may think we should take to our rocking chairs and stare down the road until she shows up, but that isn't really what either of us had planned."

chapter twenty-one

The further one walked from Puget Sound, the more the glamorous and gleaming structures of downtown fell away, replaced by old, rundown and ill-kept buildings. The streets were dirtier, the people less elegant, and the atmosphere less welcoming.

The windows of the twenty-four-hour convenience store had been bricked over from ground level to four feet high. A mesh of metal wire, which resembled chicken wire only much thicker and more durable, shielded what remained of the glass.

Lane exited the store holding her meager purchases and her stolen cup of soda. The first order of business: ditch the bag.

Grocery bags screamed wealth to the street people who shared these nights with her; she'd been relieved of one such sack on her second week alone in the city. Not one to repeat the mistake, she stuffed the four cans of cat food into her pockets and released the bag. It drifted silently to the ground.

Trash barrels stood every dozen or so feet along the sidewalk, but she hadn't even considered disposing of the bag properly. *Barrels are for civilized people.* Using it would label her a "newcomer," needlessly making her a target. Not that she wasn't a target anyway, but she saw no reason to scream it into the night.

The cup was nearly empty, and the cover and straw ended up in the gutter as well. Lane tipped the cup and dumped an ice cube into her hand. Her teeth held the cup while she stroked the ice cube around her palms, quieting the angry skin as Ray had taught her.

Ray. She swept him from her mind. *No time for pity.* Her eyes darted around the street, observing everything without lingering on anything. She marked the location of addicts in the windows of abandoned buildings, and drunks with their backs to the alley walls, clutching their brown paper bags. *Targets*, she told herself. *Just waiting for some other drunk to come take it away from them.*

Across the street, four punks hassled an old bag lady, rummaging through her shopping cart and dumping her possessions on the ground as they searched for valuables. The punks howled with laughter as the disheveled woman scrambled to recover her things: a roll of toilet paper, a half-dozen empty soda cans, a ratty sweater, a blow dryer she'd pilfered from the trash. Only God knew why.

Up ahead, a night-tagger painted intricate graffiti on the concrete walls of an overpass. Lane scanned the designs and recognized the artwork of the usual tribe, but not the new player furiously painting over one of the older tags. Her step quickened; this was no place to get stuck if a turf war broke out.

The freight yard spread out before her, dotted with small groups of the city's forgotten and abandoned people. Many of them made their homes here, or at least those unwilling or unable to acquire a bed in one of the shelters. Most of them huddled around metal barrels that spewed fire. They kept warm as the air filled with sparks set adrift by the updrafts and the stench of burning rubbish. Some of them talked, a few squabbled. Many of the schizophrenics lived here, and the slightest thing could set them off: looking at them the wrong way, walking on the wrong piece of ground, staring at them.

Lane kept her head slightly down, though her eyes remained focused ahead. She walked softly and swiftly and went practically unnoticed.

The industrial park lay beyond the freight yard. Some buildings stood close together, others further apart. Few street people gathered here because many of the businesses had night security; one such guard stood in a doorway, observing her as she strolled past.

More and more homeless people popped into view as Lane neared the underbelly of the highway system. Little clusters of people ringed burning barrels, keeping warm and passing time. This area hosted several homeless gangs, and while they maintained an uneasy truce with each other, they often defended themselves from the downtown gangs seeking payback for some perceived infraction of their turf.

At the edge of the industrial park, just before the highways converged, another group of street people had gathered for the night. The people here behaved better, many of them displaced families. They gathered wherever dry space existed—in cardboard houses, under tarps draped in tree branches, some even had little tents that they carried around with them. *Best to keep moving*, Lane thought. She sidestepped her way through the people and past the dumpster that once provided her considerable protection against the elements when she had lived there.

She cast a dead stare at the man who'd bodily thrown her out of it to protect his own family. Now, he and his wife divvied up a grinder to their three young children, all the while staring back at Lane, not quite daring her to try something, but obviously not willing to give her back her home.

A teenager stood guard in front of an old refrigerator carton. His adopted family, four other street urchins of various ages, slept inside the box, all twisted and entangled, making the best use of the cramped space. His eyes narrowed on Lane as she approached, but she posed no threat unless something of value sat around unprotected. He resumed scanning the area for real dangers.

A hundred feet further lay the unsightly understructure of two convergent highways. Not as dignified as the simple graffitied overpass, each of the two highways hosted their obligatory access ramps, steel girders, and concrete supports. Beyond that, the park that Lane now called home carved out a small bit of natural wilderness; once there, she would climb into whatever tree was handy and sleep perched out of reach of casual marauders. Sleeping in trees had been acceptable during the spring and summer, but now the temperatures dipped dangerously low, and Lane needed to make a decision about future sleeping arrangements. She could break into the church basement, but somehow that felt wrong since Father Zavier gave her food every Monday. On the other hand, she could break into some other building and then just wait for the cops to show up. A warm bed, free food. *Except that could be worse than the group home.*

Or she could just head back to Mills Valley. The physical wounds had healed, and most of the time she could run for a few hundred yards before the pain in her abdomen started. And there were tons of places to sleep and keep warm back home—seasonal campers, hunting cabins up in the mountains, and caves. Not to mention an assortment of foreclosed and empty houses.

Not that she ever got much sleep. The nightmares saw to that. Sometimes they stole just her sleep, waking her with memories of the attack; at other times they stole her breath as well, her name ringing in her ears, pounding against her eardrums and drilling into her brain. She'd have sworn the voice came from nearby, calling to her in the darkness, but she awoke to nothing—no people in the woods, no phantoms in the night.

The wind howled through the empty space beneath the highways.

The area lacked road identification signs, but the old-timers on the street recognized the interstates, and they could sometimes be heard at two a.m. muttering about their experiences on this highway or that. Lane seldom paid attention to them unless they offered real advice on how to survive. She never joined in any of their discussions and never sat with them as part of the group. Instead, she lingered at the fringe, paying attention without being obvious and picking up useful tricks along the way.

They held street-side lectures with lessons in panhandling, jimmying locks with credit cards, identifying tourists and why they remained easier marks than locals, completing snatch-and-grabs, and picking handcuff locks—a skill that she hadn't actually practiced yet. *Tonight's the night*, she thought.

A row of bobby pins lined both cuffs of her coat, just in case the need ever arose. Not that it mattered anymore. Not with her own private key. But using the key wouldn't teach her anything; better to hone her own skills just in case.

The bobby pin snapped in half after Lane twisted it back and forth a few times. The piece with the natural bend got to stay; the other half sailed into the gutter, discarded like the people who lived here. The pin slid easily into the tiny keyhole, and a little tinkering and bending eventually formed a miniature golf club.

The street professor's voice walked her through the steps. "Insert it at an angle, and then point that head at the chain. The body fits into this groove here in the lock, and the heel presses against the latch and away from the chain." With a twist of his hand, off came the cuffs.

After several tries, she still hadn't figured it out. *This will take lots of practice*, she thought. *Not like I don't have plenty of time.*

She gave up for the time being and stuffed the half-bobby in her pocket with the key. To keep the cuffs from clanging around, she locked the open cuff onto her wrist. *Since I'm already stuck with one, she mused, what difference will two make?*

She pulled out two cans of cat food but didn't bother to inspect the labels; flavors or brands hardly made a difference when one was starving to death. The two cans made nice bookends for a ten-dollar bill she pulled from her pocket.

An old couple sat with their backs to a support column. Like every night, they slept wrapped in old blankets and each other's arms; all their remaining possessions filled just two shopping bags, which they kept between them.

Lane set the cat food on the ground without a word and continued on her silent trek. With a whisper of gratitude, the old man scooped the money out of sight and gave his wife a gentle nudge. "Wake up, my dear. We've a nice can of Friskies for dinner."

Lane's eyes had already locked on a skirmish brewing in her path; her mind raced, seeking and calculating alternate routes.

An argument escalated; a homeless boy refused to give up the few dollars he'd managed to panhandle. When it ended, he lay bleeding in the street.

Cold panic washed over Lane and threatened to buckle her knees. She veered further under the highway, moving swiftly and not looking back.

Two street punks rummaged through the wounded boy's pockets and relieved him of his money. Of the two thugs, the younger was the more dangerous one, eager and quick to use his knife. He went by the name Rider, though Lane hadn't heard anyone but his accomplice call him that.

"Hey! Cherry!" He wiped his knife clean on the homeless boy's jeans before heading for Lane. "You got anything for us?"

With her hands shaking, she pulled out the bills she'd stuffed in her pants and the cup of coins from her coat pocket. She dropped it all on the ground then backed away slowly, keeping her eyes downcast. *Make them think you're easy. Just give in.*

The older of the two punks did the grunt work, and without even thinking about it, he picked up the money Lane so easily relinquished. Little more than Rider's servant, he answered to whatever Rider chose to call him, "Idiot" among the most common.

"That was easy." Rider stuffed the bills in his own pants and pushed the coins back on Idiot. "You keep that shit. I can't run with all that weighing me down."

Idiot had no complaints. He emptied the coins into his pocket and tossed the cup away.

"So easy I think there must be more." Rider grabbed Lane, threw her into a concrete column, and gave her a hard backhand to the face. Up close, his gray eyes gave him a canine quality. He stepped back and flicked his knife.

Idiot obediently stepped up to search her, groping and prodding, tossing her cat food away. It was the first time Lane had seen him eager to do anything. He pressed against her, laughed wickedly at her reaction. Then he forced her to the ground and stripped off her shoes. He laughed and handed the twenty-dollar bill over to Rider.

Lane climbed back to her feet.

Rider laughed. "Gonna have to start tricking girl, or you're gonna starve to death. You can't get by rolling drunks forever."

Lane kept her eyes on the ground, not willing to give them a reason to hurt her. She wrapped her arms around torso and held herself tight as the muscles along her neck and shoulders tensed.

Idiot glanced over at Rider. "We could work out a trade. Show her why they call you Rider. She's even got handcuffs."

Rider snorted, puffing out his lips. "Maybe you can handle the cat food breath, but I can't." He stared at Lane and grabbed her coat. "But we could pimp you out. Bet some of these drunks would pay to do you."

Lane's body shivered violently. A flash of searing white light, and a black-clad man pressed her into the ground. Another flash, and Idiot and Rider stood before her, sneering at her.

She turned away, doubled over, and barfed on the ground.

Rider laughed, pushed her back into the concrete column, and walked away. "Don't hold out on me again, Cherry."

Idiot remained, his eyes boring into her, his fingers flexing in anticipation. But Rider moved further away, and Idiot finally gave in and raced after him. "You do, and even your cat food breath won't save you."

Lane retched again, then twisted to see where her tormentors had gone. She stuffed her feet back into her shoes but couldn't find the missing cans of cat food.

The two punks drifted down the road, swaggered up to the old couple. The old man handed over the bill Lane had given him. They remained unscathed, but for the life of her, Lane couldn't figure out why. There had to have been some tidbit, some action, some street code that she hadn't picked up on.

The wind howled, bore down upon her with its cold damp breath, its whine slicing into her body. She shook, blinking back tears. Her breath caught in shallow spasms.

Focus. She surveyed the area, taking mental inventory, restarting the mechanism of survival. Three people stared out from behind other concrete columns, one holding her cat food. They quickly slid back out of view.

Down the street, the dumpster father stared back. He looked

139

down at his own three children, then abruptly stooped low and closed the cover. Further along, four boys dragged their refrigerator box away, guarded by the teenager who only moments before protected their sleep.

Closer still, the old couple gathered up their possessions and shuffled off. Whispers of gratitude and apology carried on the wind; they couldn't risk being so close to her if Rider returned.

In a matter of moments, Lane had attracted the attention of the dominant hoodlum, becoming the target of choice. The keys to survival hung in flexibility. She couldn't stay here any longer. One step, then another. *Just move.*

She stumbled past the stabbed boy, his death stare fixed on a spot in eternity. A dozen steps later, valor gave way to discretion. She broke into a full run.

chapter twenty-two

*T*he cellblock consisted of ten cells, five on each side of a solid dividing wall that had been erected to separate male from female prisoners, not that they often held both. Or any at all for that matter.

Built of cinderblocks, each cell had three solid walls and iron bars at the front. Security cameras spotted throughout the cellblock sent live feed to the dispatch area and monitored each cell, the shower, and the walkways on both sides of the divider.

Richard stood outside cell one and cleared his throat to get the prisoner's attention.

Ray peered over the top of his book, set it down, and met Richard at the bars. "What's up?" Deep sadness cast shadows in his eyes.

Richard studied his brother's face. "Isn't it enough that the entire town thinks you had something to do with the Harris girl's disappearance?"

Ray looked down at his feet, sighed heavily. He barely managed to get a word out before Richard cut him off. "Three times in six months. Doc Williams is sick of it, Ray. And quite frankly, so am I. Aren't you supposed to be avoiding children right now? What are you trying to do? Replace her?"

Ray ignored the insinuation and dismissed the argument with

a slight shake of his head. "This wasn't church business. She asked for my help."

"And her parents told you to stay out of it."

"I didn't do anything wrong. I called a lawyer. He filed the injunction, and he delivered it. The kid wants her baby. I'm not even involved really. I never even met with her."

"But you couldn't wait on the sidewalk, could you? Nope. Saint Raymond of Mills Valley just had to march right on in there."

Ray threw his hands in the air. "One step! I took one step."

"You do remember what a restraining order is, right? We did explain it to you completely, didn't we? But be sure to tell the judge it was just one step, though."

Ray knew he couldn't win. He knew he broke the restraining order when he did it, but he couldn't leave the girl standing there alone while her parents ranted and raved about her decision to keep her unborn child. And when she looked at him, almost pleading for his help, he reacted instinctively. He just didn't think Doc would have him arrested for it. He leaned a shoulder into the cement wall. "Any word on Lane?"

"Your little friend ran off. Just accept it."

Ray's lips pursed. "Her name is Lane."

"For all we know, she took up with somebody else. Maybe somebody closer to her own age."

"That's uncalled for."

"Is it?" Richard glared at Ray through the bars. "You think everybody else in town isn't saying it?"

Ray returned to his bunk. "Just for your information, the whole town does not think I had something to do with Lane's disappearance."

"Your mother doesn't count."

Ray dropped to his knees to pray. "Good night, Richard."

chapter twenty-three

*H*alfway between the dregs and the tourist areas, Lane passed into a more civilized section of the city and slowed down. No one had followed her, but she couldn't quite get over the urge, the need, to run and to keep running.

Finally, almost begrudgingly, she stopped and pressed her back into the cold brick wall of a bar, its neons flashing out into the night.

The stitch in her abdomen returned a mile earlier, turning her sprint into a hobble step while it tore at her innards. She pressed her hand against the pain, massaging it away as she leaned forward and rested her free hand on her knee.

Electricity crackled through the neon bulbs as she struggled to catch her breath, and the glow sparkled off the tiny silver crucifix dangling from her neck.

Several cars sat in the parking lot and even more lined the street in front of the bar. Loud music and laughter filtered out the windows.

Feeling safe for the moment, she pulled the half-bobby from her pants pocket and toyed around with the handcuffs for a few minutes.

The old drunk under the highway did it in five seconds flat; Lane knew it could be done. *If I can just figure it out.* The half-bobby slipped, failing again to achieve its goal.

An old foundry worker emerged from the bar, and red, blue, and green reflections danced off his balding head. His clothes still held tightly to the clay and cement he worked with, the smell of it mixing with the alcohol to create a nauseating stench that moved several feet ahead of him.

Barely able to move for the liquor in his body, he stumbled to an aged Chevy four-door, leaned against it, and fumbled with the keys. His fingers were too big for the nickel-plated strips, and it took him several minutes to find the right one and finagle it into the lock. He sagged down behind the wheel, stared out into oblivion, and promptly passed out across the front seat.

"Things are looking up." Lane smiled sadly at her good fortune but hated that she amounted to nothing more than a common criminal—a petty thief. The door groaned as she pulled it closed, and she feared it might fall off the car or alert others to her presence. The cushions were old and worn, and the springs pushed up through the foam.

The old man had three dollars in his pockets, another fifteen in his wallet, and forty-eight cents in coins dumped in the ashtray. Lane confiscated all of them.

The glove box yielded a half-empty pint of whiskey and two nips. One foray into liquor-induced sleep had quelled the nightmares, but she'd been slow to recover the next morning, and it left her unable to defend herself, unable to seek food and resources.

These three bottles wouldn't share the experience, but she might be able to trade them for food to one or two of the many homeless who preferred alcohol to food.

With nothing left to steal, she slid out of the car and stood there, staring down at the drunk for a moment. The keys, still resting in his hand, reflected light from the street lamp and issued a silent dare.

chapter twenty-four

*T*he drunk's head nestled against the passenger's armrest, and his butt pressed against Lane's hip. Fairly certain he'd sleep through the night, she drove south out of Seattle after making a pit stop at an all-night gas station to pee, refuel the car, and buy snacks for the road.

Late night often produced as much traffic as rush hour, but more of the traffic consisted of fun-seekers rather than workers. The difference didn't matter. It enabled Lane to reacquaint herself without any high-speed driving.

She cruised along at thirty to thirty-five miles per hour, stopping nicely for all yellow lights, and not drawing the attention of the occasional police cruiser that passed by. She kept to the city streets, following them down past Seatac and through Woodmont Beach.

Traffic picked up again in Tacoma. Her drunken passenger snored peacefully beside her. Moonlight sparkled off the waters of the Sound, and as long as it remained to the right of the car, sooner or later it would lead her home.

Somewhere between Fort Lewis and Olympia, the old drunk woke up rather confused by the presence of a second person in his car. The bottle of whiskey might have been traded for a few bucks or a grinder, but she gave it to her unsuspecting passenger, whose face lit up like a kid on Christmas morning. He didn't even seem to know that the bottle already belonged to him.

She merged onto the 101 and drove north toward Shelton. She'd been this way dozens of times with Ray and grew more comfortable driving with each passing mile marker. Half tempted to ditch the car in Shelton, she couldn't argue that she liked the warmth from the heater. And if the drunk woke up again, she still had the two nip bottles.

A mile before the Skokomish Reservation, she turned off the 101 and headed northwest up Mill Road. The drive from Seattle would have taken two hours for a seasoned driver on the main highways; Lane took twice as long.

By the time she hit the outskirts of Mills Valley, dawn poked its head up to prepare for the new day, the road climbed high into the mountains, and pristine forests rose up on both sides. Mist hung in the mountain air, and the windshield wipers slapped away a light rain with a soothing, peaceful beat.

Lane pulled the car onto the shoulder and parked several feet before the Mills Valley town limit sign. The drunk couldn't possibly miss it when he awoke; he'd at least know where he was.

The shoulder dropped off into a drainage ditch, then rose steeply into the forest. Younger trees used the small clearing to take root and grow out from under taller specimens. Older specimens of Douglas fir, Sitka, and a smattering of hemlock mingled about, their branches and skirts deflecting much of the rain from their trunks.

Memories boiled to the surface. Images of the rape spliced into runs through the forest. Dr. Old-Eyes stared out from Marigold's Diner. The black-clad man waited for her outside Pearce's Grocery. She threw the car door open, jumped out into the rain, and vomited by the side of the road.

Deep breaths of cool air cleared her head. For the moment, she was alone. No one threatened her. No one chased her. No one wanted to steal her money or her food.

While in Seattle, coming back to Mills Valley seemed to be the best of few viable options; she hadn't expected her first official act upon arrival to be chucking remnants of Yodels and soda. *Perhaps coming home wasn't the right decision.*

Besides herself, only two other people knew about the pull-off near the mansion: Ray and Richard. She assumed that Morgan knew something since she always ended up back inside his house. All three men were likely suspects, and she'd have to be wary of them as well as any other able-bodied man. She couldn't trust anyone.

Well, it certainly wasn't a woman. Lane figured that she could probably trust any female she ran into, believing that they wouldn't attack her first chance they got. But she couldn't guarantee their help—they could just call the cops. Cops meant Richard, and Richard meant trouble. *Could it have been him?*

Her interactions with Richard paraded through her mind. She returned to the driver's seat, fished out her half-bobby, and leveraged it against the handcuff lock.

The sheriff never confronted her using physical contact. His M.O. relied solely on intimidation of the physical and emotional varieties and his easy way of combining both. He enjoyed towering over her, glaring down his nose at her, hands on his hips or arms crossed over his chest. He always struck the pose then stared at her with his piercing eyes until she just simply melted into a puddle and oozed away.

And he had handcuffs. She slid the sleeve of her coat up, traced a finger along the scar left behind by the attack, then snorted. *Even I have handcuffs.*

Morgan. He'd been physically abusive and intimidating. He'd never intimated any sexual intent, but certainly enjoyed slapping her around from time to time.

Ray. No, not Ray. She recalled his absence that Monday night. *But he always works the soup kitchen on Monday nights. Always.*

She insisted she had no reason to doubt that he hadn't done exactly what he said. *But if that were really true*, she thought, *then why was I afraid to run into him at the soup kitchen?*

Father Zavier hosted the hungry and homeless from five until nine p.m. Ray left Mills Valley at four p.m., giving him the six to eight shift. At eight, he handed the spoons off and began his two-hour drive back home. She'd seen him at the head of the serving line and appraised him from a distance. Nothing about him appeared abnormal. He didn't behave oddly.

But Lane couldn't shake her own thoughts. Why did she always get there before he arrived or after he left, simply to avoid him? Why had she jumped out of line the two times he arrived early? *Because I'm afraid of him. Of Morgan. And Richard. And every other man alive*, she reminded herself. *Or boy.*

Jason Olsen. Maybe he'd made good his threat to get even. Or one of his friends trying to impress him. Or someone Morgan had stolen employment from. *Maybe it was a complete stranger just passing through town.*

But the location, *that particular spot*, screamed of someone with personal knowledge or experience; it didn't make sense to her that a passerby could have stumbled upon it. And that made Jason, his friends, and his father suspects simply because of their familiarity with the area.

The shock of realization struck; she might never bring the

bastard to justice or put an end to the nightmares or the fear that he, whoever he was, would find her and do it again, and maybe not leave her alive next time. *Maybe that would have been best.*

A tear trickled down her face, leaving a wet trail on her cheek before wrapping under her jaw. She scrubbed it off with the back of her hand and shook off the melancholy; for now she had to focus, had to dismiss the incident. Someone attacked her body and took what wasn't his to take. But he hadn't taken her soul, her intelligence, or her determination. She had to leave it at that. For now. *All I have to do right now is survive. Just survive.*

The half-bobby snagged on something; she pressed, and it gave way. She twisted her hand, and the cuffs ratcheted open. "Yes."

She spent another few minutes fidgeting with the other link and freed herself from it as well. If caught with them, she expected no end to the grief the sheriff and his deputies would dole out, but she knew she needed to practice this new skill. She stuffed the handcuffs in her coat pocket.

A quick inspection of the car revealed no rag or other suitable piece of cloth with which to wipe away fingerprints, so Lane pulled out a pair of socks she'd pilfered from the porn producer's apartment and slipped them on her hands like mittens.

She buffed her fingerprints off every solid surface, starting at one end of the car and working to the other. The drunk snored peacefully, the now-empty whiskey bottle nestled between his legs.

She carefully gathered up her possessions—the bag from the gas station, the snack wrappers, the soda can—and she left behind no evidence that could be used to identify her. With her hands still covered, she rifled through the glove box again, this time searching for more than just valuables. The book of matches would help her build fires, as would the reading glasses—provided there was enough sunlight to magnify. Though the drunk had already given up all his money, he had several credit cards, a few cigarettes in a crumpled pack, and a lighter. The latter ended up in her pocket as well. One could simply never have too many fire-starting materials.

Lane took two credit cards—one for jimmying locks, and a spare, in case she pressed too hard and snapped the first in half. The cards bore symbols of Seattle banks and gold embossing. "James R. Sullivan. Sorry," she whispered to him.

The trunk yielded additional treasures: a tire iron, a blanket, a travel-sized first aid kit, and a bag of trash.

The plastic sack transformed into a carry-case for the trunk's other articles once she upended and emptied it. It also became a new home for some of the crap stuffed into her coat pockets. She wiped her prints off the trunk, the door handle, and the keys.

The cold mountain air had already seeped into the car. She fired the engine, cracked open the driver's window, and turned the heater on full blast.

"Don't worry," she squeaked. "The deputies come out here all the time to catch speeders. Four, five times a day. Nothing else to do, really. They'll find you soon." Without another glance, she headed off into the forest.

The descent into the ditch posed no problem, but the climb up the opposing grade proved daunting. The tire iron came in handy, and she jammed it into the ground, clawing her way up the rise.

The sound of a car echoed among the mountains. Only Mill Road served Mills Valley Township, making traffic constant, but seldom heavy. She immediately dropped to the ground and rolled under the skirts of some young hemlocks. A cruiser slowed down to inspect the parked vehicle. It coasted past, but farther down the highway, it swung a U-turn and pulled up behind Jimmy Sullivan's car.

Lane hunkered down, pressing herself into the ground. Certain that she couldn't be seen, she lay still and smiled as the deputy rapped on the windows in an attempt to wake the old man. *He'll be OK now.*

But the deputy's attention repeatedly shifted from the car to the forest, glancing up periodically as if he suspected or knew someone was up there.

Worried that she had misjudged her invisibility, Lane pushed and crawled backwards out from under the trees, and using the widespread branches for cover, she rose into a crouch and quickly moved farther into the forest.

When trees and vegetation blocked her view of the road entirely, she veered slightly northwest. The route would take her to, or at least close to, Jensen Ridge, and from there she would fine-tune her direction further.

The Ridge rose from the forest, a narrow strip of hills that separated the main portion of the Jensen land holdings from their lakefront parcel. Jenna inherited almost everything after her parents' deaths, but Lane owned the lakefront and the Ridge.

Lane couldn't remember Gamma and Pop-Pop's faces anymore, not without looking at their pictures. She'd only been six when they died in an accident out on Highway 101. The twisted wreckage had been displayed on all the local news channels, but Lane didn't have a clear sense of what "dead" really meant back then.

Images of the investigation popped into her mind. The funeral parlor, the large closed caskets, talking with the sheriff. *I was afraid of him even then.* Eventually, the accident was ruled mechanical malfunction.

She pushed aside the pain and focused on the time she'd spent with Gamma and Pop-Pop at their house in town. They'd begged Jenna to let them take Lane for the month of July, so they could spend time with her before school started. Two weeks into August, they were dead, but July had been a great month.

Gamma and Pop-Pop spent time showing her how to cook, fish, and navigate the mountains. They toured her around town as well as Seattle and Olympia, even down to Puget Sound to watch the ferries dock. Pop-Pop took her out to the forest several times, showed her around, and introduced her to his favorite spots. All in all, they simply indulged every whim she had for an entire month, spoiling her as grandparents will spoil their first and, ultimately, only grandchild.

But their doting held a twofold purpose, and they questioned her at length about Morgan and Jenna, how they treated her, and things they said and did. It meant nothing to her then, but now she realized Gamma and Pop-Pop worked the interrogation into the fabric of every conversation. They suspected something. *If only they knew.*

Pop-Pop took her to the top of Jensen Ridge one day and told her to get a good look around. He said to climb it if she ever got lost because it was high enough to get her bearings. "Look," he said, pointing off to the south. "You can see the spires of the church. You'll always know where you are."

He showed her the borders of the lakefront parcel, and he'd taken her down to meet her only neighbor, Ray Keates.

He'd told her it was a secret that nobody knew yet and that she had to keep it that way for a while. He and Gamma had decided to give the two hundred fifty acre lakefront property to her, a very early wedding present.

"I'm too young to get *married*, Pop-Pop."

"Just the same, Gamma and I want you to have it."

"But what if I don't get married at all?"

"Then it'll be an early high school graduation present. You can build yourself a cabin out here. No prettier place in the state. But"—

he smiled down at her—"you're not old enough to handle it yourself, so I've asked our neighbor Ray to be the guardian of the property until you reach eighteen. He knows about stuff like this."

Lane smiled at the bittersweet memories. They liked to call themselves "hardy mountain folk," *and now*, Lane thought, *I can be one, too.*

The tire iron remained in her hand, more weapon than walking stick, just in case she encountered any predators. A laugh wheezed from her throat, and she choked out a few words. "Like the elk aren't dangerous enough."

She recounted the forest rules Pop-Pop had given her, his voice as stern as he could make it for a child. "If it's a bear with a hump on his shoulder, give the old grizzle a wide birth but make lots of noise." He leaned to one side, lifting one shoulder up into a hump, and he shuffled around the room.

"No hump, then you've found yourself a black bear. They're more timid, but still make noise 'cause bears don't see so good, and they get spooked easy. Some folks believe if you can duck outta sight, they'll forget all about you." He squinted at her, pretending he couldn't see.

"Blacktail, bighorn and elk and such are just plain ornery, so stay away from them. Cats with spots and standing near as tall as a German shepherd probably won't mess with you once you're big as me. But 'til then, you take a stick and you beat that bob's butt with it." He grabbed his walking stick and pummeled the rug into submission.

"But you see a great big, tannish cat," his arms spread out as wide as he could get them. "Now girl, don't run. You fight back. You grab something and wedge it in his mouth, keep him from clamping down."

She wondered now what Pop-Pop was thinking, since cougars usually attacked from the rear. How would she wedge anything in its mouth when its teeth were clamped on the back of her neck? She snickered, figuring Pop-Pop probably knew that but couldn't find a decent way to tell a six-year-old if she saw a cougar she should just kiss her ass goodbye. Still, it remained a problem if she planned to live out here in the forest.

She strolled into a mountaintop clearing and recognized it as Keates' land. Both the Keates boys hunted here sometimes, but Ray had never taken her. He told her he wouldn't take her until she could stand the sight of fish guts, and that hadn't happened yet.

The meadow held an unobstructed view of lower lands. The town snuggled in the valley, and the construction access road marred the hillside. The crews parked their bulldozers wherever they happened to be when quitting time came, and the idle machinery dotted the landscape. Neatly arranged log piles attested to the recent clearcutting, and orange-taped poles marked designs on the ground.

Lane had seen the plans by chance; Morgan left them on his desk one day when he went to work. The resort consisted of a massive main house, several clustered lodges and private cabins, a common garden area, trails, boat and bike rentals, and its own restaurant. From conversations that had carried into the attic, she knew they courted someone along the lines of Tom Del Vecchio or Gordon Rahbany as executive chef. They thought it would boost the resort's appeal, give it that something extra that other resorts in the area lacked: a first-class restaurant. She smiled, thinking about how she'd gained that information. *OK, so I was standing over the fixtures, eavesdropping,*

She mused about the boat rentals and wondered how that would happen. The south side of the lake hosted protected wetlands, which made it a salable property, but not one that could be developed. And since neither she nor the Keates family expressed interest in selling their north side parcels, the resort couldn't get to the water, though she supposed they could sue for right-of-way.

A high-pitched and eerie bugle sent shivers down her spine. Across the meadow, a young elk gave the ground a stomp, annoyed by Lane's presence. Two-point antlers turned in her direction.

An unarmed human wouldn't fare well against an elk, even a young one. Tenacious when provoked, it wouldn't matter whether he gored her with his antlers or kicked her with his forelegs. Either way, she'd probably end up dead.

In another year or two, Ray or Richard would take him if poachers or puma didn't get him first. In the meantime, she didn't challenge him for the meadow but kept a wary eye on him as she moved closer to the edges of the forest.

Rain and dew soaked through her clothing as she trudged through the damp undergrowth. Hypothermia wouldn't set in until she stopped moving, stopped forcing her blood to circulate; then her cold, wet clothes would suck the heat right out of her body. Before she could rest, she'd need a fire, a place indoors, or dry clothes. All three would be best.

The west edge of Jensen Ridge held a tributary and provided easier access to her property. Jensen Pond, known to some as Keates Lake, spread out before her, empty, deserted. Waves slapped peacefully against the sand. A small bird flew away as she approached. A chipmunk scurried across her path, chirping its surprise.

Her land contained nothing but trees; no fire pit, no cabin, no supplies, no boat. She and Ray had drawn pictures of houses she might build, sketching out the rooms, a dual-access fireplace, and a driveway. They'd even drawn lines in the sand, long since washed away, for the location of her boat dock.

Further down the beach sat the Keates' property, its boat resting for the season in the sand near their dock.

Their cabin stood hidden among the trees, but pleasant memories came faster the closer she got to it; Christmas turkey and presents with Ray in front of the fireplace; fishing on the lake; camping under the stars until it got too dark and then scurrying into the cabin with the first bobcat yowl.

Lane avoided the driveway and kept to the woods until she was closer, then stole up the front stairs. A quick peek in the window revealed no residents; she hadn't really expected to find anybody there without a car in the driveway. *Better to be safe than sorry*, she reasoned.

She drifted along the wraparound porch, walking on the outside edge of her feet to reduce noise. In the rafters on the side of the house sat a simple key, not visible from the walkway. Lane reached up, felt along the wood, and retrieved it. She let herself in, peeking around the door as if someone might be inside.

Both Ray and Richard spent a great deal of time here in the summer, less in the winter, but they seldom came together. Whether fishing, hunting, relaxing or escaping, the cabin provided a quiet respite. Lane wished she could take up residence here but knew that sooner or later, one of the brothers would stumble upon her. Plus she hadn't stored any spare clothes at the cabin; Ray was always leery that Richard might find out. *Nervous about it.*

No, she thought. Richard always hounded him. Ray just didn't want to add to the problem. She reminded herself that she'd been alone with Ray dozens of times. *No. Hundreds of times.* At the rectory, at the cabin, in Seattle, even when he took her to Disneyland. He never tried anything. *It wasn't him.*

She swept the fear from her mind and focused on her situation. For the short term, the cabin provided a fireplace, plenty of wood, and something of Ray's to wear while her own clothes tumbled around in the dryer. And, if she was really lucky, the last houseguest would have left behind a can of hash or stew. Peas even. Something edible and hot.

Or just edible.

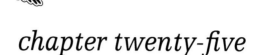

chapter twenty-five

R ain pelted the windows as Danny led Ray through the office. Just twenty-three, he remained eager to please, but he kept getting mired in pitfalls, as if the world had conspired to drop obstacles in his path. Richard's displeasure with him would eventually wane, but only if Ray would just stop making it so difficult for the deputy to perform his job; the priest made it a point to stop along the way, exchanging "Hi, how are yous" with the other deputies and an electrician he found.

The men were cordial, professional, but not particularly friendly. Pete, in his mid-thirties, had a house on Lake Cushman with his artist wife. They were expecting their first child, and Pete thanked Ray for the well-wishes before returning to his paperwork. Ed, just three months short of retiring, shuffled through the crap that his desk had been accumulating for the last forty years. People who misjudged his abilities because of his age often ended up on the ground with his knee crushing their skull to the pavement. He gave the priest a quick nod, then picked up a nearly full box of junk and carted it off to his car.

The electrician stood on a ladder in Room One, only the lower half of his body visible. Ray peeked around the ladder and up into the hole in the ceiling. "That you, Dave?"

"Hiya, Ray. I'd come down, but my hands are kinda full."

Eventually, after much pulling and tugging on Danny's part, the two men reached the dispatcher's station. Dottie looked up from her work, the silver of her hair unable to dispel the vigor and mischief in her eyes. She peered at Ray over her bifocals. "He's not happy with you."

Ray smiled. "He hasn't been happy with me in years."

"That's because you boys fought over a woman."

Ray's eyebrows rose, and his words slowed, drawing out. "That's not exactly what happened."

"Close enough."

"If I just tell you, would that put an end to the rumors?"

Dottie considered. "Yeah, no. Not really. Small town. All that really matters is the story. Besides, what makes you think I *want* to know what you did with his fiancée?

Dottie turned back to her work, stopped, and gave her best intimidating over-eyeglass stare to Danny, waggling a pencil at him. "Isn't he waiting for you?"

Danny flipped a frustrated hand at Ray. "Not exactly cooperating."

"Just because he's the sheriff's brother doesn't mean he gets special treatment."

Ray chimed in. "Don't I know it."

Dottie smiled and flipped her pencil toward Richard's office. "Hop to, Cabana Boy. You know how moody he gets when he has to wait."

Danny grabbed Ray by the elbow, dragging him away. "Guess I should be glad there's nobody else here for you to chat with."

"Why does she call you that?"

Danny had no intention of discussing it. "Dunno."

Dottie raised her voice, shouted after them. "Because he's a real charmer, that one. Always sucking up. He'd make more money delivering pink drinks with little umbrellas on some beach somewhere."

Danny ignored the jibe, knocked before opening the office door, and ushered Ray inside. He withdrew quickly when Richard didn't acknowledge him.

The office held no bells or whistles. In its old, yet comfortable style, the room stood out as a tidy example of functionality with few personal effects.

The wooden desk sat next to a window that overlooked Main Street. It desperately needed a new coat of polyurethane, as did the floor. The chair had been upgraded to include a manly plaid cushion, but it creaked with every move of Richard's body. Two wooden chairs, sans cushions, sat against the wall, facing the desk some five feet away; the distance provided a subtle intimidation that Richard often found valuable when dealing with guests to his office.

An antique bookcase, also in dire need of restoration, faced out from the far wall. Holding an assortment of reference books and old college textbooks, one shelf also held those few personal items that Richard allowed in his business space: a collection of trophies, most for sport shooting, and one for high school running.

Ray eyed the trophies, ignoring Richard's obvious attempts to make him uncomfortable. He strolled to the empty chairs and sat down. Unable to get comfortable with his hands chained behind his back, he stretched his legs out, crossed them at the ankle, and waited.

Several quiet minutes later, Richard looked up, set down his glasses, and tossed his pen onto the desktop. "New trophy?" Ray cocked his head toward the bookcase.

Richard sighed heavily, realizing Ray remained cuffed. "Regional." He grabbed his keys, gestured Ray to stand, and removed the cuffs. The restraints and the keys hit the desktop with a thud and rattle as Richard slid back into his chair.

"Doc Williams is dropping the charges. Again. I think he's afraid he'll go straight to hell if he puts a priest in jail." He pulled an electronic ankle cuff from the bottom drawer and threw it across the desk at Ray. "But I will damn well know where you are before you get into any more trouble. One way or another, you'll stay away from that clinic."

"Anything on Lane?"

Richard put his glasses back on and picked up his pen. "Nothing new. Send Danny in when he's done strapping you up."

Several minutes later, after attaching the cuff to Ray's leg, testing the frequency, and explaining its operation, Danny popped into Richard's office. "So, Ray's looking glum."

Richard motioned for Danny to pull up a chair. "I think I liked him better when he worked this side of the bars. You need to remember that it doesn't matter who is involved, the law is the law."

Danny dragged the chair over, relieved that he'd been forgiven. "Yes, sir. I was just thinking, being family and all, maybe you'd want to know. Won't happen again."

Richard lightened up. "I suppose I can appreciate that.. But Ray's made this his second home. He spends as much time here as I do. But if my mother gets arrested, I expect a call. Now, tell me about your drunk."

Danny jumped back into his deputy persona. "Jimmy Sullivan. Sixty-two. Lives in Seattle. Thinks he gave somebody a ride last night."

Richard's eyebrows rose. "And they just, what, left him out there? Can he identify this rider?"

Danny shook his head. "No."

"Any prints?"

"Not a one. Not even Mr. Sullivan's. Car was wiped down, inside and out."

"Why would we wipe the car down if we were just hitching a ride?"

"We did something we don't want anyone to find out about."

Richard nodded. "Got any money on him?"

"No. He went drinking after work last night. Says he thought he had a few bucks left, but can't be sure he didn't spend it all himself. I was thinking I'd take him down the diner, make sure he's good and sober, then gas him up and send him home."

"Good. Make sure you get receipts."

A knock at the door interrupted them, and Dottie poked her head inside. "Got a call from Pearce's Grocery. Some ratty-looking hobo is hanging around. You want Danny to go out with Ed?"

Richard's head tipped to the side. "Could it really be that easy?" He grabbed his keys and sidearm.

The rain fell steadily, beating against the windshield as Richard parked his unmarked cruiser out of sight in the alley between Pearce's Grocery and the Coin-Op Laundry. The two officers headed quickly but quietly up the stairs.

Rainwater rolled off the brims as the two men doffed their cowboy hats at the door. Richard peered in the window, getting a feel for occupants. He stepped back to let a patron exit. The bell inside the store tinkled as the door opened; Richard grabbed the handle.

Pearce's Grocery stood since the gold rush days, over one hundred twenty years. Old didn't adequately describe it; with suitable attire, people could easily be convinced they'd just walked into the past.

Antique lanterns, farming implements, and signs adorned the walls. Rough-hewn wooden shelving lined the floor, but both the shelves and the floor had warped with age. The only recognizable concession to the passing of time was the refrigeration unit against the back wall.

Lane meandered the aisles, floorboards creaking as she passed. Her clothes had dried and kept her considerably warmer; she would have been content to remain in the store longer, but the fear of getting caught urged her to leave.

The bell tinkled at the exit of the only other patron in the store, and Lane brought her selection to the register, pushing a can of cat food across the counter at the skeleton-thin grocer. She knew Old Man Pearce but hoped he wouldn't recognize her.

His thinning hair had turned silvery gray. Age had ravaged his body but never touched his mind. He remained sharp and quick-witted. When he discovered that everyone called him "Old Man Pearce" behind his back, he took matters into his own hands and created a nametag sporting the new moniker.

His frail, wrinkled hand gripped a baseball bat that he always kept hidden under the counter for protection in cases just like this one. When the waif slid a dollar across the counter toward him while watching his hand, hidden as it was, Old Man Pearce relaxed.

He rang the sale and counted out her change. "Need a bag for that?" Lane shook her head, so he slid the can and the receipt across the counter.

Glad to have made her purchase, Lane stuffed the change in her coat. She picked up the can and pivoted toward the exit.

"New in town?" Richard blocked her path.

Richard. Terror jolted through every fiber of her being, but her feet froze to the floor.

Old Man Pearce shuffled to his barstool near the window, perched himself on it. "Didn't do nothing while she was here, Sheriff."

Lane's heart raced. Her brain screamed at her to run, but her body refused to move.

"That's good, Al. But there's another matter. Thought we might go down to the station and talk about it."

Lane turned back toward the counter and snatched up the receipt. She held it out at arm's length and to her side for Richard to see, hoping it would be enough to convince him she'd done nothing wrong.

"Not your groceries I'm interested in. What's his name, Dan?"

"Sullivan. Jimmy Sullivan. Found him out by the town limit sign."

As the only new person in town, and a disheveled heap to boot, Lane knew they'd made her the minute she walked into the store. Tiny voices in her head began to chant. *Run. Run. Run.* She couldn't ignore them any longer, the muscles in her legs already tightening, but she needed a diversion.

She caught a hint of movement; white hair and a set of eyes peered out the window of the stockroom door—Old Man Pearce's wife, Lorraine. Most folks in town affectionately referred to her as Mrs. Al.

Lane's fingers shot suddenly open, releasing the receipt, letting it drift silently to the ground. Her eyes focused on the counter, not so much as darting a glance at Richard, nor the young rookie lingering in the doorway, but she sensed their eyes following the paper to the floor. She bolted toward the stockroom.

Richard followed Lane; Danny ran out the front door.

Lane hit the door hard, dancing around the old woman and knocking the receiver off the wall phone as she streaked down the aisle.

Richard charged through and came up short, grabbing hold of the old woman to keep from bowling her over. "Sorry, Lorraine." He eased around her and pursued his suspect.

Lack of familiarity with the stockroom meant Lane's capture. The sheriff had the advantage; he didn't have to find the exit, he just had to follow her. His footsteps bore down on her; she caught the support brace of a shelving unit and whirled around the corner as Richard lunged.

His fingers brushed her neck and latched on to her coat. He pulled, jerking the coat down and back, but she dropped her shoulders and relaxed her arms, easing them back and yielding only the coat to him.

She reached the end of the aisle, grabbed a rolling bread rack, and pulled it over, determined to slow his progress long enough to find a door.

The exit loomed ahead, and Lane slammed into it, flying off the top of the stairs only to find Danny charging up the alley toward her. She turned back and headed further into the alley as Richard burst through the stockroom door, only seconds behind her.

Her fingers curled around the curve of the cat food can, and she pitched it at Richard's head like a baseball. He ducked and dropped down onto the stairs; the can smashed into the brick behind him.

Lane ran for the chain link fence. She jumped onto it and scrambled up as Danny lunged.

His fingers wrapped around her left ankle, and he pulled, buying enough time so that he could get both hands on her. He braced a foot against the fence and yanked hard.

Lane struggled against him, unable to free the leg and losing her grip on the fence. He'd have reinforcements soon; Richard closed the distance fast.

The whine of a terrified animal squeezed out from her throat. In a desperate last attempt to beat him off, she let go of the fence with one hand, spun around, and kicked viciously at Danny's face.

The deputy had milliseconds to make the decision; he held on. Two quick kicks later, she pulled free and scrambled over the fence.

Richard reached Danny as Lane dropped onto the trash cans on the other side of the fence and then onto the ground. He watched as she slipped quietly away down a connecting alley.

"You OK?" He turned Danny's face to inspect the damage.

"Yeah. Glanced off. I lost my grip. You?"

"Yep."

Mrs. Al stood at the top of the stairs, holding Lane's ratty coat. Richard retrieved it, donned some latex gloves, and squeezed it all over. He found the two nips, all the bobby pins, and a trashbag-turned-raincoat.

"Think she's come home?"

Richard's eyes narrowed on the odd assortment of gear. "Didn't get a good look."

Danny donned a pair of gloves as well and picked up the cat food can. "Certainly some attitude there."

Richard nodded. "Indeed."

chapter twenty-six

*T*he rickety back porch of the rectory croaked out Richard's arrival. Rainwater dripped off his hat and splattered on the decking near his feet. Once again he didn't wait to be invited in when Ray answered the door.

Lit by the glow of the heirloom lamp, the kitchen exemplified warmth and hominess. The candle flickered, and refractions of light danced on the tabletop.

Ray stood at the counter pouring two cups of coffee. His hands trembled as he brought them to the table, and the cups chattered as he set them down. He retrieved a carton of milk from the fridge then sat down opposite his brother.

Rain slapped against the window, forming tiny rivers that coursed down the glass. The heat from the coffee escaped into Ray's cupped hands; he prepared himself for the worse.

"Is this about Lane?" Even his voice trembled.

Richard dropped two teaspoons of sugar in his coffee, poured in a little milk, and stirred it gently. "Your little friend may be back in town."

Ray's face brightened. He rose quickly and grabbed his coat from a peg by the door.

"Where?"

"I said 'may be.' Somebody stole a car with the owner in it and then abandoned both out on Mill Road. I don't know for sure that it's her, but if it is, I expect she'll be around to see you."

Ray recovered from his initial excitement, set the coat back on its peg, and returned to the table.

"What did she look like? Is she OK?"

Richard sipped his coffee, studying Ray carefully. "If it is her, she's lost her membership in the cotillion-of-the-month club. She ain't your little girl anymore."

Ray bristled. "There's no need for that."

"Hey, she's your little friend, not mine." Richard deliberately tried to get a reaction.

"There is nothing inappropriate about our friendship."

"No, of course not. You're fifty, she's what? Seventeen. Perfectly normal."

Ray had enough. *That's it.* "Just as normal as you sleeping with another man's wife."

Richard took a casual sip of coffee. "They weren't married at the time."

"But they were engaged."

"She was engaged to me first, which, as I recall, didn't stop you from sleeping with her."

Cut to the bone, Ray fell silent. His eyes dropped to the tabletop.

"Any idea why she ran off?"

Ray's hands flopped over on the table, fingers splayed wide and palms up. "Do you think my story's gonna change?"

"So you're going to stick with that one?"

"Yeah, since it's the truth. You know Morgan hit her. Are you encouraging the entire town to ostracize *him*?"

Richard headed for the door. "Not really at liberty to discuss that with you. But I'll tell you this. It'll only hurt your case, and hers, if you don't call me the minute you see her."

Ray burst out of the chair. "If she needs my help, I'll give it to her. And I don't care if you, or the vicar, or Morgan, or anybody else likes that or not."

Father Zavier entered the room. "We will call you if we see anyone out of the ordinary, sir."

Ray whirled toward the younger priest, outnumbered and outflanked. He thrust a finger in Zavier's direction. "You don't have any idea what's going on." When he turned back, Richard was gone.

In a fit of rage, Ray hurled his coffee cup toward the sink. It smashed against the wall, and tiny white ceramic shards showered down into the catch basin.

"I know you are too close to this situation." Zavier's voice remained calm, strong, and reassuring.

"She's my—" Ray caught himself. "Friend. And I'm the only friend she's got."

"Then let us discuss how best to help your friend without you ending up in jail or excommunicated." Zavier motioned Ray to a chair and went to the counter for two new cups of coffee.

chapter twenty-seven

*T*he soaking rain drilled through to the bone. Lane's teeth chattered, her limbs shaking as she peered through the darkened windows at the rear of the brown ranch. A couple hard knocks went unanswered; not so much as a dog came to investigate the visitor.

Maybe they have a kid my age. A smile creased her lips. *Or maybe just my size.*

She dug out Jimmy Sullivan's credit card and slid it between the door and lock. It took longer to pry the lock than she would have liked; the cold air made her fingers behave more like sausages than nimble appendages.

But persistence paid off. The door swung open, and she stood in the kitchen of some unsuspecting citizen's house.

Lane heaped her muddy shoes and soaked sweaters at the door, and then strolled nonchalantly through the house. She'd covered her hands in the sock-mittens and opened up all the doors and cabinets she found. She rambled around the rooms, wishing she were dry enough to enjoy the relative warmth.

A short hallway revealed opposing bedrooms—twin bunks and superhero posters in one room, and a crib and changing table in the other. And no possibility of finding clean, well-fitting garments. Not that well-fitting mattered all that much. Or clean even.

Across the living room, the door to the master bedroom beckoned, and she entered cautiously, her brain reminding her that she wasn't supposed to be in the master suite.

Her lips twisted and she rebuked herself. *Wrong house.*

Careful not to disrupt anything, she searched the dresser. The clothing presented a well-dressed woman who liked to stand out in a crowd, but a simple, casual man with much less consideration for style. The woman's clothes would fit better, but the man wouldn't be able to identify his clothes in a lineup. One black tee looked like any other.

Lane slipped out of her wet tee shirts and slid into two of his plus an unbranded, navy blue sweatshirt. For the size of it, it could have held four of her.

She checked out the remaining rooms and found the mud room that buffered the garage from the house.

Someone had tossed a brown coat with a natty Sherpa lining on the top of the washing machine with a pair of work gloves. *Bingo.* Lane snatched up the coat and tried it on for size. It hung off her; she didn't care. *Any coat's better'n no coat.* She grabbed the gloves, too, stuffing them into the coat's pockets.

She returned to the kitchen and beelined to the breadbox, absconding with the loaf of Wonder Bread she found there. Then she easily convinced the fridge to donate a half gallon of milk to the menu.

A magnet held this week's shopping list to the outside of the fridge door, and Lane perused it as she took a careful sip from the milk carton. *Toilet paper.* Something so simple. *Next time.*

She slipped a blank piece of paper out from behind the list, took the pen off its holder, and wrote a note. She dropped it on the table in plain sight.

She rummaged around under the sink, coming up with two trash bags, then searched the kitchen drawers until she found scissors. From one of the bags she hacked out rectangles, openings for her head and arms.

What it lacked in glamour, the homemade rain slicker made up in functionality. Lane smoothed it down over her body, then threw her wet clothes into the other bag and dropped them outside the kitchen door, placing her soggy shoes on top.

Folks don't like to be robbed, she reminded herself. *Not one little bit.* But here, in Mills Valley, she could at least be civil. And if she minimized the impact, perhaps she could minimize her victim's rage as well. The note would help, and if she didn't destroy their home, they might even be able to forgive her someday.

Armed with wads of paper towels balled-up in each hand, Lane polished the floor, taking special care to find all the wet footprints and all the specks of mud. She tucked the dirty mess into the trash basket.

With the house clean once again, perhaps cleaner than when she arrived, she slid back into her shoes, wiped her prints off the door knob with her sock-mittens, and headed off into the forest.

chapter twenty-eight

*R*ichard waited in the foyer of the mansion as the maid went to announce him. "Thank you, Camilla."

Camilla behaved differently at work than she had when he ran into her at the grocery store, the library, or even the gas station. She usually bubbled with life; happy and easygoing, her French heritage added more animation to the woman than any other person in Mills Valley possessed, perhaps more than all of them combined.

Today, she withdrew from him silently, not making as much noise even as a mouse. *Morgan must have that effect on everyone.*

Morgan emerged from his study. "Sheriff. I can't say this is a pleasure."

Richard didn't mind matching Morgan word for word, toe to toe. "Then it's a good thing this isn't a social call."

With a slight gesture of his arm, Morgan ushered Richard into his office, smiling like a realtor showing off a prime property.

"Ah, police business then. Since I know it isn't me, nor my lovely wife, that leaves Lane, doesn't it?"

The office held a huge mahogany desk, shined to a rich luster, matching barrister's bookcases, wet bar, and several matching chairs. Behind the desk, sliding glass doors opened onto the patio, giving a partial view of the inground pool.

"She may be back in town." Richard headed toward one of the bookcases.

Morgan motioned to a chair, then realized Richard had moved away. "Feel free to look around. You still living in that—" he hesitated for emphasis "—trailer park?"

With his hands in his pockets, Richard stared at a trophy. "Has she been here?"

"No, and I doubt she will. She never really wanted anything to do with us. Spoiled rich kid syndrome, I suppose. You should check with that priest."

Richard turned to face Morgan. "Anybody else she might turn to?"

A sarcastic grin twisted Morgan's lips. "You mean, besides the priest, right?"

"Yeah."

Morgan relaxed into his well-padded desk chair. "No one I know of." His eyes turned to the door. Richard followed his gaze.

Jenna's hand gripped the door handle, her eyes pinched in a stare that screamed hate across the room. "Your brother will spend the rest of his life behind bars, if it's the last thing I do in life."

Richard didn't actually want to defend his brother; doing so just coincided with the investigation up to this point. "No proof against him."

Jenna's elegant movements belied her hostility as she moved to her husband's side. "Maybe there would be if you weren't his brother."

Richard shrugged. He had nothing to hide. "He alleges parental abuse." Richard turned back to Morgan, a can-you-top-this smile twisting his lips. "That means you."

Jenna draped an arm around Morgan's shoulders. He reciprocated, wrapping his arm around her waist, drawing her in until her body pressed against his. Jenna spat fire. "You even breathe a word of that and Morgan's lawyers will eat you alive."

"Really? I've got pictures. Remember? Your neighbor snapped some beauties right out there in front of your house." Richard hooked a thumb over his shoulder.

Jenna jabbed a finger at Richard, veins popping out on her neck. "You don't think your brother might misdirect the investigation? Throw attention onto someone else so he could get away with it?"

Richard smiled again, his eyes narrowing on Morgan. "That could be said of just about anyone. Truth is we have no reason to believe she didn't just run away. I still think getting slapped around by your father might give you cause to run."

Morgan rose and kissed his wife. "I'll take care of this. Don't worry." He escorted her to the door.

Her eyes shot one last dagger at Richard before Morgan closed the doors behind her.

"We've been over that."

Richard feigned ignorance. "Refresh my memory?"

Morgan snorted a derisive little laugh that came as much out his nose as his mouth. "The kid never did what she was told. I lost my temper. I hit her. I expected she'd go spend time with her—" his eyes went suddenly cold, and the smile fell from his face "—what should I call him? Pimp? Sugar daddy?"

"Why not call him 'Ray'?"

"Whatever. I figured she'd spend time with him and come home on Monday. But she didn't. He was the last person to see her."

"She do that often?" Richard leaned against a bookcase, crossing his feet at the ankle and his arms over his chest.

"What? Go spend quality time with your brother?"

"Seek refuge at the church, then come home the next day. You said you figured that's what she'd do. She do it often?"

"The kid didn't listen often. I hit her sometimes, a slap here, a slap there. But she ran off to your brother whether I hit her or not. She ran to his arms if I yelled at her, if I expected her to do chores, if I cut her allowance."

Morgan straightened, his arms shrugging out to the sides then slapping against his thighs in frustration. "Hell, if I looked at her sideways, off she went. If she ran away because I had expectations, then too bad for her. Let me know how the real world's treating her."

chapter twenty-nine

*D*ay yielded to dusk. High up in the forested mountains surrounding Mills Valley, Lane dragged the last load of wood to her new home, a cave near the top of a hill overlooking Morgan and Jenna's mansion. She paused long enough to watch a police cruiser pull away. The iron gate closed behind it, but the sound of clanging metal didn't carry this far away.

They know it's me, she thought. *Or maybe they just think it's me.* She doubted they'd launch a manhunt so soon; as far as they knew, she was just a hobo passing through. She hadn't actually done anything wrong. *Well, except for trying to bean the sheriff and kicking off the deputy's face.* She prayed that wasn't enough to get their dander up.

The location provided adequate secrecy. Standing literally on the southwest corner of Keates' land, Lane had little to worry about in the way of a Keates finding her; road access to their property was near Jensen Pond, a good five miles away.

Father Ray and Sheriff Keates owned their land jointly; their mother signed it over to them shortly after their father's death. The elder Keates intended to keep the land as a sanctuary for his family, building a cabin near the mountain-fed lake, and his sons had kept it that way, prohibiting recreational vehicles, hunters, and any activities that might change the natural character of their land. It was one of the few things the brothers agreed upon, and they spent an entire summer hammering "no trespassing" signs into trees. The Keates name held sufficient favor in town that everyone respected their wishes. At least Richard's half of the name did; Ray's reputation had slipped down the toilet in recent years. As for out-of-towners and visitors to the region—they sought greater challenges, bypassing the pissy hill for the peaks of the Olympics beyond.

Ten feet to the west of the cave stood the remains of Jensen land, identified by the signs Pop-Pop had nailed up along his border. The land that Jenna had already sold off now sported signs boasting the resort's logo.

Below the hill were Morgan's landholdings, insignificant even when compared to Lane's parcel. The street that bore his name ended in an open meadow that would soon become the main entrance to the resort. But construction had stalled with the winter. The crews had all packed up and gone home; no one would stumble upon a recluse living in the forest—not until spring, anyway. Probably longer.

The natural lay of the land dictated road placement a few hundred yards further west, circumventing the hill altogether. Odds were that she could sit on her hill and watch them working and still never run into any of them.

The cave itself had been a godsend. One summer vacation of wandering the forest yielded this little beauty, and through the years she'd spent countless days here, hanging out, wasting time, and doing schoolwork. And successfully eluding Morgan.

For his part, Ray never liked Lane being out here by herself. Trespassers. Wild animals. Cliffs. A thousand ways to die. Alone. So she never told him that she spent all her school breaks hiding in the forest, as well as those times when Ray went on retreat. Nor did she volunteer that she stole away in the wee hours of the morning and only returned to the mansion in time for Morgan to catch her hard at work and sweaty when he got home.

A smile tugged at the corner of her mouth; Ray knew anyway, despite her attempts to hide it from him. She didn't know how, exactly, nor had he ever said anything more on the subject.

But his gifts, whether for birthdays, holidays, or for no reason at all, had suddenly turned more useful. It wasn't every girl who could say that her best friend gave her a compass for Easter or a season pass to the shooting range for Christmas.

Lane arranged the firewood in neat stacks outside the cave, breaking branches into manageable pieces and stowing them against the outside walls of the cave.

A day of work yielded a huge pile of tinder, another smaller pile of branches no thicker than twice the size of her thumb, and an unruly array of small trunks and large branches just too thick for her to break by hand or over her knee.

The entrance of the cave opened up into a wide room, roughly circular with a large alcove jutting off to one side. Eight feet high in the center and some twenty feet across, it acted as a natural weather barrier, blocking out rain, snow, and much of the winter wind.

Though it provided a great place to ride out a sudden rain shower in the warmer seasons, it proved difficult to tolerate in the winter. The temperature inside mimicked the surrounding forest within a few degrees; the wide entrance allowed too much air in, and the shallow depth prevented the rocks from acting as insulation.

This same inhospitableness made the cave unsuitable as dens for bear and coyote, and she'd never had any more serious an encounter than running from a skunk, which was either sick with rabies or seriously annoyed by her presence and had actually tried to chase her down.

She stared into the darkness with one hand wrapped around a stout branch and prayed that a mountain lion hadn't decided to make her cave its daybed, and that any rabid skunks had died elsewhere. She'd need to fashion some sort of door as soon as possible to keep the little beasties out.

Her eyes adjusted. The shadows dissipated to an even grayness and yielded no starving animals waiting to devour her. She entered the cave, a small bundle of tinder under her arm.

The natural alcove hollowed to the left of the entrance, and Lane had stored a few necessities there in her past visits. Two Tupperware buckets sat alone in the corner, and a quick peek confirmed that no one had touched the change of clothing, blankets, or waterproof matches that she left behind. It was a start, but not nearly enough. A smarter person would have stocked the cave better. *Weren't you here enough? Didn't you think you'd be back?*

The alcove also held a ring of stones for building fires. She arranged several thumb sized pieces of wood, standing them upright like a teepee, and she made a mental note to expand the pit in the near future.

She dug Jimmy Sullivan's cigarettes out of her pocket, withdrew two from the pack, and set the rest aside.

She broke the filter off of one and ripped the cotton wad apart, exposing more of the fibers to the air. She lit the other one and drew on it just enough to get it burning. Her runner's lungs choked on the contaminants anyway.

Orange flickered around the smoldering head as she placed it into the base of the teepee and covered it lightly with the cotton filter. A serious mountain man would laugh at her fire-starting techniques, but she didn't care. Within seconds, the wad flared up, and tiny flames licked the air in search of more fuel.

Lane obliged, adding progressively larger twigs, sticks, and branches until the young fire crackled happily, its tendrils snaking out to catch the teepee's frame. Careful placement of larger fuel stoked the fire into independence, and it spewed its warmth into the cave. Lane popped outside for another armload of wood.

It made more sense, she decided, to keep a stockpile of wood inside the cave as well so that she wouldn't have to go outside at night or when it was raining or snowing. For now, she guesstimated how much she needed to get through the night.

She watched enough reality TV with Ray to know that shelter, food, fire, and water sustained life, though the contestants always fought over which held the most importance. Lane couldn't say with any certainty; she supposed it depended on the circumstances. On a mountain, heat might be more important than other essentials. In the desert, water. Not that it mattered. She needed all of them and didn't have tribe mates to help her. Fortunately, she found the shelter years ago, and the mountain-fed tributary that fed Jensen Pond flowed just thirty feet from the cave. She only needed an easy way to secure the water without having to climb up and down the fifty-foot embankments. *No big deal*, she thought. *A pail, a rope. Maybe a pulley.*

The fire danced, licking at the feet of unseen demons. To keep that little lifesaver burning, she'd need tons more wood and would have to start amassing it before the snow fell. She also needed to handle larger pieces and to tackle some of the downed trees—not just their branches—and that required specialized equipment. But fire she had.

"Food," she said. *No choice there.* The little money she had wouldn't sustain her for long. Opportunities would present themselves, however; they always did. Food, clothes, medical supplies, towels, soap. And anything else she deemed necessary. *Toilet paper.* She'd do what she'd been doing—taking what she needed when she needed it.

Lane settled into the dirt, leaned against the Tupperware boxes, and fished around her trash bag of acquisitions for the handcuffs and the first aid kit.

She had never owned cuffs and had no way of knowing if all keys fit all models. It made sense to try hers to make sure before she did something stupid like chain herself up. The cuffs swung open with the first twist of the key.

Now the key needed a hiding place, somewhere accessible if her hands were actually cuffed together. The first-aid kit contained a tiny pair of scissors, and Lane cut a hole in the hem of her coat sleeve. She stuffed the key inside and squished it around until she felt comfortable that it wouldn't work its way back out.

Dusk gave way to night. The forest grew still. Tree frogs, crickets, and night bugs had all long since burrowed in for the winter or died. The gentle patter of raindrops and the crackling of the fire created a soothing lullaby. Curling up next to the fire, Lane waited for the nightmares.

chapter thirty

*C*louds of breath drifted in the cold air. Lane thanked God the rain let up, not that the lack of it kept her dry.

The lifeless bodies of last season's ferns, wildflowers and scrub collected moisture, transferred the leftovers from yesterday's rain onto her pant legs and shoes and soaked through, making her even colder than the brisk forty-degree temperature. She kept moving. Her life depended on it.

Before seven a.m., the town dump lay deserted, and Lane rifled through the debris and secured several useful items. But once the dump opened, cars streamed in, backed up, and chucked green and black bags of trash into the pit.

One of the citizens caught sight of her and pointed her out to the attendant. He'd charged toward her as fast as he could, mud sucking at his boots as he moved, his coveralls sagging even further with the extra weight.

By the time he reached the fence, she'd already tossed her new possessions over and climbed to safety. He continued to yell at her, as if she'd maybe climb back over to his side so he could have her arrested.

She dismissed him without so much as a glance; he'd have to

climb the fence and then chase her down. From the sound of his wheezing, she could tell the mud had sucked his strength dry; there was no way he'd catch her, even if she pulled up a rotting tree stump and waited for him.

She gathered up the salvaged items, including a frying pan that lacked a handle and had a few scratches in its Teflon. It held its smaller cousin, a saucepan with a dent in one side. Several coffee cans rounded out the morning's finds, and everything fit nicely into a dirty plastic milk crate with its corner broken off.

En route to the cave, Lane swung by another isolated house, let herself in, and helped herself to a few household items and a box of Cheerios. But the carton of milk stood guard over several baby bottles and jars of Gerber. Lane eyed it, her dead stare not intimidating it in the least.

For nutrition's sake, milk would have been a good choice. For ease of eating, the baby food, though probably the most disgusting thing she'd ever eaten, would slide down her throat easier than just about anything else. But milk and baby food? Together in the same fridge? Only a complete jerk would take them.

The milk triumphantly saved the baby food, but it couldn't save the bottle of Pepsi; Lane added the soda, a blanket, and a roll of toilet paper to her milk crate before wiping away the telltale signs of her deeds.

After dumping all the morning's treasures in the cave, Lane spent a few hours hauling stones and firewood. She pilfered all the large stones from the immediate area to rebuild her fire pit and supplemented the construction with more stones from the forest floor. The river had plenty of rocks to spare, but that was one chore she didn't want to tackle just yet.

When complete, the fire pit topped out at a foot and a half high on the sides, with a sloping back that extended another foot higher. The higher back directed more heat into the alcove, and holes along the bottom provided a constant air supply to the flames. The front of the pit remained open for easy cooking.

She tapped the side of the Cheerios box and urged a single *O* toward her mouth. It dropped in, and she chewed diligently, carefully pulverizing it before even attempting to swallow. She washed it away with a tiny swig of Pepsi, then poured out a handful of cereal and popped them in her mouth one at a time.

Meals were a never-ending struggle to locate, obtain, and then consume the food, and she was always hungry. *At least here*, she thought, *I'll be able to just sit and eat.* She'd be able to refuel at her leisure and actually enjoy a meal. *Maybe put some weight on. Get my speed back.*

She rolled the wax bag up as tightly as she could, closed the box top, and jammed it into a crevice in the rock face. *Maybe the raccoons won't get it.* She considered taking it with her, but she needed her hands to be free. "Besides," she said aloud, her voice croaking. "That'll make good tinder when it's empty."

While munching away on one dry *O* at a time, Lane headed back to town. Dark clouds threatened to drench her, but the rain held off, and forty-five minutes later, she hid behind the cars at Marigold's Diner. Two male employees stood outside the rear door, finishing up their break. They smoked their cigarettes into tiny nubs and squashed them into the wet pavement before returning to work.

With one hand on the dumpster, Lane kicked off from the bumper of a green Toyota and hoisted herself up. She had long since gotten over the repulsion of eating other people's garbage; when all else failed, survival remained.

She ripped open a trash bag, not wasting the time to untie it neatly. A three-inch end of a grinder lay under a layer of napkins and crumpled place mats. Paying no mind to the existing teeth marks, Lane nibbled off a bite and stuffed the rest into her coat pocket.

Nothing else in the bag proved edible. *No worries*, she thought as she ripped open another bag. Restaurant trash reminded her of Christmas—something hid inside every package, you just didn't know what. A small clump of spaghetti sat on top.

Spaghetti was tough. If the strings strayed too close to her throat, she'd choke for sure. With her head tipped down, she placed a strand on her tongue and ground it to a fine paste before swallowing. She finished the remaining few strings, licked the sauce off her fingers, and dried them on her pants.

Up popped a dozen French fries, then a half a burger, and all of it found new homes in her pockets. A third bag revealed several pieces of stale French bread and a nearly empty carton of orange juice two days past expiry.

The kitchen door banged open, and one of the workers ran across the parking lot. His belly protruded over his belt, and food stains smeared his apron. His unruly hair stuck out around a hair net. "Hey! What are you doing in there?"

Dead stare. *What do you think I'm doing in here, moron?* But she didn't wait around to make sure he saw it.

There were several options for escaping a dumpster. "Stacking" enabled one to climb out of the dumpster on trash stacked in a corner. If you had a lot of upper body strength, you just hoisted yourself up on the edge, like popping out at the side of a pool.

Lane "tipped" out, throwing her torso over the edge and leaning down toward the ground until her feet rose high enough to swing out. With a twist of her body, she landed on her feet and broke into a light gallop.

The short-order cook fell behind quickly. "Get a job, you loser!"

That was everybody's pat response to her. She'd heard it a thousand times. *Probably hear it a thousand more*, she thought. She glanced back; the youngster had given up.

To rub salt in the wound, she hopped a cocky sidestep, as if taking a lead off first base for the steal; he flipped her the finger and turned back to the diner. She slowed to a walk, fished out the burger and took a nibble, and washed it down with the outdated OJ.

Up the road the neon sign of Vic's Gas Station glowed against the gray sky. One of only two stations in town, it sported a convenience store, four full-service pumps, and a two-lift repair bay currently occupied by a blue Mustang and a little silver foreign job.

Lane doubled around, came up behind the shop, and rummaged through the trash. She found nothing but greasy old rags, some empty oil cans, and the boxes and wrappers from auto parts.

Wrenches clanged and curses flew as workers collaborated on some part giving them trouble on the Mustang. The lift hid their bodies, but two sets of legs shuffled back and forth in the far corner.

Closer to her, the workbench near the foreign job played host to someone's lunch, and she slipped in unseen, working her way silently along the wall toward the green box. She eased it off the bench and tucked it under her arm, then snatched the bottle of water.

A wrench slammed into the wall just inches from her head, spraying paint chips and coarse concrete powder into the air. The garage exploded with a flurry of motion and even more curse words. With the lunchbox cradled under her arm like a football, Lane charged for open ground. She stared at the box and read the owner's name off of the bottom: J. Olsen. *What have I done?*

Two options emerged: throw the box over her head and keep running, or hang on to the box and keep running. *Either way*, she thought, *I have to keep running.* She clutched the box even tighter.

The two mechanics pursued, the large bulky one giving up quickly. The smaller one continued to follow, and Lane considered chucking the water bottle at him to slow him down. After a dozen more strides, he finally gave up, but his cursing reached her for a bit longer.

chapter thirty-one

Richard stood in the frame of his office door, reading through the stack of reports. "Six? Today?"

Danny nodded, his hands riding up to his hips. "Yep, little something here, little something there. Mostly food and such."

Richard continued flipping through the papers. "IOUs?"

"If it weren't for the IOUs, no one would even have known she was in their house."

Richard handed the reports back to Danny. "Seems to be working her way into town."

"Why come back here? She's gotta know we're looking for her."

"Because this, my boy, is where the food is."

The phone rang, and both men leaned over to watch Dottie take the call. She chuckled at them, but her smile quickly faded.

She tucked the phone under her chin and waved them over with one hand as she wrote information on her call log. Richard reached her first and read the shorthand as she wrote "T-Head trash" on a slip of paper. He grabbed his hat and raced from the office, Danny in tow.

On the other side of town, out near the national forest, Morgan had built a strip mall, strategically placing it there to rake in tourist dollars. Visitors to the region encountered the Valley Plaza immediately before entering the wilderness and found it first when they realized they needed more ice, forgot their toddler's favorite teddy, or when their wives grew sick of cooking fish and hot dogs over smoldering campfires.

The T-Head, officially known as the Trailhead Restaurant, stood at the far end of the mall. They'd switched to their winter hours back in October and opened only when tourists showed up in quantity, namely Friday through Sunday.

A few of the Plaza stores remained opened year round: Gas & Go, Last Chance Liquors, Neil's Sporting Goods, Mill Hardware, and the Harris Grocery Outlet.

While the prices at the Plaza tended to be a tad higher than other establishments in town, they had wormed their way into the hearts of locals. They put up a vinyl privacy fence so their neighbors wouldn't have to look at the unsightly concrete walls, and to keep their patrons from trespassing in their neighbors' yards. The presence of the town's only liquor store didn't hurt, either.

Danny hugged the rear wall of the strip mall, easing around and peering into each dumpster he passed along the way. The suspect had hit all of them, ripping bags open in search of resources.

Further down, Lane was digging through the trash immediately behind the Trailhead. But the restaurant had trouble with dogs raiding the trash and had installed chain link fencing to block the alley behind their establishment.

The deputy eased in slowly, and when nothing else remained to hide behind, he stepped out from his hiding place and called out to her. "Hey!"

Lane whirled, surprised, but the officer posed no threat to her—he stood on the wrong side of the fence. *Rookie.* She relaxed and continued her search for food.

"What say you come on down to the station with me. We can talk about this, get you a decent meal."

Lane eyed him and noted the bruises on his cheek bone, but otherwise she ignored him.

Danny insisted. "You can't live this way forever. Probably should think about coming in now, before the snow falls."

"I think that's a good idea." The new voice was much closer to her.

Lane whipped around to find Richard had cut off her escape route. His hand rested on the butt of his pistol, and his fingers drummed on the leather holster. She panicked, her mind yelling *Run!* But she had nowhere to go. *Fool!*

The sheriff smiled deceptively, but Lane knew his pleasure came from capturing her. His chin jutted out in the direction of the fence. "Go ahead and put your hands on the fence."

Lane eyed them both. Danny posed no threat at the moment, but Richard stood just seven feet away without any obstacles to block his path.

"Only gonna get hurt if you don't do as you're told." Richard motioned to the fence again.

Lane complied, moving slowly, still searching for a way out. She threaded her fingers through the chain link and waited.

His fingers wrapped around her collar, and Richard stiff-armed her into the fence with one hand while slapping his handcuffs onto her scarred left wrist. "New coat?"

Lane drew her leg up and kicked back, expecting to impact with Richard's knee. She didn't expect him to counter her attack.

His training became evident quickly. He stepped aside, yanked the scruff of her coat and threw her face-first onto the pavement. With his knee in her back, he used his body weight to pin her down.

Lane struggled, but Richard pressed down all the harder. She soon realized that his pressing on her lungs prevented air from entering. Gasping between words, she croaked out whispers. "Can't breathe."

Richard slapped the second cuff around her right wrist. "That would be the point." He climbed off, pushing on her back to emphasize his authority and his dominance. He placed one hand on the coat and the other on her arm and gave her a gentle tug, helping her up. "To your knees first."

Once she was back on her feet, he steered her back toward the fence, insistent but not overly rough, and held her against it while he kicked her legs apart.

The pat down didn't yield any hidden weapons, contraband or identification. What Richard did find, he discarded: the stale French bread, the half-eaten grinder, and the burger and fries.

With every touch, Lane jumped nervously. When her hard-earned meal sailed through the air, her head swiveled and her neck craned as she desperately tracked the flight paths, noting where everything landed for future retrieval.

"Relax. We'll find you something *unused* to eat." His sarcasm didn't faze her; she continued searching for the food. When he was satisfied that she posed no danger, Richard peeled her off the fence, and with his hand on the cuff-chain, he steered her around the T-Head and out to the main parking lot. "Bring the car around, Dan."

The retreating footsteps echoed off the concrete walls; Lane was alone with Richard. *Alone. With Richard.* Her mind raced. *What if it was him? And now he has me alone. Again.* Logic told her that

Danny would be back in sight by the time they reached the end of the alley and that she didn't have anything to fear. He simply didn't have the time to do anything more serious than rough her up or give her a couple of slaps.

Unless he just plans to kill me and get it over with. But that didn't make sense either. The deputy witnessed Richard cuffing her; she simply posed no threat to either of them at the moment. She relaxed, talked her way out of the panic, and slowly focused her attention on escape.

How? She was cuffed, and Richard held the chain. She couldn't run and obviously couldn't overpower him. He was trained, completely unlike the drunks and losers she'd chosen to roll in the city. She played pony to his rider, steering left or right with each tug of the bit joining her hands.

Ahead, Danny pulled the cruiser into view at the edge of the building. He popped open the right rear door and stepped back, assuming his best I've-got-your-back stance.

With no choice in sight, Lane let Richard steer her to the cruiser. She jumped when he put his hand on her head to keep her from hitting the door frame.

"Just relax, Capone."

A wire fence and a Plexiglas panel separated the front and rear seats. Danny yielded the driver's seat to Richard, and Lane hoped that meant Danny would be the one to take her out of the car. He was her best chance of escape; he didn't carry himself with the air of authority or experience that Richard exuded.

With the sheriff's department just a few minutes away, Lane had to work fast. She pulled and tugged at her coat sleeve, finagling it around until the key moved into position for extraction. It popped out easily, and her hand clamped shut around it.

With a finger leading the way, the key slid around the cuff until it dropped into the keyhole. With a quick turn, the cuff gave, and Lane pulled it free just one notch at a time so it wouldn't make any noise.

"Lane," Richard said, his voice remaining casual, matter-of-fact.

Her breath caught in her throat, but her eyes focused on the floor. *Can he hear me? No*, she thought. *He's just not sure it's me. He's trying to flush me out. Or maybe he's sure and he's worried I'll tell someone.*

The cruiser pulled up in front of the station, and both men slid out. In the three seconds it took Danny to open the rear door, Lane had ratcheted off one cuff.

He reached in, motioned for her. "Come on."

Lane scooched across the seat and let him wrap a hand around her biceps. But as he helped her out of the car, she grabbed the handcuff like brass knuckles and swung at Danny's face, dropping the key in the process.

To his credit, Danny ducked, missing most of the blow and grabbing for Lane, but a second jab caught him square in the eye. He went back, slid down the side of the car, and lunged forward to grab her legs and tackle her. Lane danced out of his grasp and skirted around the front of the cruiser as Richard came around the back.

He stared at her in disbelief, helped Danny up, and retrieved the cuff key. "Give it up now."

Lane stared back, dead eyed.

Richard pulled his two-way radio from his belt and thumbed it to life. "Gonna need some help with a rabbit out front."

The station door opened, and Lane fled for the hills. She'd beaten Richard's high school record, but that was ancient history now. She had to assume that the sheriff had kept up his regular training regimen. She hoped only that his age would slow him down.

Richard pursued. She kept out of his reach, but he was surprised that she wasn't as fast as he expected her to be. His breathing remained regular and unlabored, and he pumped his arms easily, gaining on her with each step, knowing that time alone would put her back into custody.

Chest heaving, Lane sensed the problem long before she heard Richard breathing down her back. She hadn't been training, wasn't back up to speed, and wasn't eating properly. And now, several hundred yards from the next nearest officer, there was no end to the damage he could inflict on her if he wanted to.

She struggled to control her breathing and to focus, and she began to pump her arms as if she was clawing her way through molasses. Adrenaline surged; she rose higher on her toes. The transformation washed from top to bottom; her stride lengthened, and her arms drew a wider churn. Richard chased to within a few strides of her, only to watch her recover and pull away. But he didn't give up until she'd put five meters between them.

A horn blared behind him, and he swung around. He grabbed the door handle as the cruiser slammed up next to him. He jumped in the car. "It's her."

In the few seconds it took to swap modes of pursuit, Lane had veered off the street and ran through backyards toward the forest. Danny gunned the engine, getting as close as he could but coming up short; she ducked into the tree line and vanished quickly from sight.

chapter thirty-two

*L*ane limped out of the woods behind the rectory, massaging the stitch in her abdomen that doubled her over just a hundred yards after entering the woods. *If Richard had known or if he'd pursued further, I'd be in jail right now,* she thought.

A light sprinkle rippled puddles in the driveway as she approached the back porch, wondering how Ray would greet her, hoping his behavior would reveal his trustworthiness or lack thereof. She hoped she would just *know.*

The door popped open, and a black-haired priest stepped out. She saw a flash of teeth as he smiled. *Zavier?* No matter how she craned to see around him, she found no sign of Ray, not in the door nor any of the windows. The young priest stepped forward; Lane headed back into the forest.

"Wait!"

His voice lacked its usual warmth and had a nervousness that she'd never heard before; it convinced her she was right not to stick around.

He rushed back in the house, yelling all the way. But he came right back out with his hand waving furiously for Ray to hurry up.

"Lane!" Ray's desperate voice ripped through her.

She turned toward him, but her eyes didn't quite find him as they darted from his chest to his feet, and from his shoulders to Zavier and the house.

The three stairs under the porch might just as easily not have been there for all the inconvenience they posed for Ray. He raced across the yard.

Her muscles tensed under the baggy clothes, and her limbs twisted slightly. Her right leg shifted.

Eager to welcome her home and alarmed by her obvious distrust, he slammed to a halt and moved slowly closer with his hands held out in front of him. *Calm*, he told himself. *Be calm.*

Ten feet from her was as close as she'd let him get; she took a deliberate step away from him. He stopped and peered at her. Lane?" He searched her face for recognition, but she gave none.

His eyes fell on the crucifix he'd given her, but she wasn't herself at all. Since the last time he saw her, she'd devolved from athletic, well-kept and independent to skinny, dirty and desperate. Even with all the torment she'd endured living in Mills Valley, she never looked like this.

"Lane," he stepped closer, but she stepped back again. "Come in. Please." Ray backtracked toward the house and turned sideways hoping she'd see it as an invitation or at least as nonthreatening. "I'll whip you up something to eat. Mac and cheese?"

Lane's eyes darted between the younger priest and Ray, who stood before her in jeans and an old flannel shirt. She only saw him without his clerical blacks when he took her out of town.

"That's Father Zavier. He's filling in for me for a little while. Come on." Ray motioned her to follow and headed slowly back to the house, walking sideways so he'd know if she actually accepted the invitation.

His heart leapt when she took her first step toward him, and as long as he kept moving, so did she.

He motioned Zavier back into the house and away from the door, he himself moving to the opposite side of the kitchen. With ample space between them, Lane entered and scanned the room, assuring herself that no danger lurked inside.

She sidled over to the kitchen table and dragged one of the chairs back to the door, blocking it open. Rain splattered at the threshold and mingled with water that dripped off her hair and shoulders.

Zavier slid out of view and came back with two bath towels, which he handed off to Ray. Unsure how to get the towels to her, Ray simply placed them on the kitchen table then pushed the table closer to the door hoping she'd be able to tolerate his approach if the table remained between them. It worked. Lane took the towels. She used one to dry her hair then sat on it. She wrapped the other around her shoulders.

Ray whipped up a quick batch of macaroni and cheese and made small talk while it spun around the microwave. He couldn't help but notice the handcuffs still attached to Lane's right hand. "I've been worried about you, kiddo. I tried to find you in Seattle." He paused but received no response. "Have you been getting enough to eat?"

Nothing. Ray pretended it didn't feel like someone was tap dancing on his heart. She was the one person in the world that he loved like no other, and she wouldn't speak to him; she wouldn't even look at him.

He answered the microwave dinger, stirred the powdered cheese into the soggy noodles, and eased it across the table. He took a seat in the chair at the window.

Lane swooped up the bowl and carefully separated a single elbow for consumption.

Zavier slid out of the room again and returned with two heavy sweaters, handing one to Ray and shrugging into the other himself.

"Are you ever going to talk to me?" Ray asked.

Lane shifted her gaze between the two men and the backyard where she scanned for hidden threats, like the sheriff and his men. His words stung her. Everything in his behavior screamed his innocence, yet trust failed her. Her eyes found his for a millisecond before returning to the backyard. She pulled at the scarf ringing her neck and slipped it open.

The scar zigged across her throat; the doctors had saved her life, but cosmetics hadn't been important. She tipped her head back a little, exposing the hideous scar to the light, to Ray. She swallowed hard, concentrated on forming the words, and focused on expelling an appropriate amount of air.

Her words varied in pitch, tone, and intensity, creating a strange combination of squeaks, whispers, and croaks, and she hoped Ray would understand. "Doesn't work right."

Ray rocketed to his feet, paternal instinct trumping caution, but with the first step across the room, Lane rose from her chair as well, one foot out the door. Ray froze. He eased back to his chair, and his voice trembled. "How did that happen?"

Lane shrugged, settled, and slid another pasta tube into her mouth.

"You don't know?"

Lane shook her head no.

He pointed to the handcuffs. "How'd you get those?"

Lane shrugged again.

"Thirsty?" Ray rose slowly, his hands motioning at and leading the way to the fridge in an *I'm just going over there* fashion.

With Ray occupied, Lane leaned over and tugged at the junk

drawer, which was jammed full of odds and ends—screwdrivers, a tape measure, thumbtacks, menus, and phonebooks. And paperclips, which were good for freeing herself from the sheriff's chains.

They didn't work as well as bobby pins. The old drunk from Seattle said they were too flexible. It took several minutes to finally get the proper hook and to apply just enough force to pop the pin without bending the clip out of shape. She ratcheted the handcuffs off and dropped them on the table.

Ray and Zavier observed from the other side of the room, thoroughly engrossed in the process, then Ray set the glass of milk on the table before returning to his chair.

"Don't believe you don't know."

She struggled with the words again, finally giving up and whispering at him. "Richard."

Ray nodded and smiled. "No idea how you ended up with that scar?"

Lane shook her head and wiggled her fingers close to her head. Ray guessed it meant her memory was fuzzy.

"You steal a car?"

Lane ignored him, focusing on the golden elbows in the bowl and wishing she could just scoop them up and stuff them in. She slid another into her mouth, chewing it into paste.

"Answer my question. Please."

Lane shot him a dead stare, her focus remaining on him for all of three seconds. "Got a ride."

"Then why did you run from Richard?" Ray waited, but he got no response—no shrug, no whispers.

"We need to get this cleared up. You have to turn yourself in now before this gets any worse."

Lane was on her feet and two steps out the door with the bowl still in her hand before Ray even thought about shouting.

"Lane! Wait!" But he didn't pursue.

Lane moved back to the doorway.

Ray's shoulders shrugged up a little, his hands turned palm forward. "I'm not going to do anything. Please, just sit."

She took another step in, but remained standing.

"Richard will catch you. It's only a matter of time."

She disagreed with a shake of her head.

"Everybody knows you're fast, kiddo, but he didn't get to be sheriff because he could run. He got the job because he's good at it. He knows you'll come here. He's already been here looking for you."

Cold raw panic ran through her body like the water dripping off her clothes. "Relax," Ray said, his hands rising to calm her fears. "The safest thing to do is turn yourself in and get this whole mess cleared up."

The muscles rippled along her jaw, and Ray knew her answer: no. "I know you're not exactly pals, but you'll have the best lawyer money can't buy. I'll be there with you, every step. I promise. We'll get through this together."

Lane's eyes filled with tears, and she dragged a sleeve across her face. She desperately wanted to trust him. *Why would I even think twice about it?* She stepped away from the door, giving him access to the phone.

Tears threatened Ray's eyes as well. He slipped the receiver off the cradle and dialed.

Zavier stepped out of the room, and Lane took the opportunity to move further into the kitchen. She reached the door to the living room and looked around. It hadn't changed at all. A few straggling shafts of sunlight pierced the clouds and poked into the south-facing windows, illuminating pictures of her that she hadn't seen in months.

Years, even.

The bay window looked out on the old bigleaf maple that Ray claimed was older even than Pearce's Grocery. Zavier stood at the door and opened it. Danny, sporting a nice shiner with his bruises, stormed the front with his gun drawn.

Simultaneously, Richard and Ed stormed the rear.

The bowl fell from her hand, and gooey yellow noodles jumped out onto the floor. Ray's cussing echoed off the walls and chased her down the narrow corridor that led to the bathroom, the den, and the stairs to the second floor.

A heavy thud rattled the pictures on the wall, and Ray cussed even louder.

Ed shouted him down, grunting all the while. "Don't fight with me, Ray, or you'll be peeling wallpaper out of your teeth for the next month."

Lane spun around the baluster, climbed up the stairs two at a time, and bolted to Ray's room, knowing it would be the only unlocked door. She shoved the dresser across the doorway, not expecting the lock to stop Richard for more than a second or two. She didn't really expect the dresser to stop him either, so she didn't waste the few moments she had. She tossed Ray's blue jeans out of the way, wrapped her fingers around the molded handle of a black case, and pulled it free of the drawer.

The dresser wobbled when Richard slammed into the door. Another good slam and the lock popped; the dresser balled up the rug as it slid across the floor. Richard only needed enough space to squeeze his torso through, and he raised his Glock pistol. "Freeze."

Lane stopped, straddling the window sill. Her eyebrows arched high as if to say "Yeah. Right."

He blurted the first thing that came to mind. "I swear to God,

Lane. If you run, I'll shoot you."

Would he? She calculated the odds, and threw herself out the window, skittering down the slate roof and dropping off the edge.

Richard forced the dresser out of his way, but by the time he got to the window, Lane was sliding around in the mud and clambering to her feet. He had no intention of shooting an unarmed suspect. Neither did he consider climbing out after her.

He expected Danny would make a go of it, and he turned his attention to Ray's dresser— the photographs on top, the open drawer, the vacant space.

Richard returned to the kitchen and entered slowly, all the thoughts bobbing around his head vying for attention. He knew she was gone and that Danny didn't have a prayer of catching her. Ray sat at the kitchen table with his hands cuffed behind his back and Ed standing guard behind him.

Richard set a photograph on the table in front of Ray. Lane and Ray—who was in his street clothes—laughing, their arms wrapped around each other.

"Didn't see that one in the box of evidence Danny rounded up."

"Not my fault he didn't go through the storage boxes in the basement. And that was in *my* room. I'm sorry, but I didn't see your warrant, Sheriff."

Richard silenced him with a glance. "I'm thinking probable cause. What do you think, Counselor?" He didn't expect an answer. "Where was the picture taken?"

Ray stumbled. "What difference does that make?"

"Oh, a great deal I think." Richard spun the frame around for a better look. "Disneyland? I don't suppose you had parental consent?"

Ray remained silent.

"How many hotel rooms were involved?"

"Who said any hotel rooms were involved?" The chair knocked backward as Ray stood; Ed clamped onto the priest's shoulder to prevent him from going any further.

Ray tried to shake loose, but to no avail. "Not like I couldn't hear you yelling at her. Were you really going to shoot her?"

Richard toyed with the handcuffs and deformed paperclip that Lane left on the table. "These mine?" He didn't wait for an answer as he scooped them up and slapped them back into their case. "Kid's got an amazing set of life skills, Ray."

Richard dropped another photo on the table, this one of Ray and Lane in the woods. He said nothing as he pushed the photo across the table at Ray. The photo, taken from the boat dock, showed Lane and Ray in front of the Keates' family cabin. He stared into Ray's eyes and searched for an answer.

Ray's anger grew. "What?"

Richard moved closer with his hands currently tucked away in his pockets. "Have you shared a bed with that girl?"

Ray bristled. "I have never had sex with her."

Richard didn't lighten up. "Have you shared a *bed* with her?"

Ray grew more angry and repeated his answer.

Richard loomed inches in front of his brother. "Swear to me before God you didn't share a bed with that girl."

Ray smoldered, stared at his brother, and uttered the first few words of the same answer.

Richard had enough. He'd heard the gossip, and he had been seriously concerned about his brother's relationship with the girl all along. Now his brother deliberately evaded the question. And Richard was seriously pissed off. He lunged and threw his brother up against the wall with his arm across Ray's throat.

Danny jogged up the stairs and into the kitchen and found Ed peeling Richard off the cuffed priest. Richard composed himself and stalked across the room while Ed righted the chair and pushed Ray back into it.

Danny glanced between the three men, trying to figure out what had happened, but he didn't ask. "Sorry Sheriff, lost her."

Richard nodded, not at all surprised, but his eyes quickly returned to Ray. "What was in the second drawer, under your jeans?"

Muscles tensed along Ray's jaw.

"That can't be good." Richard shifted on his feet. His hands gripped the head rail of the empty chair and squeezed. His knuckles went white. "If it's what I think it is, you best tell me now."

Ray sighed. "Her Walther." He tried to minimize it. "Just a twenty-two."

"Just a twenty-two can still kill." Richard stared down at him, eyes blazing fire. "She's been breaking into houses, Ray. Stealing food and supplies. She's been pretty selective, but hell, now she's got a gun. She won't have to be so selective anymore, will she? How many rounds?"

Ray shook his head, trying to remember. "Could have as many as 120."

"Oh, is that all?"

Ray downplayed it. "There's two clips, ten rounders. And she usually stores a box of minimags in there for target practice. If she used them up last time—last time she went shooting—then she'll just have the two clips."

Richard stared at Ray with cold, empty eyes. "And you're worried that I might shoot *her*." Richard headed for the door. "Don't leave town, Ray."

Ray stammered. "On Mondays, I go into the city."

"*Don't* leave town." Richard left without another word.

Danny quickly uncuffed the priest, and he and Ed followed Richard out.

Zavier reached in and twisted the picture around, stared intently at the photograph; both Ray and Lane were several years younger. His finger pressed against the glass, and he slid it across the table and closer to Ray.

Ray snatched it up, tucked it against his side, and lashed out at Zavier. "*You* called Richard."

"I had to, you know that."

"You don't have any idea what's going on here. None. And in case you didn't hear, Richard threatened to shoot her. Still think it was a good idea to ambush her?"

Zavier remained quiet for a moment, letting the harsh words fade. He motioned to the picture. "She has your eyes, don't you think?"

Ray's mouth dropped a fraction, then he slammed it shut and left the room.

chapter thirty-three

The smoldering embers crackled greedily back to life with the addition of new fuel and a steady stream of air fanned across them. Lane stripped off her clothes, spread them around so they'd dry, and wrapped herself in a blanket before heading outside.

She'd been on the verge of surrendering, inches away from giving up her freedom, and then Richard showed up. The episode replayed in her mind over and over again as she tried to isolate the exact reason she'd fled.

Zavier's betrayal ranked up there on the top of the list, which brought up the possibility that Ray had been involved. *Not all that bad*, she thought. If he was willing to bring the police in, he probably wasn't the rapist. *Probably*.

Then the room flooded with testosterone. All those men. The surprise itself could have triggered the panic, and she decided that anybody in their right mind would have backpedaled. Or it could just have been Richard. Any doubt he held about her identity had been completely set aside. He'd be even more vigilant, and Ray was right— sooner or later, Richard would catch her.

She needed a smarter plan, something that would last several weeks and keep her out of town. And she had run out of time; winter hadn't waited for her to stock up. If she planned to survive, she needed to take drastic action.

Outside the cave, the mild autumn fled before the first blows of a cold and brutal winter. There was no hiding from the steel-gray sky pressing down on earth, nor from the howling wind, which crested the hill and swooped down into all the nooks and crannies.

A hiding place might protect her from the wind, and she squeezed herself in between the wood piles she'd been amassing. But the wind found her easily and attacked her, momentarily paralyzing her with its chill bite and sapping the warmth from her body.

She held her ground, not willing to yield the battlefield just yet. Below, through the naked branches of the dormant trees, headlights flashed as more cars pulled up to her house. *Morgan and Jenna's house.* She reminded herself that she had never been welcome there, and in light of her circumstances, she couldn't trust them anyway.

Tired of being ignored, the wind demanded her attention. It slapped her with the first few snowflakes of winter, whipping them up into a small white cyclone and pummeling them into the brazen human; she shivered but hunkered down, wrapping her arms around her gaunt frame and staring defiantly down the mountain.

Caterers in crisp bleached whites scurried back and forth, carrying heaping food platters into the house. "Monkey-suited" valets whisked away cars and ushered guests into the mansion under somber, black umbrellas.

Absently, Lane pushed her wet hair out of her eyes and wondered why Morgan hosted a midweek party. *Must be something special.*

Angered, the wind howled all the more. Physical attacks weren't working; time for another tactic. Swirling wildly, it carried on it the distant whine of a sports car—the engine raging as it ripped through the mountain road. It followed up with the screech of the flashy, red

Lamborghini's tires as it fishtailed onto the side street, then finished Lane off with the horn as the car announced its arrival and slammed abruptly into park in front of the Harris mansion.

She hadn't really cried in months, but memories slowly trickled into her mind and taunted her: the jaw-dropping slap; Morgan's fingers tightening around her throat as he dragged her out of the house and down the length of the driveway; Jenna watching at the window, emotionless, detached; the laughter of vindictive classmates after news of the incident raced through school; and the smug look on the sheriff's face when he tried to place her in the custody of the state. She did end up there, though not of Richard's doing, and in the group home, she'd learned that tears meant weakness, and that the weak became prey.

Now, watching the scene of comfort and camaraderie below, it no longer mattered; she wept, and the sobs racked her chest.

Lane didn't wait for the memories or wind to hit again. She returned to the entrance of her cave, *her home.* The glow of her small fire invited her in, and she left the battlefield in defeat, wiping rain and tears from her face.

That's OK, she thought, *you have your party. Tomorrow, I'll have mine.*

chapter thirty-four

*E*d leaned across the desk on his knuckles, looking more ape than man as he loomed over Danny, thoroughly expecting to intimidate the young officer as easily as he did suspects. "What do you mean he's taking the day off?"

Pete velcroed the closures of his bulletproof vest. All ready to go out on a "girl hunt," he joined the group that had assembled in dispatch.

Danny pointed his pen at Dottie while he continued working. "I didn't take the call." He never even raised his head.

Ed whirled on Dottie. With the slightest move of her head, she sliced his attitude down to his knees, momentarily silencing him. "What does it sound like it means, Ed?"

Properly chastised, Ed adopted a more civil tone. "He doesn't want to go hunt her down? He's not bringing in the dogs?"

Dottie peered over her spectacles. "Listen carefully. I'll say it one more time. He's taking the day off."

Ed's spine suddenly stiffened, and he stood straight up, glaring down at her. "I don't believe it. That's not like him, not with this kid. Not after what she did to Dan."

Dottie turned back to her work. "You can always bet me twenty bucks."

"Yeah, I'm stupid." He helped himself to Dottie's phone and began dialing.

"You are if you finish dialing who I think you're dialing. He said, 'No point in going after her when she'll come back to us as soon as she gets cold or hungry,' and that's a direct quote."

Ed hesitated, his finger poised over the last number.

Danny rustled his paperwork into a neat pile and chimed in. "I wouldn't want to be the one to tell him his reasoning's wacked."

Ed grew defensive. "It is wacked. She's been breaking into houses all over town."

Dottie twisted the chair to face Danny, ignoring Ed completely. "Especially today. Had that lost-in-time tone in his voice again. I suppose it might be because the girl's back in town."

Danny offered another option. "Or maybe it's because today is what would have been his anniversary."

Ed dropped the handset as if it had turned into a black rat snake—painful but not deadly. "How do you know that?"

Danny leaned back in his chair, kicked his feet onto the top of his desk, and folded his hands behind his head. "Because I pay attention, Ed, to everything. And I guess that means that I'm—" he stopped midsentence as he caught a glimpse of Dottie's face, her eyebrows arching high and daring him to take command of the office. He swung his feet off his desk and jumped up. "Taking orders from her now." He moved to Dottie's desk, plumped the pillow behind her back. "Couple days, you think? Anything I can get you? A mocha hazelnut latte thingy? I'll just pop down the diner for you."

Dottie shook her head. "Cabana Boy."

"Anything for you ma'am. Protect and serve. Or just serve."

chapter thirty-five

*T*hursday morning brought full sun, no clouds, and crisp winds. The ground froze overnight, which made hiking easier, and the light snow from Wednesday night melted away soon after the sun hit it.

Life at the Harris mansion was nothing if not predictable. The house staff had Wednesdays and Thursdays off, invariably leaving the compound to visit relatives. They dutifully returned to work on Friday, ready to supervise caterers for weekend parties.

Morgan would have left for work at seven a.m. Sharp. Jenna would return to bed for another hour or two, have a small breakfast of tea and crackers to preserve her figure, and take a long, luxurious bath.

She'd dress in her finest ensemble, hop into her Lexus, and drive into the city for her standing appointments with the hair and nail salon, the spa, and her midafternoon luncheon date.

At eight-thirty, Lane didn't worry about Morgan, who was long gone, or that Jenna might find her rummaging through the utility shed; Jenna would never stoop low enough to touch anything remotely related to manual labor.

The shed sat atop a twenty-foot square of cold, drab concrete and played home to the lawn equipment, lumber, tools, and anything that the staff might need—all items that Lane doubted Morgan would even remember purchasing. Everything had a place, and everything underwent meticulous maintenance, hosed down and towel-dried after every use.

A garden cart sat on its front lip, its basin against the wall. Lane slipped off the bungee cord that held the cart upright.

The empty bin waited as she gathered whatever she thought would serve her best: more bungee cords, a bow saw, an ax, several coils of rope, duct tape, and the magnetic box that hid the spare keys to the kitchen door.

The keys went in her pocket, but the rest of the small items thunked into an unused five-gallon pail that she found on a storage shelf.

Pails. Shiny, white, and new. And tons of possibilities. She grabbed two more and strapped all three to the side of the cart. They would help her keep track of small items and save the inside of the cart for larger stuff.

Another shelf held several two-gallon cans of gasoline, and she snatched one in each hand. They'd be the only way to set fire to wet wood. The fluid sloshed around inside the cans as she dropped them in the cart and snugged them up tight to the front edge.

Ray had told her stories about his life, shedding light on Richard's at the same time. They'd been avid campers as boys, and Richard had introduced Jenna to the outdoor life before she left him for Morgan. Since Jenna's gear wasn't in the house, the only place left to look was out here in the shed.

The rechargeable flashlight clicked free of its wall charger, and Lane headed up to the shed's attic. The angled roof made it difficult to stand erect anywhere except for the centerline, and Lane stooped low as she checked through the boxes along the walls.

More of Gamma and Pop-Pop's things lay in stacks out here, and Lane wondered if the gear Ray spoke of really belonged to them. Jenna didn't seem like the camping type; certainly sleeping on the ground couldn't be brought up in polite conversation.

Lane had no way of proving her suspicion, but she eventually found camping equipment in milk crates mixed in with Gamma and Pop-Pop's possessions. Jenna wouldn't even know the stuff was gone, not that it mattered if she did. Lane carried the crates down the attic stairs and stacked them near the utility cart.

Three tarps and several small cans of propane found homes in the five-gallon pails. The larger items, including a sleeping bag sealed in an airtight bag, a camp stove, and a set of black enamel cookware, ended up inside the cart.

For the better part of an hour, Lane perused the cabinets and drawers, swiping items she thought might be useful. By the time Jenna left, she'd pilfered dozens of items, some necessary, some convenient.

With time to kill, she settled down against a wall to wait. Deep inside, she wished Camilla and Anton were around. Anton's slight build eliminated him as a suspect, and Camilla might have been able to shed some light on Ray's trustworthiness.

But she knew if she robbed the house with them present, they'd be fired. She chose supplies instead of knowledge; the latter would simply have to wait.

The soft purring of the Lexus roused Lane from a light sleep. She peeked through the curtain as the Matador Red IS-C skirted down the driveway and up Harris Lane. She ran outside, the whine of the engine echoing off the hills as it sped down the highway and toward the city.

Alone at the Harris mansion, Lane pulled open the double doors, grabbed her coat, and pushed the cart to the servants' entrance. The cart and her shoes stayed outside as she let herself into the house, praying that no one had changed the security code. It turned green, and she sent a silent prayer of thanks skyward with her eyeballs.

She'd leave as few traces as possible, deciding against waving a big flag that said, "Hey, guess what? You've been robbed." It made sense to her to treat them like all her other victims—civil but detached—despite the treatment she'd suffered at their hands. Especially since Morgan could have been her attacker.

Across the kitchen sat the pantry with everything stacked neatly on the shelves. She snagged several black trash bags then hurried up the servants' stairwell to the attic bedroom.

Nothing had changed. The bathroom door had never been hung, her stuff sat where she'd left it, and the furniture hadn't been moved. She longed for the warmth and comfort of the surroundings but wasted no time on self-pity.

Since she had to buy all her own clothes, Lane hadn't turned into the clotheshorse that Jenna was. She threw out or recycled old clothes regularly, keeping a small collection of daily wear, a meager assortment of work clothes, and a short stack of Sunday-go-to-meeting attire.

The mountain required function in all things. Fashion fell by the wayside, and the cotton twill slacks and casual blouses for church remained on the shelf. She swept the rest of her clothes into a trash bag, filling just half the bag. She stuffed her pillows into the remaining space, tied the bag shut, and hauled it back to the attic door.

With a loud snap, another trash bag billowed open, and she filled it with supplies from the bathroom: the towels, toilet paper, toiletries, even the spring-loaded curtain rod and the blanket that covered the door.

She reached for the medicine cabinet door and stopped. The reflection wasn't hers any longer. *No wonder Richard didn't recognize me*, she thought. Dark circles ringed her eyes, and hollows sank beneath her cheeks. She dragged a slow hand around her cheekbone and down along her jaw line.

The ravages of living on the streets reached the rest of her body as well. She was stick thin and devoid of any female curves; even her hips and boobs were gone, the fatty tissue reabsorbed by the body when it went into starvation mode. Pulling the shirt taut against her skin didn't help; her anatomy barely showed at all. *I'm a boy.*

She threw the cabinet door open, peeling the reflection out of view. Band-Aids, a toothbrush, tweezers, and a half-empty bottle of aspirin all sailed into the trash bag. Tampons. She toyed with the box. She hadn't needed them in at least four months. *Bet they make good kindling.*

They slid down the inside of the trash bag, and Lane chucked the sack toward the attic door; it landed with a plop next to the first bag.

Back in her bedroom, she stuffed her bedding into two separate bags, then filled the rest of the space with food and supplies from her minifridge and pantry.

She grabbed the hiking boots Ray had given her for her birthday but scolded herself for having been too cool to buy a real winter coat. All she had were sweaters. Definitely not warm enough. *Ray did try to warn me.*

Only God knew what happened to her book bag and high school

books. But her spare book bag sat by the hutch, filled with her books from the Early College Program. She grabbed it by the hand strap and bowled it across the attic floor. It slid into the two trash bags already waiting at the top of the stairs, poofing the air out of one.

The legs of the table dragged across the floor, squealing all the way. Her fingers curled under the lip of the hutch and locked onto her pocketknife. She pried off the floorboards and pulled out all the money she had saved along with her bank account information, her wallet, license, and her camping equipment.

Memories of those camping trips with Ray flooded her mind. Eating the hot dogs raw before Ray could cook them. Stripping bark off greenwood branches to toast marshmallows. Burning said mallows black just to watch the fire bubble the sugary surface.

He kept most of the equipment at his place, but he insisted that she keep a few with her; he gave her the responsibility of managing the hand crank radio lantern. The job entailed carrying it back and forth between camping trips, cranking it to get it started, and complaining about the static.

She also kept the Sterno stove, three cans of Sterno, another set of cookware, and the compass he'd worked so patiently to teach her to use. She studiously paid attention to every detail even though she already knew her way back and forth through the mountains by the time he bought it.

Her fishing gear came next. The telescoping rod sat neatly in a little tackle box, which also held spare line, hooks, flies, neon orange fish eggs, bobbers, and sinkers. Melancholy slapped her hard, and she ran her hand down the case, remembering quiet times alone on the lake with Ray.

Neither of them would ever win a trophy for their proficiency with fishing. Ray really just liked to drift on the current and watch the clouds float overhead. Lane adopted the hobby, letting her lower legs hang over the gunwale. She usually fell asleep long before Ray did, though he seldom admitted to snoozing at all.

After a day on the pond, Ray cleaned any fish they'd been lucky enough to catch. He'd shown her how to do it a couple times, but she didn't like it, worrying too much about the fish being in pain. But once they hit the frying pan, she paid much more attention.

It couldn't have been Ray. She nodded earnestly. *He had thousands of opportunities.*

Her sleeping bag came out of the secret compartment last, and she rolled it out of the way. She eyed her Dell laptop and slid her hand over the case; without electricity, it was just a useless box.

She pushed it aside and double-checked to make sure she had everything of value, then she replaced the boards, slid the table back into place, and headed for the stairs.

The weight of the book bag bit into her shoulders, threatening to topple her over as she dragged the four trash bags downstairs, kicking the sleeping bag ahead as she went.

She skipped the third floor—no point in drawing immediate attention to her escapades. But on the second floor, she raided one of the guest baths, filling another trash bag.

Back on the first floor, she dragged all five bags out to the utility cart, dropped them on the ground, and headed back to the kitchen, where she helped herself to lunch.

Party leftovers called to her from the refrigerators. She took little bites and chewed them quickly but completely to make sure they wouldn't get stuck in her throat.

The leftovers wouldn't travel well, so she concentrated on the pantry, filling another trash bag with boxed and canned items. She swiped a manual can opener and a handful of eating utensils from the silver set, adding them to her acquisitions.

She set the alarm as she left, pressed the front gate opener, and jammed her feet back into her shoes. She dropped the heaviest bags into the bottom of the utility cart and arranged the rest on top.

The patios sat empty; all the lawn furniture was no doubt cleaned and stowed for the winter. But the Harrises had the best of everything, and lots of it. They wouldn't miss a chaise, but one would make an excellent addition to her little cave apartment. It would at least give her a place off the ground to sleep.

The pool house and shed were never locked, and Lane freed a lounger from the interlocking stack and snatched a vacuum-sealed cushion from the shelf.

All of an inch thick, the cushion slid vertically down the side of the utility cart, but the chaise had to be draped over the top. She tied it down with rope; in return, it kept the trash bags in place as she pushed the cart down the driveway and to the field at the end of Harris Lane.

Picturesque as the meadow could be during a casual stroll, it beat the crap out of the utility cart. Choppy, uneven, and full of potholes and rocks, the ground grabbed at the cart's tires, wrestling it back and forth as it bounced around on the obstacles. The cart handled easier if Lane moved slowly, but that wasn't her primary reason for dragging her feet. The key to expanding this small stash of supplies was in making another trip to the mansion, and that required getting the cart well into the forest, beyond the tree line where it would no longer be visible from the field. Free to cover and leave it, she could return for it after stealing more necessities from the mansion.

But her muscles already ached with the exertion, and she gasped air, her lungs reduced to balloons with pinholes in them. Focused on the breathing, she took slow, deep inhalations, retained the air for several seconds before releasing slow, deliberate exhalations until her lungs adjusted.

She worked her way through the field and up into the forest. The mixture of firs, hemlocks and spruce gave her ample hiding places, and Lane wheeled the cart behind a dense clump of scrub. To protect the items from rain, she tarped it over and secured it with bungees.

The cart simply hadn't been designed as an all-terrain vehicle; it had taken considerably longer than she hoped to get just this far, and she doubted she'd have time for a substantial second raid. And while she had clothes and some necessities, she only had enough food for a few days, a week at the most.

Now, with the afternoon well upon her, the Olsen kid would be home from school soon, probably with three or four of his friends in tow. She wouldn't have time to set herself up properly, not before witnesses started showing up on the scene.

A light jog did her well, revitalizing her, renewing her energy. She let herself back in the house and grabbed the green reusable "eco sacks" that Camilla liked to use when grocery shopping.

They were sturdier than simple plastic sacks and trash bags, and she stuffed them with a few more days worth of canned and boxed goods from the pantry and some hot dogs from the freezer. If she couldn't figure out how to keep the dogs frozen, she'd just eat them first.

Disappointed that she hadn't been able to rob Morgan blind and set herself up for the winter, Lane wondered if he had any spare money in the safe. *A little extra cash certainly can't hurt*, she thought.

Morgan's office had always been off-limits. She went in anyway, mostly out of spite and only when no one else was around, examining all his stuff, snooping through the desk drawers, finding the combination to the safe. The hideous painting of Morgan and Jenna stared down from the wall. As a child, Lane had always thought the portrait made them look mean and monstrous. Devilish even. Age and experience confirmed it to be arrogance born of uncontrolled power. She swung the painting away from the wall and punched in the combination of the safe hiding behind it.

Amid stacks of papers, a few thousand dollars stared out at her, but she dared not take more than a few hundred. Morgan probably wouldn't miss just a few.

Her eyes widened like a kid at Christmas. Perhaps once she was cleaned and scrubbed, wearing fresh clothes and looking like normal folks, she'd be able to walk right into town and buy the groceries she needed. Richard didn't really have anything on her and couldn't prove she'd done anything. She wondered if he could really even prove it was her that kicked the deputy in the face.

The best bet still remained avoiding him, and that would be much easier once she didn't resemble a vagabond criminal from hell. It certainly posed a better option than breaking into a different stranger's house every day to steal a loaf of bread and a half gallon of milk.

Her sleeve got caught on one of the documents, and it slid out of the safe and drifted to the floor, crashing into her foot before settling on the Oriental rug. Lane snatched it back up, absently flipped it over, and read the envelope.

Addressed to her, it bore the logo of Oregon State University. Someone had broken the seal, so Lane removed the contents and found an acceptance letter and a scholarship offer. She checked the postmark: two weeks before the attack.

Her mouth fell open, and she rifled through the other documents. The papers contained another eight letters to her, most with postmarks showing that they'd been locked away and hiding in

Morgan's office since before she woke up in the Harborview Medical Center. She snatched up all the envelopes, clutching them tightly.

The initial idea to rob the house without leaving traces died on the spot, ground into dust in her mind. She emptied the safe of all its contents, sweeping it all haphazardly into eco sacks. filling all the spaces between the boxes and cans.

The clock ticked closer to three p.m. as she rushed back through the kitchen, grabbing the last four pounds of franks on the way. They were only on hand for Morgan's version of a barbecue; Anton cooked wieners for the kids while Morgan plied their parents for investments. *He'll just have to find something else to amuse the kiddies.*

Temptation rose within her, an urge to trash the kitchen, scattering utensils and throwing food around the room, but in the long run, only Camilla would pay for that. She relented and thumbed the gate closed, then set the alarm and headed out.

In another ten minutes, the school bus would pull up, dropping off Jason and his little band of wannabe hoodlums. She jogged to the street and slipped through the gate before it slammed shut.

With the school bus still several minutes away, she could have walked, nibbling happily on a hot dog. But food would have to wait; anger burned within her, and hurt, and pain, and betrayal. She ran for the hills as fast as she could under the weight of the eco sacks, the hot dogs in her coat pockets slapping against her legs.

chapter thirty-six

*R*ichard snoozed in a chair in front of his outdoor fire pit. A small blaze burned off to one side, but coals underneath the grate roasted five steaks and a half dozen each of potatoes and corn on the cob.

An old dump truck rumbled to a stop at the front of the trailer, belching exhaust and waking Richard. He shifted a little as Wes carried a case of beer to the deck door.

"Oh, tell me you ain't sleeping."

"Don't bust my butt. I've been chopping wood all day."

"Rent a splitter, moron."

"Soon as I'm too old to raise the maul. No Maggie?"

Wes shook his head. "Says she's got no interest in watching grown men swear at the TV."

"That woman's just no fun."

Wes took the beer into the camper. "She's got her moments. You got room for this?"

Richard rose from his chair, stretched, and massaged a kink out of his back. "Absolutely."

The steaks sizzled in the heat, tendrils of smoke rising up with increasing aromas. Richard headed onto the deck to set up the TV tables and grabbed a beer before Wes loaded all of them into the minifridge.

"I hear the Harris girl's back in town."

Richard shrugged. "Yep. What else you hear?" He reached into the camper and pulled a serving tray from the edge of the dinette.

"Pulped up Dano's face."

Richard chuckled as he took the tray out to the fire pit to retrieve the food. "Nailed him pretty good. Took two to the face. Twice."

"What's wrong with that boy? No Wheaties? Couldn't pull a girl off a fence? You gotta send that boy to the gym. Make him workout with Pete. Something."

"Let's not underestimate the desperation of a trapped animal."

"Whoa, that's harsh. Don't take that boy's side. Geez, Rick, she's a *girl*. A skinny little seventeen-year-old girl."

"Nearly eighteen now. An adult."

"Oh, well, there you have it." Wes leaned against the doorframe as Richard returned with a full tray of food. "She's what? Half his size?"

"That's an exaggeration."

"I stand corrected. Dano was simply outmatched." He dropped down into the sofa. "You gotta stop taking him out with you. He's gonna get you killed. Take Pete. Ed, even. Leave Junior at the station."

"That'll certainly give him the experience to handle matters on his own. Besides, you didn't see her." Richard set the tray of food down on the coffee table. "We cornered her." His hands reached out to grab an invisible assailant.

Wes seized the opportunity to butt in. "Twice."

"We cornered her, and she turned into a rabid animal. She even growled at us."

"Yeah. The two of you. Can't pull a girl off a fence. Maybe you should retire with Ed."

"Maybe next time I'll just shoot her."

"Attaboy. Ever think maybe she's just scared?"

"She's got reason to be, assaulting peace officers."

Richard and Wes grabbed plates and forks, stabbed into the tray, served themselves up their dinner. Richard switched on the TV.

"No, seriously. Do you even know what happened to her? Maybe she's really, really scared. And there you come, all butch and what all. I bet your hand was on your gun, wasn't it? Probably scared the crap outta her. Not like she doesn't know how you feel about her."

"Who the hell are you? A shrink?"

"If her parents were anybody else, you wouldn't even know that girl was alive."

Richard pointed his steak knife at Wes. "Don't you even. I know where you're going. I'm holding a knife, you know."

"Yeah, I kicked your scrawny ass in high school. You never could fight worth a damn. And now some kid can take you. Correction. A girl can take you."

" 'Cept I ain't scrawny no more, and you give me any more lip, and I'll just shoot you, too."

Wes stuffed a monster piece of steak in his mouth and mumbled out words as he chewed. "I'm just saying that maybe you can't see too clearly when it comes to this particular kid."

"Why are you taking her side?"

"Ain't done nothing to me."

"Wait 'til you can't pay your mortgage. Hey, are we watching this game or not?"

"Hell, yeah. I'm just saying. Time for you to get over that." Wes grabbed the picture of Jenna off the coffee table and pitched it into the trash. Again.

"You know I hate it when you do that."

"Yeah. And you know I hate looking at her."

chapter thirty-seven

*M*organ leaned against his car and folded his arms across his chest when Jenna pulled into the drive. He greeted her with a peck on the cheek, but the fire smoldering in his dark eyes alarmed her. "What's wrong?"

"We've had a visitor." He offered her his arm and escorted her into the house. Jenna stood in the foyer and glanced around; nothing *seemed* wrong. He led her to the kitchen and opened up the refrigerators and the pantry.

Confusion twisted her face. "She stole the food?"

Morgan smiled and squired her into his office, nearly laughing when her mouth fell open into the most undignified gape he'd ever seen. Her eyes scanned the safe, top to bottom.

"I thought this was taken care of."

Morgan waved a carafe of bourbon at her in acknowledgment, pissing her off.

"Don't dismiss me."

Morgan poured himself a glass, took a deep slug of the amber fluid, savored it as it set fire to his throat, then his stomach. "What do you want from me? I hardly expected her to return."

"How much did she get?"

Morgan laughed, poured another drink. "All of it."

Jenna whirled on him. "A hundred and fifty thousand?"

Morgan sank into his desk chair. "No, that's gone. A few thousand. But she got the paperwork."

"The deeds?"

Morgan nodded. "And the foreclosures, appraisals, and contracts. Everything. Won't take a high school diploma to figure out we threatened half these people with foreclosure so we could steal their land for pennies on the dollar."

"If this ruins our plans—"

"What? You'll divorce me? Maybe Richard will take you back? Oh, wait. That's right. There won't be any room in his trailer for your clothes."

She glared at him, trying to muster her best intimidating stare. It worked on the staff and on attendants in stores and restaurants, but not on him.

He laughed at her pitiful attempt. "Face it, my dear. I'm the man with the money. That's why you married me, and it's why you put up with me." He took another long swig of bourbon. "And it's why you'll stay with me."

Jenna fumed, her eyes bulging, a vein throbbing in her neck. "We certainly can't have ourselves declared guardians of her property now."

"Don't see why not. We don't know it was her. Besides, the paperwork is in. We're just waiting for the ruling. No reason the judge won't sign it." A slight move of his hand swirled the drink around the glass. "We gave him a hundred and fifty thousand incentives."

He lifted the glass toward her, a silent salute. "Top that off with the current guardian's past relationship with you, and being the prime suspect in her disappearance, and this is pretty much a done deal. We'll have control of the property by the end of next week. Just too bad you weren't able to get either of the Keates boys back in the sack. We could have had the entire lakefront."

"I am not your personal whore."

"You realize that none of this would have been necessary if you had bedded that priest just one more time. If the threat of scandal wasn't enough, the monetary drain from the lawsuit would've forced them to sell their property. Lane could have kept her pissy little plot of mud."

Jenna slid across the room, her body lightly brushing against Morgan. "Is lake access so important? We should cash out now and head to the islands before this gets any worse."

He smiled down at her, amused that she thought she could use her charms on him. "The whole deal rests on it. We deliver at least one lakefront parcel or the entire deal is off. Nobody'll come to the resort if they have to get back in their cars and drive elsewhere to enjoy the water. That would be like booking a room in Aspen but having to drive to Vail to ski."

"Did you talk with the Bishop?"

Morgan nodded, set his glass down, and pulled Jenna in close. "Said it was old news, happened before Ray became a priest. Has no bearing."

"Well, that leaves Richard, doesn't it?"

"I didn't think he'd have you anymore, so it leaves Lane's parcel. If your parents had given you that land, this would already be settled. I never understood why they didn't leave it to you with the rest of the property. Maybe they knew you better than you thought they did."

He released her and strolled back to the bar. "Anyway, once we're declared guardians, we sell it, and voilá. Instant lake access for the entire resort. And if we should suddenly find out she's returned, well, too bad. By that time, all the land will belong to the resort. We acted in what we thought was her best interest at the time." He poured a cognac and carried it back to Jenna.

"We'll have to call Richard and tell him she was here."

Morgan shook his head. "We turn in our only daughter for stealing the roast beef? She's trying to survive, finds some money, and helps herself. I've already called Dean. He's handling the paperwork to get copies of all the deeds. It costs us time, that's all. We just have to get this taken care of before she figures out what she has."

Concern etched across Jenna's face, but Morgan coaxed her to be reasonable.

"You want to explain to your ex why we had all those deeds in the house? That we're planning to sell everything lock, stock, and barrel and split before anybody finds out?"

"Can't you blame it on the bank?"

"I'm the friggin' bank, Jenna. I pimped Tommy to buy all the mortgages up. He was all too willing to please me, and I knew that. He couldn't do it fast enough. Then I bought and closed the mill. I created the foreclosures, Jenna, and then I pushed Brant to liquidate them so our holding company could buy up the properties."

He topped off the bourbon again. "If either of them gets poked, they'll both squeal. They may not have been smart enough to see it while it was happening, but they'll sure in hell figure it out if somebody stuffs the proof under their noses."

He paced to the patio windows, and stared out into the backyard. "Besides, no matter what she took, it's not worth Richard rummaging around the house again, unless you're also willing to tell him about the attic."

"You were supposed to take care of that as well."

Morgan spun around and threw his bourbon against the far

wall. The glass disintegrated on impact, and amber fluid splattered against the wall. Morgan's eyes smoldered with a fury that Jenna thought could kill, and she wondered if it actually had. She knew little of his past before he came to Mills Valley.

He grabbed the telephone and thrust it at her, daring her to take it. "Who should I call? Somebody local maybe, or maybe I should bring in a couple hauling trucks from the city? Think that might raise some suspicions? Our problem right now is what she'll do if she reads through any of that paperwork."

"All right," Jenna relented. "But what if she comes back?"

"I hope she does. It'll be easier than trying to find her out there."

chapter thirty-eight

*F*our empty beer cans neatly lined the top of the minifridge and kept company with a half-empty and now stale bowl of chips. The eight remaining empties cluttered the area where Wes had been, haphazardly strewn about—some standing, some lying, some on the floor. Two on the sofa.

Richard lay sprawled in his deckchair, his feet perched atop the ottoman. Ten minutes shy of being late for work, he continued dreaming, lulled into the past by the rain as it drummed a gentle popcorn rhythm against the metal roof of his camper.

The downpour came on them suddenly, trapping them in the car. Rain beat against the windshield of the sedan, but the incessant slapping of the wipers drove Richard to distraction. He slammed the stick up, shutting the wipers off.

"What are you saying?"

Jenna leaned across the seat, her hand gently caressing his face. "I do love you. I just can't marry you."

Richard's mouth fell open as he shook his head in disbelief, but he couldn't find any words to say. He stared out the windshield, eyed the ostentatious mansion, the wrought-iron gates, and the sweeping driveway.

"Don't torture yourself, Richard. He can give me the things I want. It's no different than when I left Jake for you."

Richard dismissed the argument. "You wanted me." Her smile, a sweet seductive temptation, called to him, reminded him of pleasures they'd shared. Together.

"I still want you," she cooed.

"But you want him more."

She looked at the mansion. "I want Morgan for different reasons."

"Have you slept with him?"

"No, not yet. But I will once we're married. I may be his trophy wife, but I'm still expected to play the part." Jenna twisted sideways in the passenger seat.

"Is that what you did with me? Play a part?"

Jenna stared at her shoes for a moment. She cupped his face with her hand, kissed him and rubbed her cheek along his. She slid away, one hand clutching the umbrella, the other reaching for the door handle.

Richard grabbed her, wrapping his hand around her arm. He pulled her back.

A passionate and welcome kiss led to another, and another. Within moments, Richard had gone from rejected has-been to conquering hero, wooing her back with his prowess, proving to himself and to her that he was the better man.

He held her tightly, crushing her into his chest. His desperate hands tugged her clothing loose, and she assisted without a second thought. He lifted her hips to meet his and willed them to be one. Her back arched, their breathing came in short, tight gasps, and her nails raked along his back.

Richard lightened his grip, eased Jenna against the door but hovered close, panting. "Come home with me."

Jenna pulled her clothes back together, buttoned up her blouse, and straightened out her skirt. "This doesn't change anything."

An emotional brick slapped him in the head and instantly demoted him to yesterday's news. Richard stammered. "What?"

"Really, Richard. It's just sex. I've slept with your brother, too. Would you have me go home with him?"

Richard awoke, his leg kicking out from the ottoman as if the revelation had been a physical slap. His head pounded from the few beers he'd had; he checked his watch, then called the station to let them know he'd be late.

He showered, shaved, brushed his teeth, and ran a quick comb through his hair. Had he not been running so late, he would never have left the trailer in such a state of disarray: the bed unmade, towels in a heap in the bottom of the shower, and dirty dishes stacked in the sink, on the stove, and on the dinette table.

He sighed. "Party's at your house next time, Wes."

Jacket in hand, he stepped out and locked the door behind him. The deck, his precious deck, needed attention. This mess couldn't wait. Anyone passing by would see the swill and beer cans. Then the rumors would start, and only a lazy man would let that happen.

Richard had never been called lazy. He started with the beer cans, tossing them all toward the recycle bin. One after another, they sailed through the air; all on target they clinked into the bin with dull tinny thunks.

To save time, he decided to grab something to eat in town. He gathered up his duty items and checked his sidearm thoroughly before sliding it into its holster. His hands whisked up empty chip bags and discarded napkins along the way, and he dropped the garbage in the trash basket. Then he stopped dead in his tracks.

He eased the picture out of the pail and pulled off the sticky note that read "Loser bitch, throw me out." Richard laughed, crumpled the paper up, and let it slip back into the trash. His fingers brushed potato chip crumbs off the glass, his thumb grazing across Jenna's hair.

The picture had been taken the winter before Morgan moved to town. Richard and Jenna had gone to dinner at Marigold's, and he'd dropped down on one knee and proposed to her in the middle of the diner.

Jenna cried, the tears captured forever on film. Richard wrapped her up in his arms, and she displayed the ring to Marigold, who insisted on taking the photo. They wore matching smiles of joy.

Richard found the picture a new home next to the television. "Not gonna be so easy for him to throw you out next time."

chapter thirty-nine

Morning brought Ray to Marigold's for breakfast. He didn't want the abuse of the townspeople, but he wanted to share a meal with Zavier even less. *Smart ass. Thinks he knows everything.* He sat in the rear booth in the corner facing the wall and watched rivulets of water course down the window.

Ghosts of Lane sat across from him, the light dancing on her hair, that funny little smile she gave him when he acted more like a father than a friend, her feet on the booth next to him.

He'd stopped wearing his clerical blacks altogether. The vicar had stripped him of his position and responsibilities, so he just didn't feel very priestly these days. At first, he felt awkward wearing jeans around town, but he soon realized that people didn't recognize him as quickly in his street clothes.

He had come to expect the worse from everyone he encountered. He'd wanted to remain upbeat and friendly, but each day brought less and less civility from the townspeople. Now he chose simply to ignore them.

The other patrons at Marigold's ignored him as well, but an occasional unpleasant comment reached his ears. He pushed the scrambled eggs around on the plate and absently thanked Marigold for refilling his coffee.

Richard doffed his hat as he entered and took an open seat at the counter. Marigold stepped up, her hair freshly dyed a vibrant blonde. Richard didn't tell her it looked foolish; he didn't say anything at all about it.

She directed his attention to the corner booth. Richard considered it; he supposed it would give him time to gather additional information. "Thanks. Coffee and the three ninety-nine over hard?"

"You got it."

Richard slid into the booth opposite Ray, surprising him.

Anger bolted defensively to the surface and etched itself along Ray's eyebrows. "I'm nowhere near Doctor Death. And I haven't seen Lane."

Richard decided to take a softer tack for as long as it might last. "Every conversation doesn't have to start with a fight."

"But it will end up there. No point in wasting time."

Marigold slid a coffee across the table to Richard and left without a word. Richard stared at Ray, searching for the man he thought his brother was. Ray's eyes dropped back to the eggs, and he put his fork down. His voice softened, but not much. "So what do you want?"

Richard leaned forward, hands folded on the table. "I want Lane."

Ray met his brother's eyes. "So go get her."

Richard chuckled. "I will, but it'll be easier if you just tell me where she's hiding."

"You're optimistic. After that stunt you pulled, I can't imagine she'll come around to see me again. I had her convinced to give herself up. Hell, I was calling you when Ed introduced me to the wall," he pointed a finger at Richard. "And *you* blew it."

Richard reached across the table and rested his hand atop Ray's.

"But you do know where she is." It wasn't a question. Richard knew in his heart that Ray had a bead on where Lane would hide out.

Ray stared back, forming his answer carefully. "Of course I know. And so do you. She's up in the hills. But she didn't have time to tell me where. Besides, why would I help you imprison her?"

"Kidnapping, grand theft auto, breaking and entering with intent, assault on a peace officer, yadda, yadda, yadda."

Ray pulled his hand away. "Don't be stupid. You and I both know what I'll do to the bulk of that in court." The argument sparked Ray's appetite; he forked a pile of eggs and stuffed them into his mouth.

"So, you'll return to the bar for her. Good to know. I need to talk to her."

"Everybody talks with their guns drawn."

Silence enveloped the booth as Marigold arrived with Richard's breakfast special—two eggs fried until the yolks didn't run, two strips of bacon, and an order of toast. She dropped two checks and left quietly.

"Now *you're* being stupid. Standard procedure. I need to get her off the streets and into custody. We can work out the details after she and the rest of this town are safe."

"And if the facts prove that your case won't stand up in court?"

Richard leaned back. "That's not my concern. That's between you, the prosecutor, and the judge. Where is she?"

"Like I said, she didn't tell me." Ray folded a piece of toast in half and forked another fluff of eggs.

"It doesn't bother you that your stray may have kidnapped a man?"

"It bothers me that you refer to her in such derogatory ways, but from what I hear, your alleged kidnap victim can't corroborate your theory. You might as well chuck that charge right now."

"She'll get more brazen, Ray. Dumpster diving and stealing blankets will quickly turn into mugging, shoplifting, and armed robbery. Why won't you help me catch her?"

"Why do you hate her so much?"

"Don't be ridiculous. I don't hate her. It's my job."

Ray leaned across the table and stabbed his fork in Richard's direction. He didn't care if Richard considered it a threat or not. Spending another few days in jail would simply spare him the condemning stares of people he'd known all his life.

"Was it your job when she was six? Huh? Was it your job when you found her walking home from school? Or when you found her in a store? Or when she started playing sports? Was that just the job, or did you have another motive?"

"She told you that," Richard said, dismissing the accusations.

"No, Richard, I saw a lot of it firsthand." Ray leaned further across the table, the fork getting even closer to Richard. "Basketball games, track meets, wherever. Always finding little ways to intimidate her, even though she hadn't done anything wrong."

Richard's eyebrows rose high on his face. "I didn't know you had such an interest in girls' sports."

The fork dropped suddenly into Ray's plate. "At least I have an excuse. She's my godchild. You, on the other hand, just seem to enjoy showing up and hassling her."

Now Richard leaned forward. "What?"

"You heard me. I'm her godfather. I suspect they asked me to fill the role just to piss you off. Did it work?"

"And you accepted?"

"Why wouldn't I? The child had to be baptized, and obviously no one else in this godforsaken town would do it. He's *your* enemy, not mine. Face it. You hate her because she's Morgan's kid."

"That's not true."

Ray met Richard at the center of the table. "Of course it is. Every time you see her, you get to vent your rage at Morgan."

Richard's face turned scarlet. "Don't you lecture me—"

"What? Thought you were the only innocent one here? Sorry, bucko, but we've all got our little crosses to bear. You, me, Morgan, even your precious Jenna. Every last one of us, so just accept it. And leave the damn kid alone."

"Except that she's a criminal now."

"Then you need to try harder to separate your personal animosity from your job."

chapter forty

*T*he raid on the mansion had yielded many useful items, and Lane worked until sundown that night retrieving her acquisitions from the edge of the forest. She could have been done much earlier if she hadn't made a science out of not taking the same path twice.

But it was very important, to her at least, not to leave an easily followed trail, just in case anyone was actively tracking her. Dead tired, she settled for just getting everything inside before the sun set and decided to let the arranging wait until morning. She settled onto the chaise for some sleep, however little that might be.

Sheer exhaustion had prevented most of the dreaming, and she awoke almost refreshed. Energized. Ready for another day. *Have to try that again.*

With morning and a steady rain falling outside, the decision of the prior day proved correct, even though the cave had been converted into an eyesore with crap scattered everywhere. But at least she had the energy to attack it.

First things first, though. She was hungry. Famished. A few hard turns on the manual opener, and a can of yellow corn popped open for the having. She nibbled away, just a few kernels at a time, without even bothering to heat it up. *Hot food doesn't keep you alive longer than cold food; it just makes you feel better.*

Pacing around the cave as she chewed, mental images flashed in her mind, scenarios of where things should go and how they should be arranged. But the cave entrance had to be covered soon. *Next.*

Blocking the gaping hole would keep in more heat while keeping out the howling wind, rain, prying eyes, and curious animals. Unfortunately, it also meant that carbon monoxide could build up inside the cave. *Worse ways to go than peacefully in my sleep some night,* she thought. *Definitely worse ways to go.*

With some determined pushing and prodding, the spring-loaded curtain rod finally slipped into a nice cranny and wedged securely about a foot from the top of the entrance. She hung from it to make sure it would stay, then dug through the tarps and blankets, deciding how best to block the wind and rain. A cloth blanket would get soaked. A tarp, on the other hand, would stand up nicely to rain and snow, but she feared wind would whip it around too much to do any good.

Her feet shuffled along the floor as she paced back and forth with the wheels turning as she puzzled over the issue. *Both?*

The blanket from her bathroom in the mansion still held fast to the curtain rod hooks, so she hung it first, slipping the hooks onto the rod.

After she put the first layer up, she chose a brown tarp and hooked it on the outside of the blanket one grommet at a time. But the grommets were too far apart; she added several holes using her pocketknife and managed to get the tarp to hang smoothly.

But it still crinkled in the wind. No guarantee existed to suggest that the wind wouldn't simply toss it aside and race clean through. For added protection, she dropped a couple big stones across the bottom to prevent it from flying around.

The hole above the curtain rod allowed fresh air in and smoke out, but the cave turned very dark with the makeshift door blocking out the natural light. Lane cranked up her dynamo lantern and flicked it on. She hit the radio switch, smiling as mellow country tones whispered around the space. Her head bobbed, keeping the beat.

She slid the coverings across the rod and tested the new entrance for pitfalls. *Good as it gets*, she thought as she stared down the mountain at the mansion, wondering how their night had been. An evil, twisted grin marred her features briefly; she didn't waste much time gloating, despite the pleasure it brought her, and she went back to work quickly.

The eco sacks of food and stolen papers came next. Lane hastily dumped them in the dirt, moving aside the food, stuffing the documents back into a bag of their own, and zipping it closed. The sealed bag flew through the air as Lane chucked it into the alcove; she'd sort through those later. A smile brightened her face as she added her bank records to the pile. *It'll be like watching TV after Sunday dinner!*

The rest of the supplies had to get off the floor, or at least anything that could be damaged. *Like food in boxes,* she thought. Some of the items fit nicely into the milk crates, which stood in a column against the wall opposite the fire. They were no safer there if someone or something invaded her cave, but at least they weren't in any danger of melting or getting scorched.

She munched on corn kernels as she worked, stacking the boxes and cans by type and size, and trying to keep things together so she could find them easily when she needed them. She reconsidered the wisdom of taking boxes of food. If the cave didn't get warm enough, it wouldn't dry out; dampness would spoil the food.

A snort broke the silence, and her voice squeaked out its strange assortment of noises. "Hell, I've eaten moldy bread. How much worse can moldy pasta be?"

After a few hours, her new home had begun to resemble a little apartment just after moving day—more or less livable. *Except for the dirt floor*, she thought.

The radio played softly from the top of the milk crates. When the DJ launched into a spate of commercials, Lane grabbed one of the five-gallon pails and headed down to the river.

Her mind churned over where and how to rig up some sort of pulley system so she could haul water up from the top of the riverbanks. When the river froze, it wouldn't do any good, but it would certainly make life easier in the spring.

The trek down to the river wasn't bad; abundant trees provided ample handholds and resting stops. Five minutes later, the pail flew out over the water, a rope tethering it to Lane. It hit the water. The current slammed into it, and the bucket sped downriver.

She had stolen only three pails from Morgan's shed, and she needed all of them. One had been slated to hold boiled water for drinking, the second to hold river water for boiling.

The third would shortly become her latrine, and unless she wanted to continue squatting in the woods like the bears or forfeit a fresh water pail, she had to hang on to the one trying desperately to escape. She clamped her hand down on the rope.

Her palms stung and her arms and fingers ached with the exertion as she fought to reel the errant pail in. *Certainly won't do that again.*

She hauled back on the line, conceding that it would have been smarter just to dip the bucket in near the edge of the river, even if that meant picking up some floating debris.

The current fought back, grabbing the bucket, forcing it under the surface. If it could drive the pail deep enough, it would lodge against the rocks, and the rushing water would hold it in place forever.

"No way." Lane whipped the rope around a nearby tree and tied it off to keep the bucket from sinking any lower. When her hands grew raw from the rough fibers, she leaned her palms and shoulders against the rope and dug in.

The first lunge up hill strained her legs, and the muscles screamed their protest. She braced a foot against a tree and fought for another step. The tree provided support, but the saturated ground refused to provide a stable foothold. Sliding more than walking, Lane crashed to her knees and twisted around to give her back to the rope.

Content for the moment to just maintain the small headway she'd made, Lane gathered her strength for another push. The current continued to rush the bucket, pummeling it, trying its best to overcome the human on the other end of the rope. Lane dug her heels into the soft ground as far as they would go then pressed backward. The rope bit in to the coat but slid nonetheless; the bucket bobbed just below the surface of the raging waters. Another deep push, and the friction of rope against coat heated the skin beneath it. Lane winced. The bucket popped to the surface.

With her breaths coming in heavy gasps, Lane rested and surveyed her situation. Behind her, an outcropping of rocks presented itself as the only stable ground in sight. She dug in and pushed twice in quick succession, reaching the rocks. The bucket lay two feet from shore.

She arched her back. The rope scraped along her skin, and guided by her hands, slipped under her butt, and lodged around one of the rocks.

Lane scampered back down to the river, planted one foot in the freezing water, grabbed the handle, and wrestled the bucket to shore. By the time she had it back on land, she was tired and sweaty, and her entire body hurt. She lay in the mud, wondering if she shouldn't just pour the water out and try again tomorrow.

The five minute trek down turned into a forty-five minute forced march back. Too stubborn to yield, Lane stopped every step or two to set the heavy bucket down and find solid footing.

When she reached the cave, she struggled out of her muddy clothes, sloshed water into two pots, and set them on the fire. She collapsed onto her chaise, falling asleep within minutes.

The twenty-minute nap ended when the water boiled over and splattered into the fire. Wrapped in a blanket, she set the larger pot on the cave floor to cool, fished a box of pasta shells from her milk-crate pantry, and poured them into the smaller pot. The empty box sailed into the fire, instantly ignited, and burned furiously for mere seconds.

Spaghetti sauce required too much space, weighed too much for easy transport, and provided too little benefit, but she had swiped a shaker of butter flavored sprinkles, along with salt and pepper, and hoped the combination would make plain pasta a bit more palatable. *Like that matters.*

She'd grown accustomed to eating alone; *just as well*, she thought, considering her table manners of late. She ate like a squirrel, the food clutched in her hand while she nibbled off minuscule bits that she could easily swallow. *Perhaps if I had kept up the exercises, I'd be able to eat like normal people by now.*

She shrugged. The Shaker Exercise hadn't really been a possibility until now. On the streets of Seattle, she had no place where she could lie down flat and do neck crunches, as her therapist called them. "Head up, look at your toes, hold it, hold it, don't lift your shoulders, sixty seconds." She'd talk the entire sixty seconds, then "Down. Now rest, rest, relax, sixty seconds, rest."

Lane often dozed off in those sixty seconds, but she knew that she should have kept doing the Masako Technique. Designed to keep the tongue out of the swallowing process, all she had to do was hold the tip of her tongue between her teeth while swallowing her own saliva.

"Why didn't I keep that up?" Lane squeaked and vowed to try her therapies again.

She ate directly out of the pot, using the wooden spoon to scoop a single shell to her mouth. It was hot, fresh, and unused, and she enjoyed it. Really enjoyed it. *Like eating food for the very first time.* Her eyeballs rolled up into her head, and she groaned with satisfied delight. And now, unrushed by threats or the need to search out more food, she ate slowly, consumed as much as her stomach would hold, and relished every bite.

An hour later, she dropped the spoon in the leftovers and rubbed her sated and visibly swollen belly. She smiled and sighed. *Life may not be great*, she thought, *but this ain't too shabby.* She'd probably have a devil of a time with her guts later, but for the first time in months, she didn't feel hungry. That, however, didn't mean the search was over. The stolen food wouldn't last long, and Lane held silent debate on the importance of seeking more food right away.

It might be safer to avoid town for a few days, she thought. "Gotta be watching for me," her voice squeaking out a few words.

But when winter hit full force and the snow made it difficult if not impossible to get around on foot, the option of going into town for supplies could be lost completely. The snow itself would give Richard the upper hand, making it impossible for her to run away from him. If she saved the food she had and kept searching for food now, she'd at least have some emergency food on hand.

Then again, she thought, *I've got the money.* She upended the eco sack with Morgan's money and documents onto the chaise and counted out the bills. Three thousand dollars. *I can just buy food.*

If she didn't attract any attention, she could buy food whenever she needed it and as much as she could carry. Since she wouldn't have to break into houses, she could use the extra time to gather even more firewood and would perhaps have some spare time to read her school books.

She dropped another log in the fire and dipped a finger in the cooling pan of water. Still too hot to do anything with, she returned to the chaise and sorted out the paperwork, plotting her next move.

Her own bank records presented a variety of problems. She'd saved thousands of dollars from her paychecks, but it was all trapped in the bank. The tellers would quickly recognize her and rat her out if she walked in and tried to withdraw her money. That eliminated the bank's vestibule ATM as well because it was clearly visible to at least three teller stations.

A second ATM stood inside the Harris Grocery Outlet. Even if she could get to it without being recognized, the account had to be frozen or flagged. No doubt the sheriff would be notified within seconds.

The only way this could work depended on the cash she had on hand. She didn't pretend to be filthy rich, but she suspected that she could rent a room somewhere for a few hundred a month to get her through the winter. And she could add her "mad money" to the equation. *I don't have to live in this cave,* she thought.

But she also knew that if she spent too much money at one time or tried to rent a room in Mills Valley waving cash around, Morgan would be able to find her, as would Richard, who no doubt knew all about the robberies by now.

Besides, she thought, *who are you kidding? You're not leaving.* Producing excuses didn't overshadow the facts. Ray was here, and she felt compelled to stay.

"Why?" She didn't want to see him even though she'd nearly convinced herself of his innocence. She dwelt on it. *But I do want to see him. That's why I went to the rectory*, she thought. *He's my friend. My pseudo-dad.*

She replayed the encounter in her head. *I don't want him to see me.* Her standoffishness, the look on his face, her appearance. Her avoidance had plenty to do with the attack, but a great deal more to do with her. What she was. Who'd she become. Things she'd done.

But Ray wasn't the only reason to stick around. She was still scared as hell, scared that every man she saw was a potential suspect in her attack, scared it would happen again. She had to stick to what she knew, these mountains, these forests, and Pearce's. Without a doubt, *he was innocent.*

She set the money neatly aside while she worked on the pile of papers jumbled up on the chaise. The documents, all folded up and appearing to be similar, revealed themselves to be distinct and separate.

The college letters were easy to identify, as was her IRS tax refund, though she had no idea how to get that cashed without getting nabbed. Lane set them aside in a separate pile. A quick peek at two of the other documents revealed that they were land deeds.

They held no meaning for her; she hoped she could use them as leverage against Morgan. She expected him to hunt her down and beat the tar out of her for her effrontery. Perhaps he could be persuaded not to if she exchanged his papers for her safety. She wrapped Morgan's documents in a trash bag and stuffed them under the chaise.

The college envelopes remained. Lane unfolded them one letter at a time, read the offers, then returned them to their envelopes. Eight colleges had wooed her, two of them Division One schools, but their offers had long since expired.

Tears streamed down her face as she read the last offer— University of Washington in Seattle, Division One. The letter slipped from her hand, drifted to the floor, and crashed into the dirt. She crushed the offers under her feet and tossed the blanket onto the chaise.

She would have liked to shower at the mansion during her broad-daylight robbery, but at the time cleanliness seemed like more of a luxury than a necessity. Instead, she spent all her time pilfering resources, including those required for bathing.

The water had cooled enough to bathe, and with a sponge, a little soap, and some elbow grease, she removed months of built-up grime and odor. Lane cupped water with her hands, poured it on her hair, rubbed in some shampoo, and rinsed. The coconut smell of the conditioner drifted from the bottle.

She retrieved a hand mirror and propped it up on the cave wall, then hacked off her hair, making it easier to wash and care for. *I already look like a twelve-year-old boy.* The haircut would complete the transformation. Unbidden, the memory of her first haircut rushed her mind.

At six, Lane had no idea that Morgan would beat her to the attic door. She raced for the servants' staircase and charged up the stairs as fast as her legs could carry her. At the top of the stairs, she dashed across to the attic door and threw it open, but Morgan was already there. He grabbed her under the arm and dragged her toward the third floor bathroom. His bellowing echoed through the house as he called for Jenna.

He wrapped an arm around Lane, crushing her into his body and using his other hand to hold her chin. "Get the scissors."

Jenna just stared at him, and he screamed at her. "Scissors!" Jenna complied and held them out to him, but he shook his head. "Cut her hair."

Emotionless, Jenna trimmed the edges.

Morgan freaked and handed Lane off to her mother. "Hold her still." Lane fought against Jenna, struggling to get away.

Morgan grabbed a handful of hair and yanked hard. "Hold her still, or I'll beat her until she stops squirming." He chopped the hair off just an inch from Lane's scalp. Little jagged tufts stood up everywhere.

After several minutes of careless hacking, Morgan threw the scissors into the sink and stormed off. Jenna let go of Lane and followed Morgan, leaving the child surrounded by a pool of her own hair.

A crash sounded above her in the attic. Footsteps stamped across the creaky floorboards. Lane rushed out of the bathroom in time to catch Morgan barging out of the attic stairwell with bags of her pretty dresses. She charged him, grabbing at her dresses, trying to take them back; he simply pushed her into the stairwell and locked the door.

In the morning, he stood with her on the sidewalk while the trash man took away her clothes. The masher moved them all into the body of the truck but caught the edge of a garment and drew it back into the open hopper. The pink frilly sweater lay there, helpless, alone, blackened with grease and swill. One arm stretched out in supplication.

Morgan escorted her back to the house. From a distance, her

compliance might have been mistaken for willingness. But up close and personal, one would not have missed the dead stare. Morgan pointed her to a spot on the kitchen floor next to three brown bags stamped Goodwill Industries.

"Those are yours." Then he left.

The name on the bags meant nothing to Lane. She dug through, pulled out jeans, tee shirts, sweatshirts and sneakers. Intent on finding dresses and dainty shoes, she tossed the new clothes on the floor and found nothing more but the bottom of the bags.

She hated him. And Jenna. They'd made her look like a boy. And with the loss of her frilly clothes, the transformation was complete. The princess died. She wiped away tears with the back of her arm, hoisted up her new clothes and carted them to the attic.

The mirror now revealed few changes; Lane was older, but the princess was still dead. She scruffed a hand through her newly shortened hair, tears coursing silently down her cheeks. She donned a pair of fresh jeans and zipped them up; they sagged down over her hips.

The porn producer's belt cinched the jeans up nicely, though it created puckers of fabric in odd places. She tucked in a tee shirt and a sleeved shirt to trap body heat but left the sweatshirt to hang freely, hoping it would hide some of the more unsightly bulges.

The sweet, fresh scent of fabric softener filled her lungs as the sweatshirt rubbed along her cheek. She pulled it closer to her face, breathed deeply, then abruptly dried her wet eyes with it.

Camilla's voice echoed in her head. "You no have time to pity yourself." The mechanism of survival kicked in, swept her memories and pain away, and replaced them with visions of Pearce's Grocery.

A box of cereal, five bucks. A box of pasta, a buck. One dozen eggs, three bucks. Nine bucks provided fifteen meals to a frugal person, half that if she couldn't get food off her mind. *Better plan for the worse case.* Nine bucks, seven meals. Just two days.

She rounded it off again. Five bucks per day and $150 for a month. *Make it an even two.*

She peeled off $1200, believing that would provide food for the next six months. To be sure, she shucked off an extra $400 then split the money into four separate piles and buried them in holes around the cave to keep them safe. The money not slated for groceries was now up for grabs, and while she'd convinced herself that spending too much of Morgan's money at one time might bring unwanted attention, nothing convinced her that she couldn't use it to get even. Morgan either did not want to pay for her education or he didn't want her to have a break. It didn't matter to Lane; either way, he'd pay now. And in doing so, his money would clear some of her conscience.

She had her plan, but a belly full of pasta raged against her intestines; she ran for her latrine bucket.

Light poked out the windows at the rear of the brown ranch, a welcoming aura to those who approached. Inside, the parents and twin boys sat around the kitchen table eating sloppy joes, laughing, and joking. The baby gurgled happily and smeared strained banana around the highchair's tray.

Lane took a deep breath and hesitantly knocked. The father leaned over to see who it was, but the mother answered the door.

"Yes?" The woman's voice held a hint of suspicion, eyeing the brown work coat.

Lane shrugged out of the coat and sweater she'd stolen from them, and she handed them to the woman along with two hundred-dollar bills.

The woman eyed her up and down and took the coat and sweater but not the money.

Lane whispered to her. "Can I have my IOU back?"

The woman stared at the money. "I, I already gave it to the deputy."

Lane chewed her lip and thrust the money closer to the homeowner. "Square?"

The woman took the bills. "This is too much."

Lane waved her off and backed up.

The woman took a deep breath. "We're more than square. Next time you need food, just knock."

Lane nodded earnestly, smiled, and withdrew. She could have skipped down the driveway, but settled for a wide grin.

"Wait!" The woman called after her, leaving the door open as she ran out of view. She returned with an old blue woman's coat. "This should fit you better."

Lane stood there, silent and shocked. She pulled out more money.

Now the woman waved her off. "No. You've paid enough. We both leave this door feeling like decent people tonight."

Lane nodded. Silent, happy tears tinged with just a pinch of shame streamed down her cheeks, and she headed down the driveway, tugging the new coat on.

The door opened wider, and the father stepped out, calling after her. "Hey, we've got more bread!"

Lane visited all the homes she'd broken into and tried to collect all her IOUs. Wherever people were home, she left them money even though they had turned their IOUs over to the authorities. Wherever the victims weren't home, she left money and a note asking for forgiveness.

By the end of the day, she'd spent a thousand dollars making amends with the people from whom she'd stolen food or clothes. Only two remained—Morgan and her lunchbox victim. She had no intention of squaring herself with Morgan, and her stomach churned, threatening to jump clean out of her body when she thought about facing J. Olsen.

But feelings of pride swept both men from her mind, tempting her to relish the little good she'd done. Pleased with herself, she didn't even mind the rain pouring down on her as she trudged back to her cave, nor the pit stops she had to make to relieve the pressure in her guts. *That'll teach me,* she thought. Her arms were laden with sticks and branches she'd gathered on the trek, and she was soaked to the core by the time she reached her mountainside home.

Hunger churned around her stomach again, so she slipped into the stand of trees that overlooked the river, their low-lying branches deflecting a great deal of the rain and keeping the area underneath considerably drier than the surrounding forest.

Two ropes clung tightly to the trunk, wrapped around and tied securely, suspending their cargo in the frigid waters. She untied one of the ropes, careful not to let it slip from her numbed fingers, and she hauled it up and over the cliff, coiling it around her palm and triceps. Water dripped off the trash bag as she carted the rope and package to the cave.

A handful of kindling and a few logs quickly revived the smoldering fire, and as it licked back to life, Lane stripped to her undies, toweled off and arranged her clothes and boots so they'd dry, and then slipped into dry garments.

She untied the rope from the trash bag, finished off the coil, and secured it so it wouldn't tangle. The trash bag fell open, revealing the black cooking pot with soot etched along its sides from having sat in the fire. Inside the pot, a frozen block of leftover pasta shells stared out. She poured fresh water in the pot and placed it back in the fire; it would be edible again in no time.

With a few cranks of the dynamo, the lantern sprayed light around the dark cave. And with a flick of the switch, the radio spewed static. She dialed the tuner, dismissed the talk and rock channels, and settled on a country station. She retrieved the lunchbox from the utility cart and perched it up on the milk-crate pantry where she could keep an eye on it, hoping she could work up the courage to handle it.

chapter forty-one

The next morning did not bring a change in the weather. With her trash bag slicker stowed discreetly in her coat pocket, Lane knocked on the door and shuffled back a little.

It took Jason a minute to recognize her. "Get the hell outta here."

Lane croaked out a few words at him. "Your father home?"

"Why? So you and your old man can take something else away from him?"

A hand big enough to crush bowling balls wrapped around the edge of the door, pulling it loose from Jason and swinging it open wider. Jake Olsen towered over her, a strapping lumberjack of a man. He'd worked in the mills his whole life, barely finished high school, and was ill-suited for anything but manual labor.

Muscles built by hard work rippled under his tee shirt, and Lane considered running for her life. For all she knew, this was the man who attacked her. She reeled, flashed back to the night of the attack, and felt a man's arms and shoulders pressing against her and keeping her down. She fought the terror and prayed that Jake hadn't used her body to satisfy his vendetta against Morgan.

He opened the screen door and stepped out. Lane shook involuntarily, questioning the decision to return the stupid lunchbox.

Instinct alone drove her another step back.

"Yeah?"

Lane turned the box over, handing it to him bottom first.

"I seen you the other day. Emptying out the house." His deep voice remained soft, calm; Lane imagined it erupting like Mount St. Helens, flattening everything in its path.

His chin jutted in the direction of the mansion for emphasis as his hand closed over the container. "Police scanner says you been hitting lots of folks besides me and your old man."

Lane cast a glance over her shoulder, but didn't respond to his comment. "Sheriff tried to tie us in with you disappearing. Don't much appreciate that. Maybe you should tell me what you want 'fore I kick your ass to the curb."

Lane held out two hundred-dollar bills to him. Jason sneered at her, but his father didn't move.

"What's that?"

Lane whispered. "Squaring up."

"It was a bologna sandwich, a bag of chips, and a granola bar."

Lane peeled off one bill and held it out to him.

"That his money?"

Lane nodded. The skull-crusher hand reached out and closed on the money, two fingers wiggling until she gave him the other hundred as well.

"You living up there now?" She couldn't quite meet his gaze. "Sure don't talk much, do you?"

Uneasiness filled her, but she edged down the collar of her shirt, revealing the scar.

"Phew. Who did that to you?"

Lane shook her head. Jake chewed his bottom lip. "Hope they catch him. I'll tell my boy to leave you be from now on."

Lane nodded and headed back down the driveway. She pulled out her trash bag raincoat and put it on. Behind her, Jason laughed, but the snicker ended suddenly with a dull thwack as his father hit him in the head.

Jake called after her. "If the sheriff comes by, I'll tell him I don't know where you're at."

chapter forty-two

*L*ane strolled along the ridge and eyed the town below. She suspected that by now everyone was aware of the break-ins and keeping watch for a shabby hobo. She prayed they weren't actually looking for her, or that she had changed enough not to be easily identified.

Jason and his father figured it out easy enough. She shook the negativity from her mind. Jake said he'd keep quiet; she had no reason to believe him, but she hoped she could.

The trash bag slicker shed its rainwater inside her pocket as Lane smoothed her clean hands down the front of her hand-me-down blue coat. *It does fit so much better than the baggy work coat*, she thought, smiling. It made her *presentable*. Little things like baggy pants might be overlooked if the rest of the package came acceptably wrapped.

The tree line provided ample cover and allowed Lane to move unobserved along the edges of town. When she found a deserted stretch of road in the neighborhoods behind Main Street, she slipped out of the forest, descended to the pavement, and headed into town.

The shortest route to Pearce's was straight down Main, directly past Richard's office. The crisscrossing roads behind Main Street, however, offered cover and options. With time and just a passing knowledge of the town, a pedestrian could walk anywhere without encountering anything more serious than a homeowner.

Not one to press her luck too soon, Lane opted for the residential roads. Twenty minutes later, she ended up on the far end of the coin-op laundry with Pearce's just down the block.

The last few yards exposed her to the sheriff's office, but she walked confidently and purposefully—not too slow nor too fast—so as not to signal an obvious threat to anyone.

On Pearce's stoop, she whipped off her cap and squeezed the water out of it. The splatters created a puddle at her feet. She stuffed the hat in her pocket, using it to hide her pistol.

The bell tinkled as she entered the store; all she had to do now was act normal. She scruffed a hand through her stubby hair, threw a glance and a nod at Old Man Pearce, and grabbed a carry basket.

Rows of food beckoned, urging, and tempting her. Vegetables, meats, cookies, and butter all vied for attention. The sight of unrestricted food made her stomach growl, but she fought down the urge to go hog wild. A box of frosted cupcakes screamed for attention, but they wouldn't keep her alive for the winter.

She'd carefully designed the game plan, and now she had to follow it. Three boxes of cereal. Three boxes of pasta. Three dozen eggs. Twenty-seven dollars could produce forty-two meals if she behaved herself. *Less than two dollars a day for two weeks of food,* she thought.

She reminded herself that she couldn't be sure how long the food would last, never having put her theories to the test. Twenty-seven dollars could only amount to twenty-one meals if she suddenly lost her mind and ate everything in sight. Four bucks a day. *Still under budget.*

Technically, she thought, *I still have seven bucks to spend.* She perused the aisles as she headed for the register.

Lane hoisted the shopping basket up onto the counter and pulled off her backpack while Old Man Pearce unloaded her groceries. He didn't reach for his bat or tip off Mrs. Al to call for backup. He simply rang up the merchandise.

The eggs will need their own bag, Lane thought as she carefully arranged the rest of the items in her backpack—three boxes of cereal, three boxes of pasta, three cans of peas, and a box of chocolate cupcakes. Thirty-four dollars provided a minimum of seven days' rations and one box of simple sugary joy with absolutely no redeeming value other than to make her happy.

Old Man Pearce showed no sign of recognizing her. He counted the change as he gave it back to her and handed her the receipt.

Lane pocketed both, slipped the backpack over her shoulders, and gathered up the plastic sack of eggs. She thanked him with a nod and her clipped version of gratitude, "Q".

He countered with more emphasis. "Thank you. Come again."

Lane nodded, stepping outside the store and slapping her hat back on her head. The barest smirk crossed her lips. *Mission accomplished.*

Lack of recognition on Old Man Pearce's part meant that he wouldn't call Richard, and that meant she could return again, unmolested.

She turned up the side streets, crisscrossed through town, and headed back into the forest.

chapter forty-three

*R*ichard stared out the window of his office, still tossing around his last conversation with Ray. He understood why Ray thought he was picking on Lane, but it bothered him that his buddy Wes thought the same thing.

As sheriff, he didn't feel he'd been inordinately unfair to anyone, including Lane, but two people did, and they each had completely different relationships with the girl: one intimate, one completely absent.

When Danny knocked and entered, Richard swiveled his chair back around, dismissing the notion that either of them could possibly be right.

Danny waved a file in the air. "The fingerprint from the cat food can. It's definitely Lane. And—" he slid the folder and a videocassette onto Richard's desk "—it flagged an open police file in Seattle. Went down and picked these up myself."

Richard flipped the file open. The top picture showed Lane in her hospital gown. The caption "Jane Doe" had been crossed out and replaced by Lane's real name, and it was clipped to an older picture of Lane. "She can't be more than fourteen or fifteen here." The older picture had Ray's name, address and phone number scrawled on the back.

"Looks like Ray tried to find her," Danny said as Richard picked his way through the pre-op and post-op pictures, whistling through his teeth.

Danny continued. "Witnesses called for help after a dark sedan dumped her and sped away. There's also a warrant. They lifted her prints from a bunch of muggings and shopliftings, and possible involvement in a homicide. Picture's on the bottom. Haven't been able to find her, though."

Richard slid the bottom picture out; the death stare of a homeless boy drilled out from the photo.

Danny pulled up a chair and sat near Richard's desk. "She was in the custody of social services, but something happened at the group home. An incident. A boy touched her. She didn't like it."

"I guess I can understand why." Richard continued to flip through the pictures.

"She laid him out with a chair to the head, and then she split."

"They lost her?"

Danny nodded, pointing at the pictures. "We've got a bigger problem, though. They're fairly sure that all happened an hour or two before the witnesses called it in. While she was here."

Richard perused the photos and glanced over at Danny; he was pleased that the younger officer finally grew the stones to address harder issues. *Except now I can add Dan to my list of detractors.* "You're thinking Ray or Morgan," Richard put the pictures down. "Or me."

Danny shrugged. "Not so much Ray anymore. Even if he was trying to find her so he could finish her off, it would have been seriously stupid to leave his name and address. But Morgan or you, or any of three hundred mill men, or their families. What I'm really thinking is somebody here is gonna want to make sure she don't tell anybody else about it."

Richard nodded his agreement. "All the more reason to catch her. Sooner or later, she'll slip up, and we can get to the bottom of this."

Danny shook his head. "Been a couple days since anybody's seen her, or lost anything. I'm thinking she's moved on."

"Don't kid yourself. Ray's here. She's here."

"Could be," Danny leaned back in the chair, "but what if she's changed her appearance, cleaned herself up. Folks won't think much if she don't look outta place."

Richard's head bobbed between his shoulders. "Yep, but the prints prove it's her. Let's keep that in-house for now. If we don't press her, she might feel safe and try to move back into life somewhere."

"Pretty late in the season. Winter's set to slam us any day now. If she hasn't moved on, then she's all stocked up and holed up someplace."

"Al would've been up here hollering and yelling if he'd lost a winter's worth of supplies, and she hasn't hit enough houses or taken enough from any one of them to have stocked up. Nope, she'll be in."

"We've got no way of knowing where she'll hit next."

Richard buzzed Dottie on the phone and asked her to join them. He rose, met her at the door, and ushered her in. He pulled a chair over to his desk for her.

"Need you to put out a public advisory. Send it out over the police band so everybody with a scanner picks it up. Print out some flyers and have the guys post them: stores, telephone poles, Marigold's, the schools, everywhere people gather."

Dottie jotted down notes on a pad. "This about our hobo?"

Richard nodded. "We need folks to be concerned enough to call us if they see her. Tell them she's dangerous and shouldn't be approached."

Danny interrupted. "She's got a gun."

Richard waved to strike the comment. "Don't let that out. Everybody here's got a gun. I don't want them heading out into the mountains to hunt her down. Just say ..." he trailed off, thinking.

Danny grinned. "Mentally unstable."

Richard's head tipped to the side. "Yeah, that'll do. Say they pass the info along, should call immediately, yadda, yadda, yadda. Let me see it when you've got it written."

After Dottie left with her assignment, Richard tapped on the videotape. "What's on here?"

Danny shrugged. "Staged rape. The guy was going to edit out the consensual dialogue and sell it on the internet until she bashed him over the head."

Danny's finger tapped on his temple as he continued. "Detective Glenn said she's got some amnesia, couldn't tell them who she was. They were hoping to get her off the streets and into a program. But then she started mugging people. That tape could send her away. They plan to try her as an adult."

Richard's nose crinkled. "But she came back here. Either the amnesia was a ruse, or it's gone now."

"Maybe her memory is coming back in pieces."

"Maybe." Richard nudged his chin in the direction of the tape. "You see it?"

Danny shook his head. "No, got the gist of it from the detective."

Richard shook his head and rose. He grabbed the tape, motioning for Danny to follow. He went into interrogation room one and popped the tape into the TV. Danny stood by the door, Richard perched on the edge of the table. Ed observed from the other side of the plate glass windows.

Richard listened to the consensual diatribe, watched the first few moments. He pressed rewind, then played it forward again.

"Look at her face."

Danny got closer. "She looks scared. Probably should have thought more carefully about getting in the situation to begin with."

Richard shook his head. "No, that's not it." He let the video play a few seconds more and rewound it again. "There." Abject terror washed across the girl's face and then vanished, replaced by an empty stare when the beer bottle switched hands. "She's just gone missing."

"What?"

"She's not in there anymore. Her brain shut off."

"Then why put herself in this position?"

"For the money. She expected to roll this guy before it ever got this far. This may have been a staged rape for him, but she's not acting." Richard slapped the remote against Danny's chest. "Watch the whole thing. Then watch it again. And then tell me if you get the same gist of it." *Rookie.*

chapter forty-four

*T*he bulletin went out; for the rest of that day and all of the next, the phones rang off the hook. People had seen the mentally unstable vagabond everywhere.

They'd seen her at the gas station, at the hardware store, in most of their neighborhoods, in their woodsheds, hanging around the church and rectory—something Richard could believe—as well as the liquor store and the Harris Grocery Outlet, both of which Richard doubted.

As sworn officers of the law, Richard and his men checked out all the leads and locations, took all the statements whether they were believable or not, but found no sign of Lane.

While the sheriff and his men chased ghosts, Lane spent the time in the forest gathering and chopping firewood, stealing cut wood from the Keates' cabin, boiling water, and hooking up a pulley system so she could haul water from the top of the riverbank.

She doubted Ray would care about the missing firewood, but she'd tell him and then try to find some way to square herself with him anyway. *Replacing it will probably be enough.*

A collection of heavy rocks sat under the trees near the riverbank. Hauled up from the river and arranged like cannonballs waiting to be hurled at the enemy, these rocks would break a hole in the ice after the river froze. At least that was the plan.

At night, Lane concentrated on her school books, worked out problems, and hoped she was doing it right because she didn't have an answer key. Right or wrong, it gave her a chance to read aloud, which afforded her an opportunity to eliminate some of the odd sounds from her vocalizations. Not that it worked very well.

The crank lantern turned out to be the best gift Ray had ever given her; the light made it easier to read, and the music entertained her, softly playing country songs. A smile twisted the corners of her mouth as she thought of Ray crooning with the Falcon's radio.

And when her hands were busier than her mind, she'd pinch her tongue between her teeth and practice swallowing.

On the third day, the sheriff's office endured a new wave of calls. Victim after victim called to drop the charges they'd placed on whoever broke into their homes and businesses. The stories varied widely.

Some didn't want to annoy some unknown, mentally unstable person who already knew where they lived. Others just wanted to do a good thing. A few just fessed up: the perp had returned and made good on their IOU.

Oblivious to the goings-on in town, Lane decided to try her hand at fishing. The Keates brothers probably wouldn't be around this late in the season, but she staked out their cabin for an hour just in case.

As expected, the lake held no other fishermen. She didn't think solitude gave her an advantage in catching anything; it only meant she wouldn't have to worry about anyone ratting her out to the cops.

She'd fished here with Ray often, even late in the year. The difference between then and now lay in the timing; he seldom took the boat out in November, claiming that the weather and the waters were too unpredictable. But when she fished with Ray, eating wasn't the prime objective—companionship was.

Now, she had to eat, had to supplement her diet, and this was the cheapest way to do it. But the fish wouldn't be near the shore; they'd be out in the middle of the lake where the water ran deep.

It took all Lane's strength, grunting and groaning the whole time, to lift one edge of the aluminum boat high enough to push it over. She had no way to control its descent; as it rolled on the port gunwale, she jumped back and let its weight drop the hull to the ground.

Right side up, it gouged a trench in the sand as she threw what was left of her weight against it and pushed it to the water. She dropped her gear in, tugged it easily down to the middle of the dock, and tied it to the support post holding the oars.

The brothers had a thing about the boat. They figured that only two kinds of people would steal it: boat thieves who would take it away completely, or hooligans looking to play on the water. Boat thieves were bad enough, but neither brother wanted to be responsible for a drowning, not even of a hooligan who ought to know better.

To that end, the oars were always secured upright with the paddles in the air to make them easy to see, and the life jacket locker was never locked. They hoped that anyone stealing the boat for a joy ride would also steal a life preserver.

Lane flipped open the jacket locker, pulled out a large pail and the anchor. She pushed Richard's vest aside and dug for Ray's. A dozen black lines graced one shoulder of Ray's vest, magic-markered there by Lane and representing all the bull trout he caught but had to release because of local fishing regs.

She slipped it on over her coat and cinched it up tightly. She brought it up to her face, hoping his scent might have lingered, but it hadn't. Instead, it smelled of lake water. Or perhaps that was just fish guts.

She untied the oars and dropped them in the boat, then tossed in a pail and the anchor, which was an old milk jug filled with stones and punctured dozens of times to allow water to escape. Lane hopped in, tied the anchor rope to the bow, untied the boat from the dock, and pushed off.

The current caught the fourteen-foot craft, easing it out into the lake as Lane fit the oars into place. She rowed and steered, rowed and steered, and headed for a spot that had been particularly lucky over the years. Ray said the water ran deeper there, and underground springs kept the current moving. Fish liked that, he'd said. She smiled. *Odd, that fish like moving currents but didn't feel a thing as he gutted them.*

Using the shore as her guidepost, she found the spot, fairly certain she couldn't be more than a few feet off. If this place truly was the home of all the hungry fish in the lake, she hoped she could be off by dozens of feet and still find them. If she'd pinpointed it precisely, thcy might fight over the bait.

She gently lowered the anchor, slowly displacing the water so the fish wouldn't spook, then tipped the pail into the lake, filling it just half full.

The tackle box yielded its treasures: a collapsible rod that telescoped and locked open, and an assortment of hooks, flies, bobbers and sinkers.

Lane tied a two-shank hook onto the line, knotting it about a foot from the end. Five sinkers followed, clearly violating the regs. *What are they gonna do? Arrest me?*

The added weight would take the hook straight to the bottom, where the fish hid out, but leave the hook above the muck and rocks on the lake floor.

She rubbed the line with salmon oil and impaled a chunk of hot dog on the hook. Another of Ray's beliefs: fish loved hot dogs. She held the rod over the edge of the boat and released the reel. The five sinkers took the snack down into dark water.

When the line went slack, she locked up the reel and set the pole in the rod holder. With her hands free, she carefully secured a bobber on the line and waited.

The first nibble sent ripples along the water as the bobber jigged at the surface. Excitement washed over her, but concern seeped in as well. She'd always let Ray kill and clean the fish; now she'd have to do it herself. She'd have to experience their little deaths, and she'd be the perpetrator of them. She tried not to think about it, drawn back to the nibble. The line tugged, the bobber went under; she jerked the rod, set the line, and felt weight on the hook.

The fish struggled, pulled, wove, raced. Lane gave him room to run, pulled him back, then let him run some more. Patiently, she pulled him closer and closer until finally he flapped against the boat. She reached down, clamped her fingers around his lower jaw, and pulled him from the frigid water.

For all the fight he gave, the steelhead was legally too small to keep, not even measuring the length of her forearm. But he was a good size fish—a good meal. Maybe two. And fish soup with the head. He splashed into the catch pail.

With several hours of daylight left, fishing remained the priority, but time had to be reserved for cleaning the catch and returning to the cave before sundown. The smell of dead fish would likely bring out predators that Lane didn't want to encounter, even with the Walther.

After four hours Lane pulled anchor, and with each dip of the paddle, the boat pulled closer to shore. She returned Ray's gear and pushed the boat back up along the trench as far as she could, leaving it in the middle of the track. At least the winter ice wouldn't crush the hull.

The fish slapped against the sides, spraying water out of the pail every time Lane reached in for them. A strong and muscular fish, the steelhead would fight her; if she didn't latch on tightly the first time, they'd wriggle free and flop back into the lake.

Ray had grown up here; he fished almost daily as a boy and hadn't seen anything wrong with gutting the fish alive until he saw the look of horror on Lane's face. After that day, he systematically held them by the tail, whacked their heads against the gunwale, and dispatched them with a tad less macabre.

Lane carried the pail up to the bow. If a fish managed to wriggle free, she'd have plenty of time to recapture it before it found its way back to the water.

She took a deep breath and let it out slowly to calm her nerves; she wrapped her hands firmly around a fish. She cast her eyes heavenward as she prayed for strength, then aimed carefully and whacked the fish head against the edge of the boat.

She wasn't sure if it was really dead, couldn't be sure that the whack in the head hadn't just stunned it. If that were the case, then she owed it to the fish to just get it over with. She pulled out her knife, carefully slid it just under the belly skin, and slit the fish open. She cleaned out the innards, then washed it out in lake water and set it on the dock as the sun crested noon.

It's dead now.

She repeated the process until all seven fish lay cleaned and ready to go, then wrapped them up in a plastic bag, and buried the guts in the sand.

Shadows settled thickly in the forest early on a winter afternoon. She rolled the boat back over, several feet from its original location, but she didn't think it would matter much. Even if the brothers noticed, it probably wouldn't mean much to them; they'd just think the other had gone for a late season row on the lake.

She grabbed her gear and fish, felt for the security of her Walther, and headed home.

chapter forty-five

On the fourth day, the sheriff and his deputies slammed into a dead end. They stood around, waiting for calls that didn't come. The phones had gone silent; no one called about anything, and while Richard and his men lacked anything to do, Lane took another sponge bath and changed into her go-to-town clothes. She imagined how wonderful it would be to just stand in the shower and let the rivers of hot water wash down over her. *Someday.*

An uneventful hike took her to town, and she strolled the neighborhoods, working her way to Pearce's Grocery. Dead tired, she rubbed a hand across her eyes and dismissed the three times she awoke during the night facing the ghostly tendrils of her assailant.

She moved through town unchallenged, looking good and feeling better about herself; the desperation slipped away and contentment seeped in to fill the void. Life would be hard, but it had been for several months. The difference now was with the neighbors; there were no other street people for her to fend off. She might just be able to come into town once a week and buy what she needed. The routine would help the townspeople, too. They'd grow accustomed to seeing her, and they'd just let her be.

She climbed the stairs to Pearce's door, entered nonchalantly, and waved at Pearce. He smiled, recognized her, and waved back as she took a basket and headed down the aisles.

Three boxes of cereal. Three boxes of pasta. Three cans of peas. As Lane headed to the dairy case for eggs, the bright box of zipper-top storage bags caught her eye. She fiddled with the box and checked the price. They'd lock out moisture and keep her boxed food fresh longer. It clunked into the basket when she dropped it in.

Large spaces peered out at her from the dairy case, stock thinning out between delivery days. Only four dozen eggs remained on the shelf, and Lane quickly relocated three of them to her basket.

Hot dogs were on sale, two pounds for four bucks. Her head bobbed between her shoulders as she calculated the cost and the advantages and disadvantages. She couldn't argue with a good deal; she snatched up two pounds.

Winding through the store on her way to the checkout counter, she found herself in the healthcare aisle. A short row of analgesics stared back at her, calling to her. Further along, the dark blue box of a sleeping aid vied for attention. While it looked promising, it seemed a bit pricey for someone fighting earnestly not to starve to death. *Still,* she thought. *What wouldn't I give right now for a good night's sleep?* She dropped it in with her groceries.

The doorbell jingled. *Someone else is here.* She willed herself not to panic, returned to the dairy case, and pretended to be searching for more deals. A fat ham and cheese grinder stared out at her, calling to her. Saliva pooled in her mouth.

Reflections of an old couple danced off the glass. They stooped forward like twin hunchbacks with their feet scuffing the floor as they walked. Their heads remained down, their eyes focusing only on inanimate objects.

They picked their purchases carefully—a loaf of bread, a box of pasta, the last dozen eggs, a pound of butter, a jar of peanut butter, and a roll of toilet paper. Their plight mimicked Lane's, and she dallied, dragging her feet and marking their every move from behind racks, at the end of the aisle, and in the reflections of the refrigerator cases.

Old Man Pearce unloaded their basket and rang their purchases. "Thirteen seventy-eight."

The old couple counted out their change but came up short. The man dug in his pocket for more but only produced a couple of coins. The old woman pulled the toilet paper out of the purchases.

Old Man Pearce removed the item from the sale, recalculating the total. "Twelve ninety-nine."

The woman slid the pasta out of the pile, and Pearce recalculated again. "Eleven eighty-two."

Lane pushed a crumpled twenty onto the counter. Her words squeaked and scratched as she whispered her apology, pointing down the aisle. "Excuse me. You dropped this back there."

Their heads turned to follow the direction of her gesture, and Lane moved the toilet paper and pasta back into the old couple's purchases.

Old Man Pearce quickly recalculated and produced change for the original total, slapping it on the counter and bagging up the groceries before the old couple had a chance to argue.

The old folks exchanged a glance, picked up their purchases and left, uttering profuse "thank yous" as they went, the bell tinkling as they shuffled out the door.

Lane rushed to the window, peering out after them. The couple took turns supporting each other down the stairs, then helped each other to their car.

Lane grabbed an empty basket and raced down the food aisles, throwing everything she could think of into it. She dumped the items on the counter and ran back to the window to check on the old couple's progress.

After a second food run, she tossed the basket of canned meat, vegetables, pastas and rice on the counter and charged to the window, searching for the old folks. Gone.

Lane threw the door open and stepped out. They'd driven off, turned somewhere, and were completely out of sight. Lane whirled back into the store, arms extended from her sides in supplication.

"Relax," Old Man Pearce said. "Last house down Whistler. Shame about them. John and Shirley. Almost everything went when the stock bubble burst. Fact is, they can't afford the gas for that old beast. If it weren't so cold out, they'd be walking."

He rang up her two separate orders and doled out her change. He arranged her boxes and cans in her backpack, but put her eggs and the groceries for the old couple in plastic sacks. "You can't miss it. Butts up against that eyesore of a resort. Son-a-bitch Harris. Single-handedly destroying this town."

Lane tried to hoist the assorted bags and struggled under the weight, surprised that she hadn't made better choices.

Old Man Pearce laughed. "Hang on a sec." He shuffled off to the stockroom and came back pushing an old bike with milk crates strapped to the front and back. He pushed it over to her and leaned it in her direction until she steadied it with her own hands.

"Not much need for it anymore. Can't do deliveries. Can't keep a delivery boy. Can't afford to pay 'em more than minimum. Tips used to be good, though."

He helped Lane arrange the bags in the milk crates. "Maybe you'll get more use out of it than me. Just taking up space here."

Lane smiled, slowly and deliberately forming words. "Thank

you."

"Hang on just one more sec." He headed to the back of the store. The suction popped as the fridge opened, and Old Man Pearce shuffled back to the counter. He dropped a grinder in one of her bags. "Off you go. They go to bed early 'cause they can't afford to keep the lights on."

Lane smiled broadly and nodded her thanks.

He called to her as she left the store. "My orders come in tomorrow. Come back around if you're a mind to. Pay you seven sixty-five an hour. You work out, I'll tell folks we're delivering again."

Lane's eyebrows danced up on her forehead. She hadn't thought about getting a job, and now that she had an offer, her thoughts scrambled for attention.

Her main concern was her attacker finding her. The black knit fabric had covered his entire head and prevented identification. Perhaps if she didn't pursue him, he would have no reason to feel threatened.

But her biggest desire was to fit in more easily in the town, becoming invisible and avoiding attention. Maybe getting her life back. *Or some semblance of a real life.*

She smiled, gave Old Man Pearce a big grin and an earnest nod. Seconds later, she pedaled up Main and turned down Whistler without even thinking about Richard seeing her from his office window.

The air whipped her face and hands, biting into her skin and making her colder than she had been during her hike into town.

Even from the top of the street, the eyesore resort smudged the landscape. Bulldozers, tractors, and hauling trucks sat idle. They'd cleared and leveled a huge section of forest before the winter rains slammed construction to a halt.

The last house on Whistler sat dark. Not even the soft blue-white glow of a TV escaped from behind the curtains. Lane struggled the bags to the door and knocked, almost timidly.

After a second knock, the door opened. Shirley's mouth hung open as she stared at Lane, calling over her shoulder to her husband.

"John?"

Lane focused on the words, focused on clipping off the heavy breath sounds. "Can I put these inside for you?"

"John?"

John shuffled up to the door, and Shirley turned to him, disbelief on her face.

"Did you order groceries?"

John's eyes shifted from Shirley to Lane. "No."

Lane interjected. "No, these are a gift."

Shirley cut her off. "We can't pay for this."

"No, they're a gift," Lane repeated.

"A gift? From who?" John demanded.

Lane faltered; she hadn't thought that far ahead. Her response came out as a question. "The church?"

Shirley grabbed a plastic bag and shuffled off. John followed his wife's lead, grabbing two more bags and heading into the house.

Lane stood on the doorstep holding the remaining bag. Given a few seconds alone, she rummaged in her pockets and pulled out what little money remained. She cursed herself for not having the forethought to have grabbed more of Morgan's money, then dropped the few bills and coins into the bottom of the bag.

Shirley returned for the last bag, thanked her for the delivery, and unceremoniously shut the door in her face. Even that couldn't kill the smile carving its way across Lane's features.

chapter forty-six

*J*enna showed Richard into the great room, her manners aloof, but not as caustic as they were during his last visit.

"Drink?" She strode to the bar like an Egyptian queen holding court over her subjects.

He tried not to think of her lithe body in his arms, in his bed. He declined the drink with a shake of his head and got right to business. "Tell me about Lane."

"Again, Richard?" She waited for a moment, assuming her attitude would make him change his mind. When it didn't, she stepped to the sofa, relaxed into it, and patted the cushion for him to join her.

The change of tactics was not lost on Richard, and he chose an overstuffed easy chair several feet away.

Jenna mused over his decision. "She didn't spend much time here. She slept here. Occasionally ate here. But she wanted nothing to do with us. She spent all her time at school or with that ..." she paused and stared directly into Richard's eyes. "That priest."

Richard ignored the comment and pulled himself out of the chair. He paced about the room and ended up at the staircase. "Can I see her room again?"

Jenna rose smoothly, exuding haughty sophistication. She set her drink down and approached him. "Not if this is going to turn into another witch hunt."

Richard shook his head. His hands eased out from his sides. "Just looking for clues, something that'll help me find her."

Without a word, Jenna led him up the stairs to the second floor. At the top of the stairs, she reached out, took his hand, and pulled him toward one of the many guest rooms.

"It's been a long time since you and I were alone together."

Richard's eyebrows rose, and he withdrew his hand like he was extracting the limb from a vat of manure. "I think those days are over."

Jenna opened the door, revealing a king-size bed. "They don't have to be."

Richard peeked into the lavishly decorated room. "And your husband is where?"

Jenna laughed aloud. "That didn't always worry you."

"That was before you married him. Isn't Lane's room upstairs?" He pointed up the stairs and headed there without waiting for a reply.

The seductress fell away, replaced by an annoyed and spurned socialite.

chapter forty-seven

L ane sat on Pearce's bike outside the back door of the church, waiting. Ray usually cleaned the church brass on Tuesdays, and she hoped his routine hadn't changed.

Moments later, the door swung open, and Ray stepped out. When he looked up, his feet turned to clay and his knees wobbled. Unsure of her reaction and his ability to walk, he didn't rush to embrace her. "I'm glad you came back. I wasn't sure you would after that debacle with Richard."

Lane stared in his direction, her eyes darting around, not quite finding his.

"How are you? Do you need anything?" He kept the questions coming but paced them so it wouldn't seem like an inquisition. He recognized the delivery bike but struggled to phrase a question that wouldn't sound like an accusation.

"You've been down to Old Man Pearce's?"

Lane glanced at the bike, front and rear, and squared back to face Ray, her eyes scanning his body. She nodded and squeaked at him. "Gave it to me."

Ray's face lit up. "You working for him?"

Lane shrugged. "Tomorrow."

Ray stepped forward and stopped abruptly when Lane shifted a foot onto the bike pedal.

"That's great. Really great. A big step. But we still need to get this mess with Richard cleaned up. You have to turn yourself in."

Lane shook her head, but her eyes roamed over his body, shoulder to shoulder, head to toe.

Ray couldn't shake the idea that she was sizing him up. "Only Richard can help us with this." Lane shook her head again.

"OK. What if we just call him? We could set up a mediation. Meet someplace, just to talk. See what he has to say. Marigold's?"

Lane didn't respond, her eyes still coursing over his body. "The charges against you are minor at this point."

"Stealing your wood."

Ray smiled. "Take it all. It's yours now." He took a step forward, breaking her trance.

She slid up onto the bike seat.

Ray extended his hand to her. "Take my hand, Lane."

Lane eyed him like he had six heads, green scales, and purple hair.

Ray repeated his request, firmer, but it was met only by a shake of her head. He took a slow step forward, and she eased the bike into position for a quick takeoff. "There's only one way out of this hell you're trapped in. Take my hand."

The battle raged within Lane—the desire to trust him and fling herself into his arms bristled against the fear that he'd find out what she'd become. Tears welled up in her eyes.

"Done things. Bad things." The tears brimmed, flowed freely down her face.

Ray stepped closer, slowly. When she didn't move, he took another slow step forward, then another, and another. "You stayed alive. I don't care what you had to do."

Lane stood her ground, appraising him, waiting. She didn't want him so close that she couldn't escape, but she didn't want to pass up the opportunity to prove his innocence.

"We can get through this."

As he approached, she tried to remember her attacker's shoulders, the way they blotted out the trees and the stars.

"A boy died." Tears gushed from her eyes.

Ray's feet turned back to clay, perhaps all the way to cement. He stopped dead, emotions fighting for control of his face. There was no way to ask without accusation, but he tried to keep it out of his voice. "Did you do it?"

Relieved that she shook her head, he took another step forward. "What then?"

She sucked in several short breaths, like an infant that had been crying too long. "Watched him die. Didn't even try to stop them."

Ray closed the gap, standing within ten feet of her. His hands went out to her, and he prayed that in the next few seconds he'd wrap his arms around her. "Could you have stopped them?"

Her shoulders shrugged up a fraction of an inch, barely noticeable. "Too scared to try."

Ray took one final step; Lane flashed back; a man loomed before her, and pressed against her, his hands grabbing her.

Zavier stepped out the door, stopped abruptly, and took in the scene.

Lane's focus came back to present. She eyed Zavier and then Ray. Surely there could be no safer time.

Bolstered by her logic, she dropped the bike to the ground and flung herself into Ray's arms. She lingered there for a minute breathing in hints of cinnamon and vanilla that hugged his clothes, feeling the strength of his arms as they wrapped around her, crushing her into his chest. For a fleeting moment, she felt safe.

A flash blinded her, and a black-clad man pushed down against her. Lane buckled under Ray's grasp. His body tensed, his arms constricted; he didn't want to let her go.

Lane insisted, pushed hard against him, and he released her, allowing her to duck out of his grasp. She picked up her bike.

"Lane, please."

Another shake of her head, and she pedaled away.

chapter forty-eight

*J*enna paced as she stood with Richard outside the closed door of the third floor room. Richard took pity on her. "You don't have to be here for this."

Jenna smiled sadly and clasped her hands in front of her. "I do. If you find something, maybe I can shed light on it."

Nothing in the room had changed since the last time Richard had been there. He perused the room, fingering odds and ends, putting everything back in its designated place after he'd finished examining it. He ran a finger along the edge of the dresser.

Jenna offered an explanation. "I can't help it. I keep it ready," she paused, sniffing back a tear. "In case."

Richard ignored the dramatics and continued around the room, eyeing the white lace and ruffles. He had a hard time picturing Lane in this room at all, except that several trophies lined the dresser. *Kid's got freaking trophies everywhere.*

Richard stopped by the door and examined some scratches etched into the frame before exiting the room. "Has she been here?"

Jenna folded her arms, stared at her shoes against the brilliant shine of the hardwood floor.

Richard shook his head. "I'll take that as a yes."

"Someone was here. I don't know that it was Lane."

"Take anything?"

"Some clothes, food. A few dollars."

"And no one thought to tell me?"

Jenna bristled. "Of course we did. But what does that say about us? Our daughter might be back, takes some food and we call the sheriff? We were hoping she'd feel safe enough to come home. It's not like she's done anything. She just ran away."

Richard fell silent, pondering how to proceed. His hands slid into his pockets and toyed with the coins he found there.

"I know you too well, Richard. Just ask."

"Let's talk about Morgan's anger problem."

Jenna threw a hand in the air. "Your brother told you that."

"I've got pictures, remember?"

"Yes, the brat down the street. I thought we'd explained that months ago. Teenagers need discipline."

"A little excessive, wouldn't you say?"

"Not at all. You have no idea the hell she put us through. I'm sorry you think it looks so bad, but he slapped her, nothing more."

"What kind of hell?"

Jenna's face screwed up with confusion. "What?"

"She was putting you through. What kind of hell?"

Jenna's hand became more animated, whipping through the air like a demon-possessed painter. Her other hand sat more dignified on her hip. "I suppose you think we should have turned her in earlier. I suppose you think this is all our fault."

Richard insisted. "What kind of hell?"

Again the dismissive gesture answered him. "Drugs, sex. Sneaking boys into the house. Stealing things from us, from our friends. Shoplifting. She'd gone bad, Richard, and we didn't know what to do to stop it. To help her. She wouldn't listen to us, wouldn't talk to us. Morgan just snapped, but a slap hardly qualifies as an anger management issue."

His hands eased out of his pockets, smoothed down against his outer thighs, and presented his most professional appearance. "Jenna, she was raped."

Jenna's hand went to her mouth, and she stumbled a bit, forcing Richard to steady her. Her look of horror vanished quickly, replaced by anger and a deep, burning hatred that threatened to tear Richard's flesh off his bones. "Your brother."

"No suspects."

Jenna composed herself and descended the grand staircase. Her movements remained elegant and poised with one hand lightly grasping the rail while the other trembled. "Feel free to let yourself out."

Thoughts jumbled around Richard's head as he returned to his cruiser, where he sat for a moment, staring at the mansion. He thumbed the radio. "Dispatch."

Crackles greeted him, then Dottie's pleasant voice piped on. "Go ahead, Sheriff."

"Ask Danny to get the Lane Harris file off my desk."

"Retrieving it as we speak."

"Ask him to check the toxicology." Richard moved the shift into gear and drove in silence, save for the slapping of the windshield wipers.

Danny came on the line. "Negative for substances."

"All right. I'm heading back. Be there in five."

"Hang on a sec, Dottie's got a message for you."

Richard waited as the radio transferred back to his dispatcher. "Your brother wants you to stop by the rectory. Says it's about the Harris girl."

Richard paced through the rectory kitchen, annoyed as hell. "Did you think to call me while she was here?"

"Richard, I was trying to get through to her, trying to get her to turn herself in."

"Next time just grab her and call me."

"Don't think that's going to work very well."

"Yeah? Why not?"

"Because she can still outrun me—and you from what I hear."

Richard suddenly stopped pacing and whirled on his brother like a caged animal. "Why are your initials carved into her bedroom door?"

Ray's eyes mirrored confusion. "My initials?"

"R K."

Ray balked. "Those are your initials, too."

"Yeah, but you have a public relationship with her."

Ray snorted, almost laughing out the sarcasm. "Oh, not you."

Richard shrugged and accepted the words. "I suppose. But she doesn't have a room in my house." Richard pulled the hospital photos from his pocket, tossed them on the table, and spread them around so that Ray could see the damage done to Lane. He held nothing back, and he made no attempt to be sympathetic of his brother's feelings. "She was raped."

Air escaped slowly from Ray's lungs, leaking out through his open mouth. Unable to ignore the pictures, he shuffled them together and handed them back to Richard. His voice trembled, and his eyes filled with pain and tears.

"I suspected."

"Really? How? She tell you? I didn't think she was talking, what with her larynx having been nearly destroyed."

Ray lowered his head and averted his eyes. He couldn't protect the one person who needed him, and right now, he didn't care what his brother thought. "She has a proximity problem that she's never had before."

Surprised by the revelation, Richard stammered, thrown off his attack. "With you?"

Ray nodded. "I imagine she's got the same problem with everyone, or perhaps just males. But yes, with me. It makes sense now. She was sizing me up, probably trying to figure out if it was me or not."

"That doesn't exactly work in your favor."

"I know."

Richard's surprise grew; it registered on his face. "Then why tell me?"

"Because I didn't do it, Richard, no matter what you believe. But she's trying to figure out who did, so keep that in mind when you're chasing her down."

"She's got a gun, Ray."

Ray sat down, elbow on the table, face in his hand. "I know, but I don't think she'd use it on anybody."

"You don't *think*?"

"Look, I know the kid. If I can get her to talk to you, without fear of you grabbing her, will you give her a fair chance?"

"I give all my suspects a fair chance."

"She's not a criminal, Richard."

"You don't know her very well, Ray. She's been bashing drunks over the head and stealing their money, mugging people. Hell, she gave Danny that shiner. She's changed, Ray."

"And you don't know her at all. She's trying to survive. If we can get her to trust us, we can get her to talk."

Richard paced around the room.

"You said you wanted to talk to her." Ray hoped he'd convince his brother to lighten up on the girl.

Richard stopped by the door, turned to Ray. "Help me catch her, dammit, before she gets hurt, or hurts somebody." He saw a flash of indecision cross Ray's face. "What aren't you telling me?"

"Swear to me, before God, that you'll give her a chance."

chapter forty-nine

*M*organ closed the front door behind him, shrugging out of his coat as he turned toward his office. A cold, hard slap greeted him, tipping his head back and to the side.

Jenna faced him with her arms at her sides and her hands clenched into tiny fists.

With his eyes burning fire, Morgan's emotions raced to the surface. His hands balled up, and he glowered down at his petite wife. *Anyone else*, he thought. He forced his fingers open and stretched his hands open wide.

"I've done something to upset you." He brushed past her, knocking her slightly off balance.

Jenna chased him down, taking three strides to each of his, a poodle to his panther. "She was raped."

"What?" Morgan poured himself a drink and took a long, slow swig.

"She was raped."

The amber fluid swirled around his tongue and eased down his throat. Fire churned in his stomach.

"Don't tell me you've suddenly developed a maternal bond. I take it *he* was here. What did he want?"

Jenna poked a finger into Morgan's chest. "What kind of a man rapes a child?"

Morgan wrapped his hand around hers and squeezed, emphasizing his dominance. She recoiled, trying to pull her hand away; she succeeded only because he let her go.

"I don't know. She spent the last six months living on the streets of Seattle, probably giving herself away for spare change. I'm really not surprised she got raped." He polished off his drink, poured another, and downed it in a single gulp. "So, what did he want?"

"To talk about Lane, of course."

"That's it?"

"He wanted to see her room."

He eyed his wife up and down. "So you were alone with him."

"He didn't try anything."

"Did you?"

Jenna turned away, and Morgan smiled. "He refused you. A man of virtue. Well, isn't that scary as hell."

chapter fifty

*C*olumns of boxes lined the truck bay. Lane stacked the boxes onto a hand truck, clearing away the piles one half column at a time.

Old Man Pearce welcomed the help; he was older, slower, and weaker, and he hadn't been able to keep an employee in years. But this one had a desperation about her. *She tries to hide it, tries to act all nonchalant and what all, but I been around the track a few times…I know what that is.* He hoped that it would be enough to keep her around for a while because he doubted minimum wage alone would do the trick.

The others he'd hired had attitudes, acting as if they had done him a favor by taking the job. They'd hung around, doing little if any work, taking extra-long breaks, eating his food, and giving him lip. This one was already a better worker. And she'd been polite and respectful. *That helps.*

Lane wheeled the hand truck through the stockroom, setting boxes in front of their respective aisles. When the dock was clear and the boxes were all sorted out, the job required that she move the new deliveries onto the appropriate shelves behind any existing stock so that the oldest merchandise got used first.

She basked in the feeling of security and happiness because she was certain that no one would find her working back there. When Old Man Pearce checked in on her, he was impressed by her work ethic and the progress she'd made; she even allowed him to stroll up to her since she was convinced that he couldn't have been her attacker. He couldn't carry a box, so there was no way had he carried a human being.

"Don't know how they figured it out so quick, but I just got a call for a home delivery. Interested? You get your regular pay, but you'll probably get a tip to boot."

chapter fifty-one

*L*ane pedaled along the highway and turned into the Village Campground. A large board held announcements, items for sale, and a map of the grounds. She located her delivery site, traced the route with her finger, and peered around the sign to get her bearings.

Trailers of every shape, size, and configuration lined the roads. Some of them boasted exquisite landscaping, others none at all. Some were closed up for the winter, others obviously still occupied. Each had a green, duck-shaped number sign emblazoned with gold lettering. Lane pedaled past several campers on her way to her delivery—a clamped down pop-up, a Dutchman with a huge tarp tied over the roof and sides, and an old beater with a For Sale sign hanging off its hitch.

Lane pedaled into lot C21, appraising the park model with its large deck room. She leaned the bike up against the front wall, and began unpacking the groceries. *Whoever this is*, she thought, *they sure like their junk food.* The bags held nothing but crap—potato chips, cookies, microwave popcorn, a cheese Danish.

The sacks were light and posed no trouble; she peered through the windows, appraising the deck room with its sofa, lounger, and minifridge. Music played in the background. The door was open, but she didn't feel comfortable just walking in. She knocked and waited.

The music drowned out the voice, but she heard an invitation, so she stepped inside. Light beamed out the open front door. Two metal stairs echoed her footsteps, and she perched at the top to peek in; no one was inside. She stepped back down and turned.

Richard blocked her only exit, and the rear door of the trailer was now wide open. The bags fell from her hands; she realized then why they were so light in the first place, with no perishables or breakables.

"Welcome." He smiled a little, amused that she'd dropped all the bags. "Time to give this up." He closed the deck door and locked it. "You and I have some things to discuss. Like why your fingerprints turned up at several muggings in Seattle."

From her knees to her neck, Lane's body shook. *Was it him?* He was bigger than Ray, more muscular, and more powerful. Behind him on the TV stand stood a picture of Jenna and him, hugging and smiling. In love.

For a few moments, Richard made no attempt to approach her; he tried to talk her into a peaceful submission. "I've already told you that you'll only get hurt if you resist."

Panic swelled on the girl's face and in her eyes, and her clothes rippled on the surface in response to her body shaking underneath. "Just relax. I'll cuff you and we'll go right down to the station. Five minutes tops."

She didn't believe him and couldn't trust him. It was just a ruse to get her to submit; God only knew what he'd do to her then. Alone. In the woods. In his bed.

Richard's voice was firm but calm. "Then we'll get the cuffs off and get you squared away. I'm betting, under the circumstances, you'll get probation, so you really don't want to make this any worse right now."

She saw no way around him and no way out. He took a step in her direction.

"Just relax, Lane. This will all be over soon." He took another step forward.

That's what I'm afraid of. She wrapped her arms around herself, hugging her, comforting her, and protecting her. A choked whimper squeezed from her throat. She'd lost her options. Her attempt to return to a normal life had been shot down. Her hands reached out to stop him, and she pushed at the air as he approached.

Richard stopped for a second. With his next step, Lane's hands jammed into her coat, and her stiff arms pressed the coat down and wrapped it forward at the hip, as if it might shield her from him.

The move spooked Richard, and he reached for and caressed his sidearm.

She staggered, her knees wobbling as Richard took a slow, careful step in her direction, and her left hand came back out, palm facing him. She stepped away from him, her torso nearly concave.

Richard slowed but didn't stop.

The rubber grip fit comfortably in her hand—reassuring and strong. She grabbed the coat with her left hand and pulled the material taut as she drew the gun from her right pocket. She thumbed the safety off and brought the gun to bear in a single, fluid motion, her trigger finger pasted to the barrel to prevent accidental discharge.

Richard saw the intent and the movement, but he only managed two steps before the weapon presented itself to his face. "You drop that gun, little girl, before you dig this hole any deeper."

Lane flicked the Walther and motioned him away from the door.

He considered lunging and grabbing her and the gun, but then she dropped her aim to center mass. *Much less likely she'll miss,* he thought, remaining motionless until she pulled the slide and chambered a round. He stepped back, allowing Lane to reach the deck door.

She fumbled with the lock using her left hand, but she never took her eyes off Richard's torso. The door popped open behind her.

With his hands up to appear nonthreatening, Richard followed, keeping the pressure on as Lane backed out the door and retrieved her bike. She pushed it out onto the dirt road, trying to increase the space between herself and Richard, but he wouldn't let up. He continued to dog her.

Lane grew desperate; she let the bike go and braced it against her hips. She wrapped her left hand around the right hand, shoring up the pistol, and presenting a much more intimidating facade. She hoped the action would keep Richard from coming any closer and signify that she meant business, even if she didn't.

He took one step back, his hands lifting higher, and Lane hopped on the bike. She exerted a few hard pumps and pulled away, giving her the chance to thumb the safety and stuff the weapon back in her pocket.

She pedaled faster, hoping to escape, but the roar of a V-8 engine chased her down the dirt road, and she knew she wouldn't get away if she headed out to Mill Road. The pavement would give the car the upper hand. She veered left, heading further into the campground. Richard followed.

The car bounced and bucked on the dirt roads, but Richard gunned it, determined to stop her.

She veered again; Richard missed the fork and jammed the brakes. Lane stretched her lead to fifty feet while Richard maneuvered the turn, but the distance closed quickly. Richard was back on her trail and closing in fast.

The bike itself kept Lane from escaping. She had to ditch it but without getting run over. She searched for a likely place, but with each second Richard got closer, trying to stop her and unnerve her with his car.

He dodged and edged close to her, hoping the intimidation would freak her out, make her careless, make her lose control. If he actually hit her with the car, so be it. Once she fell off, and he did expect it to hurt, he'd rein her in and cart her off to the clinic. She'd have cuts and scrapes, perhaps a broken bone, but she'd be in custody.

She refused to cooperate with his plan, zagging and swerving, and declining his invitation to yield.

Lane broke hard, planted her foot on the ground, and let the bike fishtail around her. She threw the bike to the ground and danced out from the downed frame seconds before Richard slammed into it.

The cruiser skidded to a halt, but its weight and size carried it considerably farther than the bike. By the time he got out of the car, Lane was a retreating ghost in the tree line.

"Shit."

Richard parked in front of Pearce's and hoisted the bike up onto the front stairs and into the store.

Al eyed the bike. He shuffled over and took the battered aluminum frame from Richard, muttering in disgust. "Great, Sheriff. Thanks a lot. Finally get some help in here, and you run them down."

Richard balked, his eyebrows rising in defense. "I didn't run her down."

"Might as well have. God knows I'll never see her again. Damn good worker, too. And a decent person." Al stopped, pointed a crooked finger at Richard, emphasizing his disapproval. "A damn decent person. Lived here my whole life and never saw anybody do what she did. Well, 'cept the priest. But that's his job."

"What did she do?"

Al ignored him, dragging the bike into the stockroom. When he returned, he shook his head at the sheriff. "Still here? Wanna run my wife down, too?"

"Al, what did she do?"

"Like you care. She bought a whole bunch of groceries for John and Shirley. Delivered them herself, too. You sure? I'll go get Lorraine and have her stand behind your car. Just back on over her. Pretend you never saw her."

After two knocks, Shirley finally opened her front door. Her mouth hung open, and she called over her shoulder.

"John?"

Richard donned his most charismatic smile to reassure the old woman. "Afternoon, Shirley. I was hoping to have a minute of your time."

"John?"

Moments later John shuffled up and stood beside his wife.

"You call the police?"

John glanced between Shirley and Richard. "No."

Richard smiled. "I just need a minute of your time."

"Not a good time." Shirley tried to shut the door, but Richard reached over and held it open.

"Just a minute, really."

John grabbed the door and pushed with Shirley to close it. "We didn't do nothing wrong."

"I know. I just have a question for you."

"No, not a good time." Shirley insisted.

Richard moved into the threshold and leaned his arm against the door. "I just want to talk about the girl."

Shirley and John exchanged a glance. "Spent it, don't have it anymore."

Richard's head tipped to the side. "Spent it?"

John pushed against the door to no avail, like Underdog against Hercules.

"How much?"

"Don't matter. Spent it. It's gone."

"I don't want it back."

"For real?" Shirley leaned into Richard, her squinted eyes staring up at him.

He nodded and moved his arm off the door as a gesture of good faith.

"A hundred-forty-two and change."

Shirley slammed the door.

Rain splattered the driveway and pounded the roof as Richard waited on the back porch of the rectory. The lock clicked in its housing, the door squeaked open, and he slowly turned and faced Ray. And he waited.

Ray stared at Richard, at the look on his face, his hat in his hand both figuratively and literally. And Ray waited.

Richard shuffled forward. "I screwed up."

Ray sighed, rubbed a weary hand over his eyes, then stepped

aside and waved Richard into the house with a silent sweep of his hand. He pulled a chair out for his younger brother, offering him a seat without saying the words. He headed to the coffee pot, poured two cups, and wondered what he'd say without throwing more accusations around.

He brought the coffees to the table, set them down, and immediately went to the fridge for milk, then to the cabinet for the sugar. He couldn't think of any other way to stall, but he couldn't say he really wanted to sit across the table from Richard right now.

He settled into the chair, but Richard's attention focused out the window, watching the rain.

Ray broke the silence. "What did she do?"

Richard rubbed his hands along his face and up into his hair, then folded them together on the tabletop. "Tell me about her."

What exactly do you want to know?"

"Everything."

Ray laughed at the absurd notion. "I can't fit the last eighteen years into a coffee break. Can you be a little more specific?"

"Tell me how you two got so close." Ray's hackles rose, and Richard's hands eased off the table, his fingertips rising up. "I need to understand this damn kid, Ray."

Ray considered the question. He dumped three teaspoons of sugar into his coffee and stirred it slowly. "It wasn't planned. Things went south at the mansion pretty quickly after her grandparents died. She was six when she ran away."

He took a sip and twisted the cup back and forth on the saucer. "Camilla called me. I found Lane on Mill Road, about half a mile from the mansion. After that," Ray's shoulders shrugged. "It just happened."

Richard eased off the table and pressed his back against the chair. "You swear you never had sex with her."

"I already did, but if you need to hear it again, I swear it. I never had sex with her—not forced, not consensual. Not at all."

"But you did have sex with Jenna."

Ray pushed his chair from the table and walked away.

"Ray, I need to know."

Ray leaned against the counter across the room. "I don't want to fight with you anymore."

"Then just talk to me. Just ..." he sighed. "Just assume I have a reason to know. If it's easier, pretend I wasn't engaged to her."

Ray paced the room, one hand scruffing his hair. The action brought Lane to his mind. *Did she teach me that? No. I taught her that. Richard does it, too.* He raked through his hair again, thinking, and his other hand rose to his hip. "I'm not particularly proud of that."

Richard waited.

"I didn't want to hurt you, but I couldn't let you marry her. I'd ... I'd heard things. At court. At dinner parties. I set out to see if they were true. And then I knew they were."

"That's why you became a priest."

"Once I saw how shallow she was, I couldn't help but recognize it in myself." Ray returned to the table and settled back into the chair. "For what it's worth, I'm sorry."

"Morgan know?"

A nervous chuckle escaped Ray as he recalled the aftermath of his encounter with Jenna. "Oh yeah. Didn't do anything with it until I was ready to be ordained. Then he went to the Bishop. And don't think that it didn't get thrown back in my face when the vicar was out here in June."

Richard's lips pursed, and his brows furrowed. He couldn't find a polite way to ask. "Is Lane sexually active? Was she? Before she went missing?"

Ray shook his head.

"You're sure?"

"Much as I can be. Not like she's got any friends." He shrugged, his head tipping to the side. "And we talked. About things. Sex. And things."

Richard leaned across the table. "Does she love you? Is that a crush or what?"

"We're more like, well, family. She's the daughter I can't have anymore, and I'm—" he paused, suddenly concerned about Richard's reaction. "—I'm her surrogate father."

Richard didn't miss it. "Just surrogate?"

"Yes."

"Would she do anything for you?"

Ray considered. "If it didn't break her moral code, I suppose she would. But she's got to know I told you that she was working for Pearce. I don't know how that'll play into it. I'm probably the only person she thought she could trust, and I betrayed her."

"Tell me why she'd break into all those houses then return and pay off her IOUs."

"That one's easier. You do something wrong, you make amends for it."

Richard went to the counter, returned with the coffee pot, and filled both cups. "I'm going to tell you something, and it's really not going to be open for debate. You just have to trust that sometimes, I'm right. Understand?"

Ray stammered, but Richard insisted. "Not open for debate. You just have to trust me."

Ray quieted, certain the displeasure showed on his face.

"Next time I get a line on her, I'm gonna ask you to come and talk her in. And I don't care if you have to lie to her, or slug her in the chops, or manhandle her into submission. She's just taken this to a new level, and we have to catch her. Soon.

"What happened?"

"I cornered her, and she pulled her gun on me. Doesn't mean she will use it, but if she pulls it on the wrong person, she'll get shot."

Ray absorbed the new info, slowly. "On you?"

Richard nodded. "I don't know if she was more scared of me or the gun. But she wanted me to believe she'd use it." Richard leaned further across the table. "Tell me where she is."

"Rich, I don't think I can do this."

"I think you can live with her being angry at you. How are you going to handle it if she gets herself killed?"

Ray hung his head, interlocking his fingers on the back of his neck. "I don't know for certain she's there, but there's a cave on the hillside overlooking the mansion." His hands dropped to cradle his coffee.

His eyes stung of betrayal. "She never said, and I never pressed her. But she had to be fairly close, I think. How else could she have stayed out of Morgan's way so consistently?"

"You've been there?"

Ray shook his head. "Not recently. Not since I was a boy. Used to go there so I didn't have to babysit you. I was afraid to go." A tear rolled down his face. "I was afraid she'd run."

"If she's there, how do I get to her without being seen?"

Ray rose, pulled a paper towel off the dispenser and wiped the tears from his face.

Richard eased in behind his brother, put a hand on his shoulder, and leaned in close. "Help me save her."

chapter fifty-two

*T*he jig was up. Richard had nearly caught her, and then she pulled a gun on him. The odds increased exponentially that he'd organize a manhunt.

Even if he didn't, she wouldn't be safe in town anymore and wouldn't be able to buy groceries like normal folks. She could certainly go back to breaking into houses and buying their food, but she had to admit that she'd simply been lucky up until now, finding empty houses into which she could easily gain access.

Because of the rugged terrain, the hike to Hoodsport would be an all-day affair on a good day and a multiple day event once the snow fell. But Lane didn't have any choice except to pack up her money and some supplies and move to town for the winter.

She hadn't spent all of Morgan's money, and if she practiced restraint, she might have just enough left to rent a room, and perhaps even have a good meal daily. If she watched for coupons, she might be able to stretch that to two meals per day. Plus, nobody knew her in Hoodsport. They might not think anything of her paying her rent in cash. She probably wouldn't attract any attention at all.

She chided herself for not moving sooner and reminded herself that Ray was still here. She knew he was innocent—he had to be;

everything she felt about him and his behavior said he was. She wanted to connect with him, and he didn't seem to care that she'd done some of the most despicable things she could think of. *Maybe I can call him from Hoodsport. After I get a place.*

The keys to survival hung in flexibility. Satisfied with the plan, she dug up her hidden money, combined it with Morgan's leftovers, and put it all in a baggy to keep it dry.

She upended her book bag, put the money in the bottom, and then stacked food and a change of clothes on top, stuffing it so full that it couldn't hold much more than a pencil.

The eco sacks sat nestled in the milk-crate pantry until she snapped them open, stuffing more food into them. The weight and awkwardness would probably make the trip take longer, but the extra food on hand would more than make up for any delay, even a day or two.

But the eggs would not travel well. She'd have to set them outside before she left. *Coyotes, raccoons, hell, even squirrels would come along and polish them off in no time*, she thought.

Everything else would remain where it was. Maybe a hiker would stumble across the cave and be safe from the elements. *If not, it'll just be easier for me to come back in the spring. Unless I meet up with Ray in Hoodsport.*

She supposed she should bring Morgan's documents with her as well, so she retrieved them from under the chaise, but there were just too many papers to bring all at once. She decided she'd have to weed through them to determine what was important and what could stay behind. She certainly didn't need her expired scholarship offers— they were just reminders of what she'd lost.

With the sun already setting, Lane figured she had until morning before Richard could organize a hunting party. She upended the bag on the chaise, sat down, and quickly sorted through the paperwork.

She stacked the documents in separate piles and found that Morgan's came in three flavors: land deeds, foreclosures, and purchase contracts. Halfway through the mess, she found a document that didn't fit in the categories; she flipped it open and read the first few lines.

chapter fifty-three

*L*ane hid in the utility shed and waited for Morgan to go to work. With him gone, she'd have a chance to talk with Jenna alone. She didn't know what she'd say and didn't know how Jenna would react. *Maybe this wasn't such a good idea*, she thought. There was no guarantee that Jenna would tell her the truth anyway.

The paper crumpled in her hand used to be clean with crisp, precise folds; now it was all smudged and bunched up. She was surprised by what she'd done to it, so she lightened her grip and found that her fingers ached just a little from holding the position for so long. Her jaw ached as well from the pressure of her clenching her teeth like a tiger holding the last lamb on earth.

Seven a.m. The iron gate swung open, and moments later Morgan drove his Black Onyx LX10 down the driveway. Barely using the gas, he coasted past the Olsen house, slowly so that anyone watching could get a good look. He smiled and waved, just in case.

Morgan stopped at the end of Harris Lane and checked for oncoming traffic before pulling out. In his rearview mirror, he caught a glimpse of motion back at his house.

Lane didn't bother to take her shoes off. This time she didn't care if she left footprints, or if Camilla came back to work Friday and had to spend hours getting the stains out of the carpeting, or even if it cost Morgan a thousand dollars to get a rush cleaning.

Lane hugged the wall of the kitchen passage, easing out into the great room and past the grand staircase. Carpet-muffled footsteps approached, and Lane ducked into Morgan's office.

The footsteps drew near and changed to a gentle slapping as the slippers hit the hardwood foyer floor. Lane peeked around the doorframe and slipped out of Morgan's office.

Jenna didn't look up, her attention riveted instead to some flaw on her dressing gown.

"Forget something?" she said.

Lane forced out gravelly words. "Just how vicious you can be."

Jenna pulled up short but tried to remain calm. "What are you doing here?" She took a step away then stopped, replacing her fear with an uneasy air of authority.

Lane squeaked out a few more words. "Was it your idea, or his?" She moved out into the foyer, surprised by how uncomfortable her presence made Jenna. Another two steps and she'd succeeded in forcing her mother to retreat toward the stairs.

Jenna quickly replaced her disgust and revulsion with more appropriate emotions. "Lane? Is that you? We've been so worried. Honey, everything will be all right now. You'll see."

Lane scoffed and held out the petition she'd found so that Jenna could see it. "Tell me the truth."

Jenna exuded her haughtiest attitude, glaring her nose down at Lane. "Isn't it obvious enough?" Jenna rolled her eyes when Lane didn't seem to get it. "We need your land."

"Then why didn't you ask?"

Jenna smiled sweetly. "We did. Oh, sorry. The holding company did. But your guardian refused. Bet he's sorry now."

Lane shook her head. "How could you do this to me?"

"Oh, dear. I didn't do this to you. Morgan did. He's always hated you, you know that. You're someone else's kid. And every time he sees you, he remembers that."

Lane contemplated the words, staring venom across the room at Jenna. "Every time *you* see me, *you* remember that."

Jenna exploded, her hands whipping to a frenzy. "He said he loved me. He was going to build a house up in the hills. He was going to take a job in the city." Jenna laughed out loud. "Look at him now. That isn't love. It's poverty. Thank God I came to my senses and married Morgan."

Morgan emerged from the kitchen hallway, walking slowly and deliberately. "I knew sooner or later you'd admit it."

Lane spun and found herself staring down the barrel of Morgan's stubby thirty-eight special.

Morgan shook his head. "You never did learn to close that damn door."

Jenna thrust a hand in Lane's direction. "Just shoot her and get it over with. Look at her. You said it yourself. We couldn't know it was her."

Lane backed away. "I'll give you the deeds."

Morgan laughed. "Don't need them. Copies'll be here tomorrow. As for yours," he shrugged. "We've already got custody of your land." He motioned to the paper wadded up in her hand, using his handgun as a pointer. "Though I expect you know that. Not that it matters now. With you dead, well, the land just becomes ours."

A slight smile split Lane's face. "No, it doesn't."

"Of course it does. We're your parents."

"No, you aren't. And my will gives my land to somebody else."

Morgan's mouth puckered. "Really? You smart little bitch. I should have known you'd turn out like your mother. No matter. I can kill him, too. Not like it's that hard. Look at your grandparents." His head cocked to the side, and he aimed the gun at Lane. "It's been nice. In fact, some of it was real nice."

Lane feigned right then dove left. Morgan fired.

Jenna staggered back, a blossom of red creeping across her gown. She sagged to the floor.

Horrified, Morgan wavered off target and rushed to Jenna's side as Lane stumbled out the front door. He recovered slowly and fired several more shots in Lane's direction.

Most of the bullets slammed harmlessly into the wall, but one struck the edge of the door, peeled off a chunk of wood, and splintered it into Lane's face.

"Jenna." Morgan knelt by her side. He took off his suit jacket, folded it up, and placed it under her head. Then he stripped off his shirt and forced it against the wound while fumbling for his cell phone.

Jenna remained conscious, grimacing against the pain. "You shot me?"

Morgan tucked the phone between his ear and chin as he applied pressure to Jenna's shoulder. "I need an ambulance. Harris Lane. Who the hell else lives here? The mansion, you idiot. Hurry."

Jenna wrapped a hand around his arm. "You have to get her."

Morgan nodded, but didn't move. Jenna pushed at his arm. "I'm

OK. They'll be here soon. I'll tell them you're chasing her."

Morgan ran to his office for a handful of bullets then fled the house. By the time he reached the meadow, Lane was just a spot on the hillside, fading into the trees.

Danny pulled through the mansion gate and noted the Lexus bouncing around the meadow. He parked the cruiser close to the front door and approached the house cautiously, his pistol stiff-armed out in front of him. He peered through the bullet-ridden front door and saw Jenna lying nearby. His gun advanced before him as he swept the door open as far as he could and stepped in. Without backup, it became obvious that he couldn't clear the entire house.

"Are you alone, Mrs. Harris?"

Jenna looked at him, then beyond him. "What? Where's Richard? Of course I'm alone."

Danny eased toward Morgan's office. "Where are they now?"

Jenna slapped a hand on the floor. "Gone, you moron. She fled, and Morgan's chasing her. Perhaps if you people had done your jobs better, it wouldn't have come to this."

Danny would have preferred backup right now, but Ed had the day off and had driven to Seattle with his wife to talk to the retirement advisor, and Pete was driving in from his cabin on Lake Cushman, a good twenty minutes out.

He decided to take Jenna's word for it; he holstered his weapon and knelt at her side. Beneath Morgan's blood-stained shirt he found the bullet hole. He felt her back for an exit wound but didn't find one. "I think it's lodged in your shoulder."

Jenna smiled weakly. "Is that good or bad?"

Danny shrugged. "Depends on your point of view, I suppose. Ambulance is just minutes behind me. What happened here?"

Fake tears welled up in Jenna's eyes. "She shot me. She was hiding in the kitchen, and when I came downstairs she just ... just shot me." A tear rolled down her face.

"Where was Morgan?"

"In his office. He came running out. She opened fire on him, too." She motioned to the door. He went after her." She grabbed Danny's arm. "I'm so afraid they're going to kill each other."

"Does he have a gun, Mrs. Harris?"

Jenna feigned confusion. "Of course not. Lane's got the gun."

The ambulance arrived, its siren grinding to silence with the flick of a switch, and Danny yielded the floor to the EMTs. With someone else tending Jenna, Danny took the opportunity to snoop, and he started with the front door and neighboring wall, examining the spray pattern.

The shots were all over the place and covered a five or six foot span. He searched for blood, finding a few drops on the outside of the door.

From there, he took an easy stroll to Morgan's office and poked his head inside. Ten seconds later, he was fairly certain that Morgan had not been in the room at all. The chair snuggled under the desk with the morning paper folded neatly on top, and no cup of coffee graced the room.

The EMTs lifted Jenna onto the gurney, hoisted it to extend the legs, and carted her off. As they packed her up, Danny called the sheriff.

Richard gripped the shotgun firmly in both hands but pointed it at the ground as he worked his way through the forest. Snow mingled with the rain now, and white fluff accumulated on some of the colder surfaces. He stopped often, listened, and moved ahead. His eyes scanned for signs and tracks, human and otherwise; Lane wasn't the only dangerous creature in the forest.

His radio squawked and he lowered the volume a little before answering it. He listened carefully to Danny, but his attention shifted, apportioned between the forest, the fluttering of birds, and the wind-tousled leaves.

"She says Lane shot her and fired on Morgan."

"Where is he?" Richard crested Jensen Ridge, turned to face the church steeple, then spun one hundred eighty degrees and started down the hill. A dirt path carved through the undergrowth a few feet to his right, and he moved over to it, making his trek easier.

"Jenna says he's in the forest looking for Lane, and he may well be, but these bullet holes are huge. No way they're twenty-twos."

"So they both have weapons. Stay with Jenna. When Pete gets there, have him take over, and you head back to the mansion."

Danny balked. "You shouldn't go up there without backup, Sheriff."

"I know that, but Morgan and Lane are out here together. Armed." Richard lost his footing and slid several feet down the ridge before catching himself. He thumbed his radio. "Dispatch."

Dottie's pleasant voice returned. "Go ahead, Sheriff."

"Call Ray. Get him down to the station immediately. Tell him it's about the Harris girl. And as soon as he gets there, put him on the radio with me."

Richard signed off and continued down the grade. Near the base of the hill, the terrain leveled out quickly and ended suddenly at the banks of a large stream. He spied the downed tree that Ray had told him was the only way to cross the tributary up here on the ridge.

He wasn't a boy anymore. The tree would have been great fun thirty years ago, but now he was an adult. Ice cold water swirled below, crashing against rocks that protruded above the waterline. He shook his head and climbed onto the tree, using both hands to grab branches and pull himself along. The radio crackled to life.

"Dispatch to Sheriff."

"Figures." His eyes rolled, but he remained focused on the task at hand, preferring to let them worry a little as opposed to his taking a cool dip in the river. After three repeat calls, Danny piped up on the line, then Pete. Richard jumped off the tree and grabbed the line. "Go ahead, Dispatch."

"Got Ray for you." A moment passed as Ray took the radio.

"What is it, Richard? Do you have her? Should I come out?"

"Change of plans. I want you to meet Danny at the Harris place. Tell him how to get to the cave. I've just crossed the river. How much farther?"

"Follow the river toward its source. Maybe half a mile up there's a little clearing and a ledge. There's a cave there. If she's covered the entrance, you may not see it. Banks are deep there, really deep. Fall off and kill yourself deep."

Richard slipped between the trees and checked for movement around him. He walked cautiously, selecting his foot placement with great care, partially to stay off his butt and partially to minimize noise.

Twenty minutes later, the clearing spread out before him, and the drop-off cliff presented a stunning view of the Harris mansion. He ducked into the stand of trees on the riverbank, finding the makeshift pulley and four lengths of rope tied to the trees and trailing off the cliff.

Richard was surprised to see just how steep the banks were here, and Ray's words echoed in his head. *Fall off and kill yourself deep.* He pulled on a rope and smiled when two packs of hot dogs popped up on the other end of the line. He released it and let it drop into the freezing water as he settled onto his haunches and peered out into the clearing.

He swept the area quickly for threats, then again slower, eyeing everything as he tried to locate the cave. A plastic crackling gave the hideout away, the wind rustling the brown tarp draped over the entrance.

Rocks cropped out of the ground freely here, but where dirt showed, occasional footprints marked Lane's path. *These may not be fresh*, Richard reminded himself. But at some point she had come in from the west and jumped between rocks before landing near the cave entrance.

Scattered footprints closer to him showed her path to the riverbank, where he now sat in hiding. With a last check for danger, he headed to the cave.

The odds were great that if she were even there, she wouldn't stick around long; truth be told, he couldn't be sure that she hadn't already split. But the clearing gave her the advantage; if she hadn't left yet, she'd have line of sight on him before he could see her.

He sprinted to the rock face, pressed his back against it, and slipped around and between stacks of tarped-over wood. The whine of a wounded animal drifted from the cave.

Alcohol streamed into the wound, searing the raw nerve

endings. A whimper escaped her, but she clamped down on the string of vulgarities that really wanted to jump out. Morgan was out there somewhere. *Lost*, she hoped, *but definitely in the vicinity. No point in drawing him right to the door.*

And the deputy. No doubt he had his hands full with Jenna. "But Richard can't be far behind," she whispered. For all she knew, he was already en route. She had to leave. Soon.

A shot intended for Lane had missed its target, creating a three-inch shard from Morgan's front door that had sliced through Lane's flesh and lodged just under her cheekbone. Now it burned in the fire pit, the smoldering embers already roasting wood and blood alike. Several strips of tape held a wad of gauze on the wound, staunching the flow of blood from Lane's face.

Her packed bags sat on the chaise, already overflowing and ready to go. But this new wound would need tending; she stuffed medical supplies into the few remaining spaces. Gauze. Tape. Antibiotic ointment. Aspirin.

She rolled her coat up and tied it to the backpack with a small length of rope; she was too sweaty from the run and the adrenaline surging through her blood to wear it now.

The Walther found a new home in the front pocket of her pants. She swung the backpack on to her shoulders, gripped the tire iron, and gathered up her eco sacks. If the coast remained clear, she'd retrieve the last few hot dogs from the river before departing the Valley.

Richard inched closer to the tarp-draped entrance and pressed his back flat against the rock face when the tarp crinkled and shifted. Fingertips pushed the plastic aside, and Lane inched out.

She managed just two steps. "That's far enough," he said.

Lane dropped the eco sacks and whirled, brandishing the tire iron defiantly. Blood had already stained through the bandage.

Richard raised his shotgun just a few inches, not really pointing it at her. "Put it down."

Lane did as she was told, noting the obvious discrepancy in weaponry. Still, she refused to yield.

"Now the gun."

Lane hesitated; she slid the backpack off and heaved it toward the cave. It landed with a plop, its weight causing it to roll over.

Richard studied her and glanced at the pack. "Don't believe it's there. Don't believe you're dumb enough to leave your weapon out of reach." Her lack of cooperation didn't faze him. "We can stand here until hypothermia sets in. I think you're going to lose muscle control long before I do."

Her eyes darted to his for a millisecond, then down. She patted her pocket with her hand.

"Take it out. Two fingers. Then drop it."

She obeyed, glancing at the snow icing up the puddles at her feet, and shot Richard a disapproving glance before tossing the gun toward the backpack. It landed on the relatively dry top, but momentum carried it further, sliding into the rock face and dropping to the ground.

He moved closer and lowered the shotgun a fraction. Blood dripped down her face and onto her clothes, spattering red circles into the puddles. His chin inched forward. "How bad is that?"

The barest hint of life rippled through her body, and Richard sensed her action before it happened. "I've had enough of this, Lane. You so much as pivot, and I swear to God, this time I *will* shoot you."

He hadn't last time, and Lane saw no reason to believe he would this time. Both the tire iron and the Walther sat on the ground, and she had no other weapon. She simply posed no threat. *He can't shoot me for running. Unless he wants me dead for some other reason.*

Her brain took over, rooting through the confusion. *If he wanted me dead he'd have done it already. Unless he has other plans.* Her body shook. And her brain screamed. *Run, run, run!*

Richard lunged, easily covering the distance as Lane turned for the river. His hands vice-clamped on her shoulders, and he let his body weight and momentum bring her down. His Stetson popped off, flipped, and landed crest-down in the muck.

The crash knocked the wind out of her, but it didn't keep her from fighting. He pressed his chest into her back and wrapped his arms around her, binding her arms to her sides.

Lane thrashed around, a guttural cry escaping her as she kicked back. The terror alone spurred her struggle. *Oh, God. He's got me. He's got me.* She slipped a knee up and tried to get it underneath her.

Richard held tight. "It'll only get worse from here if you don't relax." He grappled his way up her body, planting his knee in the middle of her back.

She fought for her life, straining against him, gasping shallow wheezes driven by terror, panic, and pain. The flashbacks tripped back and forth like a toddler recently introduced to a light switch.

Richard had taken all that he would. He didn't want to hurt her, but he'd get this under control one way or another. He quickly brought her left arm around and pinned it to her back with his knee. But when he reached for her other arm, Lane resisted, rolling toward the free arm and blocking Richard's reach.

"I warned you not to fight me." Richard folded Lane's left wrist toward her forearm, and he forced her arm further up her back. She cried out.

"Stop resisting or you'll trash the tendons in this arm." Richard waited; his free hand rested on his thigh.

Still, she refused to yield. Her forehead sank into the slush, and the wheezing deepened, her lungs aching for breath.

Richard waited. Under difference circumstances, he might have forced her to surrender, but in light of her obvious terror and the reasons for it, he made it easy for her. He slid his hand down her shoulder, hooked around her elbow, and drew the arm to him. Once he controlled both her hands, he slapped his cuffs down on her wrists.

He slid off her back and rose without additional comment or intention. He regretted his arrogance in the alley behind the Plaza, regretted not knowing then what he knew now. He settled for winning without the gloating.

"Those cuffs are double locked. Don't bother trying to pick them." He snapped his radio off his belt. "I'm going to call in. Just sit tight. Relax. Catch your breath." He smoothed his hair back, thumbing the radio.

The rain solidified. Snow pattered against the ground, the dead leaves and brush, creating an eerie sound that most people mistook for silence.

Lane sucked air, nothing more than a series of short, fast minibreaths. *Oh God, oh God. Don't let this happen. Please, don't let this happen again.*

The tiny voices resurfaced. *Run, run, run.* The voices had saved her before; she had no reason to doubt them now. It would just be harder to obey this time.

She rolled right to protect the brutalized left arm, pushed off her elbow to a sitting position, and drew her legs up underneath her. By the time she was on her feet, her expression had gone blank. She charged at the sheriff. The impact sent the radio flying and Richard sprawling, creating a split second of confusion. His eyes opened wide, and a dull pain drilled into his kidney as Lane spun away and dashed for the river.

Richard's mind cleared quickly after he hit the ground. At this distance, a shotgun blast would rip a hole the size of California through anything in its path. He released it and rolled, coming up on one knee as his right hand swept the sidearm free from its holster. He brought the weapon to bear and cursed himself for underestimating her. Again. He shouted after her. "You'll freeze to death."

He had limited options. If she got away half dressed and cuffed, she'd be dead in an hour, sooner if she landed in the water. If he shot her, he'd at least have a chance to save her.

She kept running, getting about twenty feet away before he yelled at her. "I will shoot you, Lane!"

She froze, just ten feet from the river bank.

"Move back here."

Lane turned toward him but maneuvered herself closer to the precipice, inching away from him.

Richard drew his mark, avoiding body mass for the catastrophic damage it would do. He quickly dismissed a thought to aim for her shoulder; if she bobbed or veered, he'd shoot through a lung or her brain. He aimed low, targeting the outside thigh muscles of her right leg. "I will shoot you to keep you from freezing to death. And it's gonna hurt like hell, so just give it up now."

Tense moments passed; Richard waited for her decision. She let out a pained sigh, heavy with all her struggles and fears. "Just get it over with."

Richard's jaw shifted and his mouth cracked open in surprise. Lane's breathing grew labored. She fought back the sobs, shifting closer to the edge.

"I'm not kidding," he said.

Lane stopped, but Richard sensed a ruse. She hadn't given in yet, and he saw no reason to believe she would now. Her eyes darted up, met his for a moment, then she spun toward the riverbank, pushing off with her right leg.

"Lane!" Richard hesitated for a fraction of a second; he fired.

But the delay gave her time to move, and the right leg rose for its stride. Instead of tearing into thigh tissue, the bullet slammed through her knee.

Despite her efforts to gain momentum, Lane failed to propel herself from the ledge. She fell forward and hit the ground hard, her teeth gnashing against the pain.

Richard charged, holstering his weapon as he ran. He grabbed her with both hands, hauled her away from the riverbank, and flipped her onto her back, crushing her cuffed hands beneath her.

Blood gushed from the leg and created a red slushy in the snow. She railed against him, twisting, kicking, and butting him with her head while screams ripped out of her throat.

He couldn't decide if the screams were fear-based, pain-based, or both, but his frustration grew; he reminded himself that the girl wasn't exactly in her right mind. He scruffed the front of her shirt and held her at arm's length. "Done yet?"

Lane pulled against the cuffs. As Richard watched her struggle, the lights seemed to go off in her eyes. She lay on the ground, her whole body trembling, her eyes obviously not seeing him.

He gave her a shake and tried to bring her out of it. "Knock it off or you'll bleed to death."

Her eyes opened, but her terror remained, and her body went rigid. Short, strangled whispers pleaded with him. "Let me die."

"Everything I've seen tells me you want to live." He released her, hoped she'd remain still, and ripped her pant leg open at the knee.

The guttural scream caught Richard by surprise. His mouth fell open as Lane contorted, drawing her left leg up and across to her right thigh, pinching her legs tightly closed. Then her breathing changed.

The black-clad man leaned in close to Lane's face and pressed the trophy against her throat. His hand squared off on her jawline, the ring on his left hand pressing in under her jaw as he squeezed her face and forced her to look at him. Not that she could see him, but Lane knew he demanded her attention. "I've been waiting a long time for this.

Lane thrashed out wildly. Richard grabbed the left leg, forced it down, and kneeled on it to keep it there. He feared the terror alone would kill her if he didn't get this done quickly. He slipped his belt into place around her right thigh.

"Please," she begged. "Please don't hurt me."

His breath caught in his throat. *That's fear.* In the back of his mind, Wes laughed an "I-told-you-so." Richard didn't even want to think about Ray's reaction. His voice softened, choking back pity. "It wasn't me, Lane." He cinched the tourniquet tightly around the leg.

Lane convulsed. Richard had never heard that kind of noise, not even from a dying, rabid animal. And suddenly, it ended. She stared out at God knew what, her eyes unblinking, unseeing. She fell back against the ground, empty.

Blood oozed from the wound; the belt wasn't doing the job.

Richard packed the leg with snow, hoping that might slow the bleeding and dull the pain. He slipped off his tie, eased it into place just above the belt, and rooted around for a stick to place into the knot. When he finished, he had a crank. It would give him leverage and help him tighten the tourniquet until the bleeding stopped.

A quick glance revealed that the emptiness had left Lane's eyes, but the terror had returned. Her breathing came choppy, strained and uneven. She stared in his direction.

"It wasn't me."

Lane refused to acknowledge him, so he gently reached out and took her chin in his hand. Her body went rigid, and her head jerked away.

Without her cooperation, Richard couldn't save her. He leaned over and placed his hand on one side of her face with his thumb wrapping around her chin to the other side. She had nowhere to go. "It wasn't me."

He let her go, as if that alone would prove it. More snow packed against the leg turned pink, then crimson. He glanced up briefly when she turned to face him, but he didn't stare, didn't force eye contact on her.

Strangled whispers pulled his attention back, but her eyes shifted between some spot on his chest and the forest beyond. "Ray's hands are smaller than yours."

Richard's brows furrowed, and the announcement made his stomach churn. "Never thought about it."

He studied her face. Apparently she believed that he hadn't attacked her. But this new bit of information puzzled him. *Is Ray off the list? Or has she just convicted him?*

"He's shorter than me. I'd guess that makes his hands smaller, too, but we can certainly measure." He stopped abruptly as Lane

327

rolled over as far as she could and barfed in the snow.

The muscles along Richard's jaw clamped tight. *Convicted.* It's not like he hadn't suspected something inappropriate, but now he had proof. His brother had taken advantage of a child, a child who had no friends, one desperate enough to be played.

"Ray." He'd meant it as a question, but her reaction to the size of Ray's hands told him everything he thought he needed to know.

"Tell him I'm sorry."

"You don't have anything to be sorry about." Blood still oozed from the wound. "I have to cinch this tighter. It's gonna hurt." He gave the stick a quarter twist and tied it off.

Lane cried out, her torso rising from the ground. Richard caught her, held her until she spent the energy, and eased her back down. He turned to find his radio.

Morgan stared at him down the barrel of his short-nosed, five-round revolver.

Richard froze.

"I really thought she'd be dead by now. You must be slipping. Toss it."

The radio splashed down at Morgan's feet, spraying slush onto his shoes and pants.

Richard settled on his haunches. "Why do you want me to kill your daughter?"

Morgan laughed, his lips snarled back over his pearly whites. "Well, that's just it, Sheriff. She's not my daughter. She's yours."

Waves of nausea washed over Richard like crests on the ocean. His stomach rolled, lurched, heaved, and threatened to jump clean out of his body. He choked on the bile and set a free hand on the ground to steady himself.

"Named her after your twenty minutes of indiscretion with *my* wife in front of *my* house. Ray never told you?" He flicked his thirty-eight at Richard. "Your gun, too."

Richard tossed his Glock away; it landed near the radio.

"Take the cuffs off her."

Richard's tongue snaked out across his lips, and he shot a glance at Lane. He found that he couldn't look at her eyes anymore. Shame, guilt, disbelief, anger, surprise, and confusion all fought for dominion with shame in the lead. He rolled her to her side and took off the handcuffs.

Morgan flicked his fingers and pointed to a nearby tree. "Cuff yourself around it."

Richard obeyed, wrapping his arms around the trunk of the tree and binding his hands together.

Morgan kept his gun leveled at Richard, gave the cuffs a tug, then stuffed the thirty-eight in his pocket. A casual pat down yielded Richard's keys, but no additional weapons.

Morgan turned; Lane had twisted around and was crawling toward the cave. "Where do you think she's going?" He headed in Lane's direction, but Richard stalled him.

"You raped her."

Morgan stopped, smiling wickedly. "You took something of mine. I took something of yours. Seemed fair to me."

"You'll never get away with this."

"Oh, I already have. And, thanks to you, I get another shot at her." He headed back to Lane, only to pull up short.

Lane crawled further away. She managed to rise slightly on her right side and pulled herself along. Her left heel dug through the slush and found leverage to push away from Morgan.

"I had hoped to pin this whole thing on Ray, take him down at the same time, but this has advantages. After I'm done with her, I'll kill you, and well, when they find you both, they'll think you raped her, and that you killed each other. And your initials on the door help, wouldn't you say?"

He whirled on Lane. "Don't leave now, sweetie. There's so much more we can do." He grabbed her right ankle and dragged her toward the cave, feet first. "Don't worry, Dad. She'll have the time of her life, and you'll get to hear every precious moment. Oh, and one last thing, something you can take with you to hell. Killing her was Jenna's idea."

Lane screamed. She pushed at the ground, digging her left heel in, but she was unable to slow Morgan's progress. Time was running out and Richard was powerless to help her. Twisting, she slammed into the book bag and grappled with it. The move shifted her foot from Morgan's grasp. His laughter stung; Lane pulled herself along the rock face on bloody fingers. Morgan yanked the ankle again, tearing the knee even more.

Screams gurgled in Lane's throat, and Richard yelled for Morgan to release the girl. Her scream rose in pitch, winding upward in decibel and intensity.

Lane released the rock and whirled. Muscle memory brought the left hand up to cradle the rising Walther that she'd dug from the slush, but the tendons refused to work, and the arm flopped onto the ground.

The gunpowder ignited with a deafening roar. Nine rounds sped away, the slide kicking the shells free. The ninth casing bounced off Lane's face and left a black sear on the gauze bandage. Her eyes instinctively winced shut to protect themselves, but the tenth round still followed within seconds.

Blood spattered with each hit; nine struck Morgan's chest in a tight pattern, the last nailing his right cheek.

chapter fifty-four

*D*anny left Ray in the field below the hills, following the priest's instructions to the letter, and when the first shot of the Glock echoed in the forest, he dove for cover. It was several minutes later before the next series of shots sounded, nine in rapid succession and the tenth delayed.

From his training, he recognized a one-sided gun battle, but he didn't recognize the gun. And Richard's Glock didn't answer. Danny charged the clearing with his gun drawn as Morgan sagged to his knees. His eyes were saucer-wide; his lips peeled back in his wolf-smile, and he toppled over.

Danny took cover behind a tree with his own sidearm trained on Lane. "Drop the gun!"

Thunder pounded in her head. Flashbacks clouded her vision. With both shock and hypothermia setting in, she didn't even hear him. She sagged against the rocks.

Richard called to Danny. "Come let me loose."

Danny eased out from cover with his gun trained. He walked slowly, deliberately, his gun never wavering from its target.

Richard twisted around the tree. "Lane."

The movement, the sound, and the tone of his voice broke her trance. Her eyes fluttered in his direction.

Danny screamed at her again. "Drop the gun!"

Richard shot a killing stare over his shoulder. "For the love of God, Dan, get these cuffs off me."

Danny hesitated. He would have preferred securing the perp and the gun; after all, the sheriff was safe at the moment. He inched closer to Lane.

"Now, Danny!"

"But the gun, Sheriff."

"She's half dead and coming down off a terror roller coaster. And if you touch that kid, I swear to God, Dan, I'll pitch you off the ledge."

Danny shifted to Richard, but the gun remained trained on the girl.

Once he was released from the cuffs, Richard knelt beside Lane and leaned into her line of vision. He crouched down low, staring into her eyes. "You've never listened to a word I've ever said. You've never had a reason to. Let this be the first time. Please."

He searched her eyes for understanding. "Lane. Please. Open your fingers wide."

Her head turned in his direction, the barest fraction of an inch. Her mouth hung open, her skin pale and waxy.

"Please. Open your fingers wide."

Her head bobbed slightly with the exertion as she looked down at her hands, one clutching the grip, the other lying useless. She eased her fingers open wide, but the gun didn't fall free.

"Good. That's good. Listen to me. Listen to me."

Lane's head popped up, her eyes fighting to find him.

"Look at me, Lane." He dropped back into her line of vision. "Raise your hands. Straight up. Let Danny see them."

Lane focused on her hands again, struggling to raise them.

The left hand veered off sideways from her body, but the right one managed to rise, and the gun slipped free and rested in her lap. Her right hand got shoulder high but couldn't hold the position. It flopped into the mud.

Danny jumped a little, and Richard whirled on him, one hand out to Lane to keep her from grabbing the gun, and one hand out to Danny, to keep him from shooting her. The deputy relaxed.

Richard's voice remained calm and reassuring, and he gently extricated the gun from her lap. She tensed a little, her eyes batting furiously. "Relax, just relax."

Danny checked Morgan's pulse and stripped the gun from his pocket.

Richard didn't feel the need to query Danny on Morgan's condition. If the bastard hadn't already expired, it would only be minutes. He liked the idea that Morgan might live long enough to see Lane leave the area alive.

Once Danny secured the perp and the area, he radioed in for help. "Get the bus back out to Harris Lane. Now!"

Richard inspected Lane's leg but didn't see how he could move her without causing her more pain. "I don't want to die," she whispered.

Richard hesitated. "I know."

Tears poured from Lane's eyes, but Richard couldn't tell whether they were physical or emotional in nature. "I don't want to live either."

A sad smile cut Richard's face. "One has definite advantages over the other."

"Which one?"

Richard's voice turned soft, almost warm. "The one that lets you change your mind."

She met his eyes for a second. Her breathing spasmed and came in short, strained gasps. Lane choked out words that rose and fell in pitch and slurred together. "Tell Ray ... sorry ... didn't trust him." Her eyeballs rolled up in her head, and her chin crashed to her chest.

The roaring of ATVs broke the silence, and Danny hollered over his shoulder. "Olsens are heading up."

Richard scooped Lane off the ground and rushed toward the sound of the approaching ATVs.

The ambulance couldn't drive off-road and waited for their patient to come to them. ATVs were faster on the rough terrain, but Jason had stopped to let Danny recover his cruiser. Jake took Richard and Lane all the way, standing so that Richard would have ample room to hold the unconscious girl, but he kept the speed down so he wouldn't jostle her too much or bump them off completely.

The cruiser caught up with them as they reached asphalt. Richard knew the cruiser would need some overhauling, but he was glad Danny was there. For the professional support at least. He handed Lane off to the EMTs as Danny and Ray exited the cruiser.

Each of the paramedics had a task. While the woman inspected the ravaged leg, the man checked vitals, pulse, blood pressure, and the reactiveness of her pupils.

Once they finished the preliminaries, their task became one of quick, efficient, and lifesaving transport. They carried the stretcher toward the waiting ambulance, with Richard, Danny, and Ray in tow.

Lane's eyes fluttered with each snowflake that landed on them. Richard's Stetson sat in the mud back on the hill, so he held out his hand to Danny. "Give me your hat."

Danny complied without question, and Richard placed the hat

on Lane, shielding her eyes from the snow.

Ray reached in and took Lane's hand before the EMTs slid the stretcher into the ambulance. "Hang in there, kiddo, OK? I'll meet you at the hospital."

The EMTs urged Ray to release her, then slammed the door and drove away, leaving the police and onlookers in the field.

Richard watched it depart with Danny hovering at his elbow. "Did I introduce you to my daughter, Dan?"

There had always been rumors, none of which Richard or Ray talked about. Not even Dottie ever brought it up, and she had her finger on the pulse of the community. Danny clapped a reassuring hand on Richard's shoulder, headed back to his cruiser, and left the two brothers alone.

"She wanted you to know she was sorry. For not trusting you."

Ray nodded and turned to Richard. Met by Richard's devastating right cross, the priest ended up on his backside on the ground. "What was that for?"

"For not telling me."

Richard walked off, Danny, hiding a sheepish grin, waited for Ray to climb out of the muck so he could drive him back to the mansion to pick up the Falcon.

chapter fifty-five

The trauma room buzzed with earnest and focused activity. Quiet now and more complacent, Lane posed no problem to the staff, and they transferred her to the exam table. Doc Williams probed the leg, and she let out a strangled cry, struggling up before collapsing back onto the table.

In the hallway, Richard leaned against the wall and studied his shoes, twisting toward the trauma room at the sound of Lane's scream.

Jenna, who either by design, self-pity, or hospital rules had confined herself to a wheelchair, sat nearby wearing a bland hospital johnnie. Her shoulder bore a heavy bandage, and her arm snuggled in a sling. Drained from the ordeal, she remained quiet and distant, resting her head in her hand.

Danny leaned against the opposite wall, observing Richard and Jenna, waiting for his next orders.

Ray stood alone, twenty feet away, staring out the windows into the storm.

"Ray?"

Involved in his own thoughts and prayers, he hadn't heard Richard approach. Ray opened his mouth.

Richard raised a hand and cut him short. "I figure it had to be a confessional thing. I don't believe you'd have kept it from me if you didn't have to."

"I couldn't do anything about it without throwing away the priesthood. I'm sorry."

Richard dismissed it. "Not nearly as much as I am."

Doc Williams emerged from the trauma room and headed directly toward Jenna. Richard turned back, paused, and jerked his head as an invitation for Ray to join him. The brothers converged on the doctor.

"Mrs. Harris, I need you to sign this authorization."

Jenna panicked. "How is he? Is he hurt badly?"

"It's your daughter, Mrs. Harris."

Jenna's eyes grew wild, her hands animated. "Lane? Where's Morgan?"

Ray stepped up and took the paperwork from the doctor.

"I'm sorry, Ray. It has to be immediate family."

Determination swept Ray's face. For the first time ever, he was about to proclaim himself Lane's uncle, but Richard stepped up, placed a quieting hand on his brother's shoulder, and took the paperwork. He signed it and handed it back to the doctor. "Just trust me."

The doctor nodded. He slammed through the swinging door, and within minutes, the gurney, Lane, and the trauma team whooshed past on their way to the operating room.

Jenna met Richard's eyes. "Then you know?"

"Yep. I'm guessing in another hour or so, the whole town will know. If they didn't already."

Her eyes burned with hatred. "Where is Morgan?"

Richard felt no compunction to be civil, kind, or compassionate.

"Dead."

Jenna's mouth fell open, and Richard took pleasure in that small victory. Her hand covered her mouth. "You killed him? You never could get over that I left you, you bastard."

"Actually, Lane killed him. Right before he tried to rape her. Again."

Jenna morphed from a raging bitch to a battered housewife. "I wanted to tell you about her, but he wouldn't let me. You don't know what it was like, living with him. He could be such a monster. This was all his idea. Get her out of the way so he could get his hands on her land. I think he even had my parents killed."

Richard moved around behind her and rested his hands on her shoulders, caressing her upper arms. He leaned in close. "Pretty much what he said about you, without the motive. And without that little tidbit about your folks. I'll have to reopen that." Richard slapped a cuff on her and chained her to the chair.

Instantly, she converted to a wild woman, spewing vulgarities and threats, and twisting around in the chair so she could wag her fist at him. Richard shook his head in disgust and pushed the wheelchair in Danny's direction.

"Mirandize her, will you?"

chapter fifty-six

*R*ay stood by the window in Lane's hospital room, alternately keeping tabs on Doc Williams' ministerings and staring out the window. He watched a dark sedan pull out of the parking space reserved for the sheriff's department and then out of the lot.

"She'll live, Ray."

Ray pushed off the wall and moved closer. He shook the doctor's hand. "Thank you, and thank God for making you his fingers today. Will she keep the leg?"

"I'm optimistic, but we'll know for sure in a couple days."

"And," Ray faltered, unwilling or unable to say it. "The rest?"

"I've called in a consult. We might be able to do some surgical intervention for her throat. The vaginal damage has healed, but there's a great deal of scar tissue. We should be able to remove some of that."

He flipped through the pages of the chart. "We've already pulled some blood samples ..." He trailed off.

Ray knew what Doc meant. "STDs."

Williams nodded. "And other diseases. I don't expect to find anything provided she only had—" he stopped, rethinking his words. "Provided it was only Morgan. But we're also checking for vitamin and mineral deficiencies. Stuff like that."

The doctor checked the drip setting on the IV. "If she wakes up in any pain, let the nurses know."

"Doc?"

Williams paused.

"I'm sorry."

Williams smiled. "I suppose we all do what we feel is right." He strolled out into the hallway.

Ray took Lane's pale limp hand in his and sat by her side, praying softly.

She awoke, and her teeth started chattering within seconds. He leaned into her view and swept his hand over her forehead. She cried.

"Shhh," he whispered.

But she continued to weep, choking out words. "I'm sorry. I didn't trust you." Sobs racked her body and made it hard for her to talk, but she struggled to finish. "I just didn't know who ..."

Ray shushed her and smoothed tears from her face. She hadn't done anything wrong; she only tried to protect herself. But she didn't want logic right now and didn't need a lecture. She needed to know he didn't hold it against her. "I forgive you."

His hand rested on the side of her face, and he stared into her eyes.

She cried, clutching his hand tightly, but she couldn't quite look at him. She reached for him with her right hand; the cuff pulled back.

Ray grabbed the pillows off the other bed in the room and eased in next to Lane. He wrapped his arm around her, and she snuggled up against him, pressing her face into his chest.

Her fingers clutched his shirt, and she listened to the steady beat of his heart. She sniffed hints of vanilla and cinnamon and fell quietly to sleep.

chapter fifty-seven

*R*ichard sat alone in his office long past quitting time with his door closed and only his desk lamp on. He stared blindly at Lane's police file and crime scene photos.

Danny had gone home, but Dottie lingered, busying herself with paperwork at her desk. Pete, on night shift for the week, deliberately absented himself from the area, popping in periodically to see if Richard had gone, and wishing he would leave. Soon.

After an hour of staring pointlessly at paperwork, he shuffled the pictures together and stuffed them in his pocket. He gathered up his coat and keys, exited his office, and dropped the room into darkness with a flick of the lamp switch. He nodded absently to Dottie on his way out, then he stopped abruptly.

"You're here late."

She shrugged. "Odds and ends to be taken care of."

Richard nodded and took a single step toward the door. "Did everybody know?"

Dottie's playful mannerisms were gone, but her words held no malice.

"There'd been some speculating, but only the Harrises and Ray knew for sure. What matters now is what you do with the information."

Richard nodded thoughtfully, heading out. "Goodnight, Mother."

"Goodnight, Richard."

chapter fifty-eight

*L*ane's eyes fluttered open and fought to focus. She breathed deeply and gave Ray a squeeze. His eyes popped open immediately.

"Welcome back."

Though she was calmer than her previous reunion with Ray, she still fought the effects of the painkillers. "I'm sorry. I didn't trust you. Morgan. He wore black."

Ray held her close. It wouldn't be hard to imagine a criminal wearing black at night to conceal his activities. But this was Morgan. It wouldn't be any harder to imagine he'd done it to look like a priest.

"You were protecting yourself. Under the circumstances, I expect it was the best choice."

"Still," she said.

"Still nothing. You feel bad about it, and there's no reason to. I forgive you. Now it's done."

He smiled at her and held her hand tightly; she smiled weakly but averted her gaze. She scanned the room. "He didn't come."

Ray kissed her head, hugged her, and fought back his own tears. "If he can't come to terms with this, it doesn't mean a thing. There's still you and me. That's all we ever really had anyway. Though I expect a certain grandmother to be doting on you like nobody's business."

"Richard's my father?"

He nodded. "Yes."

"I hoped it was you."

"I know." A stab of pain rent his heart.

"But what if …" she paused, unable or unwilling to put words to the possibility that someone else might not want her.

Ray jumped in decisively. "Then it is me."

He grabbed a tissue, mopped her face for her, then laughed and grabbed another tissue for his own face.

Lane snorted weakly but turned serious. "Is Morgan dead?"

Ray nodded. "No doubt about that. I may even say a prayer for him. But probably not today."

"I shot him in the face. On purpose."

His lips pursed as he decided how best to address the revelation. "Think we all knew that."

"I wanted him dead."

"Me too."

Her head spun a little, her eyes locking on his chin. He smiled. "Despite what Richard thinks, I am not a saint."

"What's going to happen to *her?*"

Ray sighed. "She's got a good lawyer. Looks like she's going to claim battered wife."

"She's gonna get away with it."

Ray nodded. "Possibly."

"What if I testify?"

Ray kissed her head again. "Let your lawyer worry about that. You rest." He slid out of the bed. "I'll be back later. I have to break this to your Nana. You'll be OK for a couple hours?"

She nodded.

"Maybe I can smuggle her in with me when I get back."

The weary priest exited the hospital and hurried to his car, noticing that the dark sedan had returned to the sheriff's parking space. He pretended not to have seen it; Richard had to deal with this on his own.

Ray left, and Richard let him go, glad his brother was too preoccupied to have seen him sitting in the car. He didn't really want to talk to Ray right now. He had to think more than speak.

He'd gone up to the room earlier and found Ray sleeping in the bed with Lane, both their faces damp. But Lane looked comfortable and at ease. And Ray looked content.

He'd left somewhat angry and had been stewing about it in the car. But now, thinking about it, he reminded himself that Ray was the girl's uncle. And Ray had known it all along.

The dash light of the Falcon bathed Ray in a soft glow. His rosary laced through his fingers, and his head rested on his clasped hands as he prayed. Tears fell from his eyes, and his voice croaked as he thanked God for saving his niece. After a few moments, he headed to the house.

Dottie closed the door behind him, and Ray stooped over her, giving her a deep hug and a peck on the cheek.

"How is she?"

"She'll live. But it'll take time until she's fine."

"Is Richard there?"

"He was still sitting in his car when I left."

"She's alone?"

Ray's words slowed, drawing out. "Well, the clinic does have twenty-two full-time employees."

Dottie brushed past him and grabbed her coat from the closet. "I can't believe you left her there alone."

Ray took the coat from her hands and set it aside. He wrapped her arm around his and steered her casually toward the kitchen. "Richard needs some time to do the right thing. She's not going anywhere. He's got her chained to the bed. And she's drifting in and out. I'll take you down in a couple hours."

"I should have been first."

"How about some breakfast?"

She stopped and dug her heels in. "I should have been first."

"Absolutely. But I was first because she knows me."

Dottie sputtered. "Then I should have been second."

Ray nodded. "Probably. But Richard's the father, and he needs a chance to get his mind around this. Quickly. Breakfast?"

"So I get to be last?"

"No. You get to be next." He guided her to a chair. "Scrambled or fried?"

"Next, last. And you're changing the subject."

"Well, yeah. But I need something to eat." He glanced at his watch. "I swear. Two hours. Max. We eat, swing by the rectory for a shower and some fresh clothes, and I'll take you down to see her. If Richard's there, we join in. If he's not," Ray shrugged. "She's all ours."

"I don't like it, not one little bit."

Emotions raged across Dottie's face as her heart broke into thousands of tiny pieces. Ray could only imagine what she felt, finding out at seventy that she had a nearly eighteen-year-old granddaughter.

He slipped out of his jacket, dropped it on the back of a chair and wrapped his mother up in his arms.

After sitting in the car for another hour, Richard finally shut it off and headed into the hospital. He stamped and scuffed his shoes on the carpet to get off the excess water, but it didn't help; he still squeaked down the hallway.

The night nurse taped fresh bandages on Lane's leg and addressed him without turning her head.

"Official business?"

Richard faltered. *Damn shoes.* "Uh, no. I just came to see how she was doing."

The nurse picked up the soiled bandages and turned toward him, nodding her head. "After hours. Good thing it's official business."

Richard joined the head-nodding club. "Yes, absolutely official. Questioning a suspect, and what all."

Lane stirred and called his name, though it sounded more like "Itcher" than anything else.

Surprise registered on his face; the nurse's big eyes laughed at him. "She's been asking for you and Ray for about a half hour now. I was wondering when you'd get out of that damn car." She stepped past him and slipped quietly into the hallway.

He stood by the door for several minutes before moving closer, observing her from a distance. Another second passed before he moved to the bedside. Lane's head snuggled against the pillow Ray had used.

"Richard?"

He faltered yet again, cursing himself for this unusual display of indecision. "I'm here."

Lane's eyes fluttered open for a second and slammed shut again. Pain, pain medication, and exhaustion made it difficult for her to keep them open. "You came."

Her voice was even scratchier than before, *1-800-dial-a-friend scratchy.* Richard immediately berated himself for thinking it; he had no doubt that her ordeal and vivid flashbacks had strained her throat.

"Yes."

"They're gonna cut my leg off."

Eyebrows on the rise, Richard took the chart off the end of the bed and read through it. "They're just watching it for now."

"I'm never gonna run again."

Richard fell silent. Lane's eyes fluttered, searching him out; they crashed shut again, and she yielded.

"Jimmy was asleep when I took his car."

Richard smiled. He wondered if in her drug-induced cooperative state he might get her to talk about other things. He'd answer to her lawyer for sure, but he pulled the pictures from his pocket and showed them to her anyway.

"Tell me about this one."

Lane opened her eyes briefly. "Rolled him."

Richard shuffled the picture to the bottom of the stack. "This one?"

Lane's eyes tracked the stack of pictures, and she reached for them.

Curiosity overpowered Richard's sense of caution, and he handed her the evidence.

Lane studied each picture and separated them into piles. After several minutes, she handed one set to Richard. "Rolled them."

He pulled a pen and notepad from his shirt pocket, wrote the word "rolled" on a piece of paper, and wrapped the pictures up in it.

Lane handed him a second pile. "Robbed."

Richard noted that similarly. One picture remained on the bed by itself; the dead boy. He picked it up.

Tears squeezed out Lane's closed eyes.

"This one?" Richard's voice was soft, almost apologetic.

Lane stammered as she spoke. "Couldn't stop them."

"Couldn't stop who?"

Tears poured freely now. "Rider. Rider killed him."

Richard fell quiet, wrote "Rider" on the back of the picture, and tucked it in his pocket with the rest as she struggled to pull herself together. *Or maybe she just fell asleep.*

After a moment, her eyes peeked open, etched in pain and grief. She sought him out. "I'm never gonna run again."

To save her life, Richard had pulled the trigger. Given the same set of circumstances, he'd do it again. But he decided that it wouldn't hurt either of them less for her to know that just yet.

Richard's jaw set and his chin quivered. He fought to keep it from his voice, but he didn't succeed. "Maybe not." Richard saw the slightest hint of a nod before she shifted, trying to get comfortable. He moved closer, reached down, and traced a line down the back of her cuffed hand with his fingertip. "I'm sorry."

His eyes fixed on her hand; her eyes blinked open, following his gaze. She didn't recoil from his touch. He didn't know if that was acceptance, or just the drugs.

"You were angry," she sighed.

Their eyes met for a moment; Lane couldn't handle the depth, Richard couldn't handle the guilt. Her eyelids dropped shut as he nodded his agreement.

She didn't see his action; she wasn't watching anymore. "I was supposed to be yours."

chapter fifty-nine

S everal weeks had passed, but Richard's mood remained mired in quicksand. He had yet to figure out how to break the ice with his new-found daughter, a girl he'd treated like crap for years because he'd thought she was Morgan's child. If that wasn't bad enough, the girl's mother, the woman Richard had planned to spend the rest of his life with, was nothing more than a scheming, shallow fortune hunter who would apparently stop at nothing to obtain her goals. His brows furrowed deep across his forehead, and a scowl tainted his normally pleasant face. He stalked into the station, lost in thought while clutching an envelope in his fingers. Mumbled good mornings from his staff elicited nothing more than a grunt.

He'd been worrying, something he never did. He was afraid that this time, the bad guy would get off. He never concerned himself with that before. He collected suspects and gathered evidence; lawyers fought it out. But this time, it pissed him off. He couldn't get enough evidence. And the D.A. wouldn't prosecute with what he had.

Dottie followed him with her eyes, her head turning and openly staring. She made no bones about it and no attempt to disguise it at all. One eyebrow cocked up, alluding to her anger, though she said nothing until Richard entered his office. "Jerk."

A schoolgirl giggle rose from the desk next to her, but Danny buried his face in paperwork so no one else would catch him.

Richard tossed his coat onto his chair, spun right around, and headed down to lockup. He flipped the light on in the stairs.

Dottie rose and folded her arms matronly across her chest. She monitored the security cameras as her youngest son headed down the walk to the last cell on the female side.

Downstairs in the cellblock, Richard swung the barred door open and entered slowly. He approached the cot where Lane slept, her hands tucked protectively out of view, and he took up his customary hands-in-pockets stance, watching her sleep for a moment.

He hated to wake her. She still hadn't slept through a night. Doc Williams said to be patient, that the drugs could take up to eight weeks to reach full effectiveness. *Still*, he thought. *That doesn't help the kid now.*

He kneed the bed gently to rouse her, and she nearly jumped out of her skin. Then she rolled her eyes and let out a dismayed "Tch" before smushing her face back into the pillows.

"Sorry." He should have remembered that the cell door didn't wake her anymore. She made no attempt to rise. He kneed the bed again. "Don't make me dump you out."

A groan drifted through the pillow. "Tired."

"Community service will do that to you."

She said something, ending with "Day off."

"Yep. Weekend's coming. Come on, up. We got the court order to go up to the house and get your stuff."

Something that might have been words, groans, or expletives came out. Richard couldn't tell exactly, but then he heard, "Today?"

"What kind of sheriff would I be if I showed you favoritism?"

"Nobody else here."

"You're missing the point."

Slowly, Lane swung herself out of bed, latched onto the crutches Richard held out to her, and struggled to get upright. And without a word, she shuffled through the cell doors and hobbled to the shower room six feet away. Her awkward gait produced an odd "step, thump, step, thump" sound as the usable foot hit the floor and was followed by the thumping of the crutches.

Richard stopped her at the doorless entrance. "You know the drill." He headed in to inspect for hidden dangers.

"Nobody else here," Lane muttered, not expecting him to hear her.

"Rules are rules," he called, his voice echoing off the concrete walls. "And this particular rule is meant to protect you, so I wouldn't be too quick to dismiss it if I were you."

When he returned, Lane's eyes shifted to the floor, and she limped into the room to take her shower. Minutes later, steam billowed from the portal.

Richard leaned on the wall in the hallway outside. With his arms folded across his chest, he stared at his shoes and threw an occasional glance at the security monitor. *Don't think I don't know.*

He twisted and leaned around the doorway. "I hope you're not just standing around in there."

The water went off, and a slight smile creased Richard's face. *Why does everyone think I was born yesterday?*

The sounds of a struggle ensued as Lane fought to dry herself off and to figure out how to get dressed without getting the clothes wet. She cursed the walls for getting in the way.

The curtain slid across the bar with a metallic scrape. Lane finally emerged, dressed in orange coveralls with MVSO stamped in black, six-inch letters on the back. Balancing on her crutches, she raked one hand through her damp hair.

Richard's eyebrows danced up; he returned to her cell for her brush and handed it to her.

She dead stared his chest for a few seconds before she took it and brushed her hair. Some of it plastered down, some stuck out at odd angles. She hobbled past him and chucked the brush into her cell. It bounced on the bed as she headed for the stairs.

Richard usually led the way to the door and opened it for her, but she didn't usually have to wait this long for him to catch up. She stopped and glanced over her shoulder. He stared back, once again leaning against the wall with hands back in his pockets, and watching her eyes rise to the center of his chest. Then up to his neck. Maybe his chin. But no further. He pushed off the wall and strolled toward the stairs.

Lane let him pass and scruffed up her hair with both hands as she balanced on her crutches; then she followed him.

Upstairs at the monitor, Dottie chuckled. Danny grinned and held his hand out. "Ha! You lose! Pay up."

Dottie clucked at him. "He's not going to do it down there. Besides, day's still young, Cabana Boy." She pointed her finger at him for emphasis. "The day is still young."

chapter sixty

*R*ichard drove through town while observing Lane in the rear-view mirror. The metal grate and plexipanel separated them, but she sat quietly, staring out the window with her cuffed hands in her lap.

He wondered if she wished she had a stash of bobby pins on her sleeve, but she didn't seem to be panicking at all. Not that it mattered any more. He and the rest of the officers now double-locked all cuffs all the time. For everyone. No shortcuts anymore.

He supposed the signs had been there all along, little clues. Perhaps Ray had left them on purpose. Or maybe it had more to do with the way people passed their hobbies on to their progeny, even those of their siblings and close friends.

Early on, he'd told himself that Ray's attachment to the girl was unnatural. After that, everything Ray did compounded Richard's suspicions. But he'd never investigated it any further, convinced he already knew more than he wanted to.

He tossed another glance in the mirror; Lane's face had flushed the light pink of a blush wine. He smiled; no doubt she was stealing glimpses of him when he wasn't stealing glimpses of her.

Richard turned on Harris Lane, buzzed at the gate, and waited for it to swing open.

Camilla stood in the doorway of the main house waiting patiently while the sheriff parked, uncuffed his prisoner, and helped her out of the car. She exchanged a brief smile with Lane before returning to her work.

Jenna's lawyer demanded the paperwork and stood reading it word for word. Jenna glared across the room, her jeans and baggy sweatshirt a far cry from her normal socialite attire.

"This gives you access to her bedroom and personal items. Nothing more." The lawyer handed the paperwork back, and Richard slowly escorted Lane to the third floor bedroom. He headed into the room and turned to find her several feet away with sweat dripping into her squinting eyes from the trek up three flights of stairs.

Jenna stared harder, her eyes like daggers and her words spitting venom. "Get your things and get out."

Lane hobbled over, one eyebrow up, one down. She peered into the room.

"What?" Jenna stormed into the room, threw open the dresser drawers, and pulled out cotton twills and Sunday-go-to-meeting blouses.

Lane ignored Jenna and hobbled across the hall to the attic door. Richard followed, curiosity etched in his face.

Jenna's lawyer intervened. "You're limited to her room and possessions."

Richard popped the button on the knob and pulled the door open. Lane shuddered, recalling the first time a man had opened that door for her.

Jenna let the lawyer do the talking. "You are making this so easy for me."

Lane turned to Richard, not quite looking at him, but she

insisted. "This was my room."

Jenna dismissed her. "Don't be ridiculous. Who'd make you sleep in the attic? Your stuff is right there. You've already seen that. Don't make this any messier than it has to be."

Lane looked at Richard, making full eye contact with him for the briefest of seconds. "I lived here."

Richard studied her. His brain screamed at him. *Trust her.* His head tipped to the side, and his hand gestured her into the stairwell.

At the top of the stairs, Lane turned and headed through the first set of shelves. Most of the boxes were missing, and Lane stared through the empty space.

"We took a lot of that for evidence," Richard said in response to her unasked question. "Gonna be a lot of lawsuits. Odds are she'll lose everything, right up to the Ridge. The only piece not on the block is yours."

Lane nodded, continued down the aisle, step-thumping along the plain wood flooring. She stopped dead in her tracks, and her mouth fell open. All her things were gone. Only the furniture remained, but much of it had been rearranged. Instead of an apartment, she stared at a warehouse.

Just an attic. Disappointment threatened Richard's face, and he fought to hide it. He'd already been up here with the FBI, but logic encouraged him to believe that she had a good reason to bring him up here. Otherwise, he'd just stepped into a seriously large vat of hooey. He took a deep breath and let it out slowly. "Can you prove you lived here?"

Lane thought a moment and thrust a crutch toward the wall behind the dinette, pointing out the initials 'RK' that she'd carved into the wood.

"I saw one just like it on the door downstairs."

There was only one thing left; *at least I hope it's still there.* She hobbled to the table, leaned against it, and moved it over a few inches. The brace kept the knee from bending enough to kneel on, so she ended up sitting on the floor. But without a tool, the floorboards wouldn't dislodge. She made prying motions at Richard.

Without thinking about it, he pulled out his pocketknife, opened it, and nearly handed it to her. Then he came back to his senses. *One simply does not give a knife to an inmate.* He knelt down. "Where?"

She pointed out the board to him, and he slid the knife in. With a quick and easy twist, the board came loose. Lane caught it, set it upside down on the floor, then pulled off the other board.

Richard pulled the laptop out of its hiding place and helped Lane back to her feet. His eyes locked on the boards and the etching. Amid the drawings and names, two words screamed out at him: *Lane Keates.* His eyes locked on hers, but she turned away, her face flushing a bright, sunburn red.

He stuffed the board into the pocket of the laptop case. "Let's get the rest of your stuff."

He preceded her down the stairs and turned sideways in case she stumbled. She'd gotten steadily better on the crutches, but he didn't want a spill to sideline her.

Down on the third floor, Jenna strode from the master bedroom with long-legged, regal steps, her business suit sharp and crisp, her heels clacking on the floor.

"All dressed up," Richard said.

Jenna finished for him. "And someplace to go. You shouldn't have overstepped the limitations of your court order. We're going to the courthouse to file the complaint."

Richard smiled. "Did you know her laptop was still up there? Under the floorboards? No? Yeah, right under that fancy table. But go ahead, file whatever you like."

Jenna's lawyer stepped in and prevented her from saying or doing anything further. She headed for the stairs.

Richard smiled and directed his words to Lane. "See if there's anything in that room that really is yours." He turned to Lane and froze.

Lane's eyes narrowed, and she focused on the tapping of Jenna's heels on the floor. Dull and distant.

Her vision went black. The cold, wet pavement pressed against her face, and a sea of sparkles danced on the wet tar, reflecting the car's headlights. A shadow passed over her, the car door shut. Then echoed. A flash of white, and Richard stared at her.

Lane's face washed pale. With her eyes wide and her breathing uneven, she stared directly at Jenna. "You drove the car."

Jenna wrinkled up her face, cutting Lane to shreds with her eyes. "Don't be ridiculous." Contempt dripped from her voice.

"You were in the car. He dragged me out and dumped me in the street, but you were driving. You had to walk around the car." A wave of nausea rocked her "You stepped over me. I'm gonna be sick." She took a few steps toward the bathroom, but she didn't reach her destination; she vomited on the floor.

Richard noted Jenna's disgust with a great deal of pleasure; he himself was equally disgusted, just not with Lane. "You got a maid, right?" He latched on to Lane to steady her; she allowed it.

He smiled. "I think you've just made Ray's job a lot easier." And the cloud that had been following him the past several weeks lifted.

chapter sixty-one

*R*ichard parked the car in the spot reserved just for the sheriff, exited, but left the keys in the ignition. He helped Jenna out of the back seat, her hands cuffed behind her back. With one hand on her arm, he steered her up the stairs but paused a moment as her lawyer raced into another parking spot. The man jumped from his car, his mouth going before the door even shut.

Richard didn't hear most of it; he stood there considering the lawyer's car, parked in a spot reserved for on-duty deputies. "Thinking you should move that before I have to ticket you."

The lawyer assumed his words were posturing. "You wouldn't dare."

"Don't be betting your life on that, Counselor." He ushered Jenna into the station and left the lawyer in the street to decide the risks of parking illegally.

"I'll have her out of here in an hour. It comes down to her word against the kid's."

"Give it your best shot."

Lane waited in the front seat since she was accustomed to Richard opening and closing the door, helping her in and out, and standing ready to catch her should she trip on the stairs. But he led

Jenna into the building, and after moving his car, the lawyer rushed inside as well. There was not so much as a deputy at the door or a pedestrian on the street. No one remained to help Lane.

She stared after them, wondering if she should wait or take the chance of letting herself out of the car and getting herself inside the station. The cuffs clinked as she shifted the healing leg into a more comfortable position. The motion rocked the car; the keys swung from the ignition.

Richard handed Jenna off to Pete. "New evidence. Book her. Make sure she gets one of those new fashionista jumpsuits we got in." He stiff-armed the lawyer to a stop when he tried to press by the officers.

"You can wait in Room Three. She'll join you soon enough. When she does, you two should talk—really talk." He motioned for Ed to escort the lawyer.

Danny called over his shoulder. "I set up Room One like you wanted, Sheriff."

"Thanks, Dan." Richard headed to his office and dropped his gun in his desk drawer. In the background he could hear Dottie's pleasant voice on the phone. "He just stepped in. Can I ask who's calling, please? Thank you. One minute, please."

Richard waited, but her tone with him was bland, aloof, and distant. "Detective Glenn. Line two."

Richard nodded his thanks and popped the receiver off the cradle.

"Mike." He moved to the window and peered down at his car. He waited and searched, but he saw no sign of Lane.

"She's doing pretty good. Getting around a little better." He nodded as Mike commented, and he paced a little, returning to the window. A slight wave of queasiness washed over him, and his hands and feet got a little picky. Still no sign of Lane.

"I can't thank you enough for helping work that deal with your D.A. You ever find that Rider character?"

He snuck another peek out the window. "You picked him up? Excellent." Now he took up residence at the window with the tingling in his hands progressing to a tightening in his chest; he was glad he'd thumbed the killswitch on the cruiser.

Richard laughed at the detective's response. "His partner's name is Idiot?" Another pause. "Yeah, I'll tell her you caught them. It might help. And don't forget, next time I'm in the city, steaks and beers on me. Yeah, sure. Come on out. Wait 'til the spring though. I'll take you out to the lake, show you where the real trout swim."

He dropped the phone back on its cradle and paused as the sound of crutch-shuffling grew louder. He eased into his chair, rearranged some paperwork, and created a convincing persona of an unconcerned man hard at work.

Lane step-thumped in and waited for him to acknowledge her. She tossed the keys and the cuffs across the room at him; he caught them and dropped them in his desk drawer.

Ray entered the station and paused by the door as Richard and Lane walked up. He exchanged pleasant greetings with his brother, but wrapped his niece in a fierce hug.

Richard pointed Lane to Room One. "I'll be right in."

Lane hobbled off, leaving the brothers to talk. Ray folded his arms. "So, you make any headway with your mother yet?"

Richard shook his head. "I know she's mad, I just don't know why."

"Might have something to do with missing Christmas."

Richard's face screwed up in disbelief. "Is she not in jail?"

Ray mimicked Richard's facial expression. "Is she not your daughter?"

Richard shook his head, sighed. "You'd have me show her favoritism?"

"Don't even. No one told you to put up that shower curtain. I think that may be against regs, Sheriff."

"Oddly, I can't say I want my deputies peeping in on her, naked. So, what would you have me do?"

"Give her Christmas back. Turkey, fixings, a little tree."

"In the cell?"

Ray shrugged. "Absolutely. Or even up here. Wherever you want. Did I thank you yet for pulling in favors and fixing this?"

Richard nodded. "But hearing it again wouldn't hurt."

Ray laughed. "Thanks."

"See? Sometimes, you just have to trust me. I get to be her service coordinator. I get to be her jailer. In three months, I get to be her probation officer. And when she turns twenty-one, I get to see her record expunged."

Ray shook his head and laughed. "Yeah, you got me. You are one smooth dealer."

Richard leaned closer, keeping his voice down. "Damn straight. One other thing." He moved Ray closer to the door and farther from Dottie. "How long has Lane known about us?"

Ray couldn't hide the surprise, but his brother was, after all, the sheriff. "She was ten."

"You tell her?"

Ray shook his head. "Couldn't. For the same reason I couldn't tell you. Or Mom. Or anybody else. I think she overheard Jenna and Morgan talking." He shrugged. "Maybe they told her. She came to me one afternoon and just announced it. She knew it was one of us, just didn't know which."

Richard nodded. He raised a finger to Ray. "Gimme a couple minutes, OK?" Richard slid back into his professional mask and strode up to Dottie's desk. "When you have a sec, I need you to make some arrangements for me."

She dutifully grabbed her pad and a pen, peered at him over her bifocals, and waited. There were no quips, no pleasantries, not even a smile.

"Need you to plan a party for me. Maybe Pearce's can handle it. Or maybe even that other place." His hand flashed dismissively in the direction of the Harris Grocery Outlet. "Turkey, mashed potatoes, some pie. Oh, and a little tree, maybe. And lights. Have it all delivered here, say Thursday, seven p.m. Make sure there's plenty of mashed stuff, though. She's still having trouble swallowing."

The pen froze in mid-note. "Oh, you are smooth."

Richard smiled, his head tipped to the side. "Yep." He headed for Room One.

She raised an eyebrow, a smirk carving the side of her face as her eldest son moved closer. "You put him up to that."

"Not at all. I shamed him into it."

"Good enough." She set her glasses on her desk and crossed her arms. "What's the big secret?"

His mother felt badly enough; he saw no point in telling her that her brand new granddaughter knew about the Keates family eight years before most of the family knew about her. He decided to wow her with the day's plans instead. "We're going out to the cabin to open it back up, rearrange some furniture, and take stock of what we need to make it accessible for Lane."

"Really?"

"Uh huh. Says the trailer isn't big enough. Gonna keep it, though. Maybe spend weekends and holidays there."

"And you?"

"I'm gonna move in with them for a while, help them get acquainted."

"I meant long term."

Ray sighed, heavily. "I don't know."

"You're angry." Her words were matter-of-fact, but not accusatory. The all-knowing mother's version of spidey-sense.

"I'm actually having fun playing lawyer again. The whole 'coming and going as I please' thing."

"You're angry."

"No, I'm pissed. They didn't believe me. Well," he relented a little. "There was a minor involved, and the possibility of impropriety." The anger returned. "But the seal of the confessional prevented me from saying anything, and—" he stopped abruptly, drawn back by the smile tugging across Dottie's face. "Yeah, I'm angry. I'll get over it. For now, I just need to make sure those two 'gel.' "

"You took an awful lot of abuse to protect her."

"And I would again."

Richard joined Lane in Room One. The room bordered the dispatch area; its front and left walls had half-length windows separating the two rooms. He stood near the solid wall that separated Rooms One and Two.

Lane surveyed the room—the bookcase holding school supplies, a comfortable chair and an ottoman for her leg.

The laptop case sat on the table, and Richard removed the

floorboard and pondered it. He slid it around the table toward Lane and eased back to the wall, leaning against it. Ray had actually suggested keeping some distance between them whenever possible as a way of making her more comfortable.

She flushed, neck to crown.

"Why didn't you tell someone?"

She shrugged.

"Use your voice." His words flowed with parental concern.

Lane focused on her feet. "Morgan."

"He threatened you."

She shook her head. "Threatened Ray. And anybody else I told."

In dispatch, Danny moved closer to Dottie and found reasons to hang around, pretending to be working.

Richard changed the subject, motioning around the room. "This'll give you a place to study so you don't have to spend all your non-work hours in your cell." He took a single step closer to the table. "You'll want to take advantage of this. Remember we talked about favoritism? Goes double now that your mother has joined you in the cellblock."

Her dead stare hit him.

"It isn't every inmate that gets an end table, a radio, and three pillows. Or hourly visits from the deputies. Or smuggled contraband from the dispatcher."

The slightest flicker of emotion registered on Lane's face.

"What? Didn't think I knew? I'm the sheriff. Sees all, knows all." He pointed to her textbooks. "Principal's concerned, but says he's willing to let you try to catch up. It's a lot of work. You'll have to judge whether you can do it or not."

Lane examined the books and nodded her understanding.

Richard set a pencil down on the table. "One pencil. Anybody enters the room, the pencil has to go right there."

The dead stare returned. "Not me. Rules. You're technically an inmate. Inmates don't generally get free use of pointed objects. And don't think you've got free reign here." He pointed out the window into the dispatch area. "It's physically impossible to sneak by your Nana. It's been tried. Hell, I've tried. And if that isn't deterrent enough, you should know that I have a clear view from my office."

Lane checked. Ray, Danny, and Dottie all suddenly looked down, shuffling papers and picking up phones.

"And just to set the record straight," Richard said as he pushed off the wall and straightened. His hands slid out of his pockets and his shoulders squared. Outside the window, Dottie's fingers wiggled at Danny, and Richard read her lips: "Get ready, Cabana Boy."

The sheriff stood tall, proud and determined, but his words warmed with kind certainty.

"You are mine."

Tears welled up in Lane's eyes.

Richard moved around the table and closed the distance between them. He reached out slowly, tentatively. When she didn't recoil in terror, his hands settled on her shoulders, but she hadn't actually accepted him, nor had she glanced above the third button on his shirt. He lingered on her shoulders, giving her a moment to accept his presence and his touch, then he stepped in closer.

Lane didn't resist the hug, and she rested against his chest, the tears tracking freely down her face leaving wet streaks on his shirt as well. Her hesitancy lasted all of two seconds; she wrapped her arms tightly around her father, balling up the fabric and leaving wrinkles in his crisp, tailored shirt.

The sweet smile of fatherhood graced his face, and he looked out to dispatch to find a smile cutting Ray's face ear to ear, Dottie wiping tears from her own eyes, and Danny digging money out of his wallet to settle one more lost bet. *Rookie*, he thought.

Lane sucked up her runny nose. "How is this gonna work?"

Richard's head tipped toward his shoulder as thoughts and concerns rattled around his brain. He had no doubt that he, Ray, and Lane would be called to testify at Jenna's trial; God only knew the effect that would have on the kid. If that wasn't bothersome enough, the girl's future was completely up in the air. Richard decided that she just didn't need to worry about any of that right now.

"Don't know. I think we'll have to figure it out as we go. The story's far from over, kid, what with the trial and getting some kind of normalcy around here. But somehow, we're gonna get through it."

He pulled her in closer. Things were far from over.

About the Author

Carolyn Gibbs began writing in the sixth grade and hasn't put the pen down since. Credits include articles and essays in newspapers, poems in insurance industry newsletters, and training manuals for a local insurance company. From 2001 through 2004, she edited and published a monthly community newsletter called *The Good News of St. Thomas Parish*. She balances her time working in education and volunteers at her church.

tuesday's child

For more information regarding Carolyn Gibbs and her work, visit her website: www.tuesdayschildnovel.com.

Additional copies of this book may be purchased online from www.LegworkTeam.com; www.Amazon.com; www.BarnesandNoble.com; or via the author's website: www.tuesdayschildnovel.com.

You can also obtain a copy of the book by visiting
L.I. Books Bookstore
80 Davids Drive, Suite One
Hauppauge, NY 11788
or by ordering it from your favorite bookstore.

Breinigsville, PA USA
28 March 2011
258624BV00005B/2/P